Toquuxla

JAMES N. BRENNA

First edition: October 2023

Book Cover and Interior Design by Laura Boyle

ISBN 979-8-9890776-0-1 (paperback)

ISBN 979-8-9890776-1-8 (ebook)

For my parents, who patiently
supported me in whatever I pursued.

Contents

MAPS

MAP OF TOQUUXLA'S JOURNEY

CHAPTER 1

The Flood

It may be impossible for us to properly measure the impact we humans have had on our planet or the changes we have brought, both accidental and deliberate, to the natural world. Some say we have been a creative force, turning a wild, untamed land into one that feeds, clothes, shelters, and entertains billions and billions of people, while others believe we have been careless, hasty, thoughtless, selfish, greedy, and imprudent, wrecking, destroying, annihilating, ravaging, obliterating, and ruining the world that produced us.

Humans have been changing the world from the very first day we arrived upon it, as all creatures do, and surely nothing stays the same. No one knows how or when our road of change will end or where it will lead. There is no "master plan," and nobody is guiding or steering us. Humans *are* one of nature's wild, untamed forces.

We try to conserve and preserve bits and pieces of a natural world "untouched" by humanity, but while this is a noble and necessary effort, we only save an illusory remnant of what once was. So, we stand on a hill—or on the prairie, in the woods, in a valley, on a shoreline—and our thoughts inevitably take us back in time, and we wonder what life was like as an explorer, a frontiersman, a mountain man, a gold miner, a cowboy, a homesteader. Or else, we wonder further back to the times of native people, or, further still, to the very first people, and the first person to ever lay eyes upon a land that had never seen a human.

Looking from afar, from space, maybe about fifteen thousand years ago, Earth appears to be a quiet, little planet, but up close, on the ground, it is busy and alive and oblivious to what is happening in the rest of the universe.

A young man called Toquuxla once watched a mass gathering of ladybugs crawling all over one another; they were oblivious to and cared nothing about the larger human world.

Humans, he thought, *are doing the same thing, blind to what is going on in the larger, and smaller, world. We concern ourselves only with what lies in front of us. Occasionally, we ponder the greater universe, which often leads to spiritual thinking to help explain the world—but this is something that, apparently, the ladybugs do not do.*

Toquuxla, "Toq" for short, wondered if the ladybugs knew that he watched them. He looked up and wondered if anyone watched him or his people. A higher power, the Creator, the gods, spirits, ancestors.

He looked again at the orange-red ladybugs and thought, *All you have to do to see me watching you is look up. When I look up, I see nobody. No one watches. We are unaided and unguided, and aside from our fellow creatures, we are alone on the earth.* He took a good look around and said of the spiritual, "It's all made-up. And I am free of it."

Perhaps he is correct that no one watches, but for now, *we* will watch him.

In the time and in the land of Toquuxla's people, small bands—typically composed of several families living, hunting, and traveling together—spread along rivers and streams. People moved between bands, and bands moved constantly to keep from depleting the game that fed them. Semipermanent villages set down roots along some rivers where the fishing was good. Obvious to some, though not all, was the danger that came from too many people in one place with too many mouths to feed—whether they relied on hunting or fishing. Toquuxla had left home a few years earlier and lived with both hunters and fishers, and he had come to believe that there were getting to be too many people in both.

When a small party decided to travel east, upriver, to hopefully less populated areas, Toq had eagerly joined. They traveled overland south of and well above the river (Snake River) so they would not have to negotiate cliffs and deep coulees. About two days into their journey, they ventured down a coulee to camp near the river, among spruce and willows and where there was a great view across the valley looking north up a tributary canyon. Farther up this canyon, Toq had once visited a grand, high, and mighty waterfall (Palouse Falls) and the vertical walled canyon its waters cut through. To his people, it was a place of powerful spirits, and he'd felt deep awe of the waterfall's loud roar, its falling, muddy torrent, the foaming bottom, and the shining white mist, all while a thousand hawks and swallows zipped back and forth along the canyon's edge.

Today, the quiet, early morning broke with a clear blue sky. Toq stared up the canyon, thinking about that waterfall and listening to the sounds of ducks, geese, and other waterbirds. Then, he returned to his group and joined them in finishing their meal and packing up their belongings.

Summer is great, thought Toq. The world felt soft—not hard or harsh—and he relished these long, warm days.

Everyone put on their packs and bags, and a few men started up the coulee with a couple of the older children tagging along. They had already disappeared around a bend when the rest of the group started after them. Toq volunteered to bring up the rear, and as soon as he started walking, the geese all began honking loudly. He wondered what all the commotion was about, looked back toward the river, and then felt the ground shaking.

He mumbled to himself, "What is this?"

Everyone else had stopped to look as well, and one young man hollered at Toq, "What's going on?"

But Toq, alarmed and not knowing, only shrugged. He looked back to the north, where birds flew across the river toward his group. Ducks beat the water with their wings and feet as they took to the sky. The geese grew more agitated, until they too took off, leaving behind some goslings not yet able to fly. Immediately afterward, Toq heard the low-pitched rumble of a thousand waterfalls and smashing rocks.

Fear and panic gripped his mind and throat. He couldn't see the source of the sound or the cause of the trembling earth. He hurried to catch up to his group, but nobody knew if they should run or, if so, to where.

A young child asked his mother, "What's happening, Mom? What's that noise?"

She held his hand and said, "I don't know, son," as she looked north.

Then, another woman pointed and yelled, "Look! Look! *Look*!"

Above the hilltops, a cloud of mist formed against the blue sky.

"The gods!" Toq cried, though he did not believe in them. Then he yelled at everyone, "Get out of the coulee! Run! Run up the hill! Away from the river! Go fast!" He told one man to carry a small child, and he himself picked up another before changing his mind and handing the little one off to a different man, saying, "Go! I have to catch up to the others!"

The group raced up the hill, burdened by packs, children, and babies, while Toq ran up the coulee, glancing back just once to see the mist rising higher as the noise grew louder. He rounded the bend to find the others running toward him.

They shouted, "What's happening?"

But Toq just pointed up the hill, saying, "Get out of the coulee!" and he led the way.

The two children struggled to keep up, so he took off his bags and carried the ten-year-old on his back, while another man pulled the older child along by the hand.

The boy was heavy, and when Toq could no longer run, he let the child down and said, "You have to run! Hurry!"

Toq ran behind him, his lungs burning, his legs turning to mush. They reached the top of a small bench about halfway up the hill just moments before the others arrived. Everyone was out of breath and sweating profusely. The babies were quiet and secure, but the older children cried loudly.

One girl, with tears running down her cheeks, asked her mother, "Why are we running? Why are we running, Mom?"

Her mother only said, "It's okay. We're safe here," as she looked back north, her eyes wide with fear.

Here, they had good views up the black canyon and down into the coulee. But the hill they stood on obscured much of the valley, and they couldn't see the river. Everyone looked north at the rising mist. The growing roar cracking off the canyon walls seemed to echo off the sky. Then, at the far end of the canyon, a rushing, boiling, foaming, muddy wall of water crashed down with unbelievable speed, splashing towers of spray into the air, smashing and submerging every would-be obstacle that stood hopelessly in its way. Water filled the canyon before their eyes. Even more shocking, it began to pour over the hills as if they were mere stones in a creek.

One young man cried, "Are we safe here? We're not safe here! We have to get away! Let's go!"

Nobody disagreed. Toq worried they wouldn't be able to get high enough. He looked toward the river to see a huge wall of water spray up into the sky, and he knew the lead wave had crashed into the river wall on the south side. They ran, seventeen humans trying with all their might to save their lives.

The hill was very steep, with scattered brush and fir trees serving as both obstacles and something to grasp onto. The men carried the two smallest children. They pulled and, at times, virtually threw a couple of the older kids up the hill. Half of the group had abandoned their packs and bags, and only three, including Toq, still held their spears. From time to time, people paused to look back, but those behind them pushed them on, yelling, "Go! Go!"

Toq hung back to make sure nobody was left behind. He stole a look at the coulee below. The water was now boiling up the coulee they had camped in, razing and engulfing trees, tearing brush and rocks from the hillsides.

They reached the hilltop—a flat, grassy spot from which they could see in all directions. Some people sat or lay down, while others watched the water pouring over the hills and canyons to the north. A couple looked down at the coulee from which they had just escaped, and a couple looked west downstream of the main river, where the first big wave was barreling nearly out of sight.

The rising river became a turbulent dark brown, filled with broken trees, brush, and chunks of ice. Foam covered any still water. Toq looked down into the coulee where the leading wave pushed up the valley, then slowed and reversed direction, draining back toward the river. He saw the bodies and tusks of two mammoths, clearly dead. From atop the hill, they looked small and insignificant, hung up in the mud.

One of the older boys pointed just upstream of the mammoths. "Look! What is that?"

Shielding his eyes from the sun, Toq squinted hard until he could make out a big cat pulling itself out of the water, digging its claws into the slippery slope. It was too exhausted to shake the water from its fur and slowly climbed a little way up the hill before lying down.

"It's a long-fang (saber-tooth)," said one young man.

"It looks pathetic," said the woman next to him.

Birds of all kinds—big and small, waterfowl, birds of prey, ravens, storks, owls—flew down from the north in a spread-out, steady stream. To the northwest, Toq saw more mist rising from the hills. It appeared that theirs was not the only canyon flooding. Everywhere he looked, animals moved away from the valley: horses, camels, caribou, bison, and bears. Then, well away from the river and on another hill, he spotted a group of people waving their arms and spears over their heads, their calls drowned out by the raging waters.

Toq and a mother holding a baby pointed at this other group, saying in unison, "There!"

The eldest man, their leader, said, "We need to get over there. Is everyone rested?"

Some nodded, and a few said, "Yes, let's go."

The water below had stopped flowing back toward the river, and was now steadily rising, once more filling the coulee. The mammoths were again submerged. The long-fang stood and moved uphill on shaky legs.

Someone asked, "Where is all that water coming from?" But no one answered.

Big icebergs now floated in the water, moving upstream as the river flowed backwards.

"Unbelievable!" Toq said to himself.

His band had left him, and he trotted after them down the hill. They would have to go through a gap, then up along a ridge to the other hill. He worried about dropping into the gap; for now, it was dry, but the water was rising quickly and would certainly flood this low spot. He didn't have to warn anyone, though, as everyone hurried. As they descended, the big long-fang appeared, going up. The line of people veered aside but didn't slow down, and they barely paid the cat any attention. As Toq was still in the rear, he kept looking back to be sure the cat was not coming after them. In turn, the poor, exhausted animal only watched the people move away. It finally shook off the dripping water, as if to regain some pride, and resumed its climb.

It didn't take them long to reach the bottom. The water in the coulee had risen enough that Toq was now certain it would flood the gap. They began to climb the next hill, moving quickly at first, but soon slowing with each step. There was only so much the body could manage, even fueled by fear and adrenaline. Harried and depleted, someone was always slipping or tripping and falling, but always, they got right back up. The children struggled the most, and everyone kept an eye on them. They could run and play all day, but stepping over downed logs or up onto large rocks with short legs was much harder, and even going through tall grass and brush was arduous. But they kept going, urged along by the adults, sometimes being pulled by the hand or lifted over a log. When they reached the top of the ridge, they paused to look back at the water spilling across the gap they had just crossed.

They didn't linger. They started up along the ridge as three men came down to meet them. These men were young and fresh, and everyone directed them to the three children who were trying to make it on their own. The men lifted the children onto their backs. One by one, Toq's group reached the hilltop, where they were greeted by two more men and a boy of about twelve. They caught their breath and drank from water bladders made from deer stomachs. Toq's group profusely thanked the men for their help.

Toq recognized one man who called himself "the Traveler." He had passed through their encampment a couple of weeks ago, heading upstream. A couple of the older men in Toq's group had met some of the others years ago while scouting and trading.

One man said, "We were hunting up here last night, just before sunset, and we saw where you guys were camped. We camped a ways farther upriver. When we heard the flooding, we had an easy time getting to high ground. So, we came over here to check on you."

From here, the hills obstructed their view of the flooded river, but they could still see the rising mist and the water filling the coulee, and they could still hear the thunderous waters.

Several of them began talking: "Where is that water coming from? It's unbelievable!" "It comes from evil spirits." "What about our people, our village? How could they survive that?" "Maybe they got away. We did." "We need to go back when the flood goes down." "What if it doesn't? What if the water just keeps coming?" "It'll stop. We should go back now." Most said nothing, fear still filling their eyes.

Thousands of birds continued to fly south over the hills and waters, and watching them, Toq mumbled to himself, "Wish we could fly."

Some birds landed on the cliff tops and in the trees, some on the flatland just to the south, and some kept on flying in every direction but north.

Legends had long been told about the floods. Their grandparents spoke of "the great floods from the north," but nowadays, most people considered them only scary stories. Nobody had ever thought they would actually experience one, and no story could properly recreate its true horror and awesome spectacle.

The men from the other group said, "We need to go. We don't know how high the water will get. Come and stay with us."

"No . . ." one woman pleaded. "We have to go back to help our people."

Their leader said, "You all go on ahead, and a few of us will run back to see if anyone else made it."

Toq, the Traveler, and one other volunteered. After a brief rest and a little food, the four men ran steadily west along the plateau above the still-rising waters. It was midsummer, the days were long, and the sun had not yet reached its zenith, and Toq knew they could cover that ground—which had taken them two days as a group—before day's end. Soon, sweat ran down their faces and backs, and they peeled off almost all their skin clothing, stuffing it into their two pack bags. In these, they also carried a horn with embers for starting a fire, a stone blade, an antler blade, food, and some water. That was all. Each man carried his spear, and they switched off carrying the two bags. Two ran barefoot, while two wore moccasins.

It was late afternoon by the time they reached a prominent overlook from which they ought to have been able to see their village. But instead of a camp of about one hundred people, there was nothing but a huge lake full of floating debris: sticks, trees, brush, and blocks of ice both very large and very small. The bodies of dead animals, large and small, bobbed in the muddy waves. The wind blowing across the water smelled wet and fresh, earthy from the mud; though it smelled of wet fur, it did not yet smell of decaying bodies. That would come soon enough. A few eagles and gulls plucked some of the smaller carcasses out of the water and carried them to dry land to eat. Dead fish lined the edge of the water, some as big as a man. Scavenger birds—vultures, eagles, gulls, ravens, crows, magpies—were trying to take advantage of this feast, but the rising water made it a moving target. The frenzy was a sight to behold. Even a couple of the rarely seen, gigantic teratorns soared above the moving shoreline. People had long marveled at this enormous bird's ability to float on the wind. Its wingspan was the length of two men. It had long talons and a giant, curved beak capable of ripping off pounds of flesh. The two teratorns, with beautiful black and white feathers, circled above the chaos. Toq never did see them land.

The men squinted out into the vast stretch of water, looking for signs of human life—or death. Toq thought maybe he saw an empty canoe getting pummeled in the waves, but it was too far away to make out clearly. They scanned the shore and the lands surrounding the lake, but they were afraid to go down to the water's edge. They weren't sure they could outrun the steadily advancing shoreline.

It was the Traveler who said, "Look, there, there!" as he pointed toward a long peninsula the lake was quickly swallowing.

Toq's eyesight was okay, but he couldn't see what the Traveler was pointing at.

"What?" he asked.

"Two people coming up the hill toward us. They won't make it if they don't hurry."

Toq was miffed at himself that he couldn't see them.

One of the other men said, "They're going too slow. We have to get down there and help them."

They started down the hill, leaving their packs. Only the Traveler carried his spear. Halfway down, Toq finally saw the two human dots. They appeared to be struggling, the rising water at their heels, and Toq doubted whether his group could rescue them in time.

He took off at a dead sprint for the duo. The young man and woman were exhausted, unable to run, and stumbling along. The woman looked at him with glazed eyes.

"Toq!" she said with a weak, raspy voice.

But Toq couldn't tell who they were. They were a mess, barefoot and missing half their clothing, their whole bodies covered with mud. They both had cuts with dried blood on their hands, arms, and feet. Mud ran down off the young man's forehead, into one of his eyes, and his hands were too dirty to clear it.

The others arrived a moment later, and no one wasted any time flanking the pair, who draped their arms over their rescuers' necks.

Toq said, "We have to go fast."

They ran up the hill, the survivors' feet barely touching the ground. It was awkward and clumsy, but the two were not very big, which helped. Gritty mud and dirt, mixed with sweat, rubbed the rescuers' necks raw.

Once again, I'm running up a hill for my life, Toq thought. *Three times in one day.*

The water closed in, their legs ached, and their lungs burned. Water began pouring across the dip between them and the bigger, steeper hill that would save their lives. They ran, ankle deep, then shin deep, then knee deep. But then, they were starting back up, coming out of the water, back onto dry land, and they climbed the steep hill. Though, they weren't safe yet.

Someone yelled a kind of war cry, trying to shore up what little adrenaline was left.

With much effort, after minutes that seemed like forever, they attained the top of the hill. Lying on the ground, with arms and legs splayed, Toq's companions stared at the sky, chests heaving. But with his heart pounding,

Toq paced, trying to shake out the muscles in his legs so they wouldn't cramp up. As he walked in circles, he looked out at the water. A big shadow passed overhead, and he looked up to see one of the teratorns checking them out. After a few moments of rest, the group realized they had to get moving again. If the water continued to rise—and there was no sign of it slowing down—their hill would become an island in a growing lake.

The young man insisted he could run on his own now. The young woman was less confident. The group grabbed their sacks and spears and hurried away from the lake, down into a little valley, and up onto a higher plateau. Here, they felt safe enough to rest awhile. It was impossible to know just how high the waters would rise. It occurred to Toq that this could be the end of the world. There was no more higher ground—unless they ran to the mountains, far, far away. They could only hope the lake would stop rising soon.

The sun dropped low in the sky, hanging just above the watery horizon. The wind slowed, but the temperature dropped as the ice-cold waters of the new lake blew away the heat of the day. Now, the lake looked like a growing sea, stretching off to the horizon west and north.

Biting flies and mosquitoes came out to torment the weary group. They found a little spot to camp for the night, hunkered down behind some brush and rocks, out of any wind that might blow up—and hopefully above the high-water mark of the new lake. They split into pairs and went out looking for dry wood, clear water, and fresh meat. Water, dead animals, and fish were, of course, abundant down at the lake, but they stayed away from it.

In addition to a couple of small animals, they found a few berries and some good-sized bird's eggs. The contents of the eggs would be a surprise. The Traveler took one, held it up to the sinking sunlight, shook it, and then carefully cracked the top of the shell open.

He laughed loudly and exclaimed, "Oh, what a perfect little prize!"—though, he said it with two well-placed obscenities. He sniffed the opening, shook his head, then just stared at the egg for a moment.

The oldest man in the group said, "Don't do it. You'll be sorry."

That was all the Traveler needed. He flashed a big grin and peeled off the rest of the top half of the shell, exposing a dead, nearly completely formed bird embryo in what was left of the egg white. With everyone watching, he lifted his "prize" to his mouth and, in one quick motion, threw it back. He lowered his head and stared at the ground, chewing slowly, deliberately, with a long cord of slime dangling from his lower lip to the shell in his hand. He swallowed a couple of times.

He looked up, grinned again, and laughed, "That was a little past its prime." Then, he popped the eggshell into his mouth and ate that, too.

Nobody in this group gagged. While they'd all eaten risky things before, no one else wished to take any chances today. They cooked the rest of the eggs at the edge of the fire.

They had no bedding or fur to sleep in, and their clothes would not be sufficient to keep them warm through what was sure to be a long and uncomfortable night. They needed enough wood to keep a fire or two burning. Toq spoke with the older man about the danger of the water reaching their camp in the middle of the night, but there wasn't anything they could do about it now, except hope and pray. And pray they did—chanting and singing out to the spirits to keep them safe. Though Toq didn't believe it would do any good, he joined in anyway.

The rescued couple felt better after cleaning up and having some food and water. But still, their eyes drooped shut and their heads bobbed. They had been very quiet, speaking only a little and smiling just once at the Traveler's antics. Now, Toq recognized them, and though everyone was anxious to ask what had happened to the village, they refrained out of respect.

CHAPTER 2

The Next Day

The four older men took turns through the night sleeping, tending the fires, and watching the waters. They let the two young ones sleep. The sky was clear, and a half-moon came up to illuminate the dark landscape, reflecting on the ripples of the lake below. The night was not quiet. One could hear the odd call of some bird, and frogs, crickets, coyotes, an owl, and, at one point, two bobcats fighting down by the water. The mosquitoes had disappeared in the chilly air, allowing for a more peaceful rest.

Toq slept during the last shift of the night. When the sky grew bright, he rolled over onto his back. Someone was up and moving around. He thought he should get up, too, but his eyes felt like they'd been glued shut. Despite his bed of grass, the ground felt hard. On his body, he felt both the cold air and the warm fire at the same time. He sensed something, an itch or a little bite, just below his belly button. He reached under his trousers to crush whatever little bug was biting him, but this little bug was not going to be easily squashed. It was attached. Toq opened his eyes and lifted his head to look down at the tick. He hated them, but it seemed like he was always picking them up. Most of the time, he caught them before they could bury their tiny heads into his skin. This time, though, he held his pants up over his belly while he pinched the tick between his thumb and finger and slowly pulled up until the tick let go. He sat up and looked at the little bugger, legs waving between his fingertips.

"Little bastard," he said and tossed it into the fire.

He looked around. Three guys appeared to still be asleep. The young woman was lying on her side, staring at the fire. She looked at Toq, and he nodded and whispered, "Morning." Her lips moved, but he didn't hear anything. He stood and saw their elder standing on the rise just behind him, his spear resting against his shoulder. The sun had just broken over the far horizon, and it made this man glow before an indigo sky. He looked out at the lake while a gentle breeze pushed his long black hair back in waves, on and off his shoulders. He looked down at Toq as he came up.

Toq greeted him quietly, and the elder said, "Look, Toq. The lake does not grow anymore. The spirits heard our prayers."

Toq nodded, feeling greatly relieved. The water had come up only a little in the night. Activity on the shore had increased considerably. In addition to the birds, Toq now saw a small herd of horses at the water's edge, and a pack of wolves and four bears fishing out dead animals along the shoreline. The scavengers would get fat if they could get to this feast before it sank or floated away. Every now and then, Toq caught a whiff of dead fish. He struggled to comprehend the amount of death this flood had caused. The distant sound of flooding water was now silent, and a great calm filled the scene.

"Once the others wake up, we'll go down and try to get one of those animals to eat," the elder said, referring to the dead ones kept fresh by the cold waters.

Turning back to their companions, they were startled by the sight of a big brown bear drawing near with her two cubs. Still a little ways off, Toq and the elder ran right toward them, hollering and waving their arms and spears.

Distracted and drawn by the rich aromas of the lake, she had not noticed the humans, but when she heard them now, she stood on her hind legs to get a better look. The cubs did the same thing behind her, one leaning on his mother.

The men were nervous, but they needed to show a lot of bravado if they had any chance of running her off. Everyone in the camp sprang to their feet and joined in the loud chorus of shouting and waving. The bear looked for only a moment longer, then huffed once, spun around and down on all fours, and ran with her cubs in the opposite direction. She stopped to look back a couple of times, then they loped off out of sight.

The Traveler laughed and hooted as the group—wide-awake now and relieved—walked back to the camp.

He slapped Toq on the back and said loudly, "Now, that was exciting! But you didn't have to wake me up like that!"

This small victory, and the adrenaline, left a couple of them chattering like birds in the morning.

Back around the fires, the elder told everyone about the lake and their plan to retrieve some meat from the water. Because of all the bears, everyone would go together. So, they walked down the slope to the lake, everyone moving stiffly, their muscles exceedingly sore from yesterday.

Upon reaching the edge of the lake, it was obvious that the water had already dropped about the height of a man, leaving behind a mixture of mud, dead fish, and debris. They had chosen a point between two bears that were busy gorging themselves and barely paying the humans any attention. The horses retreated some distance before stopping to observe the people. The wolves had been scavenging half the night, so now they, too, moved away, contented and sleepy.

Icebergs floated in the lake. One gigantic, astoundingly beautiful chunk of white and turquoise ice—which the water had sculpted into fantastic shapes—was half-stuck onshore. Toq's group walked around it, running their hands along the cold, melting surface. It was three times the height of a man, but some of the icebergs out in the water looked even bigger. They used rocks to chip off pieces of ice to suck on. It tasted pure and clean—much better than the muddy, corpse-filled lake—and they filled their water bladders from trickles running off the berg.

They turned their attention to the lake, where a tree, ripped from the ground, was stuck in the mud below the surface. Its branches jutted from the water. A large, dark body floated among the branches—one side of a set of antlers sticking up from the water, the bloody remnants of velvet hanging off the newly grown crown. A couple of men waded out to the deer, the icy water up to their chest. Its antlers were entangled in the tree branches, but with much effort—and chattering teeth—they pulled the head free and dragged the animal up onto dry land. The buck's neck and legs were broken.

They had just one cutting stone to work with. They didn't bother with gutting or bleeding the animal. Instead, they cut right into its hindquarters, taking as much meat as they could back to their camp, where they cooked it and ate as much as they wanted.

For the first time, the group relaxed, and their elder finally asked the young couple what had happened to the village. How had they escaped? The young man did most of the talking. He said they'd been on a hillside with some others, about to hunt and gather wood, when they heard the flooding waves coming and saw their people—their families—running from the village below. They raced down to try to help get the elderly and the children to safety.

"But," the young man said, "it was too much water, too fast."

He saw a huge wave crash through their village, tearing everything up and swallowing it. He tried to help an old woman, but she could not run.

"It didn't make any difference. Even the fastest runners were not outrunning the water," he said.

The wave smashed into them, and he lost the old woman he was trying to help. It was so cold that all the muscles in his body seemed to lock up. He struggled to hold his breath, and he squeezed his eyes shut as tight as he could. He rolled along on the bottom of the blackness, feeling rocks and trees moving with him; how they missed him was a mystery. The water sporadically tossed him up to the surface, so he could pull in a breath of air. The wave pushed him back toward the hill he'd run down, and with his energy nearly extinguished, he happened into a relatively calm eddy.

As he struggled to keep his head up, he heard the young woman's voice behind him in the water yell, "Hey! Here! Grab on!"

She had managed to get ahold of a tree trunk floating by, and he reached out and clung to a branch. They kicked with all their might, pushing their log to the hillside, which they scrambled to climb up. "But the water was rising so quickly, and the mud was so slippery, if it weren't for some bushes we grabbed to climb up, we wouldn't have gotten out." From there, it felt like they walked and ran all day, trying to stay ahead of the water. They never saw anyone else from their village.

The young woman said, "Everything was underwater. Everyone disappeared."

"The water kept coming and coming," said the young man. "It was like a relentless animal pursuing us, like the spirits were not going to give up until we were dead. She could see the high hill, but our legs were hard to move, our tongues felt swollen and dry in our mouths, and I could hardly see. She said we were in a bad place, that the water was going to trap us, and then I heard her say, 'Toq!' And there you guys were. I felt so happy inside, but I still wondered if we would make it."

Reliving their nightmare and all they'd lost, the two young people's eyes swelled and overflowed with tears.

Struggling to form the words, the young man glanced up at his rescuers and said, "Thank you. Thank you," and the young woman, staring at the fire, nodded in agreement.

Toq felt like he'd swallowed a rock, and a profound feeling of grief over-whelmed him as he thought about the village—*his* village—being wiped away. They were hard people, used to seeing death, but this was a huge blow. The group shed tears and hugged and comforted one another as best as they knew how. Even the Traveler, who'd only passed through, was teary-eyed.

It was incredible that these two had survived, and while they all needed time to recover, right now they needed to decide what to do next. It was nearly a two-day walk back to the main group. They all agreed to spend the rest of the day searching the shore for any other survivors. They also found a better spot to camp. Three people, including the two youngest, stayed to gather food, collect wood, and make a decent place to stay, even if it was just for one night.

Toq, the elder, and the Traveler headed southwest along the shore, some-times climbing up the hills to see farther. To their amazement, the waters in the valley and coulees were receding quickly, leaving behind blocks of ice, dead fish and animals, logs, uprooted trees, and a thick deposit of mud and sand. A line of debris marked the high point of the flood. Grass stuck out of the mud in places, along with drowned, bent over bushes. Even the tops of a couple of trees poked from the surface of the lake, apparently able to hold their ground through the deluge.

The three stayed together as they searched. They couldn't risk stumbling across a bear on their own. Thousands of birds, as well as the predators and scavengers on the ground, remained, but the earlier frenzy had abated. Now, bellies were full, and the animals had retreated to shady spots to snooze. The men scoured the landscape, trying to find someone, dead or alive, even calling out into coulees and from hilltops, but they heard no replies. They dreaded coming upon a body stuck in the mud or partially eaten. But they found no one—not even a remnant of anything man-made. There was nothing left. They looked out into the lake in case someone had found something to cling to, but there was nothing. The old village site, originally next to the river, was still under water. The men looped back inland, hoping someone might have set up a camp, but instead, they found the valley to the east had flooded with its own large lake. Toq thought of the other clans down the river. *They must have all been wiped out, too.* He thought there had to be a few lucky ones who'd survived, now scattered about. In reality, the flooding was much, much worse downstream. Indeed, there were a few "lucky" ones who'd survived the flood, but many of these perished from injuries, starvation, or animal attacks.

The men returned to their new campsite just before sunset without any good news. The others had set up a fine camp with fire, food, water, and even some makeshift shelters of brush and grass. Everyone ate well, spoke about all they had seen that day, and rested, quietly contemplating the loss of the people they loved and imagining their last terrifying moments.

Toq mused as he lay on the ground, in the dark, looking up at the stars, *So many people . . . all gone. Simply vanished. Dead. Where are they now? Do their spirits roam the earth? Or have they gone on to a place of paradise? Or are they simply no more?*

He knew what the shamans said about the dead, the spirits, the gods, ghosts, the next life. He didn't believe the shamans' teachings. How did they know? They claimed to have special gifts, to be able to communicate with spirits and gods, and most people believed them. But Toq did not. He had, for a time. In fact, he'd believed passionately. He'd been taught from childhood, and ghosts once terrified him, but over the years, his skepticism grew. The closer he got to a shaman, the more he found them to be just as imperfect as anyone else—if not worse, deceitful and hypocritical. Some were honest, but Toq began to wonder who'd made them "the knowers" of the will of the Creator and what the spirits do or do not do, what is true, what is false. They seemed to have an explanation for everything.

Toq thought, *How do they know?* He concluded, *They don't. They don't know any more than anyone else. They just make shit up. They want people to be amazed at their knowledge and insight, their spiritual powers. They want to be revered and possess a special, higher status in their tribe.*

Mixed feelings filled him: deep sadness for his people, fear about what would come next, anger at the first shaman he would meet. Although it appeared that everyone from his village had perished, including the shamans, he was certain he would be meeting more of them in the camps that had not flooded—if any such camps existed. And he was also certain that any shaman who'd survived would claim foreknowledge of this flood. He would say that he had warned people who did not listen, or that he'd been told not to tell anyone—that some people must die, must be punished. Toq knew this was coming, and he knew it was a crock, and it angered him.

CHAPTER 3

Return and Begin Again

Toq felt pretty good the next morning. From their camp, he could look down the coulee toward the lake, and he saw the water had shrunk way back from its high point. There seemed to be more mud than lake now—although there was still plenty of lake. Icebergs glowed white and blue in the water. They would not last long in the summer sun, but they would leave behind boulders brought with them from the north as evidence of their presence here. Toq wondered if people would one day ask how that big rock had come to be in that spot.

Animal activity had slowed considerably. Large carnivores had largely had their fill, though one skinny, nervous-looking bear still pawed through the mud. Now, the smaller animals took their turn: coyotes, foxes, bobcats, skunks, badgers. Animal footprints indented the ground everywhere. Toq saw some bloody rib cages and legs sticking up from the soaked earth. A set of curved mammoth tusks and a large body, way out in the flat, lay surrounded by a thin sheen of water, untouched by the scavengers. Rotting fish were scattered everywhere—too many for the scavengers to eat. Several kinds Toq had never seen before. Some were very large—longer than a man—with heavy, thick, strange-looking snouts and tough skin.

The group ate, packed up what little they had, and stood together on a hill looking out at the mud and lake. They discussed staying longer. At the rate the lake was draining, they could probably return to the remains of their village in just another day. But they knew there would be no point. There would be nothing left but heartbreak. So, they began their journey east, back to the larger group. It would be a long walk. None of them felt like running, and there was no longer a need to hurry.

· · · ·

A dark mood enveloped the group during the day and a half of their return journey. Despairing their loss and anxious over their future, they questioned what they had to do next. The two younger ones felt this most acutely. The Traveler would occasionally break the silence with a funny quip, helping to lighten the mood.

They didn't know exactly where the other group would be, but they had a good idea and found the camp easily. It held around fifty people—about half as many as their home village. The people in the camp rejoiced at the arrival of Toq and his group. The women greeted them with big smiles and outstretched arms. Children ran up to them, grabbing their hands. They were exceedingly happy to see the two young survivors, and they were anxious to hear of the village's fate. Therefore, this happy scene did not last long. Toq's group had not even sat down before sharing what they had found. Tears flowed and some people wailed loudly, unable to hold in their emotions. It was a dreadful thing, seeing all this pain and sadness. Toq knew it was coming, and he hated it. He wished so earnestly for their life before the flood, but he knew those days would not be coming back.

Everything changes. It's always changing. As bad as this is, it's just another change. You have to accept it. You can't fix it. But . . . I can try to make it better. I can help. I have to focus on the living, not the dead.

He looked at the Traveler with watery eyes. Normally a lighthearted fellow, the Traveler shook his head, rubbed his own wet eyes, quietly sniffed, and walked away from the weeping people. In addition to his sadness, the Traveler also appeared restless and uncomfortable; he didn't really know these people. He walked around the camp, just outside the perimeter, and Toq thought he was waiting for everyone to stop crying before he rejoined them.

••••

Resettling with a new tribe was difficult for Toq and his group, but they needed these people and this larger encampment. Due to the aftermath of the flood, they moved farther upriver, and when they found a place to camp, they made sure it was on a bluff high above the water. They argued about it, though. Some were afraid of more floods, while others said there was little chance of another flood like that. "Not in our lifetimes."

Some looked to the shaman, who curtly said, "Whether we live here or there, it doesn't matter. It's more important how we live and if we honor the spirits."

He appeared annoyed that he was asked, but he relished the opportunity to feel important and wiser than everyone else.

In the following days, talk about the flood was incessant, with a lot of guessing, speculation, assertions, and skepticism. People got into strong disagreements. "Where did all that water come from?" "How could it appear one day, and the next day or two just stop?" "It came over the hills! Earthquakes must have opened up the springs." "Earthquakes? What, are you crazy? There were no earthquakes." "The glaciers up north, somehow it came from them." "The spirits are angry. They did it because we haven't been living right. We need to be better, pray more, and make sacrifices. We must fear the gods." Everyone nodded except Toq.

One insightful woman said, "Perhaps a giant dam, holding back a huge lake, suddenly broke open."

A couple of people said, "That's just stupid," and she said no more, but her guess was correct.

At night, around campfires, they recounted the old tales of floods. Now they had their own terrifying story to tell their children and grandchildren. They hoped and prayed they would never see anything like it again. *How many of these other myths are actually true and actually happened?* Toq pondered. Still, he did not believe in mystical explanations, and he feared the stories of this flood were already beginning to carry elements of a new mythology.

There was much to do before winter now: building shelters, storing firewood, collecting food from plants, hunting, skinning, tanning, drying and smoking meat, and making clothes, tools, spears, and everything else they needed. These resilient people had the skills to survive. The flood affected fishing throughout the summer, but by the fall, the spawning runs came, and the camp caught a good supply of fish to smoke and store.

Before the arrival of the cold weather, Toq journeyed with a group of men back to the old village, to see if they might make contact with anyone else, but the land was devoid of people, as if humans had never lived there.

The sense of loss crushed his heart, but when he noticed all the wildlife, he muttered, mostly to himself, "They'll be back. The people will be back."

The men swung by the coulee where Toq's group had been camped when the flood hit. Looking north to the hills and the canyon from which the floodwaters had poured, they tried to remember what it had looked like before. Now, it was a wasteland. All the vegetation had been stripped away. In some places, even the soil had been flushed downstream, leaving only bare rock.

In the coulee, they found the remains of the two mammoths. Bones, tusks, hair, and stiff, dried hide. They gathered up the hair and two of the bigger tusks, which slowed them down on their return journey, but the tusks were valuable and worth the effort.

Autumn came and went. Winter bore down with cold winds and long, dark nights, snow and more snow, and many cloudy gray skies. Every winter, Toq would tell himself, *It isn't so bad as long as you get outside every day.* Still, this winter was long, and he grew weary of hearing and telling stories, performing religious rituals, playing games, and doing chores. Their shelters were cramped, smoky, and dark most of the time. So, on days that were not too cold or windy, Toq escaped to hike around and breathe fresh air. It felt good to stretch his legs, get his heart thumping, look around, see the sky, and sometimes even feel the sun's warmth.

Toq went out on one of these jaunts on a brilliant, cold morning. A fresh layer of snow had fallen the night before. The clouds had all blown away, so there was nothing now but blue sky and sunshine, and not a hair moved for the lack of wind. Properly bundled up, Toq ran to the top of a hill, where, through his fur hood, he heard a muffled yell.

"Toq! Wait!"

The Traveler climbed up, plowing through the snow toward him. A small cloud puffed with each breath, but the man was barely winded. Ice was already forming on his eyebrows, eyelashes, the little bit of hair on his face, and around the edges of his fur hood.

He said, "Can I walk with you? I want to talk to you about something."

Toq said, "Sure. I was just going to walk up over that hill to see what animals might be moving around."

"Sounds good. What a great day!" The Traveler beamed at Toq and then up at the sky. Nothing seemed to faze the Traveler; he was always in a good mood, and he often went off on hikes by himself, too.

They proceeded to the next hill, and the Traveler blurted out, "I'm leaving when the snow melts."

Toq looked at him, not entirely surprised but still wishing he would stick around. "Oh?"

The Traveler did not look up from the path he was taking. "You should come with me."

Toq smiled. He was intrigued by the life the Traveler lived, the things he had seen, the different people he had met. Always moving. Free. The thought had crossed Toq's mind.

"You can always come back. I plan to come back, I think. Who knows?" said the Traveler. "I've heard stories about lands where there are no people, at least not yet. And where there are animals that no longer live here, like mammoths."

Toq said, "We saw a few in the flood."

"Yeah, but how many did we see before that? Or since?"

"Zero."

"Yeah, zero. But some of the people to the east say there are still herds of them in other places."

"How do they know?"

"Well, obviously, somebody has been there and seen them."

"Yeah, I guess," Toq said. He was thinking hard, his imagination running wild with images of an untouched land. He had witnessed the impact a group of people had when they moved into an area. If the tribe or family group was too big, the large animals would either be hunted out or would simply abandon the area. Even most large predators disappeared, though not completely.

Toq noticed the Traveler used no swear words in their conversation, an unusual occurrence, and he asked, "How far have you been?"

"Way far. Past the canyons, into the mountains, but I had to come back. I couldn't find a good route through to the other side."

"What's on the other side of the mountains?"

"I don't know, but I want to see."

"I want to see, too," said Toq.

"You'll come with me?" asked the Traveler excitedly.

"I have to think about it. Aren't you afraid, traveling by yourself, or even with just the two of us?"

"Maybe a little bit, but I just can't stay in one place with the same people, doing the same thing every day. I have to go see what's out there. I'm happiest when I'm out there. Even if I die out there, I'm willing to take that chance."

They hiked in the shade of the hill. The sun flew low to the horizon, and upon reaching the top, they broke into the blinding light of the sun on the radiant white snow. *Too much light to see,* Toq thought ironically. They looked down into the valley and across to the other side, all of it covered in sparkling white, with a smattering of spindly spruce trees. Toq held the top of his hood out just enough to shade his eyes. The Traveler slipped off his mittens and pulled his leather eye covers out of one of them. He pushed back his hood, pulled the leather band over his head, fitting the slits over his eyes, and pulled his hood and mittens back on. He looked left and right, up and down the valley, but there was nothing but an unblemished blanket of snow. No animals and no tracks.

Toq speculated, "It must be too cold. They're all bedded down, but there will be tracks by the end of the day, for sure."

They looked up along the ridge, where two snow owls perched on separate, snow-covered rock outcrops.

"They're so beautiful," muttered the Traveler, mostly to himself, to which Toq said, "Yes, indeed," and he looked at the Traveler.

It was one of the things he admired about the man. Some people considered animals only things—to be killed and eaten, to be used for clothing and shelter, their bones and antlers made into tools and weapons, their feathers, teeth, and claws used for decoration or ceremony. And it was true that they needed animals for these purposes, but many also used animals as target practice. Usually it was the younger men, but sometimes the women as well, who were trying to prove how tough, how macho, or how "skilled" they were at killing. It all seemed pointless to Toq, just something people used to puff up their chests. It made them feel powerful, admired, respected, but the pain and suffering some of these animals endured was wrong. Toq, and most older men, had gotten over that desire to prove themselves. These men hunted to live, so they hunted efficiently and made every effort to kill quickly. Hunting for a large group was often hard work. A few people, though, seemed to truly enjoy killing, and they seemed to like watching the suffering. These were heartless and bloodthirsty people, and Toq stayed away from them. Toq knew of one fellow, so unpredictable and angry, that he'd been banished from his group after beating another man nearly to death. So, for all these reasons, Toq liked the Traveler. He wasn't like other people at all. He loved the beauty he saw in the wild world. He had no desire to rule over it or conquer it. He only wanted to be in it.

They stood on the hill watching the owls, whose yellow eyes watched the two men in turn. Then, one owl turned its head and flew off up the valley. The other owl looked to see where it had gone, looked back at the men, and took off after the first.

"Ah, to be able to fly," the Traveler said.

"Yes, that would be something," Toq said.

The wind began to blow, and powdery snowflakes tumbled across the drifts.

The Traveler grinned at Toq. He said, "Think about coming with me. You'd be good company."

Toq said, "I'll definitely think about it."

CHAPTER 4

Mental Preparation and Heading Out

About one full cycle of the moon had passed, and Toq could tell the Traveler was restless. They had many conversations, with Toq asking a wide range of questions, especially about things that made him nervous. People normally traveled in groups, where there was safety in having the extra spearpoints backing you up. The Traveler seemed fearless about traveling by himself—or stupid. Even with the two of them traveling together, their journey would still be dangerous.

"What about bears, long-fangs, mammoths, moose?"

"Never had a problem."

"Have you come across bad people or an unwelcoming village?"

"Not really. Most people are very nice. Most think I'm crazy or that I've been banished from my home band, but I smile and laugh a lot, so I'm not very threatening. Some want me to stay, marry their daughters, settle down, but I always make it clear I'm just passing through. People are very generous. But it seems there's a bad-tempered person in every group. Sometimes I can befriend them. Sometimes I avoid them. Sometimes they just want to bust me in the face. That's what happened to my tooth. Got in a fight. I lost."

He showed his top front teeth and, with his index finger, touched the bottom of his chipped tooth.

"What do you carry? How much food do you carry?" "How much do you hunt? Do you hunt every day?" "How far do you walk in a day? How long do your moccasins last? Do your feet get sore and beaten up?" "Do you make a fire every night? Do you make a shelter? Isn't night the scariest time? Have you ever slept in a tree?"

"What?" The Traveler grinned and said, "No, but I've thought about it. I have spent plenty of nights wide-awake, standing guard, staring into the darkness, listening for snapping twigs, footsteps, growling. If I don't have any better options, I'll crawl into a thicket."

"What about crossing rivers and raging creeks?"

"They scare the shit out of me. Sometimes I'll walk a long way up- or downstream, trying to find a place to cross. Sometimes I'll see where other people or animals have crossed. Sometimes I can find a log across and I always kiss it and thank the Great Spirit."

"But don't you get lonely? What if you get sick or injured?" "How long will you do this? Will you ever settle down?" "How far are you going? Which way?" "Will you come back?" "Do you have family?"

The Traveler answered these and many more questions. He could tell that Toq was intrigued—and skilled and knowledgeable—but perhaps too worried about the details and lacking confidence. He thought to himself, *That little bit of hesitancy will probably keep Toq alive. He'll think twice before acting. Although, sometimes you just don't have time to think.*

The days grew longer, the sun warmer, and the snow began melting away. Toq could not make up his mind to go or stay. There wasn't anything in particular holding him back. The tribal group he was with now, although good to him, were not his family, and would welcome him back if he left and then returned. Toq helped the Traveler in his preparations, all the while making the exact same items for himself, almost unconsciously: stone spearpoints, shafts, skins, moccasins, bags, bladders.

The Traveler said the best way to venture into these new lands was to walk, not paddle, to carry their loads on their backs, going overland, staying away from the river with its deep canyons and steep hillsides. The Traveler carried two leather bags, each with a single leather strap slung over his shoulder and running across his chest. He told Toq that it got hot and sweaty with the bags pressed against his body, but he could shift them from his back to his sides, and he could even carry one in the front if he wished. The more the Traveler talked, the more Toq wondered if he could keep up.

••••

Another full moon passed, and although the nights were cold, the worst of the winter was over. Most of the snow was gone. Grasses were greening, some flowers popped up, and the muddy ground was drying. There stood Toq, spear in hand, the stone head pointing skyward. A bundle of smaller throwing spears—their stone points covered with leather for protection—protruded from the bag he wore on his back, poking up above his head. Toq didn't know if they would carry very well that way, but he was going to try it. He had two exceedingly heavy sacks on his back, but the excitement he felt pushed their weight out of his mind. He could not believe that he was standing next to the Traveler, about to leave for a new and uncertain land. The Traveler was similarly laden, but he did not bend at all under his burden. In fact, he looked even stronger.

Toq's curiosity and excitement overpowered his considerable trepidation. Some people in the band had questioned his decision and tried to talk him out of it, and he'd listened, giving them a chance to change his mind. None of them could. Most were kind and concerned about him, while others seemed angry or pissed off or jealous.

One arrogant and ambitious fellow about his age had been especially obnoxious, calling Toq "unwise, stupid, and selfish." He said, "You'll die out there," and sarcastically called Toq "my hero" in passing. He called the

Traveler an "unwanted bastard idiot" but never to his face. Toq didn't get what the guy's problem was, but he wanted to punch him in the face. He told people he planned to come back, but "not if that jackass is still here." The Traveler counseled him to just stay calm about "that jackass" and walk away. "He'll be out of your life soon enough."

Frost covered the grass on this bright, sunny, windless morning. *A good day to start out,* Toq thought, his excitement growing. They said their good-byes to their people and walked quickly out of sight. Toq felt guilty about leaving them, and he worried about them as much as they worried about him, but he also knew he had to go. A person could not stay home forever because they worried about what might or might not happen. The flood—almost a year in the past—was still fresh in everyone's minds. It made some people afraid of everything—afraid of the unexpected. For Toq and the Traveler, life-ending catastrophes pushed them to go experience all they could, knowing that on any given day their lives could be over.

But Toq pushed the negative thoughts from his mind. *They'll be fine. I have to focus on what's before me.* The Traveler thought that the next tribal encampment—if it was still there—was about a four-day walk away.

The Traveler said, "We should try to get there in three days, since we don't know what the hunting or fishing will be like."

"Okay," said Toq, but he wondered if he could keep pace.

They figured they had enough food for two days and hoped to kill something along the way, but hunting was slow and time-consuming. How could they cover all that ground if they had to slow down to hunt? They needed to hike as long and as far as they could on their first day.

Toq was in great shape and a strong walker, but the Traveler, who was a bit taller, had a long, easy stride, and Toq struggled to keep up with him on the flats and downhill sections. Toq was faster on the uphill climbs, so they matched up and traveled well together. They both started the day enthused and talkative. By midday, the energy and mental high was gone, and their speed had slowed somewhat. They walked on mostly in silence now, just working at hiking, earnestly, deliberately, watching their steps while trying to stay alert to potential dangers or an easy meal. With the sun getting higher and warmer, the frost melted away and sweat began to flow.

They had already stopped a few times to take the load off their backs, drink some water, and chew on some dried meat. A little after midday, they took a longer rest. Looking west, Toq could see clouds gathering, but he didn't think it would rain or snow. At least, he hoped not. He didn't want to spend his first night out in the rain.

The Traveler said he was amazed at how much harder it was to walk under his load this time. His feet, legs, and shoulders all hurt, and he was tired. Toq was glad to hear he wasn't alone in his weariness. The Traveler assured him that after five or ten days, they would both be in better shape for this long-distance hiking. Toq hoped that was true. Without the packs, Toq thought he could probably make it to the encampment in two days, but in this early stage, he wasn't going to get rid of anything.

They walked on through the afternoon. The sky filled with scattered clouds. The birds of spring were arriving and making a lot of noise. Mostly, it was beautiful, but of some the Traveler said, "Those annoying birds don't know how to sing. They just squawk."

They saw deer, moose, horses, ground squirrels, eagles, and big wolves (dire), but no bears or big cats. Toq was glad, because the bears and big cats made him nervous.

The Traveler told him, "Don't worry about them. They have plenty of other things to eat. Things that are fatter than you."

"Yes, but those fatter things are also faster than me," Toq replied.

"You'll be all right. You have the spear."

They finished their first day of hiking, stopping at a nice spot by a creek that ran down into the river. Some streams ran high with meltwater, though this one wasn't too bad. Even on the highlands, this early season trek was challenging. With the ground no longer frozen and not yet dry, walking through mud was the norm.

They built a fire, ate about half of their food, set up their little hide shelters, and rubbed their sore feet and shoulders. This was new country for Toq, but the Traveler had been trough here before.

Toq asked, "Do we need to have one person stay up to be a lookout?"

"Nah, we'll be all right. We can both sleep."

Toq hoped he was right, as he had been about everything so far. Toq lay under his fur, on his back, staring up and out toward the sky past the edge of his lean-to, thinking they had come a long way already and that tomorrow his muscles would be really sore. Toq had a good feeling of satisfaction.

CHAPTER 5

Journey, First Summer

The people camped farther upstream had not experienced the flood the way Toq's group had. Some had observed the river backing up and rising, but they were unaware of the devastation that had occurred downstream. Toq and the Traveler were happy to see these people—to know their group was not alone in the world, that not everyone had been wiped out.

For the next twenty days or so, the two men trekked across the land, following the trails of people and animals. They followed paths across open prairie and steppe-tundra. Streams and rivers presented dangerous obstacles, often forcing the two men to travel as much as a half day up- or downstream in order to find a safe place to cross. They were told by local villagers to go south around the big canyon (Hells Canyon) rather than east along a different, smaller river (Salmon River). There was little game to be found in the valley to the east, and eventually, they would be blocked by mountains completely encased in glaciers. The villagers had no knowledge of what lay beyond those glaciated mountains. The reality was that east of that mountain range, there was a valley that had once held the upper end of a giant lake (Glacial Lake Missoula)—the same lake that had drained out nearly a year ago, flooding the lands downstream and killing Toq's people.

So, the men traveled south and well to the west of the deep river canyon. They pressed on past the canyon country, entering a huge land of flat plains. They moved southeast along the river, passing through different human encampments along the way. They sometimes traveled with a small group, also on the move upriver. It seemed that everyone was always looking for a better spot. Toq and the Traveler never stayed with any group for long. They followed the river straight east for a while, passing several spectacular waterfalls and canyon gorges, and then the river began to turn to the northeast.

Running out of summer, with signs of autumn, and even some wintry weather, they had to make a big decision. They had traveled north for a while, until they reached a good-sized encampment that sat near a big bend in the river. The people told the two travelers that the main river was about to turn to the southeast. From an open vantage point, Toq and the Traveler gazed eastward. On the horizon, they saw a line of incredibly rugged, pointed mountains (Teton Range) sticking up out of huge glaciers—or at least, they guessed they were glaciers. From this distance, they looked like clouds. They were told the river went around the southern end of that jagged range, but the people did not know what lay beyond, since nobody had gone past that southern point. They didn't believe there were any tribal bands up there yet. If Toq and the Traveler left the river and went north, the people said they could find an open pass to the other side. But again, they believed there were no other people or camps there. This country was all new to the Traveler now; he had never been to this camp, and he did not know these people, although they had common acquaintances in some villages downstream.

"So, you're the end of the line. The last people we're going to see?" asked the Traveler, minding his language so as not to needlessly offend any of these strangers.

"Yes," replied one of their leaders. "Maybe there are more people, way north or east, but we haven't seen anyone."

This leader spoke slowly and deliberately compared to the Traveler, and the Traveler slowed his speech as well. He appeared to be measuring these people before he could relax and be himself.

This was a village of sixty or seventy people—big compared to most they had passed through. Toq saw several mammoth tusks, some simply stuck in the ground, curving up into the air, while others were used to support shelters.

He asked, "Do you ever see mammoths?"

"Oh, yeah. They sometimes come down from over the pass to the north. Lots of animals use that route. That's why we think there's good country over there. We've also seen them to the east and south."

One of the young men asked Toq, "You've never seen one?"

"A couple last year, in the flood, dead."

The young guy laughed. "You better stay and go on a hunt with us."

Toq smiled and said, "Maybe I should." He wondered how they would hunt and kill an animal so large.

"What flood?" asked an older man.

Toq told them, but to his surprise, they didn't believe him.

"Waves of water pouring over hilltops? Impossible. That didn't really happen," they said incredulously.

Their disbelief irritated him. They would believe made-up stories from shamans but doubted this? But the more he thought about it, the more he realized that if people hadn't seen it for themselves, then yes, it would be hard to believe. What annoyed Toq the most was that half of the people now thought him an untrustworthy teller of tall tales.

• • • •

After Toq and the Traveler had been in the village a couple of days, contemplating their choices, the group's two main leaders—a married couple—invited them to stay for the winter.

"We could use your help hunting this fall. It's getting a little late to travel north over the pass. You could go east along the river, but then you'd have to build shelters and survive on your own. Too difficult. Besides, you both seem to want to go north. Just wait here. The pass usually melts off by late spring."

They were right; both Toq and the Traveler did wish to go north. But the Traveler told Toq privately, "I really don't want to stay here."

He wanted to get as far as he could before winter set in hard. If the people were right about all the game coming over the pass, then there must be even more on the other side, which would make surviving through the winter fairly easy. *As if winter is ever easy,* thought Toq.

That night, a chilly rain settled on the camp, and in the morning, the wind blew in much colder air from the north. It froze the rain to the ground, the trees, and the shelters, and then it began to snow. It piled up to knee-deep that day, halting most activity.

In his usual jovial manner, the Traveler said, "So, I think maybe we should just stay here through the winter. I can't believe you were even thinking of hiking onward!"

Toq laughed and said, "I think this snow will melt. We'll have some nice days, and we could still make it over the pass. It's only three or four days to get up there. I'm sure you and I could kill a couple mammoths without much effort. We'd be all set."

His attempt at sarcasm fell flat, but the Traveler seemed to appreciate the effort. They discussed their situation more seriously and decided they would stay put. They could learn some things from this group—namely how to hunt mammoths—and Toq's stone-knapping skills could help them gain more acceptance.

Several days after the storm, on a warm day of wet, slushy snow and mud, a band of about thirty people arrived at the edge of the village. They looked pretty rough. Wet and muddy from the knees down, they'd been hit hard by the storm and had struggled mightily to stay dry and warm. Men, women, children, and some gray-haired but stout elders made them a complete band. The village took them in. Toq and the Traveler had met these people on their trek and walked with them for half a day before passing on ahead. Toq was surprised they had come this far. Their stamina, as a group, impressed both him and the Traveler.

The traveling group did not ask to stay, but many in the village feared they would move in and settle down without invitation. After several days, during which the newcomers dried out, ate, and rested, they took this fear to the chiefs, who then told the group it was time to move on. The chiefs explained there were not enough resources in the area to support such a large addition to their village. Some of the villagers thought it was coldhearted to send the visitors away. The visitors were upset, especially upon learning there were no other groups upriver. The chiefs tried to convince them that they would find good hunting country just a couple of days to the east, but the visitors grew increasingly angry and resentful. With no attachments between the two groups, there was a limit to the host's charitability. Historically, there had always been a certain level of kinship among the river's villages, even though many were strangers to each other. Now, with time and a growing population, this was breaking down. Everyone saw it.

Toq and the Traveler had mixed feelings about the situation. They understood that having too many people risked doing serious harm to their food supply—and therefore the villagers' survival. But they also sympathized with the visiting group, since it was late in the year to be going off to start a new camp in unknown territory. The Traveler thought the village leaders ought to let the children and some of the women stay until the newcomers settled on a spot, but he only said this to Toq. As visitors themselves, it wasn't their place to speak up. The men of the traveling group invited Toq and the Traveler to go with them, but they declined, explaining that they were going in a different direction come spring.

"Perhaps we can at least help them get established," said Toq to the Traveler.

But the Traveler said, "What are we getting into here? People on both sides are getting really pissed off. What are we going to do if this breaks out into a fight?"

"I don't know," replied Toq. "I've been wondering the same thing. Maybe we can act as peacekeepers. I've heard of groups fighting, but I've never been in or seen a battle. I have no desire to get into a fight."

"Neither do I," said the Traveler. "Unfortunately, some of the younger ones on both sides seem poised to attack."

"The elders have a problem. If the group stays another day, resentment will grow in the camp. But forcing the visitors to leave today will really piss them off."

"They have to go soon, and hopefully with time, everyone can leave this behind and become friends."

"I'm sure the elders on both sides are having these same discussions."

"I hope so. Some leaders are wise, some not so wise."

"It makes you want to get away and be back out there, hiking and hunting, doesn't it?"

"Definitely."

The next day, the visitors left quietly and quickly. Some were clearly angry, while others looked worried and frustrated, but most simply busied themselves with the task at hand. The leader of the visitors thanked the village chiefs for their generosity but did so with a certain amount of bitterness. The chiefs tried to give them directions, but the leader of the visitors held up his hand and said, "We'll figure it out." Then, he turned to go.

Angered, the wife of the chief said, "That was rude. And after we took them in. What a shit."

The chief did not say anything as he watched the visitors leave. He did feel some guilt about sending them away, but he believed the village was already too large as it was.

About midmorning, the Traveler told Toq, "I'm going with them. It won't take long to catch up. I'll help them set up camp and hunt with them for a few days. With you here and me there, perhaps we'll soften the hard edge between these two. I'll be back in ten or fifteen days, I think."

"Well, then, okay. Good luck."

And with that, the Traveler hurried off.

CHAPTER 6

Waiting for Spring

The days were shorter and colder, all the leaves had fallen from the trees, and nearly twenty days after his departure, the Traveler walked back into camp in new, ankle-deep snow.

He was happy, as usual, and full of news. The other group had found a great spot with a "good supply of wood, good stones for knapping spear-points, and really great hunting with moose, beaver, horses, long-horned bison, and a lot of other animals."

"See any mammoths?" asked Toq.

"No, but I did see a bunch of animals I'd never seen before. And preda-tors—wolves and big cats. Didn't see any bears. There's more to hunt there than what's left around here, so they'll be fine. They're about a three-day walk east. I'll tell ya, I didn't sleep much on the way back, being alone with all those animals."

"I should've gone with you," Toq said, excited about what the Traveler had seen.

Toq had settled into a regular routine in the village, accepted by the people as one of their own. Some wondered why the Traveler had left and seemed suspicious of him upon his return. He told the leaders about where the other group had camped and said again, "They'll be okay," but he didn't delve into the details, lest he inadvertently convince the chiefs to pick up and move the village in on *them.*

The chiefs let the issue go for now. They told Toq and the Traveler that they would be going out daily to see if any mammoths might be coming down from the north. Once the giant beasts were spotted, the hunt would begin. This news thrilled them. Life in the village had already become boring to Toq, and they still had the bulk of the long winter before them. The Traveler, of course, was always ready for any kind of excitement.

Ten days went by without any mammoth sightings. Then twenty days, then thirty. The weather grew colder, the snow got deeper, and the warm days vanished entirely. They hunted deer and horse. They still had a village of seventy to feed. Although they had dried and stored meat, roots, and berries, it would not be enough to last them through the winter. They needed to keep on bringing in meat, bone, sinew, and hide. The men hunted large animals as a group, while younger boys, and sometimes young girls, hunted small animals. Different kinds of traps were set to catch a wide variety of animals, and they fished until the river froze. Most food, however, was acquired by chasing or ambushing the larger beasts.

Their days revolved around food: hunting, gutting, hauling carcasses to camp, skinning, preparing, cooking, eating, and finding the right resources with which to manufacture hunting weapons, traps, stone axes, knives, skin "pots," and building hearths and fires. The construction of shelters and clothing took time, but once done, they required little attention, whereas food made for constant labor. Sometimes, at the end of the day, or when a storm kept them inside, they told stories, practiced rituals, played games, or even simply recounted that day's hunt. They often sang, told jokes, and decorated their clothing, hair, and bodies. But everyone—man and woman, young and old—preferred to be outside.

"You have to see the sky," said one elderly woman, "in the day and especially at night. The sky is magic. It lifts your spirit, and it sends down the fresh air. You can't stay in your hut for too long, or you'll go crazy. You need the light and the good air."

Toq agreed completely. He thought that many of the things people said, did, or believed were stupid or nonsensical, but this was a truth that everyone agreed with.

• • • •

Forty, then fifty days went by, and they still had not seen any mammoths or mammoth tracks. The village chiefs were becoming concerned about food. Each day they went out, the game was farther away and more skittish of people. Eventually, the winter would weaken a lot of animals, making them easier to get, but for now, the villagers needed to last long enough and retain enough of their own strength to take advantage of this day, when it came. The village typically relied on two or three mammoths to get them through the winter.

The optimists among them said, "Oh, they'll come. They're just late this year." Others said, "We don't need them. There's other game." The pessimists, though, began to talk about "other options" to survive. Some believed the camp should be split up. Toq agreed that it was too big, but now wasn't the time to split up. Some said half of the villagers should go to live with the visitors they had turned away, and they pressed the Traveler for information. The Traveler needed to be careful here, but he couldn't help himself.

He laughed out loud, cursed, and then scolded them, "You shitheads wanted them gone and now you're talking about going to move in with them? Or maybe you just intend to take their territory and kick them out. What is pissing wrong with you?"

This short tirade surprised everyone; the Traveler was normally the easygoing one. While most agreed with him, those on the receiving end of his tongue-lashing seethed. Where before they'd mistrusted him, now they loathed him.

• • • •

Midwinter came and still no mammoths. A group of hunters went a couple of days north but found nothing. In the four years the village had been here, this was their first winter without mammoths. Evidently, the small herd had learned that venturing south over the pass meant encountering hunters, so they simply stayed on the north side.

The village elders were perplexed, but they came to accept that the mammoths probably would not come. So, the hunters spread out to the south, west, and east and managed to bring back just enough meat to keep the village fed. People talked about moving in the spring. The religious ones claimed that the spirits always turn against you when you stay in one place for too long. The elders began saying that they wanted to move north—the same way Toq and the Traveler intended to go—in pursuit of the mammoths, and Toq's heart sank. Some decent people lived here, to be sure, but he had a notion that if there were no people up north, then he would feel like the place was his somehow. He didn't want to share it. And a large village like this would certainly spoil a new place. He felt guilty for thinking this way; these people *had* taken them in. And yet, he also thought there was an undercurrent of negativity in the culture of this group. It wasn't everyone, but angry, irritable villagers challenged their leaders every day, and this constant dripping of annoyance and petulance created a dark cloud that hung over the camp. Neither Toq nor the Traveler thought very highly of these malcontents. It troubled them to think that at any time, these unhappy villagers would suggest attacking their new neighbors, or else they might try to overthrow the chiefs or try to get Toq and the Traveler banished. Toq did not believe the leaders were dealing with these problem people strongly enough, and as a result, the troublemakers spoke out openly and boldly—especially against the Traveler. If he and Toq were kicked out in the middle of winter, could they make it on their own?

The Traveler said, "We'll just go east and stay with the other group if we have to. They're better people, anyway."

The two men did their part helping around camp, but in their spare time, they prepared for their departure, making spearheads and shafts, clothing, bags, and tools. Both men eagerly anticipated spring, hoping for an early start. They were ready to be out on their own and away from the trouble growing here.

• • • •

A couple more full moons came and went, the days grew longer, and the sun rose higher in the sky. Winter was fading, and although it wasn't yet gone, there was warmth to the days and snow and ice began to thaw. On one nice, sunny morning with a very light breeze, Toq flipped back the flap on his hut, crawled outside, stood up straight as he looked out to the horizon, and started to breathe deeply the morning air. But his expression of contentment changed to disgust as he turned, choking and coughing, rubbing his nose to clear it of the invading stench.

"Augh! Shit!" The breeze blew just right, wafting the atrocious smell of human excrement from what the group called "the shithole" directly toward Toq's hut and nostrils. People were supposed to cover their excrement with dirt, but that was difficult to do in the winter, and now, with things warming up, the villagers paid the price. A person could get used to a lot of odors but not that one.

"Just one more sign that it's almost time to leave," Toq grumbled. He looked around to see who else might be up and about. The Traveler and Toq shared a hut with a young guy who had just recently moved out of his family hut. The young man still slept, but the Traveler was already off somewhere. Toq looked for him around the village before finally finding him a little ways up the river, sitting on a large rock, meditating, thinking, praying, and very quietly singing. He often started his day this way, and although Toq did not necessarily share the Traveler's spirituality, he did respect it. The Traveler never tried to push his beliefs on anyone else. He felt that his beliefs were just for him, and others had to find their own way, just as he had.

When the Traveler spotted him in the distance, he stood on the rock and greeted him with a smile, arms raised, and calling out, "Toq!"

He's always happy, Toq thought as he smiled and waved back. Toq climbed onto the rock, and they sat down side by side looking out over the river, which flowed slow and thick with large chunks of ice.

"I have a problem," the Traveler said.

"What? Only one?"

The Traveler laughed and said, "Well, no. I have two—maybe three or four. I have women and those shithead, asshole, troublemaker problems."

"What happened?" Toq knew the Traveler had been "just having fun" with two different women, and although it was a common practice and not necessarily frowned upon, he had warned the Traveler about potential problems like pregnancy and jealousy. Toq didn't have this kind of problem. He wasn't as funny and charming as the Traveler, who he figured could have just about any woman he wanted. So, Toq concluded that it would be best if he kept to himself, kept relationships simple, uncomplicated, and emotionally detached. He avoided temptation and desire.

"Apparently, one of the assholes has taken a liking to one of the girls I've been with. So, that's okay with me. I wasn't going to marry her and settle down, anyway. It was fun for a while, but I haven't been with her for some time now, and I think she's pissed off at me. Now, the asshole is even more pissed off at me than before, even though I'm not humping his woman anymore. I think she's goading him. I wouldn't normally worry about it, but I'm thinking that whole group of assholes—who've been looking for an excuse—may be plotting up something bad for me. This may not be good for my well-being."

"Maybe you shouldn't come out here by yourself anymore."

The Traveler glanced at Toq, looked away, and simply nodded, no longer smiling. Clearly, he was truly worried, and Toq realized now the complete inadequacy of his response.

So Toq said, "It's still too early, but I think we should get out of here as soon as we can."

"Yes, I agree. Here's what I've been thinking: You're in some danger here, as well, mostly because you're my friend. I'm thinking of moving to the encampment to the east. I think they'll take me in. I'll stay there a week or two, then head north. I think you'll be safer here once I'm gone. And your calm, clear manner will hopefully keep this bunch from deciding to move in on the other group. I'm afraid if we both go to the other encampment, it will stoke the fires here to go fight them. I'll leave in the dark, so no one will know where I'm headed. When they ask, just tell them you don't know where I went, but you think I went north to get a head start. Then, we need to set a day ten or fifteen days from now to meet up at the pass. And hope the weather stays good."

"Whew! You've been thinking on this for some time. That's a lot to take in. Uh, these guys are going to ask why I didn't go with you."

"Ah, just say you got sick or weren't quite ready to go or something, and that I didn't want to wait. Or you could just say that we're splitting up and going our separate ways."

They sat quietly for a few moments, listening to the cracking ice on the river. The sounds of geese and swans came from above. They looked up at the lines and V formations of the migrating flocks. Just one more sign of the end of winter—though Toq had often said they come too early; winter was rarely over when they started showing up.

"Where do they go in the winter?" Toq wondered aloud.

The Traveler stood up, slapped him on the back, and said, "I don't know! Maybe we should go south and find out. It must be warmer! We may be crazy for wanting to go north!"

Toq stood as well, and, while brushing off the seat of his pants, he said, "We *are* crazy. Perhaps we should go north and then go south."

"Exactly what I was thinking," said the Traveler.

"As for your plan, let me think on it today," said Toq.

"All right," said the Traveler. "I've got all my stuff ready to go. I could even go tonight, if you agree."

They walked back to the village to join the other men going out to hunt. As was his way, Toq expressed concern for the Traveler; he would have to cross streams that were beginning to run high with meltwater and also deal with carnivores.

As was his way, the Traveler said with optimism, "Ah, it'll be no trouble."

As they approached the village, they walked into the zone of stench, and the Traveler said, "Augh! Shit!" as he squeezed his nose, as if trying to force the smell from his nostrils.

Toq chuckled. "That's what I said!"

A bunch of little kids played near the center of the camp, and one so young he could barely walk toddled up to the Traveler and yelled with a huge grin,

"Kupseacame! Kupseacame!" Those watching laughed as the Traveler scooped up the youngster and tossed him into the air and caught his fall—to squeals of delight. No one knew where the little one had gotten that word, but many in the village had taken to calling him "Kupseacame," as well.

Toq laughed to think how this man got along so well with women and little kids—most people, in fact. He only had a few enemies, but sometimes it only takes a few.

• • • •

That night, the brief period of warm weather came to an end. The wind blew hard, and it snowed and did not stop for two days. *So much for spring*, thought Toq. It did this every year, everywhere he'd ever lived, and even though everyone knew it, they still suffered the depressing blow that the resurgent winter delivered. Tensions between the Traveler and those he had angered did not ease, and the snowstorm served as a blunt reminder that it was still too early to go north over the pass. One alternative was to go back down the river, but neither man wanted to, and other options seemed equally undesirable. Toq finally concluded that the Traveler's first idea was the best one. But the new snow created a new problem; it was deep, and even with snowshoes, it would be tough going. Plus, it would enable the Traveler's enemies to easily see which way he went.

On the first day of the snowstorm, the Traveler decided that he would go that night, hoping the falling and blowing snow would cover his tracks. If he waited, he might be stuck here for another ten or fifteen days. Toq suggested that they should take their problem to the chiefs, but the Traveler doubted they would back them up. He feared it could make their situation worse.

So, not long after dark, after listening for the slow, heavy breathing of the young man sharing their hut, the Traveler got up and moved silently in the low firelight. He peeked outside and placed his things out in the snow. The wind had slowed a little, but white flakes continued to fall. He glanced back and saw that Toq's hand was up as he lay there watching him. The Traveler grinned, quietly grasped Toq's hand in solidarity, then pushed through the flap on their hut and without a sound, he was gone.

Toq rolled onto his back, thinking, *The Traveler is like no other man I know. He is fearless when it comes to going out there alone.* He couldn't think of anyone else who would do that—go out into the night, by himself, in a snowstorm. He stared up at the hole in the top of the hut where the smoke escaped and silently wished his friend good luck.

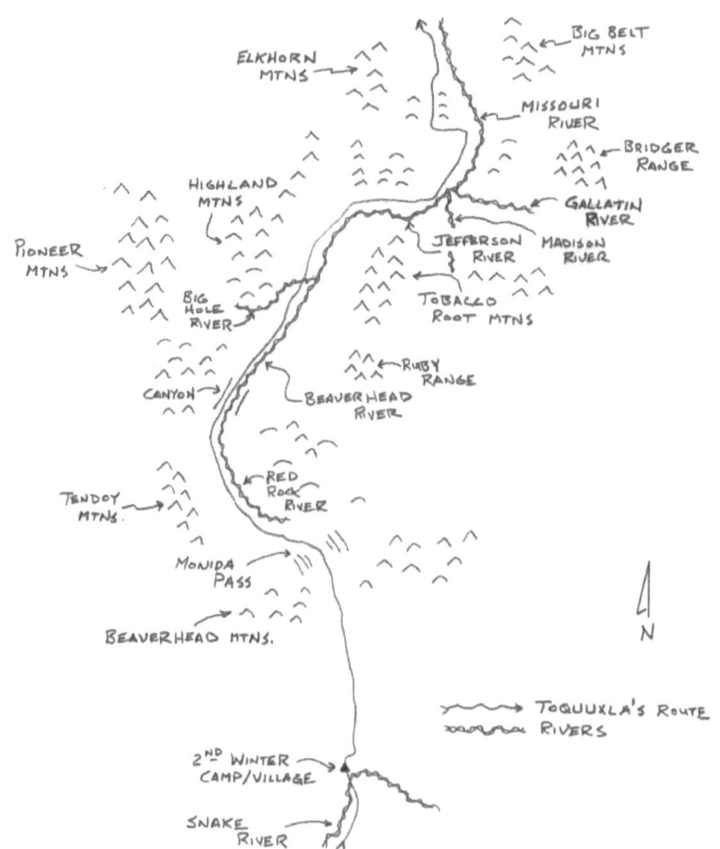

ELKHORN MTNS
BIG BELT MTNS
MISSOURI RIVER
BRIDGER RANGE
HIGHLAND MTNS
GALLATIN RIVER
PIONEER MTNS
JEFFERSON RIVER
MADISON RIVER
BIG HOLE RIVER
TOBACCO ROOT MTNS
RUBY RANGE
CANYON
BEAVERHEAD RIVER
RED ROCK RIVER
TENDOY MTNS.
MONIDA PASS
BEAVERHEAD MTNS.
TOQUUXLA'S ROUTE
RIVERS
2ND WINTER CAMP/VILLAGE
SNAKE RIVER
N

CHAPTER 7

The New Season

The chiefs seemed to accept Toq's explanation for the Traveler's disappearance. He claimed he didn't know where the Traveler had gone but mentioned his sudden departure was due to his concerns about the troublemakers. The chiefs were sorry to hear this and said they would have dealt with the problem had the Traveler only confided in them, but Toq was skeptical. The Traveler's biggest enemy called Toq a liar and guessed that the Traveler had gone to the new camp. Toq wanted to give him the universal gesture that meant "you can stick it up your ass," but instead, he just shrugged and walked away.

After that, things went smoothly for Toq's preparations. The camp procured just enough meat to keep them going, and tensions eased. Nice weather over the next ten days melted most of the snow. Toq desperately wanted to get away from this village. When the day came for him to leave, he expressed warm gratitude and good wishes to the young man he and the Traveler had shared their hut with.

Toq told him, "You'll finally have some elbow room in there," to which the young man replied, "There are already two guys waiting to move in."

He then handed Toq a piece of ivory about the length of his thumb, cut from a tusk and carved into the shape of a deer or a horse.

The young man said, "Here, Toq, take this. It's my gift to you. I had it blessed by the shaman. It will bring you good luck in hunting."

Genuinely touched by the young man's thoughtfulness, Toq told him, "You're a good person. You'll do well. You are considerate of others, and you're a thinker." He tapped two fingers to his temple. "This village needs young people like you." He pulled a beautifully shaped spearpoint out of his bag and offered it to the young man. "Here, this is for you. It's the best spearpoint I've made in some time. Not as nice as your carving, but I hope it brings you success in *your* hunts."

"Thanks, Toq. You make the best points!"

Toq nodded, smiled, and said, "Be careful and be happy."

Then, he walked to the chief's hut, where the chief and his wife sat outside on a dry patch of ground. They rose to their feet to thank him for helping in the village over the winter. They wished him well and hoped he'd be safe, but they thought he was a bit out of his mind to be going out alone. Toq thanked them for their hospitality and said he was sure they would see each other again, although he secretly hoped not. That was it. There was no big send-off or festivities. Most people seemed indifferent to his going. A few people waved or nodded as he left. Toq gave the chief one of his spearpoints, but that was it. The chief gave Toq nothing. As he walked away, Toq thought, *That's not customary. Not that I need anything.*

He was about a hundred paces outside of the village when he heard a woman calling to him. He turned to see the chief's wife running up to him.

"Here, Toq, take this. We should give you something." She handed him a leather pouch full of dried meat. He thanked her, put the food in his bag, and handed the empty pouch back to her. This fiery woman then told him, "The men are hunting out north today. Be careful."

"I will." Toq nodded thoughtfully. Then he said, "Thank you," smiled slightly, and turned to go. He stopped, looked back, and said, "You know, I probably shouldn't say this, but you should be the chief."

She said, "I am one of the chiefs."

"You know what I mean."

She smiled and said, "Thanks."

She knew her husband was a weak leader, but she wasn't going to challenge him.

Toq lifted his hand to her and said, "Be well," and she responded with a slight wave.

"Goodbye, Toquuxla."

He strode away, feeling much better about a few people in the village. But his thoughts quickly shifted to the hunters somewhere along his path north. He knew the chief's wife had been warning him that these hunters were the "assholes" who had become his enemies. He looked ahead as much as possible, going out of his way to avoid them. He didn't know if they would turn violent, but since he was alone, he wouldn't stand a chance against them if they did. He could outrun any one of them, but doing so would mean having to ditch his bags.

A line of footprints crossed a wide swath of snow. Certain these belonged to the hunters, Toq marched quite a distance east, away from them, then made a wide arc to the north, moving in and out of little stands of short spruce trees, covering a lot of ground quickly. He figured all he had to do was get a day's walk away from the village. At this time of year, the hunters rarely went farther than that.

As he moved north, he inadvertently wandered from his intended path. Cresting a small hill in the middle of the huge, flat landscape, he looked down into a gully and saw two men. Surprised, he ducked—but too late. They raised their spears over their heads, and Toq's heart sank.

"Damn it!" was all he said.

He stood tall, faced them, and raised one of his spears, too. No one said anything, but the men changed direction and began to walk toward Toq.

"Shit," he muttered.

His mind raced. He could walk away quickly, hoping they would get the message, or he could hide his stuff and run—except there was no good hiding place. He didn't want to fight. He didn't see the point, and he didn't believe he could win—what good would it do, lying dead out here? Besides, where were the others? But maybe these guys had no intention of attacking him. Maybe he was just being paranoid.

Toq didn't move. He spied a lone individual across the gully on higher ground, who turned to follow the others. Toq took about five slow steps, looking up the slightly taller hill where he'd intended to go next. Three heads popped up over the hilltop, bobbing up and down as more men walked toward Toq. They stopped and looked down at him, and one of them pointed with his spear in the direction of their mates coming up out of the gully. Toq guessed this was all of them. Six total. Three to the west and three to the north. He considered his escape routes but kept his feet planted. He raised his spear over his head in a silent greeting to the three above him. One of them responded in the same way, and they also began walking over.

Toq kept his bags slung over his shoulders and his spears upright, resting on the ground and firmly in his grip. He would try to send a subtle message that he was in a hurry and didn't have a lot of time to chat. He didn't want to come across as too unfriendly, but he also knew it would be a mistake to act too chummy.

"Just stay calm," he mumbled.

The two guys from the gully got to him first. The one lone guy trotted to catch up.

"We heard you were leaving today. Did you leave us any gifts?" one said sarcastically as he walked up.

"Well, no, sorry," said Toq, now worried they would take his spears or one or both of his bags. He could easily perish out here without his stuff. "How is hunting today?" He attempted to relax and appear courteous.

"Ha!" The jackass called out to one of the other three men as they neared. "He wants to know how the hunting is!"

"It would have been fine if some nitwit hadn't ruined it!" This came from the man who hated the Traveler the most. He jabbed his spearpoint at

Toq, pulling it back before it struck. Toq jumped aside reflexively, dropping his smaller spear to hold his larger spear with both hands. Four of the men laughed loudly. One man simply smirked.

"What's wrong, Toq? You seem a little jumpy," one said, and they laughed again.

Toq smiled thinly. *These guys are juveniles, children. And they call me a nitwit?*

The last guy walked up, breathing heavily and carrying a dead grouse.

He said, "Hi, Toq," very casually.

He was the one decent man in this group, and he and Toq had always gotten along. He didn't really fit in with these assholes.

One of them said, "You got a bird!"

"Yeah, lucky throw with a rock." He turned back to Toq and asked, "So, you're on your way north?"

Toq had barely nodded when the lead asshole interrupted, "We don't give a shit where you're going. What I want to know is, where'd that prick go? We know you've been lying. Where is he?"

Everyone looked at Toq. They stood in a half circle around him like a pack of wolves.

"I said, I don't know."

"You liar," said the asshole.

But the friendly guy said, "Oh, come on. The Traveler is gone and Toq's leaving. Who cares?"

The asshole glared. "*I* care, so you should shut up!"

A couple of the men began to look uncomfortable.

Then, the one who'd asked about gifts walked around to the side of Toq. "Well, let's just see what kind of gifts you have for us in here," and as he reached for one of Toq's bags, Toq pushed him backwards.

Enraged, the gift-seeker yelled, "Don't touch me! You want to fight? I'll fight you!"

But Toq saw more bravado in his eyes than real fight.

"No, I don't want to fight." Toq had difficulty not rolling his eyes at the stupidity of this situation.

The asshole said, "Let him take what he wants."

"No," said Toq. "I need everything in these bags."

The asshole pointed his spear at Toq's belly and nodded to the gift-seeker to help himself. The thief started to reach for Toq's bag when Toq shoved him hard, causing him to stumble, and then Toq felt the shaft of a spear cracking him across the head. The thief rushed forward and kicked out Toq's leg, dropping him on his back. Dazed, Toq reached up to feel a large lump growing on the side of his forehead, as if an egg had magically appeared beneath his skin. He looked at his fingers but didn't see any blood.

He vaguely heard the thief yell, "You piece of shit!" while the man with the grouse hollered, "Whoa, stop! What are you doing? Knock it off! Are you crazy? Leave him alone!"

Toq squeezed his eyes shut and opened them only to find the one he'd begun to think of as "the Asshole" standing over him, two hands on his spear, ready to drive it through Toq's heart.

"I'd really like to kill you," he growled through clenched teeth.

"No, this is stupid! Get control of yourself!" said the better man.

The thief said, "Do it! Kill him!"

Finally, one of the others spoke up. "He hasn't done anything. You've had your fun. Leave him be. Let's go."

The Asshole slowly straightened, fired an angry look at the two who'd opposed him, and then looked down again at Toq, saying, "If you ever come back to our village, I'll kill you."

He stepped over Toq, snatched up Toq's big spear, and slammed the point down on a rock, breaking it.

He finally walked away, but after a few paces, he turned, and as he walked backwards, he called out to Toq, "I hope you die out here! Your friend, too. Or better yet, hopefully he's already dead!"

The man with the grouse helped Toq sit up and asked if he was all right.

"Yeah, I'm okay. Thanks for the help. You'd better go, or he'll direct his wrath on you."

"You're right about that. Wait." The man ran over to a patch of slushy snow and brought back a handful, which he dumped in Toq's cupped hand. "Put it on that lump. It'll help."

"Thanks." Toq put some snow in his mouth, then held the rest to his head.

Grouse-man said, "I don't know why that fool hates you. I think I hate him now." He shook his head. "I'd be honored to see you again someday. May the spirits favor you, Toq. Be well."

Toq said, "Thank you. You, too."

Grouse-man stood up, patted Toq on the shoulder, and ran after the others, spear in one hand, grouse in the other.

Toq watched until they disappeared completely from view. The snow quickly melted on his head, trickling down the side of his face, and his hand became painfully cold. He tossed the rest of the snow and shook the remnants off his hand. Reaching up to feel his wound, it pleased him to find that—although painful—the swelling had already gone down. He slipped off his two bags and slowly stood up, happy that he'd at least landed on a dry spot of ground. Considering that he'd seen stars, he felt okay. He picked up his spear and assessed the damage.

"Well, that's irritating," he said, knowing this was an understatement.

He opened a bag and pulled out a couple of spare spear heads to make sure they hadn't broken, too. Since they were wrapped in leather, they'd survived, which was a great relief. Yes, he could make new ones, but he couldn't always find the right stones.

He walked over to the snowbank, grabbed another handful of snow, and bit off some before lying on the ground.

He laughed a little and said, "Son of a bitch! That could've been bad!" He stood back up, "You're lucky, Toq! You could be dead right now, right here!"

The adrenaline was mostly gone, and he felt tired. But anger began to boil up inside of him as he thought about what had happened. *I could've fought, but I'd be dead for sure—although maybe one or two of them would've taken my side. Ah, face it, the aggressors in that group won. They had the upper hand. There was nothing I could've done. But I'd love to catch that asshole alone.*

Then, he said aloud, "Just forget it, Toq. Put it—put *him*—behind you. That miserable piece of shit isn't worth any more of your time."

He ate some of the meat the chief's wife had given him and then set upon the task of fixing his spear. It wasn't a simple job, but he wouldn't go anywhere without this spear. When he was done, he gathered his belongings and started hiking north, briskly, with a throbbing head. He still had plenty of daylight and wanted to cover as much ground as possible. If the weather and walking conditions remained favorable, he guessed he could be at the pass in two or three days. That would be fifteen days after last seeing the Traveler, within their agreed-upon time frame. There was the little problem of the fact that neither of them had ever been there before, and both knew a pass could be indistinct and cover a large geographic area. But they figured they'd eventually find each other, even if it took a couple of days.

• • • •

Rock cairns guided Toq along the correct drainage to the main pass. On the third day, he was in new country. There was more snow, more mud, less dry ground, and while animals had left tracks in the snow—some of them very large—with the snow melting away and slushy, it was difficult to know which animals they were. Until the snow was gone and the grasses began to grow, bringing more grazers, there would be little to hunt up here. Without the game, there were no predators, either, so Toq felt fairly relaxed as he climbed through open, treeless country.

He looked forward to reuniting with the Traveler. Companionship brought comfort when problems arose, and he stopped every so often to look around, hoping to catch a glimpse of the Traveler. He watched for footprints in the snow but saw none. His moccasins and leather leggings were soaked and muddy up to his knees, but it didn't slow him down.

A little past midday, Toq walked up onto a wide, flat area that opened to the other side.

"This is the pass, I guess," he said, looking all around, seeing nothing. He cupped his hands to his mouth and called out in all directions, then listened carefully, but he heard no response.

"Well, I think this is where he would be, so I guess . . . I beat you here," he said to his invisible friend.

Toq spent the rest of the day setting up his shelter, gathering dry brush to burn, and hunting rabbits. He used his smaller spear for small game. It was much shorter, with a narrower shaft and a sharpened antler point. It served a dual purpose—also propping up his lean-to.

As he cooked the rabbits, darkness moved in over the land. Geese, swans, and ducks flew high overhead, occasionally honking or quacking. He had hoped the Traveler would be here waiting. *What if he doesn't come? What would I do? Go north alone? Go back?*

"He'll get here," Toq said to himself. "You can count on that guy."

He finished off the rabbits and crawled under his furs, with the cold descending fast. A couple of coyotes yipped and howled in the distance. He liked hearing them, feeling comforted by the way they called out to each other.

"Even though we're competing for food, there's plenty to go around," he said, as he drifted off to sleep.

• • • •

Morning came, and Toq looked out from his shelter at blue sky. Frost whitened the dead grasses. Even the mud had frozen solid, but with the rising sun, it wouldn't stay that way for long. Today, he would explore and hunt a bit. First, he climbed some nearby hills, from which he saw high, snow-covered mountains to the north and west. The only other animal he saw, besides birds, was a bobcat hunting rodents and rabbits. He figured there must be some bighorn sheep around, but he hadn't yet seen any tracks or droppings.

Toq gazed down into the gap below, just making out his little camp, hoping to see the lone figure of the Traveler. Faintly, in the distance, he heard the guttural croaking of ravens, and he spotted them on the ground a little downhill of his camp, spreading their wings and hopping up and down. Whatever had attracted them might be interesting to him, too, so Toq headed that way, thinking perhaps it might be food. He didn't see any other predators lurking around, but there did appear to be a shelter, much like his own, near the ravens.

That's odd, he thought, thinking it was probably just an illusion. He was about fifty paces away when the ravens noticed him and flew off. Toq looked hard at the shelter; it was no illusion.

He kept walking and hollered, "Anybody home?"

Was this the Traveler's or an old one left behind by one of the villagers? It appeared to have been built recently, but he thought it must have been empty or else the ravens wouldn't have been hanging around.

The shelter was built on the downwind side of a rock outcrop. Snow had been cleared from the spot, and it lay piled up on either side of the little camp. Toq walked around to an old firepit, cold. Inside, he saw a rolled-up fur bedding, two leather bags, and the contents of those bags spread out in a line at one end: stone tools, spearheads, mittens, a water bladder, and a pouch that had once held some pemmican, chewed up by some animal.

"Oh, this doesn't look good." Toq sighed heavily. This had to be the Traveler's shelter, but there was no spear here and no fresh tracks, animal or human. A few small bones had been tossed up on a snow pile, but nothing looked fresh. Signs of small animals gnawing on the leather shelter and bags told Toq that this had been unoccupied for some time.

He walked over to where the ravens had been. Nothing was there. So, he circled the shelter, looking for tracks, a path through grass or snow, or broken branches on brush—anything. A rather large thicket of knee-deep brush in a depression down the slope drew Toq's attention, and he made his way toward it. An old animal trail emerged below his feet with tracks from a few deer, heading for the bushes. The only sounds to be heard came from a light breeze and the soft crunch of the man's footsteps on dried grass. Toq was silent, not even his breath made a sound. The brush was bare of leaves, being too early for new spring growth. As Toq drew near, it became obvious that animals had been there; a lot of the brush was torn up and chewed on. He searched for clues. A whitish object shone in the sunshine—an odd-looking rock or bone. He poked at it with the butt end of his spear and then, with his foot, carefully rolled over a human skull. He froze.

For a moment, his blood ran cold, and he gripped his spear tightly, afraid he was about to be ambushed. He searched the area for any signs that he might be in the middle of some large predator's food cache. Not finding anything—no other bones, no pieces of clothing, no spear—Toq returned to the skull. He bent over and slowly picked it up. He placed his spear on top of the bushes and, with two hands, turned the skull over and over, studying it. Only bits of red flesh and matted hair stuck to it, having been picked clean by small animals and birds. The lower jawbone was gone. He looked at the teeth, where he saw a front tooth, chipped off at an angle. This was the Traveler.

The reality of it hit Toq harder than the spear of his enemy.

He groaned, "Aw . . . no," and dropped down cross-legged with the skull resting in his lap. "What happened to you?" He sat there a long time, thinking, wondering, looking over the skull. There were no signs of violence on it: no busted-out teeth, no holes, no cracks—only a few small teeth or scratch marks. Toq wondered if somehow his enemies had gotten to him, but he didn't think they'd had time to come this far. Had an animal gotten him? He hadn't seen any sign of large predators, but it was possible. Had he come early and starved or froze to death? He must have been here awhile. Why had he come so early? Was he sick? So many things could have happened, and Toq felt the frustration of realizing that he would probably never know.

"I wish I could have been here to help you, my friend," Toq said with great sadness.

The sun rose higher in the sky, bringing warmth to the body of a man whose soul had gone cold. He looked up into the clear blue sky and listened to a flock of white geese calling to each other as they flew overhead.

Life—the world—just keeps on going, whether we live or die, he thought.

He stood up, leaving the skull on the ground, and felt the seat of his pants, wet from where he sat. He wondered what he should do with the skull. He picked it up, grabbed his spear, and started back toward the Traveler's shelter.

Along the way, he noticed a long, straight stick poking out from under a bush. The Traveler's spear. It was in perfectly good condition. Toq examined the stone head, stained with dried blood—likely from a larger animal, since they rarely used their large spears on small prey. But he didn't know if the Traveler had been hunting or defending himself.

He leaned the spear against the rough structure and gently placed the skull on the ground inside, eyes facing out. He stood back, thinking. Shamans would say that, without a proper burial ceremony, the Traveler's ghost would wander this pass forever, unable to move on to the spirit world.

"How do they know about spirits? They don't know anything." Still, in the back of his mind, he had doubts. "But what if they're right? What if I end up damning my friend's spirit to this place forever?"

He looked into the face of the skull and asked, "Where are you?" Then, he thought to himself, *Are you still here? Have you gone somewhere else? Do you still exist?*

Toq wondered about these things every time someone he knew died. The Traveler had told him once that he believed everyone lived on in spirit, walking and hunting on this earth. He believed that spirits could fly, even inhabiting the bodies of birds and animals when they wanted. And he believed the spirits of animals did the same.

"So," he'd said, "nothing actually dies."

"Interesting," was all Toq replied, dubious but respectful. "And what about bad people? Do their spirits enjoy life on earth, too?"

"I don't know. Sometimes, I wish they could be punished, but then I think, *What is 'bad?'* If they changed and wanted forgiveness, then they could live on in spirit. If not, well, maybe they are just dead, even their spirit. I would do it differently than the shamans. I would only bury the bad ones—maybe smash their skulls. And I wouldn't leave any valuable items—no spears, no ocher—in their grave. The good people I would raise up, maybe put them in trees or on poles, and leave their possessions and spears with them so they'd have them to hunt. Bury? Ugh! Being stuck in the ground? They have to be free to see the sky, not dirt."

Toq only said, "Hmm, I see," thinking about foul odors and scavengers tearing at the bodies.

Now, he left the Traveler's shelter and returned to his own camp. Besides wondering what to do for his friend, he had a hard decision to make about what direction he was going to go. He hunted that afternoon, but game was slim here. And he worried there might be a large carnivore around. He needed to make up his mind fast. He still wanted to go north—even though he would be going alone—into the unknown, new country, with new obstacles, new animals and predators, new people, maybe. If there were people, they would be strangers, and they might not welcome him. No matter how he rationalized it, going alone into the north lands would surpass all other foolish choices he would ever make. And he knew it.

But the thought of going back was worse. It would be safer, but Toq had no heart for it. The Asshole had threatened to kill him if he returned to the village—although, he could likely convince the chiefs to take him back. He could bypass that village and join the smaller group of newcomers to the east, which would be logical. Maybe he could find someone from either of those camps to travel with him, but he thought that was highly unlikely, since people like himself and the Traveler were unusual. The villagers had talked about moving north. Maybe Toq could go back, get in good with them, and then go north with them—but that still didn't solve the problem of the Asshole. Besides, he simply didn't want anything to do with the villagers anymore. And he really wanted to see the land before other people got there.

His last option was to journey back home, calling an end to this whole adventure. But Toq didn't seriously consider this for long. Though he missed them, he was not yet ready to go back.

He thought about the Traveler.

"He would go north with no hesitation, no fear," he said out loud. He knew he might die; in fact, he thought it likely. "I might die if I go back, too. I'm going to die someday, no matter what I do. Forget about dying, you wimp! So what if you die? Do what you want! Go north. Let's see what's out there."

Toq came to this decision late in the day, staring at his fire while roasting some meat. All day, he had been burdened by loss and uncertainty. Now that this was settled, the weight had been lifted, though his sadness remained.

• • • •

The morning was cloudy but calm and not quite as cold. Toq felt a sense of urgency. The north side of the pass was obviously snowier than the south. It would be slow going and wet until he could walk down out of the snow zone. He was concerned about the cloudy skies bringing rain or more snow. He wolfed down some pemmican, quickly packed his shelter and everything else, and headed to the Traveler's camp, where he looked through the items the Traveler had carried. His people believed it improper to take a dead person's possessions, and the shamans claimed the spirit of the dead would haunt the thief. As it turned out, most of Toq's stuff was in better condition than the Traveler's anyway, except for the spearpoints. Toq had given two of his to the Traveler before they parted. They were good ones, and he took one of them to replace the one the Asshole had broken.

While putting it away, his fingers brushed the ivory horse he had received as a gift. He pulled it out and examined it, noting the skill and detail that had been worked into it. Neither he nor the Traveler were much interested in decorations or jewelry, which consisted of pretty stones, shells, ivory, bone, teeth, claws, hair, feathers, and whatever else might impress a person. But this little ivory horse (or deer) meant something more to him—not because a shaman had blessed it, but because of his young shelter-mate's thought and care. He didn't want to give it up, but because it possessed that much value to him, it seemed befitting to gift it to the Traveler's spirit in exchange for the spearpoint.

Toq gathered some large stones, arranging them on the rock outcrop above the Traveler's camp in a small U, with the opening facing north. He stacked the stones two and three high to form a wind break. Then, he placed the Traveler's skull in the formation, looking out. He put a couple of rocks inside the Traveler's mittens and placed them beside the skull. He put the leather eye guards between the mittens and then laid the ivory horse in front of the skull.

"Here is a talisman. May you find it useful in your next life's journey," Toq said, recognizing the spiritual side of the Traveler.

He left the shelter where it was, but everything else he placed in and around the memorial. He dug a little hole next to the outcrop, stuck the butt end of the Traveler's spear in it, leaned it against the outcrop, and stacked up a few large stones around the base to help hold it in place.

Then, Toq stepped up onto the outcrop, stood just behind the rocks and skull, and said, "Well, there you go, you bastard," laughing at his use of one of the Traveler's favorite words. Looking out to where the skull stared, Toq quietly said, "You aren't buried in the dirt. The sky is over your head. You can see where I'm going. The wind is behind you. And maybe you can ride on the wings of these birds flying overhead."

Toq sang a little bit of the song he'd heard his friend sing on occasion, but a lump formed in his throat, his voice quavered, and he stopped. He looked down, then looked straight out, tears welling up in his eyes. He sniffed and wiped his running nose with his sleeve.

"You're with our ancestors now, I guess. Maybe I'm just talking to the wind. I'm going to miss you, my friend. Who knows, I might be joining you soon."

Toq looked around at the sky, hopped off the outcrop, and, without looking back, said to the Traveler, "I have to get going. You're welcome to come with me."

He swung his two bags on, grabbed his spears, and started downhill. After just a little way, he turned back, raised his spears up high in the air over his head, and yelled, "*You* are the Traveler! May you travel forever! Kupseacame!"

Then, he continued on his way, thinking, *Ironic. The Traveler now seems stuck in that one spot. Maybe he's free to go everywhere. Maybe he's nowhere. I don't know. Nobody knows. No, I know. He travels. With me.*

The wind picked up, some blue sky appeared between the clouds, and snow pellets began to pelt Toq.

Better than rain, he thought, as he walked down into the snowy expanse, not knowing where he was going, following the valley, eyes peeled for his next meal.

• • • •

After leaving the pass (Monida Pass, about 6,870 feet above sea level), Toq spent the rest of the day slogging through slushy snow. With leather moccasins and leggings soaked through, his feet were cold and numb. Far down the valley, he saw areas clear of snow—the day's goal.

The sun had just touched down on the mountaintops when Toq reached a good, bare spot of ground. The snow had worn him out. He quickly set up his lean-to, desperately searched for some dry brushwood, little more than twigs, and built a fire. With the bit of twilight he had left, he hunted the immediate area, finding nothing. So, he ate the last of his dried meat and saved what he had left of his pemmican for the morning. Tomorrow he would need to hunt more earnestly, and he hoped to see more life. He warmed his feet at the fire, watched darkness engulf the land, and had serious doubts about his decision to move onward.

"What are you doing, Toq? You have no idea what lies ahead. What if there's nothing down there to eat?"

Then, he heard something. He stopped breathing, turned in the direction of the sound, and listened intently. Far down the valley, he heard the faint howls of a pack of wolves. He looked up and smiled at a couple of stars, feeling great relief, because he knew that where there are wolves, there is prey.

Thoughts of the Traveler filled his mind before going to sleep.

• • • •

Physical exhaustion is superb at delivering a person to the world of unconsciousness, and Toq slept well. As was often the case this time of year, the birds pulled Toq back into the waking world. He peeked out from under his fur blanket. It was still dark, but the eastern sky was lightening. He lay there, warm and comfortable, listening to the birds. He stretched out his sore legs. As the light chased away the darkness, Toq saw no frost on the ground. A light, warm wind blew.

"Where is that coming from?" he wondered.

He was hungry, which meant he had to get up and get going. He stood and pulled on his pants, then sat down to put on his leggings and boots, which had dried some in the night. He ate the last of his pemmican and packed up his stuff. The sun had barely risen above the mountains when Toq began striding down the valley, which was not yet free of snow but did have more dry spots. His number one priority today was hunting. A prolonged lack of food would lead to weakness and a loss of energy, and then he would die. So, he had to get meat.

The wolves had been silent throughout the night, and now, only the birds, trickles of running water, and the wind could be heard. He walked hard and steady, warming up his body and loosening the stiffness in his legs. Then, approaching a decent vantage point, he stopped and scanned the area below and along the hillsides, and he listened. The wind had died, and the air was still, calm, and quiet. Toq loved calm days, but they were rare. Everything was peaceful—even joyous—on a calm day, and wildlife was more active. Some birds, though, like the swallows, seemingly frolicked and played in the wind, for the fun of it.

Toq walked on slowly, stopping often, looking, listening, checking the mud and snow for tracks and scat. After a while, he heard what sounded like a large rushing stream coming from a wide coulee to the east. The land was wide-open, tundra-like country with no trees and little sign of game. Toq sped up. He reached a flat area that was freshly disturbed. Grasses and shrubs had been ripped up, leaving the ground trampled and muddy. Wolves had left tracks, but it was the large, round mammoth footprints that thrilled him, even though he saved no hope of bringing one down by himself. Besides, even if he could, he could never preserve all that meat. Still, he was eager to see them.

He walked through the mud, stepping around huge piles of dung, trying not to breathe too much, as the air reeked of mammoth urine and shit. Toq reached the other side of this elephant mess, and stepped back up onto fresh, dry grass, regretting that the foul muck now infused his moccasins. He wiped them off, dragging them across the grass, then looked around again, but still saw no animals.

So, down the valley he went, following clear mammoth trails. A short distance later, he saw the wolf pack on a hillside ahead. The undulating terrain and lack of any breeze to carry his scent had allowed him to inadvertently sneak up on them. He was about two good stone throws away, but still too close. He stopped and counted eleven wolves—all adults, black and white and gray. All but two lookouts were either curled up in a ball or lying flat on their sides, sleeping. The two lookouts sat on their haunches. The nearest one stared at Toq then gave a quiet *woof*, but it didn't bother to stand up. The other did stand up, but it casually did a full-body stretch, head down, butt up, and yawned. The bark had roused the sleepers. A couple stood up to see what was happening, while others just barely lifted their heads.

Bellies bulged, and Toq thought he saw red blood staining the nearest wolf's face and neck. This pack was full of meat, lethargic, content, and not at all threatened by Toq's presence. Nevertheless, Toq was nervous. They could tear him apart in a second. He slowly began to walk laterally away from them, making sure to stay in their sight, fearing that if he disappeared, their curiosity could be aroused and they might come running.

Luckily, they serenely watched him walk away. A couple laid their heads down and went back to sleep. Toq wondered if they had ever seen a human before.

He took his time, and when he was finally out of sight of the wolves, he checked behind him constantly to make sure they weren't coming after him. He'd heard stories of wolves killing people, but he didn't actually know of anyone who'd been attacked. On the contrary, wolves had to fear people, who hunted and set traps. While this pack had nothing to fear from a lone man, a single wolf—although bigger, faster, stronger, and fanged—could die when taking on a man and his spear.

"Those wolves have a kill around here somewhere, so there may be other predators nearby," Toq said, on high alert.

He came to a steep slope where he could see down into a distant, muddy depression; in the midst of it was a large brown bump with protruding tusks. Birds swarmed it like flies.

"Yes! Yes!" Toq's eyes widened as he thought of the meat. He scanned the entire basin, but he didn't see any other predators or scavengers. He looked back toward the wolves, but they were no longer there. He walked cautiously toward the carcass, stopping at the sight of a wolverine wrestling with a large chunk of meat and hairy hide. The wolverine's prize was twice its own size, but it muscled the meat away up a sidehill.

Impressive, thought Toq.

After another glance around, he hurried toward the mammoth. He would need to work quickly. It was still too early in the season for vultures, but he could see crows, a stork, ravens, and a couple of golden eagles standing on and around the mammoth, not too bothered by each other's presence. The feast was big enough to share, although the ravens and eagles pushed the others from the choicest sections. The birds took their fill, tearing off chunks of flesh and swallowing them whole.

As Toq approached, the eagles and crows immediately flew off. The ravens and stork held their ground a little longer, but they finally flew away, as well. Toq came close enough to smell the wet fur, the blood and guts and feces, but he didn't smell any rot or decay—a good sign. He wondered how this mammoth had died. It was not young, but based on the few he'd seen during the flood, he didn't think it was particularly big, either. He wondered if the wolves could have killed it. Even a small adult was huge. He glanced back up the hill, looking for the wolves, feeling lucky they were not guarding this meat pile.

He set his bags and spears on the grass, dug out his stone cutting blade, and waded into the mess. He guessed the mammoth had been dead a couple of days, but the cool weather and cold nights had preserved the meat. The wolves had gutted the beast, and most of its organs had been pulled out and lay piled on the ground. The stomach and intestines had been torn open by the birds.

"They're huge!" Toq said of the mammoth's innards.

Part of the trunk was gone, and the birds had worked over the eyes. Much of the neck and legs had been chewed up by the wolves.

Despite the carnage, there was still so much good meat.

There was no time to dillydally. The birds had defecated on the animal, but a large, untouched section of the hindquarter was easy for Toq to get to—and it had already been sliced open at the front. Ascertaining he was still alone, he began slicing into the hide and meat. The thick skin was tough, but once he made his first few cuts, the going was easy, and the muscle was tender with a thick layer of fat under the skin. He kept checking his surroundings. The wolverine was out of sight, while the ravens, eagles, and the stork watched from different hills. One lone eagle circled high above. He cut a big chunk of meat, fur, and hide free, trying not to drop it into the bloody, muddy mess at his feet. Heavy and slippery, Toq cradled it in his arms as if it were a child. He dropped it on the grass beside his bags. He looked around again, and this time, he saw three wolves standing on the hill, looking at him.

He stared up at them, thinking, *I wonder if the heart and liver are gone. Maybe I should try to get the tongue. There's so much here I could use. Bone, hide, food, sinew, ivory, fat, marrow.*

The rest of the pack appeared on the hill.

"That's not good," he said.

He hurried back to get his blade, then stuffed the meat in one of his bags and hoisted it up over his shoulder.

"Son of a bitch, that's heavy! I hope the bag holds together," he muttered, bending down to grab the rest of his belongings.

The ravens croaked. He looked up to see the wolves moving down the hill toward him, but they were still too gorged to care. Just as Toq was about to take off in the other direction, he noticed the wolf acting as lookout had stopped, sat down, and seemed to be staring at something beyond the mammoth. Toq did the same. A huge, dark-brown bear (giant short-faced bear) walked up the valley, heading straight for the mammoth kill. Toq felt like running toward the wolves—maybe they would be his friends. But realistically, he knew he was on his own. The wolves were to the south, the wolverine was to the west, the bear was to the north, so Toq went east toward the stream. He didn't run but moved steadily, keeping an eye on the bear, which was sniffing the air and eyeballing Toq in turn. The farther Toq got from the mammoth, the less interested the bear was in him. That bear had one thing on its mind now: that carcass.

Toq reached the stream. He could still see the wolves, sitting bunched together on the hill, staring intently down at the bear, in no shape to defend their meat against that giant. The bruin sniffed around and pawed at the mammoth but didn't tear into it. He seemed cautious, picky, even looking around a couple of times as if he had to worry about something sneaking up on *him*!

Toq walked away. *Here I was, actually thinking maybe I could camp around here, and maybe the wolves would let me steal from that meat pile once in a while. But no, I'm not that lucky. There's no way I'm sticking around with that bear here.*

He looked down at his shirt and moccasins, both covered in blood, hair, and mud.

"I'm a mess!" He laughed, and he walked on.

He felt great. He had his meat, and the excitement left him feeling elated. "The Traveler would have loved this."

CHAPTER 8

Going North

Toq followed the stream in a big loop away from the bear and the mammoth. When he felt like he had put enough distance between them, he found a safe place to gather some dead brush and dried grass. It was close to midday, and the sun was high in the sky. Normally, he would wait until evening to build a fire and cook, but he was famished after a couple of days with so little to eat. Some people, like the Traveler, would simply eat the meat raw and keep moving, but Toq definitely preferred cooked meat.

While he ate, he kept watch lest his cooking attract any unwanted predators, and by the time he was finished, Toq had consumed almost a quarter of his large chunk of meat. Seeing no danger, he lay back and took a short nap.

Toq exulted in the warmth of the sun as he opened his eyes and looked at the blue sky above. He felt something crawling up his leg. He sat up, pulled up his pant leg, and flicked away a tick. "Little bastards."

He saved some hot coals in his sheep's horn, packed up his goods, and went to drink straight from the creek. Seeing no threats, he stood naked in the creek and washed his clothes, watching the blood and mud run downstream. The ice-cold water pained his feet and hands, and when he couldn't take it anymore, he jumped out. After washing his leathers, he stepped back into the creek and, this time, splashed water all over his body, scrubbing off the grime. Lastly, he dunked his head in the water, scrubbing his scalp.

"Good enough!" he yelled as he leaped back out, shivering.

He wrung as much water from his leathers as he could, while he drip-dried in the warm sun. Cleaning up on a warm, sunny day refreshed his spirit. He dressed, figuring his clothes would dry more quickly if worn, grabbed his stuff, and started off again. Despite a belly that felt too full, he was invigorated and wanted to find a good place to camp.

He hiked the rest of the afternoon, following mammoth trails and seeing a few footprints belonging to the bear that was now well behind him. The bear's prints were huge; both of Toq's feet could fit inside a single one.

A few crocuses—the first flowers of spring—popped up here and there. Snow completely covered the mountains to the west, while the hills on the east side of the valley began to show bare ground. He passed by a prominent orange rock hill that contrasted beautifully with the blue sky. He looked far down the wide, expansive valley. Too flat, it was wet and swampy in many areas.

The farther he went down the valley, the more life he saw. Birds were more numerous. Hares were easy to spot—still mostly white with a few brown patches. A couple of coyotes watched him, and a lone fox came right up to sniff the ground where he had just walked.

"Probably wonder what I am, yes? Probably smell the meat I'm carrying. You can't have it."

"Well, there you go, Toq. You're not only talking to yourself, you've already begun talking to animals."

Pressing on, he spotted a small herd of camels feeding on a hillside across the creek. They lifted their heads and watched him, chewing. They were big animals with long necks, a giant hump on their backs, thick brown and black fur, and long legs that enabled them to cover a lot of ground. He wondered if they could outrun or fight off wolves and bears. They looked too big and slow, but he hadn't seen them in action.

Animals always have a way of surprising you with their survival and fighting skills, he thought.

He moved on past the camels and found a great place to camp among some large rocks, away from the stream and trails. Concerned about the warm day, he set up camp and sliced up the rest of the meat—which was still a considerable amount. If he could save it, it would last him a couple of days, so he cooked and ate another hearty portion, then smoked and dried the rest over a smoldering fire. He wanted to make use of the chunk of hide—perhaps as patching material or soles on his moccasins—so he scraped off the meat and fat and tried to smoke it a little bit over the fire. Darkness enveloped him by the time he had finished his work.

He wrapped up the meat in his leather pouch and piled a bunch of heavy rocks on top of it to keep the scavengers from getting to it. Everything he wore was skin, and he probably hadn't done a good enough job of washing away the blood and fat from earlier, so he worried he might be a walking call for dinner as far as the carnivores were concerned. He wished he had bigger, better weapons. He also wished he had a companion to keep watch. He wondered if he would sleep or if he should just stay awake all night.

"Ah," he growled, "you gotta sleep sometime." He looked at the stars, then crawled under his bedding.

Toq slept fitfully. He got up twice to tend the fire. The second time, he decided to build a second fire in front of his lean-to. Every now and then, he heard animals grunting, bellowing, or growling down in the valley below. He didn't recognize all the sounds, though he did hear the distinctive whinny of horses. He heard what sounded like the hooves of larger animals near his camp, but it was too dark to see them. They did not stay long.

• • • •

Toq stirred slowly. Outside, all was gray and white with giant snowflakes falling. The ground was already covered a knuckle deep. The fires only smoked now, barely alive. Toq jumped up, put on his leathers, cleared a spot under his shelter, and with a flat rock plate, carefully transferred whatever he could salvage of the hot coals. Luckily, he'd left a bundle of dried twigs under his lean-to. He had to keep the fire small under the lean-to. With no idea how long this snow might last—soaking all the wood and grass—he found a big pile of old, dried mammoth dung, knocked the snow off it, and carried the whole thing back to his shelter—though it took him several trips.

It doesn't smell too bad. And it should burn.

For a while, he got more smoke than fire, but the flames came with time. The snow was heavy and wet, and there was just a light breeze. Toq's hair dripped, and his leathers were wet again.

"I didn't need this," he sighed, although he'd known it was a possibility. He hadn't brought his hooded winter coat, mittens, or boots; they weighed too much and were too bulky. One of the many risks he'd accepted was getting cold and wet and freezing to death, but still, he thought he would be all right with his shelter, fire, food, and thick roll of fur bedding. He knew he'd been fortunate to have had such good weather so far, and this snow was inevitable.

Toq kept busy all day, brushing snow off his lean-to and rushing around collecting stuff to burn. By the end of the day, the snow was nearly knee deep, and he was having a difficult time uncovering things like brush and dung piles. He had another day's worth of meat, but all this snow was worrying.

Night came and he was up several times, building up the fire, brushing snow off the shelter, and moving it out of and away from the opening. It snowed all night. In the morning, he was tired, cold, and depressed. He sat and stared out at the white landscape, the falling snow, trying to find some opening in the sky, some sign that the storm was letting up, but all was dark gray. He grew increasingly uncomfortable sitting and lying around. But he got wet and cold every time he left the lean-to. And it snowed all this day, too.

"It's so quiet," said Toq. "No birds, no animals. Just silence. As if the world has disappeared."

By the end of the day, he had given up trying to find anything more to burn. He saved some coals in his horn and lay under his covers to stay warm, only getting up to brush off his lean-to.

He muttered, "This was a mistake. It's not going to be fun to die here. You should've stayed with your people, you idiot."

Morning came and it still snowed, but it was not too cold, so Toq thought it an improvement. Not long after daybreak, the falling snow slowed and then stopped. The sky lightened. Blue patches appeared between light, fluffy clouds. Toq immediately felt better and walked out into the snow to check the sky all around, to make sure he wasn't being teased by the gods or whomever. The snow came up to the middle of his thigh.

Now his dilemma: Pack up and start walking through deep, heavy, wet snow, risking exhaustion and the cold, while hiking for days through a white landscape, never finding food, fuel, or a dry spot to camp, or else stay put and wait for some of this snow to melt, hunting the immediate area for game, and digging for fuel. He could bring the wet stuff to camp and try to dry it out, but he knew he'd be without fire for a couple of days at least.

"Funny," he said, "you might starve and freeze to death out here. But you could've been killed by the Asshole, or the wolves, or the bear, or so many other things you don't even know about. So many ways to die, yes, but so many ways to live!"

He decided to stay. He hoped the snow would melt quickly and that another storm wouldn't come and dump even more. He watched the skies.

Once again, he would need some luck with the weather and with game. A good hunk of meat remained, enough for today, so he first went about digging for sticks and dung piles using an animal scapula he'd found. After finding some fuel—though not nearly enough—he spread it out on top of and beneath his lean-to in order to expedite the drying process. He rested and ate. By afternoon, the sun broke free of the clouds and warmed the air. Toq turned his attention to hunting.

He brought one bag, his spears, and his bolas. He wore his leather goggles to fight the blinding brilliance of the snow and sun. He hiked up a difficult hill, in the deep snow, often slipping and falling. Upon reaching a good elevation, he looked up and down the valley. The birds were active again, but they faced the same problem: Everything was buried in snow. A bevy of swans flew in a line overhead. Two eagles circled and soared their way north. Down by the creek, a small herd of horses had stomped and scraped away a sizable patch of snow, and they all had their heads down to the grass.

He saw rabbit tracks and what he thought were bobcat tracks. His gaze followed a single, deep, zigzagging line in the snow going down the valley and stopping at a large black dot. He couldn't be certain, but he figured it was a big bull bison.

He took in the view. It may have been a killing snow, but it was a most pure sight, all white and blue. A few clouds hung around the mountain peaks, and scant cloud shadows moved across the snowy valley floor.

Toq couldn't see a way to hunt either the horses or the bison successfully. Not out in the open and not by himself. The best he could hope for would be to spot or stumble upon a ptarmigan or sharp-tail or a rabbit. He stood and watched and waited, his feet growing numb. *I can't stand here too long,* he thought. After a time, he gave up and half slid back down to his camp, where he cleared some more snow from around his lean-to, so he could warm up and dry out in the sun.

In the evening, he followed his trail back up the hill. The sky had cleared and a crescent moon trailed the setting sun. The air was still and the temperature dropped sharply. Only a little snow had melted during the day, and now the slush turned to ice. The sky turned from blue to dark purple to black, and the mountains and valley seemed to produce their own light as the snow glowed against the darkening skies.

In the fading light, Toq could still make out the horses. They remained in their spot, having cleared an even larger area. But down the valley, the lone bison was gone. No opportunities presented themselves. It was quiet and cold, so Toq retreated to his camp to try to get a fire going.

••••

Staying warm through the night was impossible. Cold air, damp clothing, and a very small fire all conspired against his comfort. He got up before sunrise and climbed the hill to see that the horses had moved. His eyes grew large when he spotted a herd of twenty or thirty caribou coming down the valley in a single line, making steady progress through the snow. It would ease his mind considerably if he could get one of them. Also, if they continued down the valley, in the direction he wished to go, they would break a trail he could follow through the snow. He hurried back to his camp and packed everything up.

"You've been here long enough. Time to get moving."

By the time he was ready to go, the herd had just gone past, down the valley, toward the horses' clearing. Toq cut across an unbroken expanse of snow to connect with their trail, and just as he reached it, he looked south, where a tall camel stood still, watching him. The long, dark hairs around its neck were covered in frost and snow; frozen breath blew from its nostrils. A line of five other camels stood behind it. They were also following the caribou trail. This was the same bunch Toq had seen several days earlier. He figured a lot of these creatures had probably moved up this way, thinking it was spring, just in time for the storm to dump on them.

A breeze picked up, blowing crystals of snow—shining in the sunlight— off the animals' fur. They all waited, looking at each other. Toq backtracked away from the caribou trail, positioning himself about a spear's throw away; then, he squatted to lower his profile and appear less threatening. He removed his bags and held his spear level in one hand. He still had meat. He didn't need to kill one of these camels, but he didn't know when he would get another chance at finding food.

Toq whispered, "Let's see what happens."

He'd never seen camels get aggressive, but it was always a possibility. They stood there nervously, hesitating, seemingly weighing their options and their courage. They clearly did not wish to deviate from the trail, but they also didn't know what this man was or if he was a threat. Their fear won. The lead camel looked at Toq one more time, then swung its head around and bolted past the others. The rest turned and ran after it, back up the trail, snow flying off their feet into the air.

Toq laughed, thinking they were funny-looking animals, and he fantasized about riding one. He gathered his bags and followed the caribou trail north. The wind blew harder, filling the trail with snow, but it was a warming wind, so Toq wasn't too concerned.

The caribou had punched a nice path through, and Toq made good time. He passed through the two spots the horses had cleared and, every fifty steps or so, dodged either yellow-stained snow or caribou or horse poop.

"Horse shit, horse shit," he mumbled, while thinking it would make good fuel someday.

All day he walked behind the animals, stopping occasionally to eat. Toq saw the horses on a hillside, once again clearing snow. They barely glanced at him. Toq moved faster than the caribou, but he held back so as not to disrupt the nice work his trailblazers were doing. He wondered how far they would go like this.

Surely, they'll stop to rest or eat, he thought.

The day warmed considerably, the wind ate away at the snow, and by the end of the day, a decent amount had melted. Though tired and a bit hungry, Toq felt good. He stopped early enough to clear snow and set up camp on a hill, out of the way of the trail. The caribou were out of sight. There was nothing to burn. The dung and grass were all wet. He tried to burn the ends of some brush that had managed to poke up through the snow but without success. The mammoth meat was almost gone. He hunted around, finally getting a grouse with his bola, but with no fire, he had to eat it raw.

"Not as good as the mammoth," he said, finishing the bird, but he'd wanted to save the last of the mammoth for morning.

Toq realized that he'd seen no wolves, bears, or big cats in the last few days. Nor had he seen their tracks. This set his mind at ease for the night's sleep, although he knew something could still come ambling along. The wind continued to blow, but he was glad for it. It would not be as cold tonight.

••••

Toq was having vivid dreams of the people he knew and of wild animals when he was snapped from his dreams by the crunching of ice under the feet of large mammals. It was already daylight. His eyes were puffy, and he wanted more sleep. His hand poked out from under his fur blanket, and he felt something small and furry brush past. He jerked up his head but didn't see anything.

"Ghost mouse," he muttered.

Despite the cold, damp conditions, he stayed warm through the night. Everything had frozen again overnight. He looked outside and smiled upon seeing the same group of camels slipping down the caribou trail.

Toq picked up his moccasins and examined them, putting his finger through a couple of holes worn through the bottoms. He had been packing grass into them for extra padding and insulation, but he couldn't keep that up forever. He carried a second clean, dry pair that he used for sleeping—and hiking, if needed. The mammoth hide would be great for their soles, but he decided to try to get one more day out of the old moccasins. He stuffed in more grass, put them on, and laced them. The sun was just over the mountains, and the wind blew, though not as hard as yesterday. A few ground squirrels out on top of the snow squeaked a warning when they saw him. He was all of a sudden motivated and in a hurry to go, so he ate the last of the mammoth meat, packed up, and hit the caribou trail, each footstep crunching the ice and snow. He liked the sounds of snow—the creak of really cold snow, the muffled sound of deeper, soft snow, and this crunching of icy snow—but there was no way to sneak up on anything in conditions like this.

For a while, the trail gave Toq's feet a hard, uneven, icy pounding, and he found it easier to walk in the unbroken snow—although it was crusty and still nearly knee deep. The sun quickly warmed the white land, and soon the snow and ice softened enough to make his hike easier.

He saw hawks and eagles and two big storks flying overhead, their long beaks pointing the way, legs trailing straight out behind. They flew in silence, and Toq watched in awe. The storks were big, but the teratorns were still the biggest birds he'd ever seen. Toq marveled at the little birds, too, wondering how they survived the cold and how they found enough to eat. He saw a robin and heard meadowlarks calling out across the snowy valley.

Toq had not seen the caribou all morning. The creek grew larger the farther he traveled downstream, becoming more of a river now, and with the sun as warm as it was, the melting snow began to swell the river. He crossed a number of side streams, some with frozen ponds and wetlands.

By midday, the river valley turned to the northeast and cut through a narrow canyon. He was nervous walking through the canyon; there were too many places to surprise, or be surprised by, a big predator. Instead, he was pleased to find a small group of bighorn sheep feeding in the canyon. They moved up onto some rocky ledges above as Toq approached. He didn't hunt them; he kept moving, wanting to get through the canyon. He hiked all day with only the food he had eaten that morning to keep him going.

The river (Beaverhead River) grew larger with each step downstream, and the narrow canyon forced it up against steep banks and cliffs, impeding Toq's path. The caribou trail went into the river, but Toq did not follow it. The camel tracks had taken off into a side valley (Grasshopper Creek) going west.

"I don't know where they're going, but I'm going down," Toq said.

It took him all day, with detours up steep hills, but by late afternoon, he broke out of the canyon. Standing in ankle-deep snow, he looked north and east into a wide valley with mountains and hills flanking its sides into the distance. Spots of bare ground blotted the mostly white land. And there were animals—lots of animals. Horses, bison, caribou, a pack of wolves, two bears, and off in the distance, a group of mammoths. It looked to him like all the animals in the land had decided to congregate here in this giant valley.

"What an incredible sight. I've never seen anything like this. Maybe they gather here until the snow melts and then head to higher country."

He found a place to camp up on some hills away from the valley of critters, not wanting to be trampled or eaten. He then took his spears and went hunting.

He climbed a nearby knoll to obtain a good vantage point and develop a plan. The snow on the ridges and hilltops was stomped down, and the low spots and valley bottoms were trampled as well. Grazers had chewed the grass down to where there wasn't much left, and in places, vegetation had been pulled up entirely, leaving only mud. Melting snow had flooded the big, flat valley bottom, creating extensive marshlands. A couple of bison bulls (ancient bison) walked through one up to their knees, and only the frozen ground beneath the water kept them from sinking deeper.

You hit one soft spot, you get stuck, and you'll have bear or wolf company, thought Toq. *But I won't come after you. Too big, too dangerous, too deep. No way.*

He followed higher ground to the west to look at some side coulees. In the distance, he saw wolves chasing caribou. They had the herd on the run while some horses on a hill watched the action from afar. The bears were out of sight. At first, the caribou ran down the valley, away from Toq, but then they turned up a hill. Toq couldn't tell why. They ran toward the horses, alarming them, and the horses took off over the ridge and disappeared.

Toq watched the wolves work, admiring their speed, their stamina, how they flanked the caribou, trailed them, and even tried to get in front of the herd to steer it. The caribou were also impressive. They, too, possessed speed and stamina, but winter had weakened them, while the wolves had been eating well. The chase followed along a ridge across the coulee from Toq and was getting closer. In a second, the herd turned down the hill, heading straight for him.

He snapped out of his state of awe and squatted, his mind now racing. *Lie down? You might get stampeded! Nothing to hide behind. If I spear one, the wolves will take it. If they run by, the wolves might attack me instead.*

A straggler had the pack's full attention. They had slowed it down and stopped it, with wolves at its back, front, and sides; it was a goner. The herd continued racing down into the coulee bottom, splashing through meltwater, kicking up snow and mud. They veered somewhat, so they were no longer coming right at Toq, but they still ran up the slope of Toq's hill. He crouched as low as he could, put down his small spear, and scurried to be in line with the herd when they crested the hill.

He waited maybe two breaths, hearing their hooves clicking and heavy breathing, until they topped the hill and turned to go up along the ridge and away. He was about five running steps from them. It was now or never. He stood quickly and ran toward the middle of the herd. They jumped and started to turn away, when Toq reared back and pitched his spear at the nearest caribou.

The spear sank deep into the unfortunate creature's side. Toq heard a thud and what sounded like the crack of a rib. The animal ran a ways back down the hill, the spear stuck in its side, while the herd kept running up the ridge. It stopped, blew blood from its nostrils and mouth, dropped to its knees, and fell over on top of the spear, dead.

Toq ran back to get his little spear. He looked down at the wolf pack, tearing into the dead caribou. He breathed heavily, excitement and adrenaline circulating through his system. He looked around for any threats, then jogged down to his kill. Toq was a conflicted man. Hunting was exciting; he enjoyed it. But he hated killing anything besides ticks and mosquitoes. He looked down at the dead animal and felt sorry for it. He felt sorry for the caribou killed by the wolves as well. The world of beasts and men was brutal and merciless. He would rather watch and wonder about these animals than kill them. He solemnly patted the female caribou's white and tan fur, then rolled it over to pull out his spear, which thankfully had not broken.

He quickly gutted the animal, disappointed to find the spear had nicked the stomach on its way into the lungs, but fortunately, it had not contaminated anything. This female did not have an unborn calf inside her, which was fine with Toq, but he acknowledged that they were very good eating. His goal was simple: leave the guts, take the heart and liver, and drag the carcass back to camp. It was heavy, and pulling the caribou uphill wore him out. The sun was just about behind the mountains when he arrived. He worried about the two bears he'd seen earlier; if they didn't have food of their own, they might be drawn to his dead caribou. With no trees to hang it from nor ponds to sink it in, he was left trying to cover it with snow, mud, and rocks. Adding to the difficulty, everything was still too wet for a fire. That meant Toq would again be eating raw meat. He needed fire in the next day or two or three, so he could cook, smoke, and dry some meat.

You might need to stay here a few days, he thought, which would give the grass and dung time to dry out—and would give him time to process the hide for new moccasins.

• • • •

Toq had a restless night. The valleys, plains, and hills below were more raucous than he was used to, and his senses amplified every sound—a breath of wind, a flap of his shelter, a vole sniffing around, a trickle of water. But no bears or wolves showed up in his camp.

Morning came, and Toq forced down a filling portion of raw meat. The animals in the valley had mostly vanished. The wolves were still hanging around yesterday's kill, but there wasn't much left of it. The gut pile Toq had left was gone. It amazed him, all the animals that could live off a pile of guts. He saw no bear tracks. The wolves watched him as he walked around on the hill above them.

The mammoths had moved closer. Toq counted eight of them, and though he was not familiar with their behavior, he cautiously walked toward them as they meandered toward the canyon. They cleared snow with their long, curved tusks and feet, exposing grass and short brush, which they curled their trunks around and pulled up out of the ground. They knocked off the mud, shoved it into their mouths, and took two steps forward.

They looked pretty docile, but Toq knew that in order to survive in this world, they must have a tough, aggressive side. He approached slowly, from behind. These were the first live mammoths he had seen, and he imagined they could outrun him, so he tried to resist the temptation to get too close. But his curiosity about these magnificent beasts drew him in.

They didn't walk in a line. Rather, they each took their own path, except two that were half the size of the others. Toq guessed they might be a year or two old. They followed behind the big mothers in front, picking at the uncovered grasses. The wind favored Toq, so they didn't smell him, but they were well aware of his presence. The nearer he came, the more impressive their size. He had only been up close to a dead one, so to stand near these living, breathing mammoths bordered on rapturous, like a fantasy.

They had been silent, and Toq only heard their tusks and feet crunching the snow. When he got within a stone's throw of them, the two big ones in the rear turned to face him. Their ears faced out in his direction, and their trunks curled up as if trying to feel the air. They tried to get a whiff of him, and one let out a very low, vibrating rumble. The rest of the group stopped and turned, too, all eight noses waggling in the air. Toq stood still, then backed up. The giant matriarch pushed through and delivered a loud elephant call—a sound Toq had never heard before. He felt it in his chest. It sounded like nothing else in the wild, except maybe a hundred hoarse geese honking in unison.

The agitated beast bore down on Toq. He ran, but the slick ground was not conducive to quick movements. Though he slipped, he didn't fall. He glanced back to see her stop. He ran a bit farther, paused, and looked back. She watched him, flanked by the two calves. The other giants had already gone back to their grazing, unconcerned about this man. Toq turned to walk away, and she did the same, nudging one of the little ones with her muddy tusks.

The people of the village had explained how they went about hunting mammoths, but now Toq appreciated the danger involved. Also, now, he had no desire to ever kill one.

"Your heart is too soft," people would tell him. "They're just animals, put here for us."

But Toq sensed, from his first encounter, a higher level of intelligence, and he was intrigued by them, drawn to them.

He could watch them all day, but he had work to do. He returned to camp to gather grass, peat moss, dead shrubs, and old dung, spreading them out on the driest piece of ground he could find. He uncovered his caribou and skinned it, then sliced off thin strips of meat down to the bone. With the sunny day, he wasn't sure the snow would last long enough to keep the meat cold. So, he counted on being able to get a fire going. He stripped off tendons and sliced them to make cords of sinew. He saved the bones for later, when he would smash them open to dig out the marrow. He cleaned the flesh from the bottom of the hide and scraped the hair off about half of it. He figured he'd use the bare skin for moccasins and patching clothing and keep the piece with fur just in case—although his bedding was still in good shape. He picked the ticks out of the scraped-off fur and saved a good bit of it for padding.

He had to rework his stone blade and scraper many times to keep sharp edges. He skinned the head and defleshed it a little on one side. Then, with a large rock, he smashed open the skull enough to remove the brains. He lamented that he didn't have the resources to do things properly.

"You use what you have and don't whine," he chided himself.

He mashed up the brains on a flat rock and spread them across the hide. He added a bunch of snow until he had a good, mushy mix, which he then worked into the skin using his hands and the end of a bone. It would have been better if he could soak the hide over time, but this was the next best thing.

Toq staked the hide out on the ground with busted rib bones, then periodically went back to work it with the bone to keep it pliable and to prevent it from shrinking too much. He worked steadily all day, pausing only to eat and to look out for bears or scavengers. He took a short nap, then gathered up the finest, driest grasses and dung, forming a nest-like bundle. Then, he repeatedly struck a piece of pyrite with a piece of flint, creating sparks to generate a fire. He blew a flame to life and set about nursing the reluctant fire. He began roasting and smoking meat, eating it almost as fast as he cooked it. He'd go work the hide, go get more fuel, go back to the fire, go work the hide again—and around and around he went.

By dusk, he was used up. Working hunched over on his knees most of the day had greatly fatigued his back. His work was still far from finished, but he decided to take one last stroll up the hill above his camp to get a good look around.

The warm day had melted away almost all the remaining snow in the valley; only a couple of stubborn snowdrifts persisted on the hills and ridges. A thick blanket of white covered the distant mountains. Toq looked for the mammoths, but they had disappeared up the canyon. He wondered how far they'd gotten and if they'd made it all the way through.

From the hill, Toq saw no bears or wolves, though far off, he saw what he thought were bison and horses. Satisfied and feeling somewhat secure, he returned to his camp to cover the caribou meat with rocks and mud, then took a quick walk down to the wolves' caribou kill. The wolves were gone and had left only the caribou's skull and pelvis bone.

"That didn't take long," Toq said. Staring at the skull for a while, he couldn't help but think of the Traveler and his fate. He drew a deep breath and let it out, trying to rid his mind of gloomy thoughts before they ruined his day. "It's okay to think of the past. Just don't dwell on it. Focus on today and tomorrow. The past is done. It's gone. You don't get it back. Move forward."

He started back to camp, turning once to see a weasel, mostly white with brown patches, appearing out of nowhere, sniffing around the caribou skull.

"Too late for you," Toq said to him. "There's nothing left."

Light faded quickly from the land, and a crescent moon hung bright in the sky. Toq had one thing on his mind now and that was sleep, and sleep did not elude him, carrying him away from the world the second he crawled under his fur.

• • • •

Toq woke to the warbling of spring's birds and the ruckus of some bird landing on his lean-to and chattering away. Outside, only a hint of light shone in the eastern sky.

"You're up early," he mumbled to the bird, which chirped and flew off.

He heard heavy breathing and a munching noise. He lifted his head and peered out. Against the dark landscape, he could just make out the black shape of one gigantic bison, with long, thick horns sticking straight out from the sides of its head, grazing only ten steps away. Toq was suddenly wide awake, but he didn't move. He had known a few cocky young men who were now lame, or dead, because of these beasts. Bison were good to eat, but they were not easy prey.

This close, the last thing Toq wanted to do was startle or agitate the giant, causing it to charge in self-defense. He lay quietly, waiting, watching, and hoping the animal would not destroy his camp. The monster—with a massive hump rising above its shoulders—only took a step here and a step there, chomping grass, rarely lifting its head.

Don't lie down, don't lie down, Toq pleaded, lest he be trapped there for half the day. He was suddenly aware he needed to piss. The bull apparently had the same urge, and it sounded and looked like a waterfall. At first, a gentle breeze carried the strong odor of bull urine to Toq, but then, the wind shifted, carrying it away. Something, or some smell, got the bison's attention. He looked in Toq's direction and stopped chewing. Toq held his breath. Then, the big bull turned around and sauntered away. As soon as it was out of sight, Toq leaped up and let loose his own smaller waterfall.

He spent the day eating, cooking and drying meat, and making a new set of moccasins. Toq ate as much as he could. Resting and eating were vital to restoring his body and mind, and the warm, sunny weather lifted his spirits. But it soon became too warm, and the meat would spoil before he could eat it all—unless he buried it in the frozen ground or immersed it in one of those bogs down below. But he felt the urge to get going. So, today he would rest and eat, and tomorrow he would pack up as much dried meat as he could carry, and then he would move on.

CHAPTER 9

Spring

In the morning, the sky was cloudy, but it did not appear to threaten rain or snow. Toq packed up his bags, freshly reinforced and patched, and loaded them with extra meat and the remnants of the caribou hide. He hoisted them up over his head, groaning at the added weight. He would eat his way to a lighter load, but that would take days.

He took a good long look at the route ahead, checking for potential trouble. Most of the beasts in the valley had wandered off, leaving only horses and bison behind: no camels, no caribou, no mammoths. He hiked north along ridges and hills, attempting to stay out of the flat, boggy valley bottom. Ice on the ponds melted quickly now, and already the croaking of frogs filled the air.

"Another sure sign of spring," said Toq.

A blue heron, tall and thin, stalked the shallows around one of the wetland ponds.

You're a bit early, he thought, but then he said, "Spring might be late. Hey, trees can't be too far away if you're here."

He hadn't gone far when he heard the howl of wolves. Were they gathering to hunt? Warning of danger? Were they lonely? A little farther and Toq saw them on a hill right in his path.

"Crap," he said, looking for the best way around. They hadn't noticed him yet. Going right of them meant going into the wetlands. Going left meant walking sidehills, which was tough on the feet, unless he could find an animal trail. He went left. The wolves saw him, and one by one, they left the hill and trotted in line right for him.

"Oh, that's just great!" he said out loud. He looked around, but there was nowhere to go, and he couldn't run, so he stood his ground and watched them come. When they were fifty paces away, Toq raised his arms and spears over his head and yelled loudly, "Hey! Go away!"

He doubted whether this was the right thing to do, but the pack did pause. Then, they continued on toward him. Toq thought about the blood on his leathers and the meat in his bags, but he wasn't going to leave those things behind to feed the wolves. He lowered his arms and pointed both spears at the wolves. They slowed to a cautious walk as they approached him. Toq could tell they weren't in an excited, hunting state of mind. They were controlled, trying to figure out what he was. Was he edible? Was he dangerous?

Toq's heart pounded, but he stood still, watching them, remaining calm. The wolves walked around him, sniffing the ground and air, their piercing eyes watching his every move. One advanced from behind. Toq slowly turned and pointed his spear toward it, and it moved away. He now stood with both spears held out in a V.

The smell of the meat was a lot for them to overcome, but they were more curious than hungry. And as for this man, they were more careful than curious. They didn't know it, but they were within a killing reach of this human's spear. Toq didn't know what would happen if he killed one; would the rest run off, or would they attack?

After circling the man once, the lead canid seemed to get bored, sat down, and started looking around. The other wolves—six in total—began milling around, and a couple casually nuzzled the neck and head of the sitting leader, sensing that he had little interest left in this two-legged creature. Toq was hopeful upon witnessing this calm. Then, the leader stood up and trotted away down into the valley. The other wolves didn't even look at Toq; he was not a threat, and he was not prey, at least not today. Their eyes followed the leader, and they all left to run after him.

Toq breathed a huge sigh of relief and bent over, hands on his knees, his spears leaned against his shoulder, trying to get his heartbeat back to normal.

He straightened up, looked toward the wolves, and said, "Damn it! These tense situations are gonna kill me!"

He felt the same as when he'd been surrounded by the Asshole and his men. The only difference was the humans had actually attacked him. Did that make the wolves better than people?

"Maybe not," said Toq. "Next time, the wolves might attack." It was enough to make a man loco. Everyone, and everything, might be out to get him.

He hiked on, his legs feeling a bit wobbly, as if he'd been running all day. He wanted to sit, but he needed to put some distance between himself and the wolves. After some time, he stopped, drank from a stream, and ate some meat. He lay back for a spell and closed his eyes, but not for long. Feeling better, he got going again, constantly on the lookout and reflecting upon his wolf encounter.

"Maybe you were never in danger. Maybe you don't have to get so afraid. Some people claim they've befriended wolves. But I'll bet anyone, by themselves, surrounded by a pack of wolves, would shit their pants. *I* didn't shit my pants." He laughed, counting that a success.

Toq hiked the rest of the day without incident or trouble, crossing small streams and passing deer, horses, and bison. He saw one bear rummaging around in the valley bottom. He stayed west of the main river (Beaverhead River), which continued to widen. There was a little more brush, but this was still a treeless country.

He wondered, "What if I never see a tree anywhere up here? Can a person get through a winter burning sticks, grass, and dung? Maybe." But he didn't relish the thought. Trees and wood were useful for shelter, fuel, and weaponry.

"Maybe that's why there are no people here," he mused.

He wondered more and more about people and when he would run into them. As much as he wished to be the first one to see a new land, he was certain that somewhere up ahead he would find people. Would they be friendly? Would they be different from his people? Would he settle with them? There was no way for him to know this, but there were no people where he was going—anywhere. He was the first human to set foot on the land that lay before him. Nobody coming after him could ever make that claim. Everyone else who would ever live would forever be walking in another's footsteps, looking at mountains and valleys and plains that other human eyes had already seen.

Toquuxla, though, only walked in the footsteps of animals. The land and the creatures he encountered had never seen his species before. This one man was the forerunner of a species that would radically and profoundly change the land and the beings living there. It and they would never be the same. Although, this was never Toquuxla's intention. He had no wish to see these places changed by humans. On the contrary, he dreamed these lands, and their inhabitants, would remain as they were: rich, wild, dangerous, and exciting. He knew the land and its creatures might kill him, but that made him feel alive. It made him feel like he was a part of it, like he was inside the world—not set apart, not outside. He was in it. He didn't just look out from the safety of a group of people or a village. *A false safety,* he thought, *because people might turn on you more quickly than a pack of wolves or a bear.*

Still, he missed people—at least, the people who seemed to actually like him. But he didn't miss them enough to wish to go back. Not yet. He had to keep going. He had to see what was out there.

But pain entered his belly, and dysentery crept into his life. It began in the afternoon and worsened toward the end of the day. He quit eating until he could get all the shit out of his system. He was thoroughly spent by the end of the day.

Too much raw, uncooked food, or maybe some bad water. It's not an evil spirit, but it feels and smells evil, he thought.

• • • •

The wind blew hard this morning, but Toq didn't mind. He knew he'd had a pretty nice stretch of weather, and though windy, the sun shone brightly. This morning, he was thirsty but not hungry, so with a somewhat settled stomach, he packed up and headed out, seeing how he felt as he went along. Even lacking his usual vitality, he nevertheless made slow, steady progress. He endeavored to only drink from clear-running streams, but with large animals wading through and pooping in the water, it was challenging. By late morning, he arrived at a very large, prominent rock hill (Beaverhead Rock) with a cliff facing the river, and he hiked to the top to have a look around.

The hills and valleys, now snowless, were brown and tan. Only a few wildflowers had popped up. Toq had been admiring a higher range of mountains (Pioneer Mountains) to the northwest, all white, and though he couldn't tell for certain, it looked as if there were glaciers on them. He had crossed a couple of streams that were milky gray with silt, which he thought was a sign of glacier-fed streams. The valley to the north looked very flat and braided with multiple channels of water. It ran off into the distance as far as he could see.

He left the hilltop, walking northeast and staying west of the river channels. At midday, he was tired and hungry, a good sign that his illness had passed. He rested and ate a little bit of meat. Rejuvenated, he hiked the remainder of the day. But as the day wore on and his body grew weary, he questioned his own sanity.

Every day he asked, "What are you doing out here? Where are you going? Why are you in such a hurry to get there, and where is 'there'? How are you going to know where to end your travels? Is there an end? Are you just going to wander around forever?"

But after resting and relaxing, he felt good again about what he was doing—whatever that was. He said to himself, "Just enjoy every day. You don't have to be anywhere. You don't have to please anyone or do what they say.

Do whatever you want. You're free!"

Toq passed many animals, hardly noticing them, and they paid little attention to him. The wind was strong at his back all day, helping him to make great time to nowhere in particular. He would hike to the end of the day, then do it again tomorrow.

• • • •

Toq listened to the patter of raindrops on his leather lean-to. He rolled over to look out at the dreary day. The mountains across the valley to the east had disappeared behind the gray. He was certain it was snowing again on the mountains, and even a few snowflakes mixed with the rain around his shelter.

Rain was more difficult than snow, because rain soaked his leathers. He'd tried to waterproof some leathers with melted caribou fat, but there wasn't much left. So, today, with the clouds low on the mountains and filling the valley, he wasn't going anywhere, or else he'd be wet all day—and maybe for several days beyond.

It wasn't comfortable, lying under the shelter all day. A person needed to get up and move around, and Toq's shelter was so small, it was difficult even to sit up without his head rubbing against the ceiling. He could have a larger, cozier shelter, but that would mean carrying more. He lay on his back until he got sore, then rolled onto his left side, got sore, rolled onto his right side, flipped onto his stomach, tried to sit up for a bit, and went outside to relieve himself. All day he did this. His eyes felt puffy and swollen from lying flat so much.

He was warm enough, and only a very slight breeze blew, so he didn't fret about a fire. He had plenty to eat. It was quiet. Even the birds were quiet, though a few poked around in the grass. The rain would let up for a while, then return. Around midafternoon, Toq had just dozed off when he was awakened by a rumbling coming from the ground. *Weird*, he thought, wondering if it might be a herd of large animals. Then, the land began to shake.

"What is that?!" he cried as he jerked up, then braced himself as his lean-to shook. It stopped suddenly. All was quiet and calm again, while the rain pattered atop the lean-to.

Toq wondered if it had been a huge avalanche. He stepped outside but saw nothing but the gray. Then, off in the distance, he heard the unmistakable sound of a thundering avalanche coming from the mountains to the east. It was far off, so he wasn't worried. But then there was another one from the mountains to the north.

"Wow," he said, staring into the blankness, wishing he could see what was happening. The ground shook again, softly, just for a moment. Toq was mystified. He'd never felt the earth quake like this before. It was much stronger than before the flood, but he was certain there was no flood coming, as he heard no rushing water.

He had a strange feeling of being alone with this earthquake, the avalanches, the fog and rain, and no animals in sight. Suddenly, he wished for the comfort, companionship, and comradery of living together with the other creatures that roamed this world. He felt like he alone had just experienced this strange phenomenon. He wondered if people south of the pass felt it. He wanted to call out to the animals, asking, "Did you feel that? What was that?" But all was now quiet, still, and foggy.

Then, a little red fox appeared out of the grayness, trotting straight toward Toq.

"Oh, thank you. The world hasn't come to an end. How you doing, little buddy?" he said quietly to the fox, which was still too far away to hear him.

Toq ducked back down under his lean-to and watched the fox. It stopped and stared at him, then changed direction to go around the camp. Curious about the camp that had invaded its territory, the animal—with fur darkened and wet from the rain—curved in closer. Toq reached into his bag and, though he knew he shouldn't be giving his food away, tossed a small strip of meat toward the fox. It jumped back, looked at Toq, and sniffed the ground. The little, furry animal didn't know what Toq had thrown and couldn't smell it, and so it didn't investigate. Instead, it trotted off behind Toq's camp. Toq got up in time to see it fade away like a shadow in the fog. He retrieved the piece of meat and stuck it in his mouth.

"Well, if you don't want it, I'll eat it," he said as he chewed.

•••

The rain stopped in the night, and Toq arose well before sunrise. The gray and fog were gone. Through a partly cloudy sky, he saw a few stars. Though the valley was still dark, the clouds had lifted off the mountainsides enough to reveal a fresh covering of snow. What little snow had made it to the valley bottom did not stick.

He took his time, eating and shaking the water from his shelter, and when the sky lightened enough, Toq packed up and cautiously walked north into the half-light, looking hard at every dark, shadowy bump that lay before him.

By the time the sun cleared the mountains, he'd reached a river that came down from the southwest (Big Hole River). As big as the river he had been following, it was sure to be no small obstacle. With the rain and melting snow, there was a lot of water coming down both rivers. Toq stood on a hill looking up- and downstream for a good place to cross. He could see far enough downstream to guess where the two rivers converged. He stared over at the main river, wondering if it would be easier to cross, putting him on the east side of the valley. He could not know which side of the valley would be better to travel down. There were no trees and therefore no downed logs to cross on. If he couldn't find a wide, shallow crossing to wade through, he would have to swim in the icy current. If he'd had a large animal bladder or stomach, he could keep some of his stuff dry, but he didn't, so most of his stuff would get wet.

The river moved fast, and the murky water appeared thick with mud and silt and the occasional large chunk of ice. Toq walked upstream for some distance, but it looked hopeless. He found a path where animals had crossed, but with no fresh tracks, he guessed it had last been used in the late summer. He went back downstream into the flat bottomlands, and as he searched, he considered it might be impossible to cross at the peak of the snowmelt.

Finally, near the confluence of the two rivers, he found a wide spot in the river, forty paces across, with a muddy, wide trail filled with fresh animal tracks of all kinds. He saw another trail going east to cross the main river. Toq checked both crossings but came back to the first one. The river slowed and spread out here, and some of the blocks of ice had even become grounded on sandbars. But it was very wide, and he was certain it would be deep in places. The morning air was chilly, and Toq shivered just thinking about the icy water, but as the day warmed, the water was likely to rise. Now was the best time to cross. He walked onto a little hill, sat down, and pondered his route, hoping to see some animal come along to make the crossing.

He didn't have to wait long. A bear sow showed up on the other side of the river with two tiny cubs. She was about half the size of the bear he'd seen at the dead mammoth site, and she moved cautiously, looking for any signs of danger. Toq sat still, watching them, thinking she surely wouldn't try to ford the river with those two cubs. She paused at the water's edge, sniffing the air. The energetic and curious cubs stood on their hind legs, leaning against their mother. They were undeniably cute and playful, but Toq knew if he got too close, the sow would kill him. She hadn't seen Toq and couldn't smell him, and although she wanted to cross the river, she did not. Instead, she turned and moved upstream, staying on the north side, two little balls of fur and legs scrambling right behind her.

Toq was relieved to see them pass out of sight, and he again focused on the crossing. The sun shone warmly upon him. He looked at the sky and saw no sign of any impending storm. If he did get his stuff wet, he could dry it out. He stood up and, with no large beasts in sight, marched straight down to the river, where he took off all his clothes and jammed them into his bags. He considered making two trips, carrying one bag at a time, but to save time and minimize his exposure to the cold water, he decided to try carrying it all in one trip. It was going to be awkward keeping two bags above water with one hand and holding two spears in the other. The spears would help stabilize him, planted upstream in the river bottom as he moved across.

He stepped into the icy stream. He couldn't see the bottom through the murky water, so he stepped cautiously. His bare feet felt the painfully cold water and, thankfully, a mostly sandy, muddy streambed. He moved quickly at first, but the soft bottom gave way to a rocky bed and a faster current, making his footing precarious. Halfway across, his feet were numb, and the water rushed just above his knees, trying to push him off his feet. He glanced at his intended exit and saw a small herd of five or six horses watching him.

He wobbled as he almost lost his balance, then refocused on his feet while saying out loud to the horses, "What are you looking at?"

As he worked his way along, the horses plunged in—directly on the same line Toq was going to take. They were nearly swimming. They moved fast, pushing a wave as they rose up out of the deep water, high-stepping right around Toq, their hooves splashing up glittering droplets of spray, brilliant in the sun. In two seconds, they were on the other side, shaking the water from their manes. They briefly sniffed the ground, then trotted off. Toq felt like a weak little man as he continued his struggle across.

"Show-offs," he mumbled.

He was nearly across when he reached the deep spot where the horses had entered. The current wasn't as strong here and the bottom had become sandy again, but the water was now up to his butt, and the river bottom sloped down. He held his bags up high. Then, he took his smaller, antler-pointed spear and threw it over onto the bank. He did not throw his big spear, fearing it might break the stone point. He considered trying to throw his bags across, but it was too far and they were too heavy.

Gripping his spear in one hand, he hoisted his bags up onto his shoulders. Now, he was top-heavy and unsteady. He inched forward and down, saying, "If your stuff stays dry, you'll be very lucky."

Three steps, water up to his waist. Three more steps, water over his belly.

"Control your breathing," Toq said, gasping at the cold water enveloping his body.

Two steps more, water nearly up to his armpits. Although the current was slower, it still pushed Toq over, and he lost his footing completely and swam. He kicked with all his might, while the bags—not yet soaked through—provided some buoyancy. Only his head, hands, and spear were above water. He reached for the bottom with his feet and pushed hard off the streambed, grunting loudly with the effort. He progressed into shallower water but stumbled over the now rocky bottom, not able to stand.

"Itshla!" he said, frustrated with feet too frozen to work right.

Breathing hard and shivering mightily, he pulled his bags to shore. That last push had nearly filled his bags with water. He quickly turned them upside down, the flaps swinging open and water spilling out. He hadn't lost anything, but pretty much everything was soaked. Though no animals were in sight, he had to get away from the crossing. He hurriedly put on his drenched clothes and packed everything back up. Grabbing his spears, he walked quickly on frozen feet with stiff legs to a place far off the animal trail and away from the river.

••••

Toq spent most of the morning trying to dry out his leathers and meat, feeling lucky that it was a warm, sunny day. He made no attempt to start a fire. The river had snuffed out the ember he'd kept in the horn. He put up his lean-to and hung a couple items on it to speed the drying process. He turned his bags inside out and flipped other pieces over to maximize their exposure to the sun. He ate and gazed at the glacier-covered mountains to the east (Tobacco Root Mountains). They were high and rugged and almost completely covered in snow and ice; only a few cliff faces showed through. There were no trees. Glaciers capped the higher peaks and flowed down the mountainsides into hidden canyons. Even from some distance away, Toq could make out gigantic cracks and crevasses in the glaciers, and the brilliant white and shades of blue ice were beautiful.

Nothing can live up there, he thought. *It's an impossible land. A man could never cross those kinds of mountains.* But somehow, he felt a pull, a compulsion, to try. *Not today, or tomorrow, but maybe . . . someday*, he mused.

White torrents of water flowed loudly down from the glaciers and into the valley to join the river just below him. The valley bottom and hills were just beginning to show a light hint of spring's green. The sky, between the clouds, was a deep blue.

Toq said, "What a sight. So glorious." He felt lucky to be there, at that moment, that day, to see it all. He wished someone else could have been there to see it with him, but, he said, "It's okay. At least I get to see it."

By midday, he was impatient to get moving again. His leathers were not completely dry, but he trekked north anyway. The river pressed up along the west side of the valley, forcing Toq to walk on the hills above it. He had numerous side streams to cross, but none were as big as the morning's crossing. Animals were scattered, plentiful, and diverse. Toq never felt alone among them, and he had no confrontations that day. He hiked steadily and hard, and by late day, he stood above a healthy flowing creek (Cherry Creek). The valley to the north opened up, so the walking tomorrow looked flat and easy. High, ice-capped peaks bordered the valley. This wide little valley, squeezed between mountains, was the only habitable zone, and the wildlife thrived in it.

Toq decided to camp here and went down to the creek to get some water. On the edge of the creek, half buried in the mud, a shining nugget of gold contrasted sharply with its drab surroundings.

"Whoa! Look at that!" Toq said as he picked it out of the mud. He washed it off.

It was half the size of his clenched fist, smooth and irregular in shape. He marveled at its weight. He had seen gold a couple of times but nothing this big. It was beautiful and his people might keep a bit in their homes, but it didn't have any real use and it was heavy to carry. Some people pounded smaller pieces flat to use as ornaments in their clothes or hair. Some said it caused trouble and envy. Nothing like other rocks, it felt cold in one's hands. He put the gold down on a flat stone and struck it several times with a round rock, and sure enough, it changed shape and did not shatter or break. He held it up in the sunlight, wondering what he could do with such a prize.

••••

The next morning, Toq was up with the sun to see another clear blue sky and a thick layer of fog blanketing the valley bottom. His food supplies were getting low, and he would need to hunt again soon. After eating, he packed his bags and returned to the creek. He held the gold nugget for a while, looking at it, wanting to keep it, to possess it. "Maybe it'll bring good luck." But he couldn't carry every unusual thing he found, and good luck or not, he decided it didn't hold any special power, and he couldn't think of any good use for it. So, he dropped it with a wet thud onto the mud at the creek's edge, where it glowed in its new place.

"Goodbye, golden rock," Toq said to it. "Perhaps someone else will find you one day." He then strode barefoot across the creek, never thinking of the gold again.

He scanned the terrain for dangerous animals and potential hunting opportunities. His bags were considerably lighter now that he had eaten almost all of the meat, and he felt like he could run with such a light load.

He watched a herd of white swans on a large, marshy pond, so big and majestic. He wondered if they would nest here or move on. He walked along the edge of the pond but found no nests with eggs. The swans and honking geese swam away from him, while most of the ducks flew away. There was little chance of getting any of these birds for dinner. With no cover and no eggs, he moved on.

As the day warmed, the fog disappeared. The wind began to blow, and by midmorning, it blew hard. He came over a small rise to a view down to the river. Multiple braids of streams ran left and right, curving back and forth, going every direction except straight. In the middle of these streams, a sizable herd of mammoths worked over the vegetation, sucking up water and spraying it from their trunks onto their heads and backs. He watched them for a while. The wind blew their long hair and carried off the spray. Those mammoths with longer tusks pushed them down into the stream and back up again repeatedly. A couple of giants rolled back and forth on their sides in the icy water. Some of the herd swam across the deeper stream, holding their trunks up. They crossed to the other side, emerging from the river with waterfalls flowing from their fur, soaking the ground beneath them. They had begun to shed their reddish winter coats, and they rubbed against each other and rolled on the dry ground to try to rid themselves of the old hair. Toq wished to stay, but he finally left them and walked north.

As the day wore on, the wind blew harder, making it difficult to walk straight. Toq's black hair whipped in the wind, and though he tied it back into a ponytail, it still snapped at his face. He took breaks behind hills and rock outcrops just to get some relief. Hawks, eagles, and other birds soared in the wind, but other animals did the same as Toq and found places of refuge or else lay down. Many simply stood with their butts to the wind. Toq laughed at the sight of horses' tails blown between their legs. He had a theory that horses *liked* feeling the breeze on their ass.

The wind might help him in a hunt. If he found the right spot, a bedded-down animal wouldn't hear or smell him. He would keep an eye out.

Despite the wind, Toq marched on. He passed many animals but had no chance at anything bigger than a rabbit. He saw a couple more bears and another large pack of wolves, luckily on the other side of the valley.

By the end of the day, after crossing a substantial creek (Whitetail Creek) that flowed down a valley from the north, Toq found a spot to camp out of the wind. He noted the hills looked much greener today than they did yesterday.

No doubt about it, spring is here, finally. He admired several flowers popping up: crocuses, as well as yellow flowers, purple flowers, and little white flowers. Still, the land grew only grasses, forbs, and knee-high shrubs. No brush, willows, or trees. This continued to weigh on Toq's mind.

The sky remained clear, but the wind, rowdy, blew all night, making sleep a difficult companion to find.

• • • •

Toq figured he had about a day's worth of meat left, with the rabbit giving him a little extra. Scavenging an already dead animal would be ideal, since it would be easier and less dangerous, but it risked a confrontation with other predators, and the hide was usually unusable. He thought there must be fish in these rivers, but the water was too silty to see through, making spearing impossible. Making a net or hooks and lines would take time he did not wish to spend.

Coming down the valley, he'd constantly come upon the bones of animals, large and small. Old, rotting ones and new, fresh ones still stained with blood. If they were fresh enough and hadn't been busted open, he could crack them open and get to the rich marrow. But Toq wasn't too worried about eating; prey was abundant.

He lay on his side, under the lean-to, downwind of a rock wall, listening to the wind blow and watching the eastern sky turn bright orange, red, and pink. It was brilliant. The land glowed as the pink light spread its way west. Pink-bottomed clouds floated above the mountaintops, their reflection turning the white mountains rosy. Toq got up to look around, and in a few moments, the bright colors were gone, replaced by the white and gray of the clouds.

He felt tired and grouchy after a poor night's sleep. He gazed east, following the river (Jefferson River). It seemed to run up against the mountains and disappear.

"Where does the river go? I'll find out soon," he said.

He didn't want to leave his little space of calm amid the windstorm, but he did. He went east, toward the rising sun, which popped in and out of the clouds, forcing him to shield his eyes.

He came upon a large, scattered pile of mammoth bones. The skull lay on its side, one huge, curving tusk in the air, one partly stuck in the ground. The lower jaw lay a couple of steps away. He approached from upwind, and as he neared, a gray and white fox peeked out from behind the massive skull, which it had been using as a windbreak. The fox took one look at Toq and bolted, its long, slender body flying across a grassy hill and disappearing. Toq marveled at its speed.

"Sorry for disturbing you," he said.

He examined the bones of the long-dead giant. No soft tissue or hide remained. He found a large stone and, after multiple attempts, split open a thick leg bone, but the marrow inside was putrid.

Toq winced when he got a whiff of it. "Ho, shit!"

He poked around the bones some more, wondering if he could learn what animals had fed on it, or how old it had been, or how it had died. He ran his fingers over the massive, flattened, rippled, and worn molars. This animal was so different from all the others. He wondered how it had come to be. He didn't accept the mythologies about the origins of the animals, but he had no explanation of his own. He had many questions, but he did not linger there long to ponder them. Before he left, he grabbed a tusk and tried to move it, but it was stuck tight in the dirt and the weight was too much. It did not budge.

Toq continued east until he reached a decent-sized valley coming down from the north, and with it, another large stream (Boulder River). Fortune favored him when the stream hit a large, flat area before joining Toq's river, spreading out in a wide delta where there were multiple braided channels allowing for a well-used, shallow crossing. But after the crossing, the main river funneled into a narrow and steep canyon. He would have to go up and around. This would be his first time wandering away from the river since entering this country.

He looked up at some ridges that ran to the northeast. They would be terribly windy, but they were not too steep and were mostly free of snow. After a break, he began his climb up onto the hills.

"At least I'll get a good view of this country," he said.

The wind blew hard at Toq's back, aiding his ascent and keeping him cool and dry, but he felt ravaged by the relentless thrashing of this invisible beast. He hurried to the top and looked down at the valley. The wind buffeted him so badly he couldn't stand steady, so he sat down and tried to make out the route he had come. Everything looked so different from high up; the river was much smaller, and the big animals below were merely dots. Eyes watering from the wind, he looked northwest at a wide valley and mountains, and he looked south at the magnificent, glacier-crowned peaks and valleys of the mountain range (Tobacco Root Mountains) that had held his attention for days. Today, those mountains looked cold and ominous.

He stood up and walked north and east, attempting to escape the wind-battered perch. He crested a big hump, and a large, wide, flat area lay before him, sloping downhill to another new land. He saw tall white mountains in the distant north (Elkhorn Mountains), a giant valley took shape to the east (Gallatin Valley), and a distant, snow- and ice-covered range stood on the eastern horizon (Bridger Range). On the open flat in front of him, several different groups of bison fed on the grasses. They were the only animals in sight.

Toq was a little elated. With the wind at his back and an easy down-sloping plain before him, he felt like he could fly. He crossed the open plain quickly, moving between the groups of bison, keeping his distance. They watched him closely as he passed by. He saw quite a few newborn calves, light tan in color, all bedded down out of the wind. He didn't see any grouchy, old bulls around, but the giant mothers still kept him on his toes.

Speaking to some of the nearer ones, he said, "It's okay. I'm just a little man, just passing through. No need to attack me."

He had no idea if this calmed the animals, but it helped his own nerves. Indeed, he felt small among those giants; their backs stood much higher than the tallest man's head.

Finally past the bison, Toq decided he would go around a herd like that in future. Though successful, he'd taken quite a risk. His thoughts turned to hunting. All those new calves confirmed that this was the birthing season. Predators would be after them, and while his own people considered the young animals to be especially good to eat, Toq didn't like killing them. Just beyond the bison, he saw a dark-brown object lying in the grass, and he moved toward it, looking frequently behind. He was a few steps away when he identified it as a dead bison calf.

"You were probably born just last night," he said.

No scavengers or predators or birds had touched it yet. The wind had dried the slime on the fur, but underneath, it was still wet. He wondered if it was born dead or if its mother had simply walked away from it. The calf was smaller than the others he'd seen. He grabbed the front legs and dragged it a safe distance from the herd, where he quickly gutted the animal. It looked and smelled fine to him. He kept a couple organs, placing them back inside the chest cavity. He dragged the body a little way, stopped, and used dead grass to dry up the blood and slime on the fur. Then, he picked up the calf and draped it across his shoulders, continuing on his way.

"Come on, little guy. I'm sorry you died, but you're going to taste good tonight."

Through the day and the wind, he walked on, although much more slowly with the calf. He came to some parallel running ridges with a little valley between. He walked the south ridge, seeing many animals below in the trench, somewhat out of the wind. As the day wore on, the wind finally, gradually, lost some of its force. The scattered clouds blew away, and the sun shone brightly as it fell nearer the horizon. Toq reached the end of the ridge line and decided to camp just below, out of the wind, among the rocks of an east-facing hillside. He had no trouble making a fire, and he set about cooking and eating the little calf. Ravenous, he ate the heart, liver, half the tender and delicious meat, and some bone marrow. The rest of the meat he cooked and dried out. He carried what remained of the calf away from his camp, so as not to attract any unwanted visitors.

• • • •

The night brought welcome relief from the fierce winds. The sky was clear and starry, and the moon, more than half-full, lit the landscape of the night until it followed the path of the sun and disappeared behind the mountains. Toq kept two fires burning. There seemed to be a lot of activity here: coyotes, wolves, horses, bison, mammoths, and some new creature whose call he couldn't identify. It was a fair distance away, but it was loud and ferocious, a roar that went on and on and on, before stopping and then beginning again.

"What the piss is that?" he mumbled softly. He kept his spear and stone knife right by his side, sleeping very little for the second night in a row.

••••

The eastern sky began to brighten, the wildlife quieted, and Toq finally fell into a deep sleep. The world did not wake him until the sun was halfway up in the sky and blazing into his lean-to, heating him up to the point of sweating. He rolled over and squinted into broad daylight. He hadn't slept this late on a nice day for a long time. He was still tired, but he got up. He stretched tired, sore muscles and looked around. Just below, moving up the hill, in and out of the rocks and onto some short cliffs, a group of five or six long-legged bighorn rams were coming his way. The lead rams stopped often to look ahead. Toq froze, hoping he would not be noticed, but he was. The group all looked right at him, then they ran, single file, around the hill and out of sight.

Wide-awake now, Toq grabbed his spear and ran, hoping to intercept them if they turned uphill again. Getting one would be a huge gain for him. He reached a large rock outcrop where he slowed, ducked behind it, and cautiously moved around it until he could see the other side. He gazed intently into the rocky land, looking down, up, and finally to the northwest, where the six rams were already a long way off and running up the gulch at a pretty good clip. He turned and walked back to camp.

Toq ate about half of the meat he had left, packed up, and hiked down into a drainage with a nice, clear stream, one that was not fed by a glacier and so did not taste like dirt. Just below was his river (Jefferson River), which had curled around through the canyon and now flowed northeast.

He hiked up onto some steep hills, where he had another superb view of the mountains and the lush prairie, braided with rivers and streams. Everywhere Toq looked—on the plains, the hills, the riverbanks—there were large animals of all kinds.

"This place is rich," he said.

He set out to the north, avoiding the marshy wetlands, then worked his way downhill toward an open bench area, where he spotted some animals directly in his path. He couldn't tell what they were, so he started to angle away to go around them. He went into some hills, where he was able to walk out of sight of the animals. He walked this direction until he figured he was straight west of them, then he slowly walked to the top of the slope, where, on the other side, it stretched down to where the beasts were. As he neared the top, he crouched as low as he could and then stopped and slowly rose up to look down at them.

"Itshla!" he said under his breath, shocked to see a large pride of lions (American lion) lounging in the grass. Little cubs ran around, wrestling each other.

Toq was suddenly, unusually afraid. But in the next instant, he knew he couldn't let fear control him. He slowly ducked back down and quickly moved northwest below their line of sight, hoping they wouldn't catch a whiff of him. He and the Traveler had heard of lions from various villages last summer, but this was his first sighting, and being alone, this close, with no place to run or hide, Toq struggled not to panic. He trotted away, constantly glancing behind him. He started up another hill, and when he was high enough, he turned back to see that the pride had not moved. Either they hadn't seen or smelled him, or they didn't care. It bothered him that his mind had responded that way, with fear almost paralyzing him.

"You can't let that happen again. You have to stay smart, wary, and calm."

Toq heard roaring coming from the northeast, the same kind of roar he'd heard last night. Then, two big males in the lion pride roared back. All the lions stood, their attention focused in the opposite direction of Toq. The two big males moved toward the first roars. Toq turned again to head away and uphill.

"I've got to get out of here," he mumbled to himself as he ran up the hill.

This was a volatile situation. He didn't know these animals or their behavior, and he feared that the lionesses might move the cubs away from the fight—in his direction. Once he'd gotten a little farther away, breathing hard, he looked back to see four figures in battle, raising a cloud of dust, fighting for dominance, fighting for life. The ferocity of their roars, delayed because of the distance, filled the world, and all the wildlife stopped to look and listen. The fight didn't last long. Toq saw two animals running away to the north. The two behind followed a short ways, roaring after them in victory and warning. The pride moved toward their defenders.

Toq felt better now that there was distance between him and the lions. But as the rounded hill leveled off, he saw a huge bull bison staring at him, not more than twenty steps away. Toq froze, his heart again pounding.

"Godsdamnit," he said in exasperation, as he moved right, eyes locked on the bull. Then, he looked away.

He heard a deep, rumbling growl come from the animal, and Toq looked to see the bison blowing snot from his nostrils, lowering his massive head and horns—and then, charging. As fast as lightning, Toq pulled off one of his bags, crouched, and at the last second, threw it at the bull's face before diving to the side. The bull grazed past Toq. Toq scrambled to his feet and faced his assailant. The bag's strap had looped over one of the bull's horns, and the bull ran away, tossing his head up, down, and sideways until the bag flew off. The beast trotted away, turning only once to look at Toq, then disappearing behind a hill.

The man was filled with emotion: excitement, fear, anger, irritation. He retrieved his bag. Miraculously, nothing had fallen out and the strap had not broken. A large glob of bison snot splattered one side, which Toq wiped off on the grass. He put the bag back on, looked all around, and checked the lions' location. They hadn't moved; only now they were small, fuzzy spots. He headed straight north.

Feeling frazzled and alone, he said, "Well, you knew you'd get some of this sooner or later. Best thing now . . . hike, eat, drink, hunt. You have to get some meat today. You'll also need to rest soon."

Talking to himself calmed him. He ate while walking, saying, "What a day."

He worked his way north, giving a wide berth to any big animals in his way. His people would gladly take this bountiful paradise from the lions, but by himself, this area was perilous, and he wanted to put it behind him. He made his way into some hills. The new river (Missouri River), having formed from three (Jefferson, Gallatin, and Madison Rivers) was out of sight, and while he didn't want to lose it completely, he was beginning to wonder if following it too closely would mean more lions and bears. The hills might have lions or bears, too, but they may also have places of escape, like a rock wall.

He had lions on the brain all day, but he didn't see any more. He found a place to camp in the hills, in a deep coulee, up against a rock cliff. He successfully hunted a deer, cut off a hindquarter, and buried the rest under stones. The smell of cooking meat floated on the air, attracting a pack of curious wolves. They sat on a hillside opposite, watching Toq and his three fires, never coming too close, and he watched them as he ate. Finally deciding there was nothing there for them, they left.

Mentally and physically exhausted, and with a full stomach and well-stoked fires, Toq fell asleep quickly. But even so, he woke several times in the night to build up his fires. While he heard some animals, he heard no roaring lions.

●●●●

Toq felt good in the morning, up with the sun and ready to go. He packed up and went to retrieve the animal, planning to take some meat with him, but when he got to a place where he could see it, his heart sank.

"Oh, crap!" he said.

A big, old bear had uncovered Toq's cache and was busy eating his kill. So, he moved on and spent most of the morning crossing the highlands, getting glimpses of the river below to the east, now of a considerable size. To the north, the valley opened wide and mostly flat. White-capped mountains were to the northwest (Elkhorn Mountains) and northeast (Big Belt Mountains). Animals were everywhere.

Toq walked down off the highlands into a flat wetland expanse cut with multiple streams. Numerous mammoths loved it here, but birds dominated, and they were raucous. All kinds of ducks, swans, geese, long-legged waders and shorebirds, and tall-grass-loving birds flitted and flew here and there; some seemed to be raising their voices to be heard over the others. Singing frogs added to the racket. The grasses in these marshlands were greener and higher than everywhere else, and Toq thought there might even be some taller brush, possibly willows, growing on the opposite side of the wetland. He was relieved to see some sign of larger woody plants.

It was a long way across the marshland, and Toq wasn't about to try going right through it. He attempted to skirt around the edge but kept running into soggy ground. He walked much of it barefoot to spare his moccasins. He was in awe of the abundance of life here, more than his eyes and ears could take in. He stumbled upon a duck nest. The female flew off while squeaking loudly; he would never have seen her if she hadn't moved. Toq picked out two pale-green eggs, leaving four in the nest, and walked away, gently shaking them. He held them up to the sun, then carefully cracked the top open with his spearpoint. It was fresh, so he tilted his head back and poured the contents down his throat, then did the same with the second egg. His mind went straight to the memory of the Traveler eating the old egg at the flood. He smiled briefly, but a twinge of sadness hit him, so he put the thought out of his head and moved on.

The day ran long; the marshland had made for slow going. The wind picked up, and the temperature cooled as thick, low clouds moved overhead, and by evening, it had begun to drizzle. Toq was in the middle of a large, wet flat, and he didn't want to camp there. He hurried to reach a prominent hill (Lone Mountain), where he would feel more secure—though he acknowledged that predators often used high points as well.

Toq approached the hill in the dim light of a rainy evening. The marshland was mostly quiet now. The drizzle didn't worsen, but it fell steadily enough that Toq's hair and shoulders were dripping wet. He found a dry, narrow spot just below a cliff face. Although it was hard and lumpy, he figured with enough grass to soften it, he would have a comfortable bed.

He had to work hard to find grass, brush, and dung to burn, and the cool, wet weather made lighting a fire all the more difficult. Toq had three options for starting a fire: the ember in the ram's horn, his hand drill, or using his flint and pyrite to get a spark. People were experts at creating fire, but if conditions were especially damp and his ember went dead, a man could be without a fire until things dried out. Toq would not be without a fire tonight.

It was black as a raven by the time his fire was burning. He wasn't completely comfortable, but because of the weather and his narrow ledge, he made only one fire, knowing it would be a challenge to keep even this one burning through the night. The damp, cold air chilled his body, and he gladly crawled under his fur robe. The misty rain continued. Except for the occasional bird calling out, the night was quiet.

• • • •

The drizzle turned into snow during the night, and by morning, big, fat flakes fell straight down. There was no wind; there was no sound. Snow covered the ground, but Toq's spot by the cliff was dry. He looked out at the gray sky and white land and wondered how long this snow would last. Suddenly, a large gob of white bird poop struck the top edge of his shelter, splattering onto the ground in front. Droplets hit Toq's face.

"Well, son of a bitch!" he cried, as he sat up and wiped the shit off his face.

He got up and cleaned his hands and face with snow, then looked up above his camp to see a raptor's nest on a ledge of the cliff straight overhead. While rushing in the dark, Toq hadn't noticed he'd practically set his camp atop a bird latrine. He looked at the nest of sticks for a while, but he couldn't see the birds. He decided to move camp a few feet away. He had no idea how long he might be here, but it was dry, and for as long as it snowed, he would stay.

Having eaten the last of the meat the night before, he now was hungry. He collected more eggs and managed to spear a muskrat—enough to get by on. He wondered if he could live off these smaller animals and birds.

"For a while, sure, but sooner or later you're going to need new hides and furs," he told himself.

The big snowflakes slowly petered out, and by midday it was back to a light rain. Toq cooked and ate the muskrat, watching the weather and the world. By late afternoon, the rain stopped, and in the early evening, some patches of blue sky appeared. It was too late in the day to move on, so Toq went to hunt some more food. Most of the snow had already melted, leaving the grasses looking much greener than before. He decided to try sneaking up on a goose—even though geese were notoriously impossible to sneak up on, since they saw everything and alerted everyone. But a goose on a nest might stay put and stay quiet. But they might also be done nesting, he thought; he'd seen some goslings in the marsh the day before. Still, it was worth a try.

He spotted a possible nest from the hill and swept around out of sight. He then crawled over grass, mud, and goose shit until he was nearly upon the supposed nest. It was empty, but he kept his head down, hoping to catch something unaware at the water's edge. He had his spears and bolas, but he didn't want to risk throwing any of his weapons into the water, lest he lose them.

"No geese here," he whispered.

He crawled a little ways more. He raised his head slowly over a bump in the ground, and that was all it took. Four big ducks—two with bright-green heads—flew away, quacking. Toq stood up and watched them fly in a circle overhead. He looked around for any stragglers, but all he saw was a bobcat, nearly completely flat on the ground, staring at Toq. It quickly spun around and ran away.

"I guess I ruined your hunt," he said to the cat.

He looked around, but he only brought home a couple of frogs to eat. His meals were getting smaller. Before sunset, Toq hunted the hill he was camped on but again came back with nothing. He finished the day somewhat hungry; it wasn't a new feeling, but it did give him a greater sense of urgency for tomorrow.

He sat at the edge of his camp in the dark, just outside the firelight, looking and listening for anything that might make the mistake of sniffing around too close. There was nothing. He went to bed and watched an almost full moon light up the clouds in the eastern sky, illuminating the night world below.

"Such a contrast between last night's darkness and this night's brightness," he said. "Predators will hunt tonight."

• • • •

The next morning, well before sunrise, Toq cautiously, silently, slowly climbed up the hill. It was risky being alone in the dark; he could easily become something else's prey. The moon now hung in the western sky, about to set on the mountains. A large, brilliant star shimmered in the eastern sky. It was cool, but the dew on the grass did not freeze. He made it to the top without incident just as light began to show on the eastern horizon. The moon disappeared, a bright shooting star blazed across the sky, and Toq sat on a rock, peering into the still, dark landscape below.

He said quietly, "A shooting star. Does it bring good or bad? I don't know . . . probably neither. It's just one of those unexplained, beautiful natural wonders. What does the Traveler think? Well? What do you think?" He whispered, "I can't hear you. Speak loudly and clearly. Come on. Nothing? You just leave me here to figure it out on my own? Well, okay . . . fine." He paused, listening, then said, "How about sending me a deer or something?"

The shadow of the earth and mountains gradually gave way as sunlight moved down the mountain range and filled the hills and valleys. Toq waited patiently for the world to give him something to eat.

He saw game everywhere except on the hill itself. On a dry plain to the southwest, there were a few white and tan spots that Toq believed were pronghorns. Not too big or dangerous, but they had great eyesight, were hard to get close to, and were exceedingly fast. On the other hand, they sometimes became curious and stupid. Toq would be lucky if he could get one by himself, but he had to try.

He moved quickly down the hill, careful to stay out of sight. They were a ways away, standing on a large, open area. There was no cover with which to sneak up on them. By himself, this was impossible. He eyeballed some brush at the bottom of the coulee, but he doubted even camouflage would allow him to get close enough. Perhaps they might walk close to the edge of a coulee, where he could surprise one. He lay prone, watching them, getting a feel for where they might go, trying to come up with a plan. There were four females, no fawns. If any were pregnant, they must be close to giving birth. They were constantly alert, taking turns eating and keeping watch. They barely moved. Toq's neck grew weary and stiff.

"This might take forever, and I could still get nothing for it," he muttered as he pushed himself down the slope and rolled over onto his back.

He caught movement out of the corner of his eye. He looked down the coulee to see a coyote working its way to him. Blond-gray and scraggly, the coyote's ears were perked up; it sniffed at everything, hoping to snarf up whatever it could find. It took a while before it noticed Toq, who did not move. Finally, the coyote stopped and looked at him, sniffed the air, and loped around in a half circle, never taking its eyes off him. Toq wondered if he could eat him. Not that he wanted to; he felt a kinship with certain animals, but if he were starving. . .

The coyote approached skittishly, ready to run away, but unable to resist the strange smell, the possibility of an easy meal. His head moved up and down, back and forth, sizing up this thing lying on the ground. He jumped back a couple of times but then moved closer. Toq's tired neck muscles began to shake, so he moved his arm around to support the back of his head, and the coyote retreated again before coming closer. His courage seemed to be growing, and he came close enough to sniff the man's feet.

Toq said, "What do you think you're doing?" and the coyote darted away from him and looked at his face.

Toq rolled to his side, grabbed his spears, and—hunching down to keep out of the antelopes' sight—moved down the hill a little so he could stand up. Now, the coyote decided he wanted nothing to do with him. The coyote trotted away, looking back at Toq a few times, and Toq watched him. The coyote walked up the hill in the direction of the pronghorns, stopping when he saw them.

"Ah, crap," Toq said under his breath.

He went back up to his spying spot to check on the antelope. The coyote glanced at Toq then refocused on the antelope. The antelope all stared at the coyote, and one began walking toward him. Most old, smart coyotes wouldn't bother chasing antelope, but this young and hungry one sprinted at the nearest speedster. The four pivoted and easily ran away without ever reaching full speed. The coyote gave up quickly. He sat down and watched them run away, then looked back to see Toq observing the whole debacle. The man shook his fist at the coyote, and the coyote moved off toward the hill.

Toq called out to him, "That's it?! That's all you've got? That's all the effort you're going to put into it? You should be embarrassed! You ruined my hunt!"

The coyote glanced back at him, unabashed. Across the flat, the antelope had stopped and were watching him.

"Oh, well. My chances of getting one were slim, anyway."

He spent the rest of the morning getting a couple ground squirrels and finding a few more eggs. His belly wasn't full, but at least he had something. By midday, Toq was packed up and hiking around the marshland, staying on the drier ground of the hills. He crossed a couple of streams that flowed into the wetlands and continued on, straight north. Hills loomed to the east (Limestone Hills), so he climbed through a wide gap just to the west of them. After negotiating his way through and around some steep hills and canyons, he came out onto a wide, gently sloping plain from which he could see the river.

The valley spread wide-open on both sides of the river, with snowy peaks to the east and west. It was late in the day, so he decided to camp in the hills. There was plenty of wildlife out on the flats, but Toq did not pursue them, managing instead to get a marmot while searching for a campsite. The marmot would make a decent meal, but the skin was too thin to make good moccasins. His shoes were falling apart again, so he needed to get a good, thick animal hide. He spotted some bighorn sheep at twilight and planned to hunt them in the morning, if they stuck around.

• • • •

The eastern sky was turning light as Toq moved like a ghost amid the still, dark hills. He was determined to get one of those bighorns. It was difficult to see in the dark, but he stopped often to look and listen. A big, lone deer jumped up from where it had been bedded down and bounded noisily away across the hillside.

"Damn it," Toq whispered, startled and frustrated that he had not seen it sooner.

Now, everything nearby was on alert. Toq waited to see if anything else might reveal itself. All was quiet except for the early morning calls of a few birds. He proceeded around the base of a hill, where, in the growing twilight, he could see a ram standing on a steep, rocky area, head down, eating something. Toq spotted four more—one bedded down on the grassy hillside, the others spread out, feeding, moving away from him toward the rocks. A small cliff stood above the scree that the group appeared to be headed for. Toq circled back around the hill and climbed up the other side of a little ridge that separated him from the rams. He had to climb well above the rams before he could cross over to a spot directly above them. Then, he descended, slowly, quietly, looking and listening often.

At the top of the cliff, barely breathing, Toq approached the edge on his hands and knees. He heard at least one animal's hooves clinking the loose stones just below him, but he waited to take a peek for fear of being seen. The cliff was not very long, and Toq knew the rams could come up around it on either side. He didn't know where they all were. He couldn't see any of them.

He waited and listened, clutching both spears as he contemplated his next move. He didn't want to throw his spear on this steep hill, fearing it would break if the stricken animal fell and rolled.

Toq stopped breathing when he heard hooves on stone and small rocks falling as the animal scrambled quickly up toward Toq's right. He let go of his small spear, rose up on one knee, and pulled his arm and big spear back into the ready position.

The big ram flew up onto the cliff, as it had a dozen times before—but this time, a man was there, only a spear-length away. Without hesitating, Toq moved as fast as a cat and, in one fluid motion, jumped to his feet and grasped the spear with both hands, leaping forward with an underhand thrust into the front of the ram's chest. Toq had intended to thrust his spear in and pull it out, but the ram spun and pulled away, and Toq couldn't hang on. The ram reared back on its hind legs, and in its panic, stumbled and fell off the cliff. Toq rushed to the edge to see the animal roll a couple of times down the rocky slope. It looked dead. Toq looked around just in time to see the white backsides of the other rams vanishing around the hill.

Exultant, Toq picked up his small spear and started to give a loud, victorious yell, but he squelched it, fearing it might attract other predators. He hurried down to the ram, anxious about his spear, which protruded out of the creature's back, just missing the spine. It was bloody—and broken.

"Shit," he sighed. He looked around for the point and found it a short distance up the hill, wedged between some rocks. The tip of the bloody, stone point had broken off, but the point remained attached to a piece of wood about the length of his forearm. He saved it, hoping to salvage something from it. He went back to the ram and muscled the heavy beast around and onto its back; then, he grabbed the end of his spear and tried to pull it back out. The blood made it slippery, and the stick was wedged tight against bone. He dried his hands in sandy dirt and tried again, turning and pulling until it slid out.

Seeing no predators, Toq left his kill and ran back to his camp to get his bags and stone knife. Then, he spent the rest of the day gutting, skinning, and butchering the ram under the watchful eyes of some ravens perched on the cliff top above. He made four or five trips back and forth, carrying the meat and hide. As the morning warmed, he took off his leather top, held it up, and looked at it in disgust. It was stained with mud and goose shit—and now, blood. He tossed it under his lean-to.

The ravens bothered him. Each time he took a load to camp, they swooped down on his animal. He'd come back and chase them off, and they'd fly back to the cliff, squawking. He was afraid the birds would attract bigger, more threatening animals. So, he worked as fast as he could, and by late morning he had taken all that he wanted, including the head, feet, and a couple of leg bones with sinew. Before he left for the last time, he created a depression in the rocks and covered what remained of the ram—mostly bones, bits of flesh, and guts. He walked down the hill and looked back to see the ravens poking around the kill site.

"They won't find much. Maybe now they'll leave."

Toq spent the rest of the day cooking and drying meat; scraping, stretching, and tanning hide; and replacing the broken spearpoint with one of his spares, now affixed to a shortened spear shaft. He ate and ate some more. He took his leathers to the creek and washed them the best he could. He used what was left of his caribou skin to make new moccasins and do minor repairs on his lean-to and bags. The ravens circled his camp and landed a short distance away, watching him. He kept throwing rocks and running after them until they finally flew off for good.

"Fly away and stay away," he said, worried about carnivores raiding his camp.

Some hunters had a kind of spiritual idea that an animal would give or offer itself to the hunter so that the hunter would have sustenance. Some believed that spirits or gods delivered the animal to the hunter or assisted in some way. This inspired them to lay hands on the head or the body of the animal and thank the beast for giving itself to the people. Toq believed it was good to be thankful, but he didn't believe animals willingly or gladly gave themselves up to humans. They might be old, weak, tired, sick, stupid, or wounded, and then they might appear to be giving up, but his experience told him that animals felt fear. This was a savage, violent world with no mercy, and there were no feelings of kindness between predator and prey. The ram and the hunter had just happened to come face-to-face; the ram had not offered up its life, but rather, Toq took it. Although he thanked the ram, Toq thought his gratitude required less pretense. He couldn't be certain, but he figured that other carnivores didn't wrestle with the feelings of their victims. Only humans. But on the other hand, perhaps most people lacked the capacity to understand the feelings of another creature, whether it was food or not.

• • • •

A beautiful full moon brightened the dark and cloudless night, even casting shadows onto the ground. Toq was up and down throughout the night, keeping three fires burning and squinting at dark things moving in the dim light, things that made him nervous. He heard things—some that he couldn't identify, and though he tried to sleep, he rested very little.

Once the sun was up, the beasts quieted down. He slept most of the morning and decided to stay all day in this place. He could use the rest, and he had far more meat than he could carry. He gathered combustible materials, finished drying the meat, ate all that his stomach could hold, and sat on a hill watching the animals spread across the plain.

He reworked his broken spearpoint. It was considerably smaller now, but it would make a decent spare. That left only one good, new replacement point, so he needed to keep an eye out for any workable stones. His broken, shortened spear shaft was a problem, though. He needed to get into some wooded country where he could find a stout branch or small tree trunk. A long bone could be manipulated to extend the length of the spear, but it would take some time, so for now, he would just live with it.

He strolled over to the buried remains of the ram. Something had tried to dig it up. He covered it with more rocks. He glanced back up at the cliff and was startled to see a big, furry animal looking down at him. A wolf. He glanced around to make sure a pack hadn't surrounded him. Seeing only the one wolf, Toq returned to his camp, looking over his shoulder along the way. His camp was not in the safest of places, but he could build bigger fires. He added fuel to one fire, ate, relaxed, and slept until late afternoon, knowing he would again be awake most of the night.

Toq was having bizarre, vivid dreams when he was slowly roused from sleep. His eyes felt like they'd been glued shut, but he wiped a bit of drool from his lip and listened. Faintly, he thought he heard light footsteps in the grass and quiet sniffing. Immediately, he was wide-awake. He slowly turned his head to look for the source of the sniffing—though one eye was a blurry mess. The wolf stood right next to the fire, smelling the ground and clearly eyeing one of Toq's bags full of meat. He was so close, Toq could almost reach out and touch him.

Toq quickly sat up and took hold of his spear. He uttered a loud, guttural, "Get out of here!" and the wolf jumped and scooted away, looking back at the man as he ran.

Toq might have been able to kill the animal, but he'd had no desire to do so. He stood up, wiped both eyes to clear them, and watched the big wolf reach the bottom of the hill, cross the creek, and go up the hill on the other side.

"Hmph. Are you by yourself?"

Lone wolves were not unheard of, but he figured they lived with a large disadvantage.

Just like me!

There were stories of people befriending wolves or even trying to raise wolf pups to be a part of their tribe, but Toq had never seen it himself. The idea intrigued him. There was something attractive about wolves: They were in some ways like humans, and humans were in some ways like wolves.

But Toq didn't know if or when a wolf might turn and attack, so he thought it best that this big male ran away. He prepared for a long night. Tomorrow, he would depart from this place. He would have to leave some meat behind, but he planned to eat and carry as much as he could. As twilight came, a great calm fell over the land. Most birds went to roost, and the animals on the plain dispersed. Toq began to relax, thinking that perhaps the big predators had moved away as well. Still, he decided to keep three fires—"Or maybe I'll build four." He settled down, just outside the fires, to watch the moon rise. It still appeared to be full as it rose above the hills and mountains, noticeably later than the night before. The sharp outline of the hilltop contrasted with the big, bright moon behind it. The black silhouette of the wolf appeared and sat on the hill, clearly facing Toq's camp.

"Well, I guess you don't scare so easily," Toq said.

••••

Toq placed all the meat in his bags and covered them at the back of his lean-to, and then he stayed up guarding it off and on throughout the night. He no longer saw or heard the wolf, but he was certain it was nearby, sizing up the situation. When Toq did drift toward sleep, he wondered if he would wake up to the wolf stealing meat or clamping down on his throat.

But nothing exciting happened. At sunrise, Toq got up and broke down his camp, again eating as much as he could. Then, he refilled his bags and looked at the pile of cooked meat left on the ground.

"What a waste," he said, but there was no way to carry it all. He was already going to be so weighed down that he worried about tearing out the seams or the straps on his bags.

He considered staying until he'd eaten everything he couldn't carry, but he was itching to get back on the move. Guilt and doubt troubled him but not enough to change his mind. With an already warm sun rising higher, he was about to lift a bag when he caught sight of the wolf again, sitting, watching him from a little ways off.

"Well, how long have you been there?" he asked, no longer feeling bothered or threatened by this particular wolf.

He picked up a piece of meat the size of his hand and tossed it toward the wolf. It backed away, then cautiously approached the piece of meat, sniffed it, then, in two bites, swallowed it down.

"Impressive," Toq said. He noticed the animal seemed thin.

Toq threw him another larger chunk, and again the wolf devoured it and looked back at Toq. He picked up his two heavy bags and groaned under their weight.

Toq grabbed his spears and motioned toward the meat pile, saying, "There you go, the rest is yours."

The man began walking away. He looked back to see that the wolf had come forward, stopping when he stopped. Toq walked a ways and looked back to see the wolf standing over the pile of meat, eating fast, ravenously. Despite his mixed feelings about giving up good food to a wolf, he shrugged, and said, "I guess it's not wasted."

He left the hills and walked out onto the plain. Scanning for predators, he proceeded across a long flat, aiming for some hills directly north. He wondered if he ought to hug the hills, but that would be slower going. As it was, the extra food slowed him down considerably, and he stopped twice as often as usual to take the weight off his shoulders.

The plain made for easy hiking, and he moved quickly but stopped often to look around. It was dangerous on the plain with no place to hide or defend oneself. He feared the lions the most.

"Probably because I don't know them," he said, trying to understand his fear.

But he didn't see any lions. The plain sloped gradually down to the widening river, where willows and taller brush grew along its edges.

"Great spots for lions and bears to hide out." He stayed far away from them.

All he saw were a few herds of horses on the plain and some mammoths down among the willows. Late in the morning, he spotted a lone wolf off in the distance, a little behind, staying closer to the western hills and moving parallel with Toq. He was fairly certain it was the wolf from his campsite, but it was a bit far off to tell for sure. He watched it for a while as it walked and trotted north, then it glanced in Toq's direction, stopped, sat down, and stared at Toq.

"What are you doing?" Toq asked quietly. He felt some amusement and even comfort in saying, "Maybe I have a friend."

He began walking again, and sure enough, the wolf did, too. Toq wondered if the wolf might serve as a lookout. "Probably not. You're thinking you're going to get more easy meals from me. Oh, well, we're all ultimately selfish. Question is, what are *you* going to give to *me*?" He stopped and looked at the wolf, thinking. "Amusement and company. And . . . maybe you *will* warn me of danger . . . or kill something we could share. Could I drive a wolf off a kill?" After a long pause, "Maybe, maybe not."

Toq hiked all day to get up into the lower sections of the hills (Spokane Hills). With aching shoulders and feet, he longed to relieve his body of its burden. He had seen only one bear, far off, down by the river. "His" wolf had disappeared by midafternoon. The day had been warm and sunny, but now clouds moved in overhead. He found a place nestled up against some large rock outcrops where he thought he could sleep safely. He set up his shelter, built his fires, ate, and rubbed the sore muscles in his feet and shoulders. Then, he bedded down. There would be no bright moon tonight. He closed his eyes, and none of the sounds out of the darkness would rouse him from his sleep this night.

• • • •

The days grew longer and the nights shorter, allowing more time to hike and less time to sleep. It was early, getting to be day, when Toq woke to a sky that was a solid sheet of gray. At least the clouds were high above the mountains, not hanging down on the peaks, and the air didn't smell of rain. It was simply a cloudy day, good for travel. He sat up, threw back his robe, and looked across the dry gully to a hill.

"Well, would you look at that?" he said very quietly to himself. The wolf was curled up, asleep on the hillside, only a stone's throw away. "Amazing." His fondness for this animal grew. "How did you come to be alone?" he wondered.

No other animals were in sight, and Toq's fires were out. He placed his hands close above the ashes, but there was no heat. Using a stick, he poked down to some warm coals, hoping to salvage an ember to carry in his horn. He checked on the wolf, which was now awake and watching him again. He wondered how long the wolf would follow him. Toq ate and packed up his camp; the wolf never took his eyes off him. Though conflicted about feeding the animal, Toq couldn't help himself. He threw a piece of meat to the wolf. It did not jump back this time. It calmly walked down and quickly devoured it. Toq didn't feel too bad. He had a lot of meat, and giving some away would lighten his load.

"That's all you get," he said to the wolf, which gazed at him. "You seem to be so docile."

Toq donned his bags, picked up his spears, and walked slowly up the hill. He didn't get far before the wolf went to sniff around the campsite for food.

Toq called out to him, "Sorry, buddy. Nothing today."

The wolf glanced up at him and went back to sniffing around.

"Let's go!" Toq said as he rounded a curve, wondering if the wolf would still follow—and soon the wolf emerged, walking in the man's footsteps. Toq pulled out two strips of meat from his bag. He stuck one in his mouth and dropped the other on the ground before moving up a ridge. The wolf came to the dropped piece of meat, ate it, sniffed around, looked up at Toq, and then continued following.

Toq suddenly realized he was paying too much attention to the wolf. He needed to be alert to danger. He climbed the hills to see what lay ahead. A herd of camels appeared on the hills above him, as well as a few big elk with new antlers, fuzzy with velvet, having grown to just above their ears. They looked at Toq with curiosity and without a hint of nervousness. But when the wolf appeared, the camels grew uneasy and trotted away, while the elk watched closely without moving. The wolf clearly saw them, but he simply sat down and looked, knowing they were too big for him to try alone. Toq took mental notes, thinking up ideas for hunting alongside the wolf.

"Ahh! You're probably crazy. You can't work with a wolf!"

He started to walk away, and then the wolf darted toward the elk. The elk scattered, keeping their distance, but they didn't run away like the camels had. The wolf made a half-hearted attempt at chasing one, then another. One by one, they ran away, then turned and stopped to watch him. The wolf sat on his haunches again. Toq laughed at him and walked away, and the wolf followed.

They climbed higher into the hills until cresting a long ridge. The ridge ran to the north, and Toq followed it to its end, where he could see the river below and a wide valley plain (Helena Valley) to the northwest, dominated by marshland. The southern mountains were fading from view, while mountains to the north and east, not so high and rugged, were much closer now. The river, though, dove into a deep, narrow canyon, emerging onto a flatland and then wiggling its way into the mountains. The mountain snow seemed to be melting quickly, replaced by new growth of green grass and colorful wildflowers. The lowlands were a darker green, and the willows and shrubs sprouted new leaves.

It was a little past midday when Toq descended the hills, angling to the northwest. The wolf would disappear, then reappear, sometimes behind him, sometimes beside him, but always a safe distance away.

Once, the wolf appeared in front of him, and Toq grinned and said, "How do you know where I'm going? You want to lead?"

But as they neared the bottomlands and willows, the wolf hung back, stopping often, looking, sniffing the air, ears up. Toq daydreamed of meeting people. With more woody growth around, he was certain he would find humans soon. He came to a hill looking down on a creek, and turning back, he realized the wolf was no longer in sight. He should have paid better attention to the wolf's cue.

He crossed the creek and walked across a flat plain toward the marshlands, keeping well away from what had become a thick band of spindly willows. He could hide and move unseen in them, yes, but he could also surprise something dangerous. The only beast that couldn't hide there were the big adult mammoths.

The wolf was nowhere near, and Toq grew nervous, thinking the wolf knew something he did not. He stood on a hill to survey his route. The plain ahead was thick with wildlife—mostly horses, bison, and pronghorns—and right in the center, a large pride of lions tore into a hulking buffalo carcass. The beasts roared as they squabbled over the best place around the feast. Ravens gathered a safe distance away, and a pack of wolves—with more members than Toq had ever seen—moved casually toward the lions. A couple of lions noticed the pack, and soon the entire pride rose to its feet, on alert. The wolves split up to circle the lions and the carcass. A couple of lion cubs climbed up on top of the bison. Toq wasn't sure if he was safe here, but he figured the lions and wolves were too absorbed in each other to notice him. He couldn't take his eyes off them.

The wolves far outnumbered the lions, but the lions were giants, and they were powerful and fast. They stood their ground. Two huge males with reddish-tan manes and rippling muscles emerged from the group of lionesses to face the wolves. Neither stupid nor reckless, the wolves knew they were no match for these lions, but with their speed and numbers, they could conceivably run the lions off their kill. So, they tested the lions. A couple of wolves moved closer from opposite sides until one of the lions roared loudly and charged a wolf, swiping at it with its massive paws. The roars echoed across the valley, causing the bison and horses to move farther away. The wolves were fast enough to stay just out of reach, and the lions were becoming increasingly annoyed. Finally, the two males charged the wolves on one side, scattering the wolves in all directions. Except one, who was a little slow to get moving, and one male quickly closed the gap between them. She ran with her tail between her legs and, at the last second, spun around to face the lion. Fierce and infuriated, he was as big as five wolves, and he completely overwhelmed her in an avalanche of flesh, claws, and fangs. Toq heard his drawn-out roar and her high-pitched yelp, and then she was dead. The lion then took off after the other wolves but couldn't catch them. The wolves gathered together a safe distance away, where they appeared to check on each other and stared back at the lions and their lost sister. The lions returned to their feast, ignoring the dead wolf and glancing at the wolf pack only occasionally now. This wolf pack would not be so bold in the future; lions were too much, even for them.

Toq stood alone on the hill, the wolf pack far from him and the lions in between. He turned to go east, away from both groups, but when he looked back, it was to the unnerving sight of one of the lions looking at *him*. A second lion stopped eating to look at the little man on the hill, wondering what he was, wondering if he was a threat. Panicking, Toq hurried away, suddenly feeling like the distance between them wasn't nearly enough. The lions watched him disappear behind the hill, then resumed eating. They were somewhat curious about the unusual, upright creature; they had never seen a human before. But luckily for Toq, they weren't curious enough to chase after him.

Toq decided to try crossing downstream of the marshland. He walked quickly to the east, then curved around to the north, checking over his shoulder the whole way. It was getting late, but he needed distance between himself and the lions and wolves. Far away, he heard the howls of the wolves, who would be hunting. He still saw no sign of "his" wolf. He neared a stream and wrestled with camping in the willows, to hide, or else building a big circle of fires away from the stream.

Now that the lions were far behind and the wolves had plenty of other game to chase, Toq felt less frantic. The sun never made an appearance all day, and soon twilight was upon him. He hadn't seen any safe places to camp, and there were only a few small patches of willow along the bottom of the hill near the stream, so there was likely to be plenty of competition for hiding in them. Toq breathed a heavy, frustrated sigh. The hills on the other side of the stream rose up higher; he would feel safer over there, but he feared getting completely soaked and cold and having to set up camp in the dark. He thought about it for a long time, not liking his options.

"Yah," he growled. "Just go for it," and he headed to the stream.

There was no time to search for the best crossing point. He stopped at the water's edge to put his ram's horn with the fire's ember into a stiff, dry bladder bag, just in case he did have to swim. He took off all his clothes, stuffed them into his bags, and marched barefoot into the water.

"Don't get deep," he pleaded as the ice-cold water shocked his feet.

The stream was not rushing, but there was no way to tell how deep it would become. He felt the mud, sand, and moss squish between his toes, but not for long since his feet quickly grew numb. The water reached his thighs before it started to get shallow again, and he splashed to the other side in knee-deep water. He stepped out of the stream, climbed a steep bank, and went a little way up the hill before stopping to put his clothes back on.

He spread his arms and hands out toward the sky, looked up, and said, "Thank you. Thank you for the easy crossing." Just then, a couple of raindrops landed on his upturned face. "Okay, okay, have to get going."

He picked up his bags and looked back across the stream. The wolf was on the opposite bank, staring at him.

"Hey! There you are! Come on!" Toq called and waved, but the wolf simply looked at him.

Toq could barely see him in the growing darkness. He started up the hill in search of a place to camp. The wolf waded into the water, swam, then walked and jumped the rest of the way, stopping to shake off the water before he was completely out of the stream.

Toq was glad for the company. "You may not talk as much as the Traveler, but I'm happy to see you."

He knew the wolf was also frightened of the lions and the big pack, so he dropped some meat scraps and continued searching for a campsite. By the time he settled on a little, flat spot and cleared the piles of animal dung away, it was pitch-black. He set up his lean-to in the dark and went to gather some material to burn. He made his way back to camp, but somehow, in the darkness, he missed it, and it rattled him. He stood, peering into the blackness in all directions, but he couldn't see it.

"Shit!" he said in exasperation.

He thought he was right where his camp should be. The rain began to pick up.

"Be careful here, dummy," he said, realizing he could end up far from his lean-to, never finding it, lying out in the rain with no shelter. He tried to retrace his steps slowly, working in a zigzag pattern, barely seeing where he stepped. Now completely disoriented—unsure if camp was in front of or behind him—he knew he would have to walk right into it if he was ever going to find it. Then, directly in front of him, he glimpsed the white parts of the wolf's fur—the only light things that broke through the darkness.

Toq whispered, "Hey, wolf," as if the wolf could help him, but the white spots moved silently away and vanished like a spirit. Toq moved toward where the wolf had been and almost ran into his lean-to before seeing it.

"Lucked out again," he said.

He got under his lean-to and fumbled around in the dark, out of the rain, realizing the wolf had been sniffing around for food.

"Lucky he didn't run off with a bag," he said as he pulled out the ram's horn.

Almost completely blind, he prepared his fuel and made his fire. Once lit, the small, dancing flame allowed him to see again. Now with a beacon to guide him back, he made a couple more trips out for fuel. He settled in under his shelter, ate, and listened to the gentle rain softly pelting his lean-to. Toq looked out past the fire into the blackness and saw the white parts of the wolf faintly showing in the firelight.

He said, "Thank you, wolf. Even though you were trying to steal my food, you probably saved me."

He tossed a couple pieces of meat out to the wolf and curled up under his robe to sleep.

• • • •

The rain stopped well before sunrise. Toq got up when it began to get light and saw a partly cloudy sky. He wanted to get moving, even though the wet grass and brush would soak his pants and moccasins. In the cool, damp air, he could see his breath, and fog filled the valley to the west. The wolf was gone. Bird chatter filled the air—meadowlarks, red-winged blackbirds, robins, and gulls—but the valley of lions and wolves was quiet. A couple big marmots barked high-pitched warnings about him from the gray rocks up the hill, but Toq was more concerned about his larger adversaries.

He packed up and made his way north, above the marshland's stream. He saw the wolf down below, hunting ground squirrels, voles, and mice.

He whistled to it, and the wolf looked in the opposite direction, and Toq chuckled. He whistled again, and this time, the wolf looked up at him before going back to hunting.

Toq walked past the junction of the marshland's stream with the main river, which ran straight north into a valley with steep hills. He went up to avoid walking the sidehills. He spent six days climbing up into rocky, cliff-strewn mountains and back down out of them, wandering into gorges and box canyons, wondering if he would be able to get back out. He hiked out of mountains onto flat plains or wide valleys, only to walk back into them. He detoured far from the river, catching glimpses of it from high above, before coming down and meeting up with it once again. He saw incredible views of the mountains and the curving river. Gray-white cliffs dominated certain areas along the river, while in other places, the rock was brown, red, and yellow. The rocky paths tore up his moccasins so badly they hardly lasted a day before they required patching or replacing. His feet took a beating on the rocks. This was not like cruising across the grassy plains.

"One good thing: no large packs of wolves or lion prides," he said.

But he did see a lot of eagles and hawks, bighorn sheep, and, for the first time, shaggy white mountain goats walking the faces of cliffs far from fangs, claws, and spears. He surprised a cougar—a solitary cat much smaller than the lions, but which still weighed as much as the man. It fled.

He crossed numerous streams, but one (Dearborn River) was deep and fast, and he had to swim, using his bags as floats. He went up and down countless times as he crossed hills and valleys and scooted through gaps between stony towers. He complained when the easy, flat going was on the other side of the river and rejoiced when it was on his side. The weather favored him. Hills and mountains were treeless, snow still covered the higher peaks, grass turned a darker shade of green, leaves popped out of the willows and bushes, and purple, blue, orange, red, and yellow wildflowers overwhelmed even the grass in places. Although the river was gray-brown and murky, he could see fish making waves and ripples. Toq stopped often to marvel at the beauty of this rugged mountain-hill country.

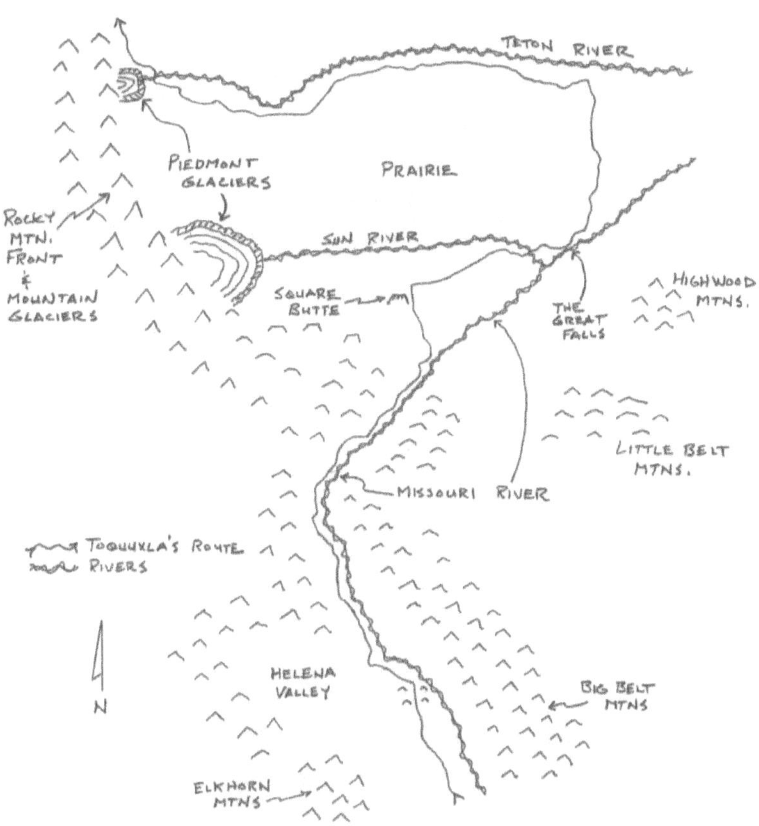

TETON RIVER
PIEDMONT GLACIERS
PRAIRIE
ROCKY MTN. FRONT & MOUNTAIN GLACIERS
SUN RIVER
SQUARE BUTTE
HIGHWOOD MTNS.
THE GREAT FALLS
LITTLE BELT MTNS.
MISSOURI RIVER
TOQUUXLA'S ROUTE
RIVERS
N
HELENA VALLEY
BIG BELT MTNS
ELKHORN MTNS

CHAPTER 10

The Prairie

The wind blew hard off the mountains and out of the canyons onto the eastern prairies. Half of the orange sun had broken above the distant, flat horizon. Toq stood on a high hill, watching the sunrise. There was too much for his eyes to take in: isolated mountain-hills, big, flat-topped buttes, an expansive prairie running away to the east, where it was interrupted by a distant mountain range (Highwood Mountains) sitting blue and white on the horizon, and to the northeast, the prairie extended out to forever, the sky coming right down to the earth. The river (Missouri River) reflected the sky's brilliant blue as it meandered across the valley plain, which held numerous ponds, oxbows, and flooded flatlands.

Animals of all kinds were everywhere—in the water, on the water, at the edge of the water, on the plains, hills, mountains, and buttes, and in the sky. The willows seemed thicker, taller, and stouter, and for the first time since leaving the village, Toq saw a few scattered spruce trees in the distance. They were short, skinny, windblown, and battered. Toq looked for any sign of people but saw none. But he believed that with more wood, there would be people.

Then he thought, *What if I'm the only one here?* The idea scared and excited him. *Maybe I am the first. Maybe all of this is my land! Maybe . . . but you can't live for long without other people.*

The wolf followed Toq through the mountains. He disappeared for a day but came back, and a couple of times came almost close enough to take a piece of meat from Toq's outstretched hand. But the animal always stayed just out of reach, which was all right with Toq; those few times the wolf had gotten close gave him a deeper admiration for just how big and intimidating the wolf actually was and how large his fangs were. The wolf never snarled or snapped at Toq, but still, Toq wasn't keen to test him. He liked having the wolf around, but he knew the animal was finding his own food elsewhere, and he wondered if the wolf might join another pack or find a wandering female. But whenever wolves howled or appeared, "his" wolf went the other direction.

"So, you're not a dominant male," Toq said to him. "But you know how to survive."

Toq stared intently into the wolf's amber eyes, while the wolf looked everywhere *but* Toq's, mostly looking at the food in his hand. "But will you ever have pups? Do you want to?" Then, the man wondered, "Do I?"

Toq scanned the valley for trouble before leaving the hill. He looked at the wolf, who was only ten steps away and who also scanned the valley. His eyes moved to his shortened spear, and he began hiking to the nearest spruce, "Or whatever kind of tree that is." The wolf stayed close to the man.

Toq was disappointed to discover the tree had lived a tough life on this little patch of ground. It had been thrashed by horrendous winds, antlers, horns, and tusks. Neither the branches nor the trunk were straight enough for a spear shaft. It was gnarled and broken and only twice the height of the man. And yet, its twisted, tortured form was beautiful.

"None of us has a choice about where we get stuck," Toq mused. "We do the best we can, wherever and however we start."

He looked at the wolf. "Just like you."

He started for the next tree, thinking aloud, "Just like me."

The trees were widely scattered; this was no forest. More than half were as beat-up as the first, but Toq was able to select a young tree with a nice, straight trunk and a perfect diameter. Using a makeshift stone hand axe, he chopped and sawed the tree down, knocked off the branches, and cut it to length.

"Mmm, this pine smells *so* good," he said, inhaling deeply as he worked.

He whittled off most of the bark and smoothed out the knots. He cut a notch in one end, took the spearpoint from his old spear and, after softening a long strand of sinew in his mouth, wrapped the stone spearpoint onto the new shaft. He smeared pitch from the tree on the sinew wrapping to strengthen the binding.

All the while, Toq remained vigilant. It was too easy to get caught up in one's work, forgetting that, with his head down, something could ambush him. The wolf waited patiently, never straying far, and Toq knew it would see anything coming their way. Once finished, he pounded the butt of the spear on the ground a couple of times, looked it over, and said, "That'll do for now." Having a longer spear gave Toq a bit more confidence.

He went up a rise onto a flat plain, where he could see the prairie had been chewed down to the dirt and trampled by herds of animals. There were piles of shit everywhere, but the prairie was empty for now. He looked down toward the river, where a large herd of mammoths walked above the far bank, the largest group he had yet seen. Toq hiked northeast, keeping to the hills above the wide river valley. He had not seen any lions or wolves yet, but the river attracted their prey. He saw two bears wandering separately along the wetlands—one very large, one much smaller, one eating something, one walking along through the brush.

He walked out of the overgrazed area onto a beautiful, treeless plain, seemingly untouched by the grazers and covered in green grass and wildflowers, with wind gusting across the grasslands in waves. Only a few small groups of pronghorn and horses grazed here.

"Wonder why this hasn't been worked over."

It energized him to walk across such a pretty place, and the walking was easy. Sometimes grasses grew in rounded clumps, making for difficult walking on uneven surfaces, but not here. He had eaten almost all of his food, his bags were light, the day was warm and breezy, and he traveled fast. He stopped to ponder his course and where he might camp tonight. The large, flat-topped butte (Square Butte) straight north had vertical cliffs, and Toq was certain he could find some degree of safety there.

He hiked toward it, across a wide, flat bench with depressions holding small lakes with no clear inlets or outlets. Every lake and pond overflowed with ducks, grebes, geese, gulls, terns, swans, and myriads of different shorebirds from short and noisy to tall and quiet. Falcons, hawks, and eagles patrolled the water, looking for meals, causing panic among the waterfowl. As the man and wolf made their way around these ponds, the birds either paddled away to the other side or took flight. Toq kept an eye out for easy meals, as did the wolf, and attacking birds swooped down on them, trying to protect their nests or young. Toq looked back once to see the wolf devouring something he found on the ground—something dead, maybe, or baby birds, or eggs.

"I wonder if wolves eat eggs," he said as he turned away. "Probably."

He dropped down into a coulee, out of sight of the wolf. He was relaxed and feeling good about the day. He looked to a flat area upstream and spotted an animal, blond and tan, crouched low, hugging the ground, clearly facing him. Toq immediately tensed. He looked hard at the animal, barely breathing, his heart beating faster as his mind raced.

It was too far away to tell exactly what it was, but it was clearly focused on him. Toq didn't want to look away but still glanced quickly around, and seeing no other attackers, he returned his attention to the animal, which had risen and moved closer. It was a cat, and it froze in place when he looked back at it. It wasn't a lion, but he had never seen a cat like this before. And he had no place to run.

"He's going to knock me down and go for my neck."

He removed his bags, unsure if he should use them as shields or weapons. The cat began moving forward, even with Toq watching him. Toq dropped his small spear and held the strap of one bag in one hand while gripping his new, large spear in the other.

The cat—long and slender, not nearly as big as a lion—picked up speed, and then it exploded forward in a sprint. Toq spread his feet wide and prepared for contact, intending to swing his bag first, then lunge with his spear.

Surprisingly, Toq became calm, focused, and ready to fight, and he roared at the cat as only a human voice could, "Come *on!*"

The cat let up, slowed down, and finally stopped about twenty paces away. It looked at Toq but didn't seem to know what to do. It was used to things running away. Toq stood tall, at the ready, as the cat opened its mouth wide, showing its fangs, then closed and licked its lips.

"We're okay here, yes?" Toq said in a low, calm voice, and the cat's ears perked up momentarily at the new sound.

Suddenly, it looked up the hill to the south and turned sideways, raising its head and neck to see better. Toq figured he could probably spear the cat now, but he no longer felt in danger. He took a good look at the cat; it had fairly long, thick hair, with blond, brown, tan, and black coloring, some black spots, long legs, a very long, muscular tail, a long body, and a rather small head. "It" became "she," and Toq guessed she might be about the size of the wolf, maybe a little smaller. She started panting and turned to go back the way she had come. Toq followed her gaze and saw the wolf trotting over. Obviously, the cat didn't want anything to do with the wolf, as she surely had confrontations with wolf packs in the past.

Toq smiled at his wolf and watched the cat disappear. He didn't know what kind of cat it was; it wasn't a long-fang (saber-tooth), bobcat, lynx, cougar, or lion. (It was an American cheetah.) He wondered, "How many kinds of cats are there, anyway?"

It would not be the last of these cats he would see. The wolf sat down a little distance away, some blood on his muzzle.

"Well, I see you had something to eat. You missed the excitement! That cat nearly had *me* to eat! You didn't even see it, did you? You don't even care, do you? No, all you care about is your belly!"

It relaxed Toq to make fun of the wolf, as if the wolf could understand him. He picked up his bags and spears, ate a bit as he walked, and pulled out his bolas to carry around his neck, saying, "You never know what might present itself."

He felt unusually serene after that encounter. He didn't know if it was because he was getting used to danger or if the cat simply didn't scare him that much.

He needed to get fresh meat. Anything would do. He wasn't too concerned, since food was everywhere—flying, swimming, walking, digging, crawling, climbing, and sometimes just lying there, already dead. He recognized some of the plants popping up out of the ground, but many were new to him. He knew of some that he could eat, or that had an edible root, but aside from berries, he wasn't confident he knew what was good and what was bad. In the villages, the women collected plants. Toq had always thought he ought to learn from them, but he never took the time, and now he wished he had. If he was uncertain about a plant, he might take a little taste, but mostly he just stayed away. The bulk of his diet was, by far, flesh.

After slogging through a shallow, boggy valley, Toq and the wolf arrived at the flat-topped butte with plenty of daylight left. He looked up at the vertical walls of stone and saw a hawk's nest on a ledge in the middle of the wall, and a small group of bighorn sheep on top. They walked around to the east side, where a wall of cliffs guarded the top of the butte. Cuts or gaps in the wall allowed animals an easy route up. The cliffs showed clear bands of horizontal layers, and he admired the beauty of the vertical faces, cuts, and fins and columns of stone. Some of the cuts had steps to the top, thanks to the horizontal layers breaking off separately. Chirping swallows swarmed the cliffs. Wanting to find a spot at the base of a cliff, Toq climbed up a steep, grassy slope scattered with fallen boulders. He clambered over a pile of large rocks and lucked out when he found a flat, grassy pocket.

"The perfect spot," he said, looking around. "Just a little sheep poop."

His only concern was that certain predators might work the bottom of the cliffs, but he still thought this was better than an indefensible place above or below. As he set up camp, the sky grew dark, and the sunlight left the hills to the east. The butte blocked his view to the west so he couldn't see what was coming, but it was too early for sunset, so he knew clouds were moving in.

The wolf found a flat rock, not too near, not too far from camp—which Toq had just finished setting up when he heard thunder coming from the west.

"Wow. First thunderstorm of the year," he said, feeling a little excited. "I wonder how much time I have."

He took his spears, bolas, and an empty bag and carefully jogged down the slope to get a look over the top of the butte. A big, dark cloud boiled toward him, and thick, bright bolts of lightning struck down.

"No time to hunt."

He quickly set about gathering brushwood, working his way back up to camp. Halfway there, he saw dust blowing off the top of the butte. The little birds were gone, and the wall of wind hit Toq. He raced back as the wind blew harder and thunder rumbled the air and shook the earth. Large raindrops began to fall just as he reached his lean-to. The thunderhead moved directly above, thunder cracked the air, and rain and hail fell in a torrent so heavy it was like trying to look out from inside a waterfall. The hail piled up and water pooled under the lean-to.

"Ah, that's just great!" he growled. "I should have known. But it was so nice and clear all day." He looked out to check on the wolf, who was curled up on the rock, soaked and covered in hail pellets, shielding his face with his tail.

The storm lasted a while, and Toq dashed out a few times to grab rocks to place beneath his shelter and on which to stack his belongings so as to keep them dry. Drenched, he sat on one rock and hunched over with his feet on another rock. His butt quickly became sore, but all he could do was stare out at the rain, getting cold. He looked at the little pile of sticks he had collected, now all wet. The rain began to let up as the dark-purple thunderhead moved east, lit by the occasional flash of lightning. Thunder rumbled quietly now, off in the distance. The wind stopped, and soon after, the rain did as well. Toq went outside, stepping through the cold water and hail, and he breathed in the wonderful, fresh-smelling air, listening to drops of water still falling from rocks into puddles and grass. The thundercloud—now a floating mountain in the eastern sky—shone brightly in the sun, reflecting brilliant, roiling pillows of cloud. A double rainbow appeared, adding to the spectacle for a time. This was nothing new for Toq; he had seen these wonders before, but he was forever captivated by it all. His people had stories explaining the lightning, thunder, and rainbows, but as was his nature, he was skeptical. He was certain there was *their* explanation for these phenomena—how they were formed and what they "meant"—and then there was the reality, and he didn't believe anyone really knew what this all was or what caused it.

The wolf was gone, probably hunting.

The water slowly drained out of his campsite, and with a pointed rock, Toq made a small ditch around his shelter and away down the hill, just in case another storm came along. He searched along the bottom of the cliff for dry sticks and killed two grouse with his bolas. He saw the wolf hunting the land below, not far away. The movement warmed him, but he was still wet, and his leather clothing would not dry now until tomorrow.

He spent considerable time searching for enough material to burn, then cooked both birds, ate one, and saved the other for morning. By now, the thundercloud had floated almost out of sight, but with more clouds coming, he figured he could be in for more rain. He gathered dry grass to place beneath his lean-to. He hadn't been able to find enough dry material to keep a fire going all night, but he was okay with that. With the light quickly fading, he looked for the wolf one last time but didn't see him, and as he crawled into his bedding, rain began to fall gently on the camp.

• • • •

It rained all night, hard at times. Light seemed to be very slow to come. Toq's camp hadn't flooded any further, but his clothes remained wet, and he didn't bother to put them on when he went out to relieve himself. He shivered against the cold rain and hurried back to his warm bed. It rained all morning, too, and Toq stayed under his shelter. He ate the grouse and what was left of the dried meat. Now, he was out of food. The wolf—sodden, but largely unbothered by the rain—appeared once to check on the man. Toq tried to coax him under the shelter, but he had nothing to coax him with, and the wolf walked away to search for food. By midday, Toq figured he had little choice but to go out to find food, as well.

With a bare head, wet leathers, the bolas, a bag, and two spears, the man went out in a steady rain. Clouds and rain hid the distant mountains, hills, and horizons, but the grassy plains glowed a brighter shade of green. He had no desire to do a big hunt in this weather and hoped to find something small and easy. No bighorns were in sight. The birds were mostly quiet, but some searched the grass and brush for food. Visibility was poor, so he could just make out a few scattered horses, bison, and pronghorns on the plain below. He worked his way north, above the plain, just below the cliffs, moving over and around the large boulders.

Coming around to the north-facing side of the butte, something caught his eye: a small group of pronghorns on a large, flat plain that sloped down, away from the butte. A couple were bedded down, most were feeding, and all were alert. It was a group of males with nice-size horns. Pronghorns were a common sight, but what really grabbed Toq's attention was a blond and tan cat with a long tail, sneaking up on them from an adjacent coulee. Toq stopped his own hunting and fixed his eyes upon what was happening below. The cat moved slowly—imperceptibly slow, from Toq's perspective.

Rain fell on all of them, and Toq sat down in the wet grass, shivering a little, and saying quietly, "Now hurry up. I don't have all day."

The pronghorns saw him but were not alarmed, knowing they were a safe distance away.

Toq thought, *This would not be a good time for the wolf to show up.*

Mist occasionally obscured his view, as rain and fog slowly blew east. The cat was the same kind—maybe even the same one—as yesterday. It inched closer, and the two bedded pronghorns stood up. The whole herd now looked at the cat, freezing it. The cat focused on its quarry, looking for any sign that the bucks were about to bolt, the tip of its tail flicking back and forth. It was out of the coulee now with only shortgrass prairie between it and them. The pronghorns did not look for long. Within moments of identifying the cat, they spun around and began running. Their speed didn't surprise Toq; he had seen many a pronghorn race across the plains, and once they ran, nothing caught them.

"Well, so much for that," he said. As soon as the pronghorns ran, the cat sprang forward, and Toq laughed, "Oh, you have no chance now!"

The cat accelerated rapidly, flying across the ground.

"Whoa, the gods, he's fast!" the man said, eyes wide, forgetting about the rain.

Indeed, nothing traveled across the ground as quickly as these two animals. The distance between predator and prey shrank, and the pronghorns' path began to curve, enabling the cat to cut the distance more. The five bucks strung out in a line, and while the cat would never catch the leaders, a couple at the back had all the pursuer's attention, with the cat right behind them. One pronghorn, second from the rear, stumbled in a hole, momentarily slowing it, and that was all the cat needed. The pronghorn in the back sped past the other. The cat changed its course slightly and quickly overtook the pronghorn that stumbled. It lunged at the buck, knocking it off its feet. Mud flew into the air, and the cat and its prey slid across the wet grass. The cat's front paw went around the buck's neck to hold it down, and the cat's jaws quickly searched for and clamped down on the buck's windpipe. The pronghorn's legs kicked the air until it died. The other bucks faded far from view in the rain, still running. The chase had lasted only ten heartbeats. Toq wasn't certain the cat would have caught any of them had the one not stumbled.

The cat held the pronghorn in its jaws long after it had stopped kicking. Toq kept watching. It finally let go, stood up, and looked around to make sure it was alone, but it didn't see the man. It began to tear into the buck, stopping frequently to look for enemies. If a bear, wolves, or lions showed up, the cat would lose its meal. Toq contemplated rushing the cat to chase it off its kill, but he didn't know if that would work by himself. It could backfire, and the cat might turn on him. After seeing its speed and power, Toq was hesitant to take the risk. He looked around and saw the wolf sitting a short distance away. Maybe together they could scare off the cat, but this particular cat and situation might be vastly different than yesterday, and he wondered, "What if the wolf runs away?" He couldn't explain his plan to the wolf, and he didn't know what the wolf was thinking. So, they sat in the rain, watching the cat and the buck, mulling over what they should do.

Toq stood up. He thought about trying to scare off the cat with a wolf howl but worried it might attract a pack. The wolf stood up with the man. Toq took a few steps down the hill toward the cat. The wolf followed.

"Huh. Maybe this will work."

He walked right toward the cat. The wolf started to go straight at it, but then began veering to the right, as if to surround it, to intimidate it. The cat spotted them, paused, then ate faster, before finally stopping and standing up, warily watching the unnatural pair approaching. Lone wolves and cats typically avoided each other, but wolf *packs* chased and killed cats.

Rain washed over Toq's hands and head, and he tried not to show his apprehension. Instinctively, the wolf moved to the side of the cat, which stood its ground, not wanting to lose this kill. Toq kept looking to see where the wolf was and thought this might not be worth the risk, but with a surge of adrenaline, he charged the cat, waving his arms and spears like a wild man, yelling, "Hyah! Go on! *Hyah*!"

The cat crouched, and the wolf moved closer, ignoring Toq's antics. The cat jerked its head left and right as it tried to track both of its antagonists. Finally, bullied off its kill, it jumped over the pronghorn and ran a little ways off before turning around to see what these thieves would take. The man and the wolf got to the buck simultaneously.

Toq wondered if the wolf would snap and growl to keep him away from the kill, so, taking no chances, he aggressively placed himself between the buck and the wolf, saying loudly, "No!" as he pointed his spear at the wolf.

The wolf seemed to get it, stopping and sniffing the ground with no snarls or growls. Toq was relieved. He glanced at the cat, now two stone throws away, pacing, clearly agitated. Toq felt bad about stealing its kill but not bad enough to stop.

"I'll leave you some," he told the cat.

The cat hadn't gotten far into feeding. The pronghorn's belly was partly opened, and the hindquarter was chewed only a little. Toq turned the buck over and used his stone blade to quickly cut off the other hindquarter and leg. The wolf came closer, sniffing the ground. Toq was well aware that he was lucky this wolf wasn't an aggressive, dominant male.

"There, that's all I want," he said to the cat, which had backed farther away, and now sat and watched more passively.

To Toq's amazement, the wolf seemed to be patiently waiting. He sliced the belly open more completely and pulled out most of the guts, warming his hands in the steaming organs. Finding some choice pieces, he tossed them to the wolf, who quickly devoured everything thrown his direction.

"Shit, man. You can't possibly taste it when you eat that fast," Toq said. He would have taken some of the organs with him, but he had no clean way to carry the slippery things. Some would have tried to drag the whole carcass back to camp, but Toq would not, saying, "It wouldn't be fair to the cat. And it would make my back ache."

The rain washed the blood from his hands. He picked up his spears and the hindquarter and backed away from the buck. The wolf cautiously moved in, sniffed a little, nibbled a little, then tore into the feast.

"Be quick," Toq said as he eyed the cat. He stood watching the wolf and cat for a while, constantly looking around in all directions. The wolf gorged himself, and Toq finally said, "Let's go," and hoisting the hindquarter onto his shoulder, he walked away. But the wolf kept eating and didn't notice the cat creeping closer.

"Ah, shit!" He called back, "Hey! Let's go!" but the wolf ignored him. Dropping his load, Toq ran back to the wolf, spear at the ready, not wanting his buddy to get killed. Only once Toq reached the buck did the wolf break off its obsession and jump back, his face and neck red with blood.

"Come on!" Toq said, glancing at the cat—which backed away again. The wolf only looked at him, and Toq charged him to chase him away from the carcass.

"He's not going to leave this meal here," Toq realized. He looked at the wolf and the cat, who both looked at the man. "All right, let's see if you can defend yourself." Resignedly, he walked back to the meat he left on the ground. He picked up the hindquarter and swung around to see the cat watching the wolf eat.

"Godsdamnit!" he said, feeling cold, tired, and hungry. He looked down, thinking, exasperated, then looked back at the animals. He shook his head and walked on.

"I have to get back," he muttered, not really believing the cat would attack the wolf. He was wrong. Toq walked a little ways and turned around in time to see the cat moving quickly toward the distracted wolf.

He yelled, "Hey, *wolf!*" but neither creature seemed to hear.

He dropped his load again and ran toward them. At the last second, the wolf finally turned to face the cat, but the cat slammed into him at full speed, sending the two carnivores tumbling over the pronghorn. The wolf yelped with pain or perhaps surprise. They were a blur of fighting fur, the wolf snarling, the cat growling. Then, the animals parted, facing each other. The wolf growled, but he backed away. Toq heard no sound from the cat. Neither animal wanted to go for a kill; neither wanted to be injured. The cat had taken a big chance in attacking the wolf, but it won, and the wolf walked away with his tail down.

Toq stopped running. In only a moment, the fight was over. Neither animal appeared to be hurt, and the cat reclaimed its kill. Amazingly, the wolf came right up to Toq and, with tail held down, rubbed his flank against the man's leg.

"Wow, that's a first," Toq said in shock. He patted the wolf on the side a couple times, and the wolf moved away, stopped, and looked back at the cat and the pronghorn.

"You're lucky," Toq said to the wolf as they walked in the rain to his camp.

The butte loomed large above them; the rocky cliffs enveloped in a white mist. As they approached, a single bighorn ram stood up in front of Toq's lean-to and scampered away along the bottom of the cliff. The grass where it had been lying was matted down and dry.

"Sorry for taking your favorite spot," Toq said. Then, "Why do I keep talking to all these animals?"

That evening, the wolf curled up in a somewhat sheltered place out of sight, and Toq curled up under his robe with a full belly, listening to the rain patter on his lean-to. He slowly warmed up, closed his eyes, and dreamed about the cheetah-cat, the wolf, and the pronghorn.

••••

It rained all night and most of the next day, and Toq hardly ventured out from under his shelter. He went for long stretches without seeing the wolf.

"I hope he's not going back to that carcass," he sighed.

He lay flat, tossed and turned, sat up, fidgeted, and stared out at the rain. His soaked clothes would never dry in these conditions, and he spent most of his time out of them, under his fur bedroll. He slept, he was bored, he was uncomfortable, and he worked on a couple of pairs of moccasins. When the rain let up, he roamed around, looking for good stones to knap or something more to eat. During one break in the rain, he found an opening in the cliffs, where he climbed up on top of the butte to see if there was any sign of blue skies, but all was enshrouded in the same dull gray. He was surprised to see bison and camels on top of the butte, but he retreated to his shelter when it began to rain again. He wondered what his people were doing at that moment. He wondered how they were, and then he thought about the Traveler.

"He would have loved this journey. He would have loved the wolf."

He thought about the legends of people long gone; he thought about the flood, and he thought about the future and the people who would come after his time. He thought about his own future. After thinking too much, he just wanted the rain to stop so he could get going again.

••••

The rain quit during the next night, and finally, a few blue patches of sky appeared. For the first time in days, Toq could see the hills and prairie instead of only fog. A light breeze came up, while water dripped off the rocks of the cliff. Toq stretched and smiled at the new day, a day without rain—hopefully.

If he left now, the wet grasses would soak his feet, but he said, "So what? I've been wet for three days, anyway."

He packed everything up and whistled for the wolf. The wolf had been responding to his whistle, but this time, he didn't show. Toq started east, then turned north at the bottom of the hill, listening to the meadowlarks' songs. He was in a great mood, and as he rounded a curve in a hill, he looked down at the spot where the pronghorn carcass had been. A couple of magpies called and seemed to laugh at each other over the remains, but the cat had dragged most of the kill away. Toq liked magpies, but he hadn't seen any of the beautiful birds since leaving the village. He looked around for the cat and spotted it sitting on a huge boulder on the butte, watching him. Toq was very curious about this animal. Although impressed by the cat, he wasn't scared of it. They looked at each other for a while until the cat jumped off the rock, walked to the steep, rocky portion of the butte, and suddenly shot upward in three or four giant leaps—climbing a nearly vertical rock face with such speed and grace it was as if there was no such thing as gravity. Again, Toq's jaw dropped.

"You are such an amazing animal!" he said, wondering how any prey could escape such prowess. It would have to be either very big and powerful or very fast, with a solid head start—or else very good at hiding.

The last of the clouds were breaking up, and sunshine finally brightened the landscape. A couple of large birds of prey soared over the flat-topped butte.

Toq looked at the butte and asked, "How did you come to be the way you are? You look like a mountain that's had its top removed. . . . Hmm."

He wondered how everything had come to be: the rocks, the water, the mountains, plants and animals, people, the sky, the sun, the moon, the wind.

"So many unanswered questions."

Suddenly, the wolf galloped toward him across the green prairie.

"Ah, there you are."

Looking east, Toq began hiking. He went down into wide coulees that would normally be dry but now ran with muddy rainwater. Large, barren areas were now almost impossible to walk across due to the slick mud. He slipped on it and sank into it, it sucked at his feet, and stuck to his moccasins, doubling or tripling his foot size and weight. He went around these areas as best he could, trying to step on rocks or grass wherever possible. The mud showed signs that other animals had passed through, as well: large and small hooves, bears, cats, canines, and even a set of mammoth tracks, which left deep depressions full of muddy water. He crossed a coulee and climbed up onto higher ground, where he could see a small family group of mammoths along his route, and he decided to detour around. He reached a prominent point where he saw a large river valley (Sun River) to the north; it ran east, where he guessed it met the big river. He was going to be forced to cross it. From this spot, Toq viewed the isolated mountain range (Highwood Mountains) to the east and a seemingly continuous line of lower peaks (Little Belt Mountains) to the south. To the west, there were the buttes in the foreground—flat tops and round tops—and behind them, higher mountains formed the background, white with snow. As the day wore on and the clouds left their positions on the mountains, their departure revealed a line of high peaks extending north as far as the eye could see—brilliant white in the sun and rising abruptly from the gloriously green hills and prairie.

"One wondrous view after another . . . everywhere a man looks. Dreary, rainy days followed by days like today."

The man and wolf traversed a good amount of territory, and by day's end, it had grown quite warm. Toq considered camping on the flats, but he worried about getting trampled. They hadn't seen any predators. He managed to find a good place against a small outcrop of rocks, overlooking the river valley. The wolf stayed close throughout the day. He appeared to be nervous and reluctant to go where they were headed. Because of this, Toq stayed alert. In the twilight, as Toq prepared to settle into his bed, he heard wolves howling in the valley. The wolf moved closer to the lean-to, stared off in the direction of the howling, and eventually curled up on the ground just outside. They slept only a little, with wolf packs on their minds.

• • • •

It had been a clear night with no moon and an abundant array of stars. Toq arose before the sun, the horizon glowing red, pink, orange, and yellow. The air was perfectly clear and dry, and no fog or haze or smoke obscured the view in any direction. He could see forever. By daybreak, he stood on a hill looking down at the north valley. The wolf never wandered off in the night and now stood nearby. Toq searched for predators and a possible river crossing. He had second thoughts about using a popular animal crossing, as predators likely frequented those areas. Spruce trees sprinkled the floor of the valley, while thick stands of willows guarded the riverbanks. It was quiet. Only the songbirds could be heard, and a light breeze blew Toq's hair. The air smelled of grass and wildflowers and distant conifers.

Seeing no predators, Toq headed down to a clearing by the river. He stopped often to look, listen, and smell. If a dead animal lay rotting in the brush, it might belong to, or attract, a possessive carnivore. He made his way through waist-deep brush to get to the bank of the river. The wolf followed close behind with its tail down.

"You're awfully nervous," Toq observed quietly.

It was a large river, thick with silt from mountain glaciers. No animals were in view, but a dozen dark ticks crawled up Toq's pant legs. He flicked them off while mumbling his usual, "Little bastards."

Swarms of mosquitoes whined overhead, though they didn't bite. He knew that with the longer, warmer days, his time of peace would soon come to an end. The ticks would be gone, but biting flies and mosquitoes would take their place.

"Maybe we'll be lucky. Maybe this won't be a bad year for them," he hoped.

The river was wide, and he could tell it was deep. This would be the biggest crossing he had faced so far this year. The river flowed quickly, and the cold could chill his body and kill him. The opposite side was clear and open, while upstream and downstream, dense thickets of willow clogged the banks. This was where he wanted to cross. He searched for some wood or a log he might be able to use. If he wished to spend the time, he could fashion some kind of boat, but he was in a hurry, not wanting to stay here that long. Only a few spruce trees were close at hand, and so there were very few downed logs—a couple of old and crumbling ones, a tree much too big to handle, and pieces too small to be of any help. Eventually, though, he found one he thought he could use. The trunk was almost as big around as he was and about two body lengths long, and it still had branches attached. He busted off the skinny top end and some of the branches and dragged it to the riverbank.

This is going to be awkward, he thought.

He pulled the log into the water to see how it would float, then pulled it back out to break off a couple more branches.

He tested it again, saying, "All right, let's try that."

After wedging his bags between some branches and loosely tying his spears to the trunk, he waded into the water with his clothes on, hoping they would keep him a little warmer. The wolf watched him the whole time but often looked around for the danger that only he could smell. Toq scanned the area one last time. A large bull bison walked out of the willows upstream to take a long drink. Toq looked at the bull and looked away and tried to estimate how far downstream he and the log would be carried.

He looked at the wolf, then the cold river, took a deep breath, and said, "Time to go."

Walking deeper into the water, pushing the log in front, he held his "raft" steady so his bags wouldn't fall off.

Without looking at the animal, he said, "Come on, wolf!"

The water was quickly over his head. The cold shocked his body, and for a moment, Toq struggled to catch his breath. He clung to the log, pushing and kicking with all his might. The current carried him downstream. When he was halfway across, he looked back to see the wolf was in the river, a little upstream, swimming much faster than he could. Toq shivered, his muscles tensing, and his leathers feeling more like a heavy burden than protection from the cold. He struggled to keep the mostly submerged log straight and upright, while the bottom of his bags sat in the water. The current was faster than he'd thought, carrying him farther downstream than he guessed. The wolf reached the other side, climbed out of the water, and shook off. Toq's hands and feet grew numb; soon, they would be hard to move and useless. He pushed and kicked harder until he felt the log touch ground. Holding onto his raft, he struggled to stand. He rose out of the cold water into the warm, dry air—immediately feeling better, warmer. He pulled the log out of the river, tossed his half-wet bags up onto the bank, and with stiff fingers, untied his spears.

Seeing no danger, he said, "Son of a bitch!" and lay back on the grass, catching his breath, feeling the sun's warmth.

He only allowed himself a few moments of rest. Then, he took off his leathers and wrung out the water from them and his bags, ate a little, drank some silty river water, and then put his wet clothes back on and readied to go. It was still early morning, and the day was warming quickly. Toq welcomed it.

He and the wolf waded through a wide section of brush, picked off ticks, and climbed a hillside. They looked across a beautiful, green, expansive valley, split by the big river and filled with a small forest of larger trees and open meadows. Further downstream, mist rose up from the river. Birds flew in and out of the trees, bison occupied the meadows and brush, and a couple mammoths moved through the willows.

"If there aren't any people here, then there aren't any people anywhere in this land," he said to the wolf. But he saw no sign of a human.

The draw of this place was too much to resist, and against his better judgment, Toq headed straight into the valley of trees. He followed a well-used path through the brush, past some of the tallest spruces he had seen in quite some time, weaving his way cautiously through thickets of willow well over his head, and arriving at a stand of birch trees, where he reached out to stroke their smooth white bark. He looked up through the new green leaves, dancing and clicking in the breeze, the sun filtering through from a deep blue sky, casting shadows everywhere. He had not stood in the shade of trees for a while, and it felt secure, sheltered. He closed his eyes and breathed deeply the springtime smells of this little forest sanctuary, while birdsong filled his ears.

He heard the snapping and cracking of dead branches and was jolted from his moment of reverie. To his surprise, a mammoth passed by, silently but for the few dead sticks it stepped on, close enough to hit with a stone. Toq was equally surprised the mammoth didn't seem to have noticed him—or else didn't care. He stood still and watched the massive beast slowly make its way through the trees.

The man and wolf made their way through the thick growth to the river (Missouri River), now very wide and full of life. Most of the activity seemed to be centered around a couple of islands partly covered by trees and willows; birds flew all over them, perched in trees, and hunted along the shores and in the grass. A huge bear walked the river's opposite shore.

"That's what we don't want to run into," Toq said to the wolf, pointing at the bruin. He picked up a rock and threw it as far as he could, watching it splash about a quarter of the way across the river.

Downstream, the mist, closer now, rose like a cloud. He looked along the riverbank, and although believing it may be unwise, he followed it downstream. The nearer they got to the mist, the more obvious its source became. The sound, at first, was like the wind blowing through the trees, but once they reached the spot where the flat river dropped off into the cloud, it roared with a deafening noise. This was not the first big waterfall Toq had ever seen, but it was still immense and impressive (the Great

Falls). He stood on a rock ledge to get a good view, while the wolf hung back. The waterfall drowned out all other sounds, and the mist carried upward, where it swirled in the breeze and floated away. Below, an immense volume of water crashed onto rocks and poured over terraced ledges in a series of drops that created a white, foaming, silt-laden cascade. It pushed up so much mist that Toq couldn't quite see the bottom of the falls. He was thrilled by the spectacular sight, but the wolf didn't understand what the man was looking at, seeing no food in the falls.

They made their way down the hill on the north side of the falls, taking care not to slip. Halfway down, the swirling breeze brought the occasional whiff of rotting flesh, in stark contrast to the fresh air of only moments before. Toq stopped to search for the source of the odor, and the wolf perked up and hungrily sniffed the air, though he didn't move away from the man.

Toq glanced all around and said, "Can't stay here."

The hillside to his left was clear of animals, so he made his way over to it and climbed halfway up. He could see more of the waterfall, although the blowing mist continued to obstruct his view. No dangerous animals were in sight. Below the waterfall, the water had cut into the hills, creating good overlooks, and Toq went down to one, where he removed his bags and crouched low as he approached its edge. An eagle—dark-brown and gold—jumped off the ledge just below and flew off to the other side of the valley. Startled, Toq watched to see where it would go. His thoughts flashed back to the giant flood, nearly two summers ago, conjuring bad memories.

He peered over the edge. The river flowed away from the falls in rapids, moving around and over huge boulders. One spot pinched a portion of the river between the near bank and some large rocks, and a pile of dead mammoths plugged the gap. Tusks and bones stuck out of bloody red flesh, while some still-intact bodies looked as if they had just died moments ago. Legs jutted into the air, a limp trunk waved back and forth in the water, and the rapids poured over some that were lodged deeper in the pile. Toq guessed there might be six mammoths there. Three large bears pulled at them with their claws and teeth; one stood on top of the pile, one hovered at the edge of the riverbank, and the third was knee deep in water below the carcasses. Toq counted four other bears nearby, either lounging or hanging back. Now, when the breeze turned the smell in his direction, it almost made Toq gag. A few ravens and magpies perched on trees and rocky ledges, waiting for a spot to open on the heap.

Toq turned away, looked at the wolf, and said, "This is a dangerous place. Let's get out of here."

They started back up the hill as Toq thought, *There weren't many birds scavenging around those bears. And where are the lions and wolves? I guess they don't mess with that many bears.*

"What happened to those mammoths?" he wondered aloud. "They've been dead for quite a while. I'll bet they fell through the ice above the falls in early spring. Bad day for them." He remembered the dead mammoths he'd seen during the great flood, and said, "Too many dead mammoths."

They climbed to the top of the hill, on constant lookout, with the roar of the falls fading away. In the east, a few more wisps of mist floated up out of the river canyon. Toq looked back at the falls one last time, marveling at the amount of water pouring down.

They walked across mostly flat country north of the river, trying to avoid having to cross a never-ending series of deep coulees. They ended up on the southeast side of a basin holding a decent-sized lake (Black Horse Lake). Spruce trees were scattered around the area, and Toq set up camp next to one, thinking he could climb it in an emergency. Food was abundant here. Although eggs had become harder to find, there were plenty of small mammals and birds, and tonight, he ate porcupine. Wood was plentiful for once.

The sky was clear, the air was alive with the sounds of wildlife, and Toq did not feel alone. He shared some meat with the wolf, and then the wolf wandered a little ways off to find its own food. Toq was confident it wouldn't rain, so he didn't set up his lean-to. He watched the sunset as a couple of big bull caribou—with already large antlers, in velvet—moved toward the lake. He smacked a mosquito on his neck and looked at the spot of blood and flattened insect staining his palm.

"And so it begins," he sighed.

The wind died down with the setting sun, granting the mosquitoes easier flying weather, but they weren't bad . . . yet. It grew dark, and the wolf returned. Toq lay on his back looking at the night sky, listening. He closed his eyes as an owl hooted in the distance, and it comforted him. Then, the high-pitched whine of a mosquito tormented him, and though it was impossible to see in the dark, he swung at it anyway. He rolled over and pulled the robe over his head to escape the "little bloodsucker." Images of the day occupied his thoughts before sleeping—crossing the river, the lush, wooded valley, the waterfall, the dead mammoths, the bears.

"Good day," he mumbled.

••••

Toq slept well. The land around was already light when he heard the wolf sniffing around his head. He opened his eyes, stretched up his arms, and yawned loudly, contentedly, causing the wolf to step back.

Toq sat up. "Good morning, wolf!"

The sun hung over the horizon in a partly cloudy sky. He stood and looked around to see what animals had moved in during the night, then packed up and went northeast. They hadn't gone far when they saw, coming from the river, six or seven wolves on their trail. The wolf spotted them first. His tail was down and ears erect—and then, he suddenly changed. Clearly scared, he ran away a few steps and turned to look back, repeating this a couple of times. Toq jogged quickly to a nearby tree. He started to leave his bags on the ground, then decided to hang onto the bag with the food. The tree was difficult to climb with its spindly, dead branches below and thick, new growth above. Toq clung to his big spear, which made climbing all the more difficult. He finally got his hand around a branch big enough to hold him, and he stood on dead twigs no larger than his fingers, just barely out of reach—he hoped—of the wolves. He didn't know how long he could stand there, but he couldn't get any higher, as the branches above were too close together to pass through.

"Shit!" he grunted.

Toq looked for the wolves, who were nearing, taking long, loping strides. He spotted his wolf a little ways away, panicked and unsure what to do, looking for a place to hide or cower.

Toq yelled, "Run! Go! Get out of here!"

There was a chance they would accept him into their pack, but he feared the more likely outcome would be the death of his friend. Something in Toq's voice snapped the wolf out of his indecision, causing him to turn and flee with all the might and speed he could muster.

The pack sprinted past Toq's tree, with only one wolf glancing up at him. Toq watched them go and, with aching feet, jumped down and ran up a small hill to see where his wolf was. In the distance, he saw his wolf crossing a flat plain, impressively swift. The pack chased him, but it looked like he was leaving them behind.

"Ha! Run, wolf, run. Run like the wind," the man said quietly. "Don't let those sons of bitches catch you."

They all vanished over a hill. Toq didn't know what to do, so he retrieved his other bag and spear and began jogging after the wolves, thinking all the while that he shouldn't be doing so.

Toq jogged quite a distance, past a herd of wary horses, but he didn't see the wolves. Sweat ran down his face, and his palms and feet were wet. He took off his leather shirt and shoved it into a bag. Too many animals had passed through the grass for Toq to be able to track the wolves. A cool breeze began to blow, and he walked straight north—the last direction he'd seen his wolf go. The chase may have turned at some point, though; it was impossible to know. He crossed a couple of wide plains, valleys, coulees, and hills, passing marshlands and isolated ponds, and always, the beasts of the steppes. He was walking across a wide, treeless valley when he spotted movement going over a hill far away to the west. The pack was making its way back south, and Toq stood motionless, hoping they wouldn't notice him. They trotted across the valley, briefly distracted by some nearby bison, before going up a hill and out of sight.

Toq hiked in the direction the wolves had just come. He feared he would find his companion dead—but still, no sign of him. Feeling that he was far enough away from the pack, he called and whistled for the wolf. Nothing. He walked farther and called again, but no response.

Heartbroken, Toq mumbled, "He's either dead, or he's still running to the end of the world, scared out of his mind."

He continued on, trying to stay hopeful. By midafternoon, he had covered a lot of ground over easy and vast terrain. He stopped to rest and eat and decided to keep going north. Although it looked like it was taking him farther away from the river—and possibly other people—he was ready to break from the pull of the river, anyway, and besides, his wolf might be going this way. He laughed to think he now followed the wolf. So, Toq worked his way through various basins filled with multiple lakes and ponds (Antelope Coulee and Antelope Flat), feeling lucky that a stiff breeze was keeping away the mosquitoes. The mountains in the southeast (Highwood Mountains) now dominated the view in that direction, deep blue in color and covered in large patches of snow. A couple of prominent buttes rose up in the distance on the east side of the mountains (Square Butte and Round Butte). Another isolated mountain range showed itself far away on the northeastern horizon (Bears Paw Mountains).

Toq passed through the region of lakes, ponds, and marshes and arrived at a place where he could see another large valley to the north, though he had yet to see the river (Teton River). Toq sat down to think. He could follow this river down to where it, probably, joined the big river, or he could cross it and continue north—except that he no longer felt the pull to go north—or he could follow it west, back toward the mountains.

"Well, wolf, if you're still alive, which direction would you go? Where would the Traveler go?"

Toq felt a strong compulsion to go back toward the western mountains.

"Why not? What else am I going to do? I want to see them, and there ain't nobody around here to tell me I can't."

Setting his mind to it, he turned west and hiked until sundown, camping at the edge of a large coulee (Berry Coulee). He sorely missed his wolf buddy's comforting presence.

• • • •

The next morning, Toq pulled on his shirt and wrinkled his nose after getting a whiff of it.

"Damn! If it smells that bad to me, it must be really bad."

He hunted for food, cooked, and ate, and before midday, he was hiking west. He crossed the large coulee and a flat bench and arrived at a second coulee from which he could see down to the river, flooding the valley below.

"Good choice, Toq. You would have had to cross that thing if you'd gone north."

A wolf popped up out of a deeply eroded head cut. Toq couldn't believe his eyes; it was *his* wolf.

He grinned broadly, waved, and whistled. "Hey, wolf!"

The wolf saw him, looked backward once, and started trotting up the coulee toward the man. Suddenly, a second wolf appeared in the coulee, making Toq a bit nervous. The second wolf followed his wolf until she was about a stone's throw away from Toq, where she stopped to watch. To Toq's delight, his wolf came right to him and rubbed his face and neck against Toq's leg. Toq patted him while eyeing the female. He saw no battle wounds on his friend, who was happy, energetic, dancing playfully up and down, and running from Toq to his new mate and back again. Toq smiled. He had never seen the wolf act like this, and he relaxed once he realized the female wasn't going to attack.

"Who's that?" he asked. "She with you?"

He had no food to share with them, so he sat down, and his wolf immediately jumped over to him. The female took a few cautious steps closer, but she came no nearer.

"Boy, am I glad to see you're all right!" he said to his wolf. "So, you've found yourself a mate. That didn't take long. Good for you! Now you have a pack. Are you going to come with me still? Whatever you do, though, keep away from those other wolf packs."

The wolf gradually settled down, his mate turned away to sniff around the area, and he began to do the same thing.

After a while, Toq stood up and said, "Well, I got to get moving. I don't know if I'd fit in with your little pack there, but you can come with me."

He turned and started walking away, looking back to see what the wolves would do. His wolf started to follow, and then the female began following her new mate. Toq was amazed. He worried he'd be leading them through a lot of new territory already claimed by other wolves, whereas this here might be an area they could call their own, but Toq didn't attempt to dissuade them. They hadn't gone far before Toq noticed the female falling behind. She had her own agenda, and it did not entail following this man. She wanted to hunt. Her nose was to the ground, and it led her off toward the river. Clearly torn, the male wolf looked back and forth between the man and his mate, barking out a call to the female—the first time Toq had ever heard his wolf bark like that. But still, the female did not look. Toq tried his whistle, and she glanced up for a moment before going back to her task. She soon moved out of sight, going down into the valley to the north. Toq and the wolf watched her go. They looked at each other, and then the wolf turned around and trotted away from Toq. Toq watched him until he, too, disappeared into the valley. Toq stood there for a while, hoping they might come back. He wasn't going to stay here—to live here—and he was now certain they would not be coming with him.

"Maybe they'll follow . . ." But he was sure they wouldn't. "I wouldn't go with me, either, if I had a new girlfriend."

Toq felt nearly as dejected as he had after losing the Traveler. He was surprised and partly angry with himself.

"What's wrong with you? It's just a stupid wolf." But he'd grown attached, and he couldn't help but feel the loss and, suddenly, the loneliness.

Toq called out, "I'll see you again someday!"

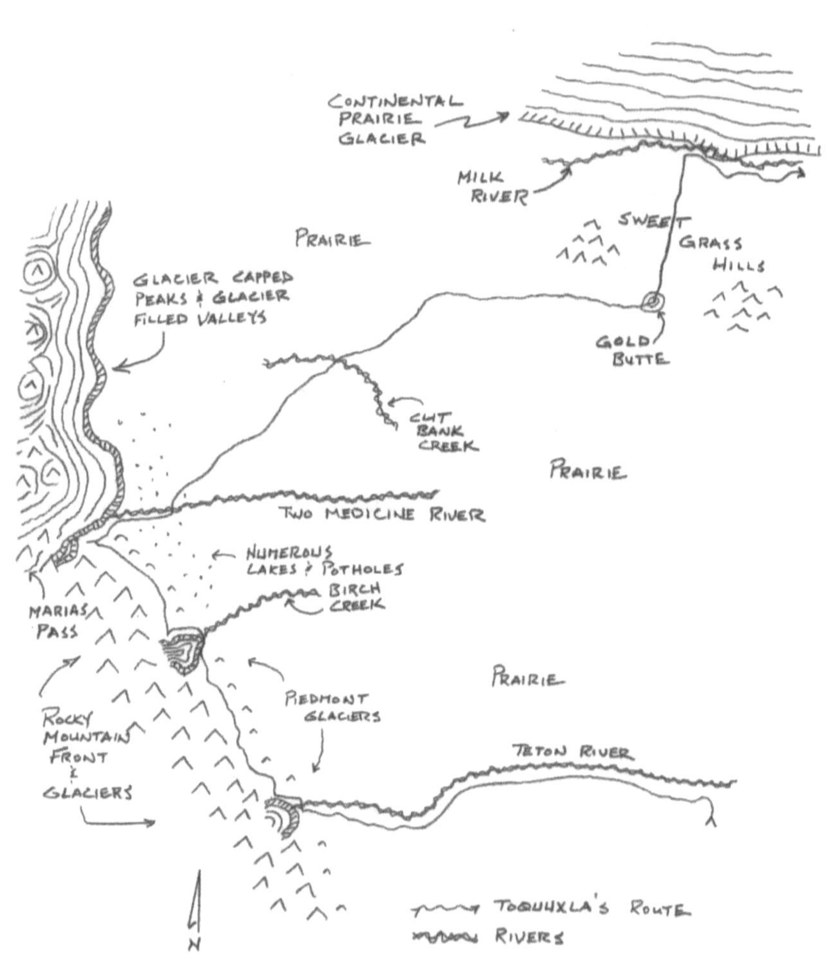

CONTINENTAL
PRAIRIE
GLACIER
MILK RIVER
SWEET GRASS HILLS
PRAIRIE
GLACIER CAPPED PEAKS & GLACIER FILLED VALLEYS
GOLD BUTTE
CUT BANK CREEK
PRAIRIE
TWO MEDICINE RIVER
NUMEROUS LAKES & POTHOLES
BIRCH CREEK
MARIAS PASS
PRAIRIE
PIEDMONT GLACIERS
ROCKY MOUNTAIN FRONT & GLACIERS
TETON RIVER
N
TOQUHXLA'S ROUTE
RIVERS

CHAPTER 11

Mountain Glaciers

The wind powered off the peaks and through the canyons of the western mountains with such force Toq struggled to walk. He stood on a rise, look-ing west, with a river behind him (Teton) and the large creek he had crossed the day before to the south (Deep Creek). An impressive wall of mountains pushed up from the prairie. He'd spent two days crossing easy, flat prairie to get here. Now, the plains were gradually giving way to wider valleys, steeper hills and buttes, more ponds and lakes, less brush, no trees, and the willows in the river valley had become scattered and sporadic. A lush green blanketed the landscape, and while short grasses dominated, bountiful wild-flowers added a burst of color.

Without a single cloud, the sky was a perfect, unblemished sheet of blue in every direction, and the white mountains stood tall against the azure heavens. Toq knew he wouldn't be able to get through those mountains with all the snow and ice. Even if he had the means, he would probably starve to death. But he felt the pull to get closer, to maybe climb up some peak. Just to be in the presence of such massive giants. They felt alive and like they could protect him—or crush him. He thought that if there *were* anything divine in this land, anything spiritual, it would probably be attached, somehow, to these mountains.

With watering eyes, he squinted into the wind. To the southwest, he saw a single male lion slowly crossing a plain toward a small lake in a coulee. He opted to go northwest, away from the lion, staying on higher ground and nearer some buttes (Teton Buttes). He approached a rock outcrop and a small patch of exposed dirt, where only a few tough plants struggled to grow. If he were not constantly on the lookout for workable stones to turn into blades or spear points, he could have easily missed the bones embedded in the dirt. He stood there for a moment, trying to work out what he was seeing. He had seen the big bones, tusks, and teeth of mammoths, but these were different. An obvious leg bone was as long as Toq was tall, and the bones were not white or gray but rather the orange-tan of the rocks. Shattered bone fragments littered an area downhill of the leg bone, and a couple of steps away, a giant skull—unlike any he had ever seen—stuck out from a mound of dirt. He picked up a vertebra the size of his head, shocked at how heavy and dense it was—like a rock, not bone—but it was fragile, and a piece of it broke off.

He turned it over and over in his hands. "Itshla! What was this thing?" He looked around, wishing he could ask somebody.

He had heard of "stone bones," even seen some fragments, but this was bigger than anything he had ever seen before. He examined the partially buried leg bone. He dug around the end that wasn't buried as deep and slowly tried to pry it up out of the ground. It snapped in half, and Toq immediately felt bad for breaking it, knowing this was an unusual and unique find. Even broken into two, half of the leg bone was nearly more than he could lift. In the dirt, under the displaced leg bone, he saw other bones, and he picked at them until he determined they were foot bones with two long, curved claws. He put one of the claws in his bag. Then, he went to the skull, saving the best for last. The ground around the skull had been trampled by some big animals, and the skull—nearly as long as Toq's out-stretched arms—lay on its side, half buried in dirt. The upper back portion was broken, and Toq fitted some of the pieces together. The jaw held no grinders; all the teeth were pointed, serrated, and brown. Some were longer than his hand. He carefully worked a tooth out of the jawbone and held it in the sunlight to get a good look at it.

He looked down at the giant's skull, trying to imagine what this beast had looked like, how big it had been, what it had eaten. "Probably ate mammoths," he guessed. He wondered, too, how long it had been dead.

"How can an animal have rock bones? Was it cursed? It would weigh too much." He speculated, "Bones must turn to stone after a long time." He thought for a bit. "How does that happen?" He wondered if any of these beasts still lived here. "It would not be a good day if I met up with one."

He continued trying to envision this animal in its day, adding flesh, muscle, skin, fur, and eyes. He contemplated the fossil bones for some time until he came to some conclusions: He did not wish to meet one of these creatures and would avoid it if he saw one; he would never know how its bones had turned to stone; and people would make up all kinds of stories about the bone-stone-fanged monster.

He smiled about that last one. "Maybe *I* should make up some stories about it."

He placed the long tooth in his bag, too, before continuing on around the buttes—and then between more buttes. Then, he walked west until he stood on a high point looking into a large basin filled with water. It blocked his route and stretched into the distance to where Toq could see a glacier at the western end. He pondered his choices. He could go south around it, but, "Then what?" If he went far enough south, eventually he would end up back where he'd started. Or, he could go north and keep exploring new country. He observed three different groups of mammoths on the lake's near shore.

He looked north into the valley, where there were multiple creeks and rivers to cross. "Difficult, but I can do it."

So, north he went. He crossed one creek, then a big stream (McDonald Creek), then another creek, and multiple marshy areas in between, until he came up on a dry bench, where he looked down on a swollen, silty river flowing east (Teton River). On the opposite side, he could see dry, high ground.

He dreaded it, but he followed his usual method for crossing icy rivers, saying, "At least it isn't as big as some."

Upon reaching the other side, he shivered while getting back into his clothes, glancing upstream in time to see several large blocks of ice floating down the river. "No wonder it was so damn cold. I wouldn't want to get hit by one of those chunks of ice," he mumbled as he pulled on his moccasins.

He hiked hard away from the river, trying to warm up. The wind died down, the sun dropped onto the mountaintops, mosquitoes swarmed his hands and head, and another large blue lake dominated the view to the northeast. Toq set up camp and began to question his decision to go to the mountains. There was so much water—lakes, marshlands, creeks—and he hadn't even gotten to the glaciers and mountains yet.

"Tomorrow . . . we'll see how far up there I can get, and then I think I'll get out of here."

• • • •

Toq was up with the sun and tired. He rolled some yarrow flowers and leaves between his palms and spread the juices on his exposed skin to help keep the bugs off. He hiked west along a ridge, feeling great now that he was moving again. It was still early morning when he stood on a hill looking down at the lake. Birds flew back and forth across the shimmering water. A thick river of ice flowed out of the mountain canyon, and where it spilled onto the flatland, it spread like a giant fan, flowing around the higher hills, creating brown and green islands in the white expanse. Rocks and soil littered the surface of the ice. Some areas showed huge crevasses, revealing beautiful blue and white ice. A portion of the ice lay in or against the lake, where a vertical wall stood high above the water's surface. The wall—broken and jagged—had towers of ice that appeared ready to fall at any moment. Large pieces of glacier, which had broken off, lay stuck in the lake, grounded on the shallow bottom, while smaller pieces of ice drifted on the surface, slowly melting, finding their way to the lake outlet and down the river, where they might clobber an unsuspecting human making his crossing. Toq heard the water rushing from the glacier, and the echo of cracking and breaking ice. Warm morning sunlight shone directly on the wall of ice, loosening its connection to the glacier, and Toq was rewarded when a large mass collapsed silently into the water, creating a gigantic splash of white spray and mud. Moments later, the thunderous roar reached his ears. A series of waves spread out across the lake, sending ducks and ice bobbing up and down.

Toq quietly held his arms out, with two spears in one hand, as if to embrace the gift of this sight. "All the things that happen that human eyes never see."

He moved toward the foot of the glacier, climbing over a pile of loose rock and dirt. Only a few patches of plants lived on this barren piece of earth. He surmised, correctly, that the glacier must be melting back, leaving fresh ground to be colonized by new plants. No wall of ice prohibited him from walking up onto the glacier; it was an easy step up, and he walked a ways on the flat, crunchy surface. The ice was blindingly bright in the summer sun, and the reflecting rays off the surface warmed the air above.

"No mosquitoes," Toq noted, appreciatively.

Caribou droppings on the ice proved he was not the only one to find relief from the insects on the glacier. But it was too bright, and he was uncertain what obstacles he would run into—like deep crevasses—so he circled around to the north and jumped off onto a hill. He skirted along the north side of the glacier, moving west. He crossed a couple valleys, followed a ridge, and climbed a hill, from which he stood looking down at the sprawling ice sheet pushing far out to the plains. From this elevated position, he saw several small turquoise pools of meltwater on the glacier's surface.

"Wow, this is spectacular," he said in a subdued voice.

As he went up, the plants were shorter, growing close to the ground, adapted to high winds and cold weather. The higher alpine vegetation became sparser with more exposed rock and soil. Most flowers had yet to bloom.

He looked west, where giant snowdrifts still covered the ridges and expansive fields of snow spread across hills and valleys. It was too early in the summer; not enough snow had melted to allow him to climb up on top. Just above, he counted eleven white mountain goats feeding on new vegetation.

Below, some caribou dotted a big green hill. Toq worked his way southwest up some steep mountainsides and around cliffs, crossing sun-softened snowdrifts. After slopping through meltwater, he obtained the top of a giant ridge. The west side of the ridge dropped down into another deep valley. This was as far as he would go. High peaks, covered in snow and ice, soared above, while the canyon below, filled with a narrow but deep river of ice, wound its way down from between huge mountains. Straight across the canyon, a lone mound and ridge separated two drainages coming out of the mountains, both carrying glaciers. The one at Toq's feet spread out into a wider valley and then pushed through a gap in a ridge before it finally found the unconfined freedom of the prairie. His view in that direction was partially blocked by a butte, but it appeared that the two glaciers converged just to the east.

He turned in every direction to behold the wonder of it all: white mountains, blue sky, white glacial rivers of ice, green hills and prairies, blue and turquoise lakes and ponds, and silty streams. Several ribbon-like waterfalls ran down greening mountain slopes and off rocky cliffs. Goats and squeaking pikas and a few tiny birds kept him company. A light breeze carried the sound of streams, while distant waterfalls, rushing torrents, and falling rocks echoed off mountains and canyon walls. Toq felt that, at this moment, he was in heaven, and he could not ask for any of it to be any better. There was no flaw in this land—except, perhaps, for this one human. But for now, he was a part of it, and he left no mark on the purity of this place.

He found a crystal-clear stream trickling down the ridge and got down on hands and knees to press his lips to the surface and drink in the fresh, cold liquid. His long black hair trailed in the water. He reached his cupped hands into a small pool, lowered his head over the water, and somewhat ceremoniously, wet his face and neck and cleansed his spirit. Water dripped off his face, his eyebrows, nose, and lightly whiskered chin. To his side, among the brown grass, bright-green moss, and orange, lichen-covered rocks, a small patch of tiny pink flowers bloomed.

"Everything—from the giant and mighty, to the small and fragile—is perfect," he said. "I wonder if I'm the first person to stand here." He was.

He noticed his footprints in the grass where his weight had bent the blades over, and down the hill, he saw his tracks across a snowfield. These faint marks would soon disappear without a single sign that he had ever been there. He gathered some stones to stack on top of the ridge to let people know—if anyone else came up here—that he'd come first, that this was in some way his mountain now.

He stood back and stared at his work. The stones only stood as high as his knee, but it was obvious that somebody had stacked them; this couldn't have happened naturally. He looked around at what nature had created and suddenly, profoundly, realized how stupid his miniature monument to himself was. His creation, his "mark," didn't fit in with what nature had created.

"Who cares if I was here? Who cares if I was first? It's not my mountain. It's not my land. The mountain belongs to itself. No one needs to know I was here. It's between me and the earth, no one else."

He dismantled his rock pile and put the rocks back where he had found them.

"Now, only the earth, the sky, and I know I was here," he said. "Maybe the Traveler sees me."

He picked up his stuff and noticed a mountain goat had come near and was watching him.

He pointed to it and said, "Aha! You see me! You know I was here! Good enough!"

• • • •

The next morning, Toq was clear about where he was headed, as he traveled north, following the foothills along the edge of the mountains. The route meant going up and down and up and down, crossing countless ridges, valleys, and streams. The line of impressive peaks was never-ending—like a parade of mountains, except the parade stood still, watching the lone man pass by.

Game was plentiful, and newborns were everywhere: horse foals, pronghorn fawns, mammoth and bison calves, ground squirrel kits, ducklings, goslings, bear cubs, and lion cubs. Everything on the earth was fresh and new: the grass, the leaves, the flowers, and even the animals, although many adults still looked pretty scraggly as they shed the remnants of their winter coats. Predators shifted from hunting the winter-weakened and scavenging the winter-killed, to finding and pursuing the young. The newborns had their defenses; some, within hours or a day of being born, were already fleet of foot or good at hiding, while others had their mothers or family groups to keep the predators away.

Toq shared the hilltops and ridges with numerous species trying to keep out of the buggy, boggy valleys. Caribou, bison, bighorn sheep, even a few small herds of musk oxen, and long-legged llamas—the first of these animals he had seen. The farther north he went, the fewer horses and pronghorns he saw. There were no trees here, and even the brush was small and sparse. Grasslands dominated. He passed by huge, ominous peaks in the west—some capped by glaciers clinging to the tops, carving at the sides, opening giant cracks as they inched downhill. Ponds and marshlands increased. Several streams were large and dangerous to cross.

He arrived at the southern edge of a large piedmont glacier that flowed from a mountain canyon (Birch Creek). No single, large lake attached itself to this glacier; instead, multiple torrents of meltwater gushed freely from beneath the foot of the ice, merged into one stream, and flowed away into the prairie. It looked like a thousand small lakes and ponds dotted the land to the northeast—as far as Toq could see. Near the edge of the glacier, separate, gigantic pieces of ice lodged in the ground. Wetland birds were everywhere. A bear with three cubs worked its way through the wetlands and around the ponds, searching for an easy meal. She walked onto a hillside, and lying on her back, sprawled out, she nursed the cubs gathered on her midsection.

The glacier lay directly along his desired path. He considered crossing on the glacier. To go around to the east meant either negotiating the wetland-lake region or else going quite a lot farther to avoid it entirely. He decided to cross the lake region, hoping it might be hilly enough to keep him on dry ground most of the way.

He walked down to the edge of the glacier. In most places, it sloped gently toward the ground. Those steeper, rough sections seemed to be where giant pieces had separated from the main body and were left stranded—icebergs on the plain. Toq walked to one of these icebergs, which towered above him, surrounded by a moat of meltwater. Trapped in its own bowl, the giant had no way to escape; it would simply, slowly, melt away until the only evidence of its existence would be a pond, which would gradually fill in with sediment, becoming a marsh, and then a meadow. About twenty-five paces separated the berg from the glacier. The farther from the glacier, the smaller the ice chunks in the ponds. He guessed this glacier was also melting back, shrinking into the mountains.

"I wonder if it comes back in the winter," he mused, intrigued.

He wound his way through the lake region until he arrived at a raging torrent of a stream. Finding no safe crossing points, he went back to the glacier, climbed up and crossed over on the ice. He never worried that his bridge over the water would collapse since it felt solid and much safer than swimming. On the other side, Toq jumped across a deep gap separating the glacier from the hillside and continued north.

He spent a night next to a pond and, the following day, journeyed northwest through a vast land of hills, valleys, creeks, bogs, ponds, and lakes. With each passing day, the mosquitoes and biting flies seemed to get worse. He wished he could just get used to them, or ignore them, but when the bugs were this bad, he longed for windy days and even looked forward to the end of summer. He wasn't alone in this. The little devils tormented all the wildlife, making them swish their tails, waggle their ears, twitch their skin, shake their heads, jump, kick, bite, scratch, and run. Nothing was ever easy. Mother Nature gave them this warmth and the abundance of summer's growth, but she made them pay for it. Some animals escaped the tiny bloodsuckers by standing in rushing water; some fled to windswept ridges or moved up the mountainsides. Others rolled around in the mud or dust, but many simply stood there and took it, given over to their misery.

As Toq progressed farther north, the glaciers appeared larger and more numerous. Nearing the end of an exhausting day, with clouds moving in, he stood on a hill looking north across a vast piedmont glacier spreading from the mountains onto the foothills and plains. To the northeast, beyond the glacier, he could see the prairie, but the northwest was an ocean of ice. Clouds obscured the upper half of the mountains west of the glacier so all Toq could see was ice rising into the gray of the clouds. In the distance, lying in a low spot on the glacier, a large turquoise lake gleamed in the sea of white ice. He heard the ice crackle and break as it slowly melted and settled into new positions. He shook his head with wonder and exhaustion and decided to camp here. The bugs were not too bad, so he could rest a bit, hunt, and decide what to do tomorrow.

He hunted and killed one of those long-legged llamas. The animals didn't know what to think of him, and they did not see him as a threat until he threw his spear. Now, this herd knew the human was dangerous. To the famished man, the llama was delicious.

For a fire, Toq had only dried dung to work with, and not a lot of it. After cooking and eating, he dragged what remained of the llama into a bog, where he placed large stones inside of and on top of the carcass to submerge it completely. This would preserve the meat while also hiding it from scavengers and predators. He made his camp far away from the bog, on a ridge overlooking the big glacier, exposed to a light breeze. With the arrival of the cool night air, the mosquitoes vanished completely, allowing Toq a peaceful night's rest. The ridge, standing above the glacier-cooled air filling the valleys below, was comparatively warm.

• • • •

First one, then two, then ten whining bugs roused Toq from his sleep. He grumbled as he pulled the robe up over his head, but it was getting too warm to stay covered up for long. When he finally gave in and got up, he stood on the ridge next to his lean-to and soaked in the stunning view. Only a few clouds feebly attempted to obscure the mountains, and they were quickly dissipating.

Toq took only one bag and his spears and climbed to the top of the mountain immediately to the west. As far as the eye could see, glacial ice rose up to meet the horizon, blindingly white below the blue sky. It undulated over hills and cliffs, filling valleys, cracking when it bent around, or over, or down. To the south, a couple of higher peaks—mostly covered in snow and ice—stood tall. To the west and northwest, even taller mountains rose above their glacier-covered sides and valleys, their high, rocky cliffs free of ice and snow. Dark rock mixed with red rock and dirt, falling onto the ice from the mountainsides, left the pure white and blue glaciers soiled in streaks of debris. Toq guessed that some of the boulders—which appeared tiny to him—were actually the height of several men. One mountain away to the northwest was completely engulfed in a glacier, except for the very peak, which pierced the surface of the ice like a new horn from the skin.

Below him, the glacier largely surrounded the mountain he stood upon. The snow had melted enough that it was now easy to distinguish the snow from the ice. The dazzling turquoise lake on the piedmont portion of the glacier captured Toq's gaze for a long time, its color and radiance incomparable to anything else he'd ever seen. He saw little sign of wildlife on this relatively small peninsula of bare ground and grass. He walked to the northeast side of the mountain, where he could just barely make out his camp far below. He spotted the little herd of llamas near the edge of the glacier. The glacier clearly sloped down on its way to the prairie, until it finally reached its end. The sound of rushing water and waterfalls echoed up to Toq. A small river of meltwater raced down the glacier on the near side. Having carved a large, blue channel on the surface, it ran across a gently sloped area, then down a steep section where it disappeared into a crevasse.

Toq walked down the mountain toward the glacier for a closer look. About halfway down, not far from the edge of the glacier, he stopped to watch the llamas feeding on the short green plants. They occasionally looked up warily. There were five adults—no young crias. They weren't yet alarmed by his presence, and proceeding, Toq gave them a wide berth. He was watching where he stepped when he heard the sound of hooves running across rocks. He was at first surprised that he had disturbed them and stopped to look. All five ran hard and fast down and across the hill right below him.

"What's happening?"

Then, where the llamas had just been grazing, a large tan bear went sprinting after them. Toq immediately crouched. "Oh, shit!"

With eyes wide open, he tightened his grip on his spear, and his heart pounded. He watched the big, lean bear race across the hillside, just below, with long, fast strides. Completely focused on the llamas, the bear didn't notice him.

The llamas turned and ran straight downhill toward the glacier, and the bear followed. Relieved the bear wasn't after him, he marveled at the speed of the ungainly, long-legged llamas, but he was even more amazed by the speed of the bear. It seemed to be gaining on them. Toq jogged across the hillside to a spot where he could see better. The llamas, in their panic, had split up. Three reached the glacier's edge and turned west, following along the ice, dashing up a hill. The two llamas at the back leapt onto the glacier, and the bear didn't hesitate to chase after them. The animals were silent except for their heavy breathing and the sound of hooves and claws on the crunchy surface of the glacier. The llamas turned to go up the glacier, but the one in the back lost traction, and its rear legs slipped out from underneath, causing it to fall. Its companion raced on while the llama quickly regained its feet. It knew exactly where the bear was—nearly on top of it. The llama darted to the right, heading further out onto the glacier, just missing a collision with the bear, which slid across the ice, spraying crystals into the air as its claws dug in to gain traction, scrambling in pursuit. Toq rooted for the llama, although it occurred to him that had someone been watching him hunt the night before, they might have rooted for the llama, as well.

"The bear has to eat," he said as he watched the drama.

The llama went straight for the glacial stream, and with the bear only two or three strides behind, it planted its back feet and jumped with all its might over the clear water. The bear hesitated, stopping short and sliding across the ice with his front paws out in front to arrest its momentum, vocalizing a frustrated protest. The bear saved itself, but the llama did not. It almost cleared the stream, but the melting ice and running water created an impossibly slippery surface on the other side. Upon landing, the llama's feet slipped out from beneath it, its shoulder landed on the ice bank, and it slid into the fast-moving stream. The current, the large volume of water, and the streambed of ice made it impossible for the llama to get its footing, and it bawled loudly as it was carried quickly downstream.

The bear, beside itself with excitement and indecision, woofed a couple of times as it ran alongside the stream and the struggling llama. It started for the llama a time or two, then backed away and kept running. This caution would not last. With saliva dripping from its jowls, the bear ran ahead and jumped into the stream on top of its prey, pushing the llama down under the water. The current carried both animals downstream. The bear rode on top of the llama, stuck its head in the water, and came back up with the llama's neck in its jaws. Blood fouled the clear water. The bear straddled the llama, hanging on with powerful jaws, and turning itself so it faced upstream, trying to dig its claws into the icy bottom. But even this giant brute could not hold against the power of the water. Toq clearly saw what lay ahead of them. The glacial slope steepened, and the speed of the current increased. Realizing its predicament, the bear let go of the llama and fought to save itself. Toq now rooted for the bear. The dead llama, surrounded by red water, was swept down the slope and disappeared into the crevasse. The bear managed to slow its own progress but couldn't get out of the stream. It lunged for the sides, slipping back each time. The beast roared loudly, then struggled silently in the water until the stream carried it down into the glacier.

All was quiet. Only the sound of rushing water carried up to the man. Toq was stunned. The two animals, there one moment, had completely vanished the next.

"God!" was all he said.

He looked up along the glacier's edge. The four remaining llamas, reunited on the hillside, looked back for the bear and their companion. Spooked, they retreated further uphill.

"That herd has had a rough time lately," he said.

Toq wondered if the bear could have survived the fall into the crevasse. He waited to see if the bruin might crawl out. The temptation to go look into the depths of the glacier was strong, but if the bear had lived and found a way out, Toq would be an easy meal. So, he returned to his camp, where, after considering whether he was safe here, he decided to stay, certain the bear was dead. He felt sorry for the two wasted lives—killed and soon forgotten by an indifferent, unconscious universe.

He spent two days on the mountain, gathering what little dung and sticks there were to burn and retrieving his llama from the bog. He skinned and butchered it, cooking and drying the meat, and working the skin so he could fix his worn goods. He also collected some workable stones to make new cutting blades. The incident between the bear and the llama played out in his mind over and over, but he wasn't concerned about coming across any more bears since there was so little prey. Only the llamas and a passing wolverine provided company. Sunny skies, light breezes, and warm temperatures made for perfect weather, and Toq often interrupted his work to admire the views that surrounded him. He couldn't get enough of them and wondered what was on the other side of the glaciers and mountains. He missed the wolf and the Traveler. He thought about his people and his family.

"I'll see them again," he reassured himself. With each passing day, he grew more certain that there were no other people anywhere in this land.

"You're it, Toq. You're the only one here," he said as he slowly turned, looking in every direction.

• • • •

The morning of the third day, he packed up and left, leaving behind a good portion of the llama.

"Something is going to eat well when I go," he said, thinking of his first encounter with his wolf. Nothing in the wild went to waste.

"Well . . . maybe that bear and llama at the bottom of the crevasse."

He wondered why he felt more sadness for the bear than the llama.

"We're both predators," he reasoned.

He hated leaving this spot with its sublime landscape, but there was more to see. He didn't know where he would go next, but he did know the land would decide where he could or could not go. He left the mountainside and backtracked east, recrossing a creek (Deep Creek) and turning north to go around the front of the glacier. He was back in the land of ponds and lakes, mosquitoes, and multitudes of wildlife. He hadn't traveled far when he came to the high bank of a large, rushing river thick with silt (Two Medicine River).

"No way. Not even going to think about crossing it."

He turned back toward the glacier, thinking he might be able to cross that way, as he'd done before. After walking a little ways, he stood on a hill, with the river raging below on the northside and the glacier looming large to the west. Toq looked at the glacier for quite some time, rising high overhead. Most of its front was ominous, and he couldn't see any easy places to climb up. It was either too steep or breaking apart into giant, jumbled ice blocks and spires. Directly in front, a monstrous, dome-shaped cave opened wide to spew forth the river, which leaped and crashed in waves of white water. Toq couldn't see any way to get up and over from here. Going back south and west, where he'd been able to easily get onto the glacier, would require walking a long way on the ice with no guarantee of safety or success.

"It's decided," he said. "Follow the river until I find a place to cross," and he turned back again to journey east.

Toq spent the rest of the day following the south side of the river. He traveled from the lake region into a drier area. As he moved east, the view of the mountains and glaciers changed. With a little distance, he was now able to see peaks and valleys, and he still felt the strong pull of those magnificent giants. He stared off toward the northwestern peaks, wanting to explore there, but knowing the terrain would be difficult, and besides, there were other lands to see. Animals were plentiful, and it was only a matter of time before he met another predator, so he needed to cross and get out of the river corridor.

•••

Toq spent a nervous night near a creek (Little Badger Creek) that flowed into the river. All kinds of beasts were in the vicinity. He heard raindrops on his shelter halfway through the night.

"Ah, crap," he mumbled, hoping for only a passing shower. He jumped out of bed at first light. A drizzle of rain dampened everything, and the mountains were covered up by clouds, fog, and mist. Toq didn't want to travel in this weather, but he had to get out of this valley.

He packed everything and moved downstream, noticing one of those cheetah-like cats watching him. The river valley widened, and the river slowed and spread out, creating a good place to cross. A large, lone mammoth stood still in the water, just downstream, facing away and occasionally dipping its trunk in the stream. The water wasn't high enough to reach its belly, so Toq was hopeful it would be a shallow crossing. He was not so lucky. He ended up swimming across a section, which carried him a bit too close to the mammoth for comfort. He hauled himself out of the ice-cold water only a stone's throw from the beast and looked back across the river to see the cat walking away. The drizzle turned into a steady rain. Shivering, Toq headed north, away from the river valley. He hiked hard, but his cold, damp body could not generate enough heat to warm him, so he stopped at one of the best spots he could find, and with cold, shaking fingers, he set up his shelter, got out of the rain and his wet leathers, and crawled underneath his robe. He shivered for a while but eventually warmed up, ate some meat, and spent the day listening to the rain.

By the end of the day, the rain had ceased, the clouds broke up, and the mosquitoes attacked. He slept off and on throughout the night and saw a star or two peeking out.

"That's a great sign," he said, hoping for a dry day to come.

CHAPTER 12

Sweet Grass Hills

For three days, Toq hiked northeast across broad flats, down into deep coulees, crossed multiple streams, and enjoyed warm, sunny weather. At times, he was too warm and hiked without his shirt and pants. He considered the breeze a blessing. He tried plant repellants to help with the bugs, which worked some, and he also tried applying some mud, but it was exceedingly uncomfortable and gritty, rubbing his skin raw. He found an old bison carcass, cut off the tail, cleaned it up, and hiked while casually whipping it around his shoulders and back. The biting bugs made it difficult to remain alert and aware of dangerous animals.

Early one morning, he stood on the west side of a broad, shallow valley. A lot of water, glistening in the morning sun, extended far to the north and south, creating a long, narrow lake. Waterfowl were everywhere. Toq cautiously followed some well-worn animal trails southeast, hoping they would lead to a crossing, which they did. He stood on a little bluff and watched as about twenty-five bison waded across a narrow spot separating two wide bodies of water. Even the calves made it across without having to swim. No vegetation grew around the thoroughly trampled crossing, a sign of high traffic. Toq scanned the area for bears, lions, and wolves, certain they would frequent an area like this.

He watched the bison coming his direction. The calves seemed happy, running and jumping onto dry ground. Their hooves weren't muddy—a good indication that the crossing was solid, perhaps gravel. Out of the corner of his eye, he saw something big moving out of an adjacent coulee toward the crossing. An enormous bull mammoth stepped toward the bison, then paused to watch them. The bison were relaxed around the mammoth but kept their distance nevertheless. The herd moved toward Toq. He hurried down off the bluff to get out of their way and avoid the wrath of a bunch of mothers. He watched them wander over the hill, and then he turned back to the mammoth.

This big bull was easily the largest mammoth—indeed the largest *animal*—Toq had ever seen. It was taller than two men stacked one upon the other and had a massive, domed head with ears flapping back and forth. Its back sloped down, and its tail whipped the air and bugs. It was covered in a relatively short coat of reddish-blond fur, having shed all of its long, thick winter hair. Toq didn't know if the bull was aware of his presence until it turned its trunk—which led its eyes, which led its massive head and tusks—toward him. It wasn't alarmed by the human, but it had never smelled or seen one before. It didn't appear frightened or aggressive, and Toq watched with wonder the control and dexterity of the animal's trunk. The tusks looked to be as long as the bull's body—though the tip of the right tusk was broken off.

A deep rumble from the mammoth resonated in Toq's chest, and he took it as a warning to keep his distance. The mammoth turned its head toward the crossing and gracefully, silently moved forward. Patches of dried mud stuck to its back, and there were scars on its head and backside where the hair no longer grew.

"This big, old beast has seen some battles," Toq murmured.

To his amazement, the bull heard him and stopped for a moment to listen. Then, it walked on into the water, where it drank and continued on.

Toq cautiously approached the shoreline, looking around for danger. When the bull was halfway across, Toq stepped into the water and followed the mammoth. A solid gravel bottom covered by a thin layer of silt kept Toq from sinking into mud. In the deepest sections, the water only came up to his butt, and if there was any current at all, he couldn't feel it. He was halfway across when the mammoth exited, and Toq looked back to see that a small herd of horses had appeared on the bluff, watching them.

"Don't come yet," Toq said to them, hoping they would wait for him to get out of the way.

When he reached the far shore, he glanced back to see the horses were gone. He was glad for an easy crossing and glad to see the bull still walking away to the east. Glancing back again, this time he saw a giant, dark-brown (short-faced) bear on the bluff looking across the water at him.

"Damn it! That's why the horses disappeared," he said, worriedly.

In this flat, wide-open land, with no rocky cliffs or trees to climb, animals had evolved to either fight or run. But Toq knew he could not outrun that bear, and to fight would be near suicide. At best, he could stand his ground and, with a lot of bravado, make the bear think twice before attacking.

"Not likely to succeed. . . ."

Toq started after the mammoth, and he looked back to see that the bear had moved down toward the water.

"Son of a bitch! He's coming," said Toq, realizing this could be his end.

He picked up his pace, trying to catch up to the mammoth, unconsciously attempting to find an ally—or comfort, or something, anything. The bear was now in the water. It was big enough to easily look in Toq's eye while standing on all fours. He fought the feeling of panic. He ran, trying to get around the mammoth, to place it between him and the bear. He was catching up to the bull when he glanced back again and saw the bear starting to run even before it was out of the water. Its long legs carried it easily through the shallow stretch, its paws splashing the surface. It reached dry ground and increased its speed, not bothering to stop and shake off. Shining drops of water flew from its legs.

Panic-stricken, feeling like a child, Toq began to lose control of his legs as he tried to run faster, but they buckled, and he fell. He slipped off both bags and raced toward the mammoth with a spear in each hand, his lungs burning. He heard panicked noises coming from his own throat. The mammoth stopped and turned sideways toward him, its trunk raised. Toq looked back, seeing the bear quickly coming up on him, and now knowing it was useless to run, he stopped to face his attacker. To his surprise, the panic vanished, and while fear still crushed his heart, his mind was regaining control.

"Time for the bluff," he panted.

He spread his shaking legs, trying to get a solid base. He watched the bear gallop over his bags, never taking its eyes off the man. Toq's mind raced.

He didn't see it, but when he stopped and faced the bear, the animal had the slightest flicker of hesitation. It didn't know what a human could do, but the bear rarely backed down from anything, and this little man looked like easy prey. The bear was so focused on the man, it hardly noticed the bull mammoth. Toq threw his small spear at the bear, hoping for a lucky strike, and then gripped his big spear with both hands. The small spear bounced off the bear's face, doing no harm, and the bear lunged forward. Reminiscent of the attacking cheetah-cat, Toq let out a yell as he prepared to be crushed. He would try to drive his spear into the front of the animal's chest between its front legs.

The bear was only a couple of strides away—an awesome and ominous mass of muscle and fur. Toq—yelling with all his might—was suddenly drowned out by an ear-piercing, high-pitched call coming from behind him. He glanced back in time to see the charging bull mammoth nearly on top of him. He dove to the side, just missing the tusks. The mammoth charged over the spot where Toq had just been, while the bear—nearly one ton of carnivore flesh—was suddenly face-to-face with ten tons of mammoth flesh. The bear, swerving too late, collided with the mammoth with a loud thud. Both bodies shivered from the impact, and dust and water droplets flew into the air. At the last moment, the bear tried to rise up to strike the mammoth's face, but he couldn't get his front legs up in time. His jaws opened wide, and he bit down on the bull's face at the moment of contact, but the force of the impact and the mammoth's surprising speed were too much for the bear. The bull lowered his tusks, which skipped off the ground and bounced up, the left tusk going under the bear's body, while the broken right tusk went under its chin and neck, lifting it up and driving it backwards.

Knocked back and tossed into the air, the bear tried to land on its feet, but instead rolled across the ground. The mammoth charged forward relentlessly, rolling the bear again, seemingly determined to kill it. Both behemoths roared, and Toq felt the earth shake. He stood up and backed away.

After knocking the bear down again, the mammoth hesitated, taking half a step back, raising its trunk, and bellowing loudly. The bear quickly regained its feet and rose up on its hind legs, roaring and showing its massive fangs. Astonishingly, the bear's head was now almost as high as the mammoth's. The bear tried to intimidate but to no avail. The aggressive, irritable, old bull charged again, shrieking furiously. The bear quickly dropped down on all fours, spun around, and raced away. The mammoth pursued a short distance, but the bear was too fast, and the bull stopped to watch it retreat. Toq was amazed the big bruin was still alive, albeit limping. It looked back a couple of times, but it kept walking away, back toward the water.

Toq mumbled to the bear, "You're not eating me today."

With his heart still pounding, knowing he had just barely escaped, he raised his arms, the spear in one hand, and let out a wordless victory yell. But he quickly shut his mouth, realizing how stupid it was to draw attention to himself.

The mammoth turned to look at him, sniffing the air. Toq started walking away, keeping an eye on the bull.

"Easy, big guy. I'm no threat," he said softly.

Still highly agitated, the bull flapped his ears, raised his tusks, bellowed loudly, and charged. Toq wasted no energy on words, and he ran, again, with all the speed he could muster, the question racing through his mind: *Is it worse to be crushed by a bear or a mammoth?* This time, he maintained control of his head, feet, and legs. He ran, knowing there would be nothing to save him this time, and he expected to be launched into the air or crushed underfoot at any moment. The moment didn't come, but he did hear the mammoth call from well behind. Toq slowed, turned around, and stopped. The bull hadn't chased him far. It watched him for a few moments, then—feeling it had thoroughly established its dominance and space—resumed its trek east, stopping every now and then to listen and sniff the air.

"Lucky. Again. Sooner or later . . . one of these days . . ."

Toq had escaped unscathed—except for the friction burn on his hand from when he'd hit the ground. His knees and left shoulder were grass stained. He caught his breath, then trotted back, nervously, to get his bags. There was no sign of the bear. He figured it might be lying down somewhere, recovering. Toq knew that both he and the bear were lucky to be alive. He retrieved his undamaged small spear and turned to follow the mammoth. The big bull was certainly the most dangerous animal around, but if it didn't kill him, it might keep predators away.

As Toq walked along, he imagined a horrible outcome to his recent encounter: When he'd turned and ducked the mammoth, the broken tusk could've caught him in the flank, its sharp and ragged ends piercing his leather shirt, his skin, his ribs, his lungs, and crushing his spine. The force of the bull's tusk would have bent him awkwardly backward, his head striking the base of the tusk, while his feet flew about unnaturally. He imagined remaining conscious as the bull tossed its head and launched his battered body off its tusk, through the air, and right on top of the bear. He thought of the bear striking him with a heavy paw and biting down on his head. Toq could feel and hear the teeth on his skull. The mammoth would then charge the bear, which would stand atop the man, snapping his arm and shoulder. When the mammoth collided with the bear, it would push the bear off him, and Toq imagined himself barely conscious, taking his last breaths, feeling no pain, and only vaguely aware that he was being crushed to death by the great mammoth.

"My god, you have an awful, morbid imagination. Why do you always have to think up the worst possible scenarios?" he chided himself. "Well, I can answer that. It's because that easily could've happened."

Toq trotted to catch up to the mammoth, staying back and off to the side, careful not to follow directly in its tracks. He tried to remain on hills and ridges, where he had a better view. He didn't know where the bull was going, but it was taking a direct route, not stopping to graze. The prairie grasses were lush and green, but they were shorn close to the ground due to all the grazers. Toq guessed the bull was headed for better feeding grounds or perhaps to find a mate. They passed other mammoths—a small group of younger males, a larger herd of females, juveniles, and calves, all moving east—but none with the bull's single-minded determination. The bull was aware of the man but no longer bothered by him.

They turned to go northeast for a while, but then went directly east again. A large massif towered over the plains to the northeast (West Butte of the Sweet Grass Hills), but these treeless mountains held no glaciers, and only a few patches of snow remained on the higher peaks. A separate conical peak stood tall straight to the east (Gold Butte), and behind it, Toq saw another group of mountains (East Buttes). Along the way, they passed caribou and musk ox, pronghorn and bison, horses and camels, a cheetah-cat, and a small pack of wolves. Crossing the prairie was quick and easy, with only a few small creeks to cross. Toq was in superb condition and had no trouble keeping up with the mammoth; in fact, he often had to slow down so as not to get too close. He could walk all day without tiring; the only thing that stopped him was sunset, since hiking in the dark was too dangerous.

They were straight south of the west butte of these high hills when the day came to an end. The plains had become hillier leading up to the base of the mountains. Toq stood on a rise looking down into a coulee, where "his" mammoth had paused. The bull drank from a creek before kneeling down in the water and rolling over onto its side, rocking back and forth and kicking its legs. It got up on its knees and rolled onto its other side, then stood up, raised its trunk into the air, walked a short distance upstream, and began pulling up grass and brush to stuff into its mouth.

The sun dipped down into a thin layer of clouds hanging over the mountains. With each passing day, the glaciated peaks grew smaller. Now, it was the mountains to the north and the east that loomed large. Toq saw a single bull caribou in the coulee with the mammoth—the only two animals visible within shouting distance. All was quiet except for a few prairie songbirds and the mosquitoes. It wasn't a great place to camp, but he had few options. He planted himself on the hill and hoped nothing would disturb, trample, or attack him in the night.

• • • •

In the darkness, flashes of light awakened the man, along with softly rumbling thunder. Lightning flashed in the sky, illuminating a landscape that disappeared just as quickly back into the blackness, and the thunder—louder this time—shook the ground. Toq rolled onto his back and listened, wondering if he was about to be pounded by strong wind, rain, or hail. He was wary of lightning; it seemed so random and unpredictable. Most people sought shelter or hunkered down behind rocks, but there were some who believed that if they ran around like fools, the lightning would not strike them, figuring it only hit things standing still. Toq took his chances. He lay still and quiet, thinking, *Maybe the lightning won't see me.* The cloud drifted northeast, taking its light show with it. No wind came, and only a few raindrops fell, and Toq could see the mountains alternately lit up or silhouetted. Relieved, he fell back asleep.

• • • •

Nightmares of bears and mammoths disturbed his slumber. He kicked his feet and swung his fist in his sleep, groaning loud enough to wake himself up. His mind found peace when he realized he was dreaming. He opened his eyes and looked out to the east. The sun was just about to come up, meadowlarks were singing, and the thunderclouds were long gone. He was tired, his eyes were puffy, and he felt sore from yesterday's dance with the bear and mammoth. He wanted to sleep more, but he forced himself to get up.

"What a beautiful day!" he said when he looked around, feeling like he lived for these kinds of mornings: birds singing, green grass, flowers, no wind, blue sky, a few puffy clouds, only a couple of mosquitoes. "Fantastic!"

He saw some deer and a coyote in the coulee, but no caribou and no mammoth. He wondered how and if the mammoth slept. He thought he saw his bull heading toward the north hills, now only a fading spot on the huge landscape.

"Should I follow him?" he asked himself. "Nah."

He didn't wish to go north. He'd been looking east to the lone, conical mountain. He ate, packed up, and walked straight for it. The sun occupied the large, flat gap between the mountains.

"What a fine day to be alive," he said, thinking about yesterday, his spirit soaring. He even grinned. The air was sweet with the aroma of grass and flowers. Bees and tiny flies flew from flower to flower, and in some areas, there were hundreds of butterflies: little blue ones, white ones, yellow, orange, brown, spotted, and striped ones.

"The land lives."

He crossed numerous coulees and creeks until, close to midday, he reached the base of the mountain and began to climb steadily up the west side. With dead calm and sun-warmed air, he began to sweat, necessitating the removal of his shirt and pants. As he climbed, he stopped often to admire the view. Bighorn sheep moved out of his way. He traversed wide, grassy slopes and loose, rocky ones. The rocks made quite a clatter and were almost impossible to walk across quietly. The higher he went, the more visible the line of mountains and glaciers were to the west. Below, he could see every coulee, creek, pond, and lake. Even mammoths became small dots. Crows and hawks followed his progress, squawking and screeching at him. He looked across the prairie gap at the mountains to the northwest, and as he went up, they appeared to shrink, and he felt as if he flew with the hawks.

About halfway up the mountain, Toq had a good view north, and on the horizon—on perfectly flat prairie—a white line appeared, extending east and west.

"What is that?" he asked, mystified. "Fog? Snow? Can't really be snow, can it?"

The mountain slopes were steep but easy for him, and Toq reached the barren and rocky peak before the middle of the afternoon. Only a little grass grew there. A good-sized snowdrift clung to the east side. The peak was rounded and oblong, with a nice, although rocky, flat spot. A couple piles of deer and bighorn scat littered the area, and Toq wondered what they were doing up so high. He sat down on rocks covered with orange and green lichen. First, he faced north, where the white-lined horizon was clearer. Now, he was certain that he was looking at a vast, flat glacier covering the prairie.

He looked northwest, where the neighboring mountain group clumped together—its highest peak appearing to be a little taller than this one. He looked east, where a third mountain range rose out of the prairie, more spread out with multiple peaks and valleys. Toq's mountain was different from those other two groups—his being a single, lone peak. The crystal-clear air revealed—far off on the southeastern horizon—a low, sprawling set of mountains, only small blue bumps (Bears Paw Mountains). On the southern horizon, little blue mountains (Highwood Mountains) showed themselves on the other side of an ocean of prairie. To the west, the white mountains from which he had come capped the horizon (Rocky Mountain Front). A sea of green hills and plains, coulees and ridges, and multiple, shiny blue ponds and lakes surrounded the mountain he stood upon. His eyes traced the route he took across the prairie, and he wondered where the bear and the mammoth were now.

His thoughts turned to the wolf, guessing that they'd last seen each other somewhere straight south. The wind picked up a little, making it cooler here than down below, so he put on his leathers and looked at the sky. Thunderheads were definitely building—the clouds growing and thickening, with white, puffy tops and flat bottoms turning dark blue. Smaller clouds cast dark shadows, and Toq was captivated, watching the shadows race across the prairie below.

"Those thunderheads are probably headed my direction," he said, but it was late afternoon, and he didn't want to leave, so he scrutinized the rocky surface of the mountain peak and decided to spend the night here, on top.

He gathered rocks and stacked them on the west side of the little flat spot, creating an L-shaped wall about hip high, then stood back to admire his work. "That'll break the wind. Yeah." He set up his lean-to behind the wall with a view to the east. Excited about spending the night on top of the mountain and feeling relatively safe from predators, he said, "This'll be great." But then he looked to where the storm clouds loomed larger. "Those damn clouds may be a problem," he said. "A normal person doesn't stay on a mountaintop in a storm." He circled the peak, trying to gather enough grass to soften his bed of stone. There would be no fire tonight since there wasn't enough to burn. The sun vanished behind the clouds, and beams of white sunlight streaked through the air above and below the clouds, creating a magical, heavenly scene. It grew darker as the plains below became more and more cast in shadow, while the ice, glowing on the northern horizon, remained bathed in sunlight.

Sitting beside the wall, Toq ate and watched the advancing thunderheads. One giant cloud outgrew the others, its top reaching far up into the atmosphere, its uppermost parts flattening and spreading out—dominating the sky. From afar, its spectacular beauty disguised the darkness and fury growing within and beneath it. Toq saw a couple of thick bolts of lightning, bright as the sun, connect the bottom of the cloud to the earth. It was a strange perspective, looking down on lightning. He ran to the east side of the peak, where he scooped up some snow, put some in his mouth, and carried some back to his viewing spot to watch more of the show.

The cloud began to rain out underneath, obscuring the view below it. Toq heard thunder. The cloud developed a weird, gray, rolling, wall-like front, and everything below it vanished. Lightning flashed inside the cloud, momentarily giving definition to the dark pillows. He looked north; the sun no longer shone on the ice sheet, and though he could not see it, he thought the sun must be close to setting. To the southeast, more thunderclouds assaulted the plains. The big storm looked like it was going to miss him and go around to the south, but it would be close. The wind picked up and the temperature dropped, and Toq crawled under his shelter. He listened to thunder and peeked out every once in a while to see where the storm was going. It grew darker, a couple of raindrops fell, and the wind blew, but the mass of the storm was now to the southeast, headed straight for the mountains to his east.

He reclined beneath his lean-to, listening to the top edge flutter in the wind, watching the thunderstorm bearing down on the mountains. The mountains had been growing darker when suddenly they were alight with a bright, reddish hue. A corner of the cloud blazed pink. Toq rolled out from his shelter and looked west. The prairie was dark, but the sun, glowing like an ember in a fire, slipped into a sliver of clear sky between the clouds and the horizon, gushing its last light of the day.

"So beautiful," Toq said.

The thunderstorm attacked and, like a colossal beast, began swallowing the mountains in wind and rain and dust. Thunder growled. The sun set on Toq and the mountains, but the pink light shone off the cloud, reflecting a strange glow onto Toq's mountaintop. Lightning flashed and lit up the mountain as the storm drifted over. The pink light was replaced by the last vestige of daylight still touching the cloud. The mountains took a big bite from the thundercloud, which moved off, the thunder fading into silence. Now and then, the cloud lit itself up as it floated away over the ice fields.

Toq stood on the mountain with only a faint light remaining in the northwest. There was no sound—no wind, no animals, no birds or bugs. Not even mosquitoes. Silent flashes appeared in the dark, far away. Stars filled the gaps between smaller, scattered clouds, sparkling brighter at this elevation. Toq wrapped his robe over his shoulders as he sat and watched the night sky. The earth below was completely black, while the stars and Milky Way lit the sky above. After a while, the eastern horizon lightened until a nearly full moon popped up and rose in and out of the clouds. The clouds gleamed, and Toq could now see their shadows moving across the moonlit plains. The ponds and lakes reflected the moonlight, adding to the splendor.

"This does not look real," he said.

Toq was wide-awake, feeling a supreme sense of peace, contentment, and safety as he took in the wonders of the universe. Until he heard rocks clattering down the side of the mountain. He focused his attention down the slope, suddenly filled with the dreadful thought that it could be a bear. It was quiet. He reached under his lean-to and picked up his spear, letting the robe fall off. There were more footsteps on loose rock. Toq moved down to a position where he could see better and waited. The heads and curled horns of two bighorn sheep rose above the curve of the slope, followed by a third head.

Toq whispered, "Oh, thank you, spirits."

He stayed still. The rams didn't see or smell him as they came right to the top, where they paused. This was their peak, but something was different; this wall of stone was new. They approached it cautiously, and one of them snorted a couple times. They sniffed the wall, while one walked around to the man's camp, where it looked and sniffed and pawed the ground.

Nervous, they did not stay, lie down, or eat. Instead, they trotted off the north side of the peak and were gone.

Toq walked up to his camp and peered down into the dark, but he could no longer see the bighorns. Only the occasional clatter of rocks could be heard as they moved to their second favorite spot.

"Sorry, fellows, but tonight the peak is mine," he said quietly.

• • • •

The deep croak of a raven awakened Toq. The sun was well above the horizon, and the sky was clear and blue. He looked at the eastern mountains, where a few low-hanging clouds mingled in the valleys below the peaks. It was calm. He got out of bed and stood on the peak, staring down in astonishment at a thick layer of fog covering the earth. It made the little human feel like he was a bird or a spirit looking down from above the clouds. He knew that below the fog, it was dark and gray, but here he stood in the blue sky and sunshine.

Exultant, he raised his arms and disrupted the peace and quiet—an unusual thing for him to do—by calling out as loud as he could, "I am here! *Toquuxla is here!*"

That mountain, which had never before seen a man, now heard him, but the sky absorbed his proclamation, and it did not echo back, and aside from a small bird and a ground squirrel, no other ears heard him, and the universe did not care if he was there. He knew this, but he still reveled in the glory of it all.

In no hurry to leave his mountaintop, Toq lounged, ate some meat and a little snow, and watched the fog melt away in the sun. He plotted his next route. Southeast of his mountain, far below and much smaller, another pointed butte stood alone on the prairie (Haystack Butte). He wondered at this unusual little group of mountains, smack-dab in the middle of all this flatland.

By midmorning, he was ready to go. This time, he didn't dismantle the rock wall, leaving the first and only man-made structure anywhere in this boundless, unpeopled land, thinking he might come back here one day. The wind picked up, and the fog quickly faded with only a bank of it shielding the ice sheet from view. He followed the bighorns' path down, setting a course for the ice fields. It was rougher going down than going up. This side of the mountain was nearly all rock, and he slipped and slid, his feet quickly becoming sore and tired. No animals lived here. He came off the rocky section and hiked down a grassy ridge that led back to the rolling hills and the land of wildlife.

Eventually, Toq walked onto flat country dotted with small lakes, ponds, marshes, and little streams. He followed a small stream running north (Breed Creek), and the farther he went, the richer, greener, and thicker the grass was, making for easy, soft walking—mostly. Large boulders to tiny pebbles, brought from the north and left behind by the retreating ice sheets, littered the landscape. Some hid in the grass, where they rudely interrupted Toq's path. After stepping on too many of them, the pain of stubbing his toe on one culprit caused him to wheel around, point at the rock, and curse it with every obscenity he could think of.

He jabbed at it with the butt of a spear, snatched it up out of the grass, and hurled it away, yelling, "Get out of my way, you son of a bitch!"

Immediately feeling better, he laughed at himself for cursing at a rock, as if the rock could hear him, cared what the man said, or even had the ability to somehow get in the man's way in the first place.

The grasslands attracted an abundance of grazers, and while in some places, the grass was knee high, in other places it had been grazed down low. Toq walked on cautiously, watchful of predators. The sun was descending from its zenith when the fog finally evaporated from the northlands. High, wispy clouds, shaped like feathers, arced across a blue sky, while the northern horizon held a thick white line, with green hills and plains pushing up to it.

"Green, white, blue . . . it's beautiful," he said, trekking north.

He tried to take a direct line, but the beasts of the prairie caused him to weave around. Some moved out of the way when he approached, while others stood their ground or ignored him, and he kept his distance from mammoths, bison, and musk oxen, as well as the big carnivores. He saw the paw prints of wolves and lions in the mud, and as a result, he checked behind frequently. Most of the water was good to drink, clear and not stinking, but he often found that it had obviously been wallowed in—the vegetation trampled and ripped up, the water muddied, and sometimes reeking of urine and feces. Many animals enjoyed a good bath—to cool down and ward off bugs—but mammoths loved it the most. They often took more of a mud bath than a water bath. On the other hand, he also watched many animals—like bison—lie down on the bare ground and roll in the dirt, raising a cloud of dust. They were so covered that, when they walked away, dust wafted off their heads and backs with each step they took.

Near the end of the day, he entered an area with deeper coulees and some badlands, and as he considered setting up camp by a sandstone caprock, he saw three female lions. Two sat on their haunches, looking down into a valley from prominent positions, while another reclined behind them, watching four young cubs wrestling in the grass. They were a good distance away, and although he didn't see any males, Toq knew they could turn up anywhere.

He walked east to get as far away from them as he could. Feeling hot and stressed, he hiked hard, trying to beat the coming darkness. As he walked along the top of a coulee, he periodically came upon large and small sinkholes. Given all the creatures that took shelter in holes, he figured he would be willing to try one. In a deep cut in the side of a coulee, he spotted a couple of dark holes, and he scrambled down to the edge of one. There were no tracks in the hard dirt around it, and he tossed a few rocks into it. Removing his bags, he got on his hands and knees, pointed his spear into the black hole, and slowly poked his head down after it. He saw nothing but blackness. He pushed his spear slowly down until it hit bottom.

"Too deep. I'll never get out," he said to himself.

So he moved down the gully to a second hole that opened onto the side of the hill instead of straight down. Again, he tested it, and though its opening was much smaller, he decided that if he could squeeze into it, he would occupy it. There was even a separate, small hole in the top letting in a bit of light.

These coulees and hills with the badlands had only the occasional clump of grass or brush. The ground in the gully that held Toq's hole was a dry, hardened, light-gray soil, along with brown sandstone and the scattered rocks left behind by the ice sheet. He had to chip away at the opening to make it large enough for him to fit through, and the sun was setting when he crawled into the hole.

"Barely bigger than a grave," he mumbled.

His eyes slowly adjusted to the darkness, and he peered into the dark corners.

"No bats?" he inquired. "Maybe a few spiders, no problem. . . . Toq, I hope this thing doesn't cave in on you."

He pointed his spear toward the exit-opening. If he hunched, he had room to sit up, and he had just enough space to spin around and exit headfirst. The floor was sloped and uneven, and rabbits had hidden and pooped in the hole, but Toq didn't care. This hole could save his life. He lay back with his feet near the entrance, uncomfortable, but it was good enough. He wondered if wolves could get in, or if they would even try. He didn't believe a lion could get to him, but a bear could easily dig him out. He knew he was well hidden, and hiding was his best defense.

"What a way to live, hiding in a hole. From the mountaintop to a hole in the earth." Then, he mumbled, "I am here, I am Toquuxla," mocking himself.

He ate some meat, closed his eyes, and drifted off to sleep. The little cave was quiet, muffling the sounds of the night.

•••••

Toq was unconsciously aware of the dirt wall pressing near his face. His sleepy brain did not recall where he was, and he panicked. The thought screamed in his head, *I'm trapped! I'll suffocate!*

He tried to get up, but his head hit the ceiling. With his hands, knees, and feet, he tried to push up and out—and crying out, he finally fully woke himself up. He lay on his back, sweating, remembering where he was and feeling foolish.

It was nearly completely black inside the hole, but Toq could see moonlight through the little opening above and the exit by his feet. He listened for any sounds but heard only a single cricket chirping just outside. *A comforting chirp,* thought Toq as he slowly fell back to sleep.

•••••

Toq's ears picked up something, and he jolted awake. He lay motionless, straining to hear. Moonlight still shone outside. He rolled onto his side and looked out the opening near his feet. A big, heavy animal jumped down into the gully, its padded feet landing on the hardened dirt, and the creature softly exhaled as the large body touched down. Toq looked up at the little hole and saw nothing, then he looked back down at his exit hole and listened. The beast moved so silently it made him wonder if it moved at all; then, he heard the soft, careful footfalls. A large shadow darkened the ground just outside the exit, and Toq heard the animal sniffing near the upper hole. Then, it jumped down in front of the exit and quickly stuck in its front paw all the way to its shoulder, growling low and soft as it swept the floor to the side wall, completely blocking the light. Toq felt the air move from the swiping paw, and he pulled his feet and legs and bags up to the back of the hole as far as he could go, but the spears were too long to be pulled out of the animal's reach. The paw disappeared, and the head of a lioness peeked in and sniffed. Then, the head pulled out and the other paw came in to sweep the other side of the hole. The lioness was far too large to get through, but she might be able to rip the hole open. Toq gripped his big spear and raised the tip to the ceiling, above the lion's sweeping arm. The small spear got knocked around, but it didn't break.

Toq hardly breathed. The lioness pulled her paw out of the hole, and the face appeared again, trying to see into the blackness. She knew something was in there—she could smell it. She sniffed, then huffed and pulled back. The lioness's breath filled the hole with an awful odor. An irritated growl emanated from outside. Toq smiled slightly. The shadow was suddenly gone, and it was silent again. Now, even the cricket was hiding and quiet. Toq waited and listened for a long time before stretching back out. He pivoted to peer out of the hole, but he saw no sign of the lioness. Still, he feared she was nearby or might come back.

He returned to his sleeping position and whispered, "This could be a long night." He wondered why that large animal would be hunting for things in small holes, telling her, "You should be chasing horses and bison, not rabbits and people."

He rested his head and tried to quiet his heart and mind so he could sleep a little before sunrise. But a small animal came sprinting into Toq's hole, and he jerked and grabbed his spear—but it was useless inside such a cramped space. He tried to make out what it was, finally determining it was a rabbit. Toq was almost out of food, and normally he would kill and eat the rabbit, but the unjust irony of killing this little animal, seeking safety in its own home, in the same place where Toq himself had sought—and found—safety, would not allow Toq to kill. Instead, he welcomed the furry "little buddy." Sometimes he felt kinship with predators, but right now, his kin was this rabbit.

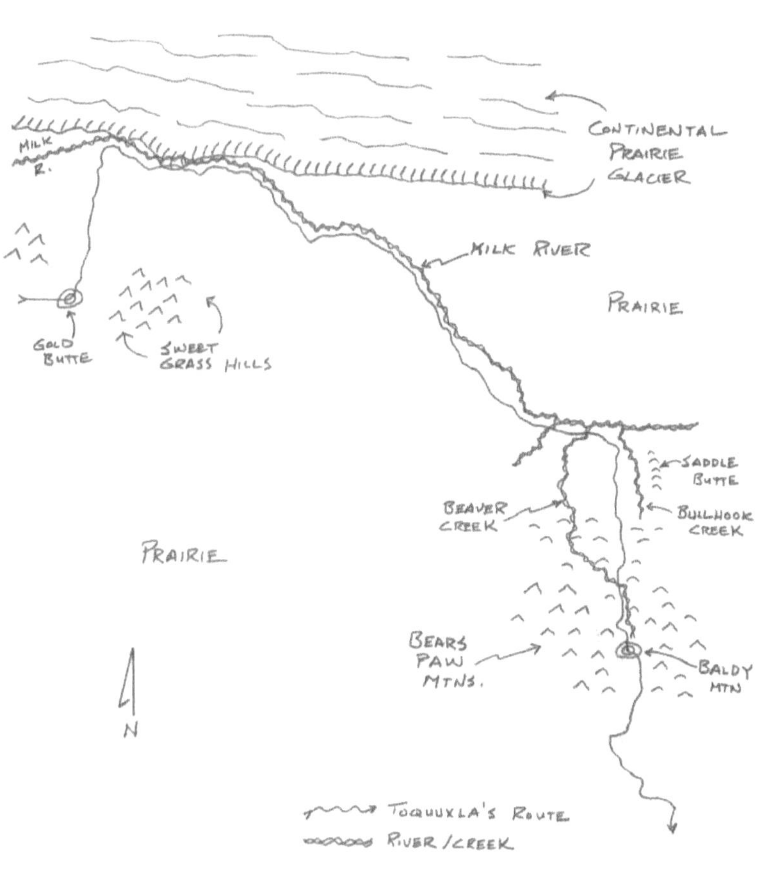

MILK R.
CONTINENTAL PRAIRIE GLACIER
MILK RIVER
PRAIRIE
GOLD BUTTE
SWEET GRASS HILLS
SADDLE BUTTE
BEAVER CREEK
BULLHOOK CREEK
PRAIRIE
BEARS PAW MTNS.
BALDY MTN
N
TOQUUXLA'S ROUTE
RIVER/CREEK

CHAPTER 13

Prairie Glaciers

Toq slept late and had to force himself to get moving. Sunlight shone on the ground outside. He swapped ends and looked out the opening, listening. It seemed to be clear. He pushed one bag out through the hole. Nothing attacked it. He poked both spears out next, laying them just within arm's reach. He left the second bag inside, near the exit, and he squeezed out, headfirst, moving slowly to start and then hurrying to get out of that vulnerable position. Grasping his big spear, he squatted and spun, looking in every direction, but there was nothing there. He gathered his bags and his other spear and immediately, carefully, walked up and out of the gully. He had no desire to stick around. He hiked up onto a large, flat benchland with a good view.

"No lions," he said. At least none within sight.

The sun was bright, and the wind was warm. The three large buttes of the hills stood tall to the south, and a prominent, thickening white line extended along the horizon to the north. Toq hiked and ate at the same time, stopping to drink from the first pond he came upon. He walked toward the ice sheets over flat plains, avoiding the little valleys, nervous about the lions.

The farther north he went, the greater the changes in the grasslands. They were no longer as lush or thick or tall, and the wildlife thinned as well. Toq thought this might work in his favor. Fewer herbivores meant fewer carnivores—he hoped. He reached the end of the big flat and stood at the edge of a badland area that broke up the prairie, sloping down into a wide and somewhat deep valley that held a rushing, muddy river (Milk River). It flowed east, spilling out of its banks and flooding the flat bottom of the valley here and there. On the north side of the valley, the giant, continental glaciers overlaid the land, guarding whatever lay beyond.

Toq had watched them grow larger as he approached. They extended as far as he could see to the east and west. Green and brown grasses spread almost to the base of the ice. Getting up onto the glacier looked easy if one could get across this river. Giant blocks of ice lay like islands on the plains, cut off from the main mass of the glacier; some had melted down to mere bumps, while others loomed tall as any hill. A little downstream, the thick ice extended farther into the valley, where the river ran along its edge, cutting into the ice and leaving a cliff face high enough to kill a man if he fell from it. Most of the ice glistened white and blue in the sun, but dirt and rock—even large boulders—peppered much of the interior of the glaciers and the ice cliffs hanging over the river.

Only a few animals could be seen, and even birds were fewer here. One large mammoth slowly made its way down the valley bottom.

"Huh, another loner," he said.

He decided to go east. He hadn't seen any wolves, lions, or bears, so he felt somewhat relaxed, and he needed to hunt. He worked his way along the south side of the river valley, watching for any opportunities.

After a while, he went down to the edge of the riverbank. The water ran swift and deep, and it carried a load of silt and mud, making it the color of the earth. He swallowed grit when he drank from it. Large streams of water flowed off the ice, cutting into hillsides before merging with the main river.

Toq walked along the river. It was too wide, too fast, and too danger-ous to try to cross. The body of a small horse bobbed along in the current, too far out to safely retrieve. Just ahead, another ice cliff towered over the river. Two large, dark eagles perched on its edge. Suddenly, a thunderous cracking rose above the noise of the river. The eagles gracefully leapt off the ice and flew away as the cliff collapsed. The near side shattered into small chunks and fell into the river, while one large tower tilted out and crashed down with a gigantic splash. A large wave—as tall as a mam-moth—pushed out, crested, and broke on the opposite bank, momentarily flooding the adjacent land. The wave rolled rough and turbulent upstream toward Toq, seemingly changing the direction of the river's flow. Toq trotted away, watching the water, until he was sure that the river's current would overpower the wave and push it back. Soon, the wave disappeared, leaving only puddles where it had flooded.

Only a large chunk remained stranded on the south bank, and down-stream, a thick slurry of ice chunks was being swiftly carried out of sight around the bend. In the river itself, there was no evidence of the massive ice fall. He looked up at the new cliff face, many lengths back from where the old cliff had stood. The water began cutting into the base of the new front immediately. The two eagles circled high above. Toq walked downstream, where he noticed the wave had carried much further out from the river, leaving pieces of ice here and there.

The ice fall and the wave had left something else: a few dead fish and a large one still flopping around in the mud. Toq picked up the live one, carried it to the river, and threw it back in.

He gathered three dead ones and said, "What a lucky break." These were the first he had gotten his hands on since leaving the village, but they were different than any he had seen before. The stripes, spots, fins, snouts, whis-kers, and colors were different. They were as long as his arm and fat. He ran his small spear through their gills and carried them up a hill at the edge of the valley. No predators were within view, but his eye was drawn to a dark object farther downstream. Two large wings fanned out from atop the object.

"What's that? Those eagles found something, and it isn't fish," he murmured.

He took a moment before deciding it was worth a look. He carried the fish with him over to where the eagles were busy tearing into flesh. They looked up at his approach, and then took off, leaving their find behind. It was the small dead horse he had seen floating down the river.

"Lucky Toq," he congratulated himself.

The little horse was probably only a month or two old. It was partially covered in dirt and mud and had light-brown fur, a black mane and tail, and faint black stripes on its legs. The eagles had ripped open a spot on the rear flank, and Toq bent down and sniffed the open wound.

"It's good," he declared.

He picked up the fish, grabbed the foal's front leg, and dragged the body up to the hilltop. He took a long look around. A flat plain stretched off to the south. He was in an open, exposed place, but he saw no large predators, so he quickly gathered dried grass and dung. He carved up one fish and about half of the foal, and then he made his fire. He used the horse's ribs and piles of stones and bones to suspend the meat over the smoky flames, keeping a constant eye out for intruders. He saved the foal's skin to patch up his lean-to, but he discarded all the innards because they were quickly going bad. Flies pestered him terribly, and the constantly changing wind caused the smoke to sting his eyes.

As the sun made its way down to the horizon, he decided he had better get going. A coyote approached from downwind and sat a little ways away, watching intently as Toq crammed food into his mouth and bag. He packed up and walked east, and the coyote scurried out of his way, circled around, and boldly went after the fine pile of food left behind. Toq glanced back at him, reminded of his wolf, but he didn't believe the coyote would behave the same way. He walked on, and when he looked back at the coyote again, he saw smoke blowing in the wind. He thought for a moment, then hurried back to his fire. He made an aggressive move toward the coyote, and reluctantly, it backed away, snarling. Toq picked up the foal's rear leg and used it to stamp out what remained of the fire. The last thing he wished to worry about was a wind-driven grass fire racing his way. Satisfied that the fire was out, he tossed the leg at the coyote, which jumped out of the way, and he resumed his journey east.

Toq hiked steadily, following the river valley, staying on hilltops as much as he could. The lone peak he had camped atop was out of view, but he could still see the west buttes. Wildlife was scarce, and yet some living creature, large or small, could always be seen. Compared to some places, he now hiked across an uncrowded expanse.

The sun neared the horizon, and he decided to take the next safe camping site he came across. He walked into a deep coulee and up the opposite side, then followed a ridge out toward the river for a better view of the valley. The first thing to catch his eye was the big, red-blond mammoth in the valley bottom, the same one he had seen earlier. His gaze slowly took in whatever there was to see of this magnificent and beautiful land. The river rushed in from the west, ran against and along the ice mass—where it created another white cliff—then vanished beneath the ice, while the glacier spread across the valley all the way to the south side like a giant blanket.

"Awesome," said the man.

The sound of the raging river came from the west; the east was still and quiet. Toq wanted to dwell here for a while. Little was left of the day, so he weighed the risks of camping on the point or down in the coulee. There were no sinkholes to hide in, but he had seen no killing predators all day, so he chose the point, and the sun set just as he finished putting up his lean-to. The ice glowed against the darkening sky in the east where the earth's shadow spread up overhead, the deep purple turning black.

In the dusk, Toq could just make out the form of the mammoth down below, seemingly content where it was. He made no fire, only watched the stars come out, listened to a coyote, and crawled into bed. He thought about the lions, knowing he would be killed right there if they found him.

So what? he thought to himself, weary of being on constant vigil. *Tomorrow, I will be careful again.*

And he slept well.

••••

Nothing disturbed him during the night except a mouse. He awoke early to a clear sky, with a couple of bright stars struggling to maintain their prominence in the growing light. The occasional rumble and crack of ice breaking off the cliff face across the valley were the only sounds to be heard above that of the river. Even the birds were silent. Toq dressed, checked around, and ate quickly. The sun poked up above the glaciers by the time he'd finished packing up his camp. The mammoth, to his surprise, was still in the same spot, and he wondered if there was something wrong with it.

The first thing he wanted to do was to check out that mammoth. So, he walked down into the valley and slowly, deliberately approached the huge creature, thinking, *This animal sure looks familiar.* The mammoth stood in a small patch of tall grass, slowly ripping up big clumps with its trunk. It swished its tail and occasionally flapped an ear. A little brown bird hopped across its back, pecking at bugs. A path of destroyed vegetation marked the mammoth's progress through the field. Toq kept his distance, studying the mammoth. There was no wind—not even a breeze—and yet the mammoth stopped eating, turned its massive head, trunk raised, ears out, and looked in his direction. Every mammoth had a different curve to its tusks, but the broken right tusk set this mammoth apart.

"Well, what do you know?" Toq said, finally recognizing the bull that had saved him and then nearly killed him. His heart beat a bit faster, knowing this mammoth had an aggressive disposition. He stepped back and knelt down, unsure if he should walk away, run away, or just look small and be calm. The mammoth stared at him, strained to listen, sniffed the air, and then moved its huge body a few steps closer.

Even if that giant is just curious, it could still turn bad, he thought.

The mammoth stopped. It appeared to relax and resumed eating. Toq relaxed, too, but he stayed put.

"I ought to name you," he mumbled.

It dawned on him that the traveling mammoth with the broken tusk was like his friend with the broken tooth, the Traveler. Both were comfortable being alone, but the Traveler had never tried to kill him.

"Old Busted Tusk. There's your name. You like it? Original, one of a kind, huh? Ya, you don't care what I call you."

Busted Tusk kept an eye on him and carried on eating. Toq sat and watched the animal until he had enough of the flying bugs around his face.

Busted Tusk turned and worked his way toward the glacier, mostly ignoring Toq now. Toq slowly stood, then cautiously circled around out ahead of the mammoth and marched directly to the foot of the glacier.

As with the mountain glaciers, there was a narrow zone around the edge of the ice where the vegetation changed, and then, right near the ice, there was bare rock and ground and mud. He wondered what was under all that ice.

He walked along the edge going east, staying out of the mud, ponds, marshes, and streams of water running down off the ice. He came upon a hairy brown beast frozen in the ice right at the base of the glacier. Only now, after hundreds or thousands of years, buried and carried along inside the ice, had the beast been revealed. Some bloody bones and a little fur stuck out into the sunlight. Toq couldn't figure out what kind of animal it had been.

He asked, while thinking about the bear and the llama in the crevasse, "So how did *you* come to be encased in the glacier?"

He walked on until he found an easy slope up onto the ice. Grit stuck to the bottom of his moccasins gave him enough traction to climb up. The glacier was pretty flat on top, but walking was treacherous on the slick meltwater, and it quickly soaked through his moccasins, numbing his feet. He went north a ways, but the sun on the ice was blinding and surprisingly hot. He went east until he came to a ditch in the ice, full of water streaming off the glacier. He closed his eyes for a moment, and tears welled up to fight the burning.

"All right, that's enough," he said, and he followed the stream down, shielding his eyes as best he could.

He reached the edge, but it was too high and too steep, so he had to go back west to find an easier, gentler slope back down.

"Damn it! This was a bad idea, you dummy."

Down on the ice-free hill, a small group of caribou watched him. Still a ways away from where he'd climbed up, and beginning to feel desperate, Toq fell a couple of times on the rock-hard ice. The first time he fell, he said nothing. The second time, he landed hard on his elbow and tailbone and hollered in pain, "Augh, shit!"

He stood slowly and checked that he hadn't broken his spearpoint, then rubbed his elbow and backside, trying to alleviate the pain. Continuing on, he approached a place to descend—but soon, the slope steepened. It was rough and uneven, but a narrow ribbon of blown-in sand had melted into the ice, and carefully, he followed it down. When he reached the last little section—much steeper and now free of sand—he saw there was an open marshy area at the foot of the glacier. With burning and watering eyes and bruised, tender bones, he inched his way down—but soon, there would be no more inching, only sliding and accelerating into the marsh. He worried about losing control and tumbling down, breaking a spear or a bone. He inched down a bit more, and then sat on his butt, preparing to slide, the cold, melting ice soaking through his trousers. He pressed his fingers into his eyeballs to try to squeeze out the tears and wondered if he could chop steps into the ice with his stone hand ax.

"No way to do that," he mumbled. Angry with himself, he said, "You idiot. You have to think before you do something this stupid."

His tailbone throbbed; sliding down on his butt would be painful. He dug into a bag and pulled out his bedroll, which he straddled, skin side to the ice. It offered a bit more friction. He arranged the items in his bags to minimize damage, then set them on his lap. He threw his small, indestructible, antler-point spear as far as he could down the slope and off to the side, listening to it bounce off the ice and into the water. Through blurry eyes, he noticed that Old Busted Tusk had walked to the edge of the marsh.

Toq knew he needed some good fortune, because once he started sliding, he would have no control over his direction or speed. He grasped his large spear in his right hand with the point uphill, the shaft resting against his shoulder, and gripped the front of his bedroll with his left hand. He leaned into his bags on his lap and began hopping his bedroll downhill. He successfully made it down several body lengths before beginning to slide. As predicted, there was now no stopping the slide, and Toq bounced down the slope, hair flying, eyes streaming. His bags flew off his lap and were dragged behind him by their straps. He held onto the bedroll, leaning left and right, while holding his spear up above the ice. He hit a bump that threw him off the bedroll, and he hurled his spear down into the marsh, butt end first. Having lost control, he spread his hands behind him, fighting to keep his feet in front, and nearly free-fell the last bit into the shallow marsh. His feet shot deep into the mud, and his torso and head lurched forward into the water in an awkward, unnatural way.

Water and mud flew in every direction, splattering the glacier foot as well as Toq's face. He struggled to push himself up out of the mud. He hadn't struck any rocks, but the icy mud held his feet fast. He reached for a bag, still somehow strapped over his shoulder, and he pressed it down into the mud to try and gain some leverage so he could straighten up. His feet, legs, and hands were in pain from the glacier-fed water. Once upright, he placed his bags in front of him and to his side, so he could lean on them as he tried to free his legs. As he struggled, he saw both spears, near each other, in shallow water; the small one floated, and the large one stood upright, pointing to the sky. He lay to the side to try to get pressure off his feet and work them back and forth, until, finally, they were free. He stuffed his muddy bedroll in a muddy bag and leaned forward on his bags as he tried to keep from sinking too deep in the mud. The mud—an icy, slippery gumbo— stuck to his feet. He attempted to move quickly to retrieve his spears, but being up to his knees in mud and water, it was slow going. Upon reaching them, he looked around for the nearest way out. He laid his spears flat in the watery mud for leverage and pushed for dry ground. He pulled himself along on all fours, losing feeling in his legs and hands.

The mammoth watched as Toq got out of the water, but he still had mud to get across, and this mud—although warmer and not quite as wet—clung to his feet in globs, accumulating like balls on the bottoms of his feet, making walking even more difficult. He tried to scrape the mud off, but his feet quickly globbed up again. He finally reached dry ground and grass, where he fell onto his back, absorbing the warmth of the sun. After a few moments, he tried to wipe the mud off his moccasins and found that one of them was gone.

"Shit."

Rubbing his feet and legs, he tried to get blood flowing in them again. As feeling returned, throbbing, intense pain came with it.

Toq squeezed his hands, and tears came to his eyes as he cried out, "Aggh! Shit!"

The pain subsided, but his eyes still burned. He cleaned off his muddy hands in the grass as best he could and rubbed his eyes, then he took a blurry look around. The only animal he saw was Old Busted Tusk, slowly walking around the marsh toward him.

"Gotta move, Toq," he said.

His hands and feet still felt tender and swollen, but he stood up and groaned as his knee and back complained.

"Gah! In one morning, you went from a healthy youth to a crippled old man!"

The mud-covered man slowly, gingerly, picked up his mud-covered bags, spears, and single moccasin and walked barefoot through the grass, wincing at the pain in his knee.

He limped to a small stream, where he cleaned his body and belongings. Then, he spread everything out to dry in the sun. No large beasts were nearby, and Old Busted Tusk was at least momentarily out of sight. Toq's hands and feet recovered fully, but his eyes still burned, and they were sensitive to the intense sunlight. While his back was sore and stiff, it was his knee that worried him the most, and he kept trying to bend and flex it, but it hurt to stand on and it was becoming stiff. Most men were injured doing stupid things—usually fighting or hunting—but this was the first time Toq had injured a joint like this.

Some old guys carried their injured, unrecovered bodies with pride and honor, while others had warned him, "Be cautious, Toq. If you hurt yourself too badly, you will never be the same." Young men often challenged one another to do risky and dangerous things. Toq had avoided most of these unwise actions, until now, and now he didn't even have a witness to his daring and foolish escapade.

"Just as well," he said, feeling exceedingly humbled.

Now Toq felt even more vulnerable, concerned about his ability to run and hunt. He limped around the area until he found a spot to camp, not far from the little stream. It was not yet midday, but he was going nowhere. He set up camp and lay under his shelter, out of the hot sun, throughout most of the afternoon. He dozed, ate, listened to flying bugs and cracking ice and, when he got up, limped to the stream, where he applied mud to his knee. He tried to find material to burn and plants he could crush into a poultice. He didn't know if mud or a poultice would help, but he had to try.

He contemplated different outcomes, in which he'd broken a leg sliding off the glacier, or landed on his spear, stabbing himself in the neck, and he sighed, "Dwelling on the worst again."

Late afternoon found Toq sitting outside his shelter tending to his knee, sweating a bit in the sun, and looking down the gully at Old Busted Tusk, who now lingered at the bottom where it opened into the river valley. The big mammoth barely moved. Toq was concerned. He looked at his small pile of combustibles, painfully aware it wouldn't last half the night. He doubted a little fire would stop a mammoth. The wind shifted to a northwesterly breeze. Clouds appeared in the west and north, and by early evening, the sun was gone. The breeze grew into a strong, steady force, and the temperature dropped to where Toq had to put on his clothes and crawl beneath his shelter. By late evening, the entire sky had turned gray, and rain fell on his lean-to. Only a couple of growls of thunder came with this storm. Toq pulled his fire materials in under the shelter and contemplated starting a fire. Small pellets of hail began pouring down, piling up on the ground, and Toq slipped under his robe, thankful that it had dried in the hot sun.

"Fire can wait," he said as he watched the downpour.

The hail stopped, the rain stopped, and by dark, the wind let up a little. He never did bother with a fire, falling off to sleep, snug, warm, and dry under the fur, hoping Busted Tusk would stay away.

••••

Toq slept uncomfortably with his throbbing knee, aching back, and tender elbow and tailbone. He became chilled a few times, and the flapping and fluttering of his lean-to in the wind roused him throughout the night. He didn't hear rain, and when he rolled over to look outside, he saw nothing— no moon or stars. An ambient whiteness came from the ground in front of his shelter, and he reached out his hand, sticking it into snow. He scooped up a little and put it in his mouth.

"Oh, that'll make everything easier," he said sarcastically.

He slowly sat up and felt around the edges of his shelter to make sure snow was not blowing in and covering his stuff. He brushed off some spots and cursed the wind. It was damn cold out, and it shocked his body, which had sat in the sun sweating the day before. He lay back down and pulled the furs up over his head.

• • • •

The wind died down, bringing calm and quiet, and the man slept. Something big walked by the little shelter, the snow softly crunching under the footsteps. Toq's eyes popped open, and he strained to hear. He slowly turned over to see a gray and white world with large flakes of snow falling straight down from the sky. Snow piled knee-deep around his shelter and caused his lean-to to sag badly, nearly collapsing. Toq discovered he was in a hole with hardly enough room to move, insulated by the snow from the night's cold wind.

Two more soft footsteps came up next to his shelter, and a deep, gentle rumble came from massive lungs and vocal cords. More footsteps, and the tusk appeared with the muscular trunk following right behind, audibly sniffing the air. Old Busted Tusk towered above Toq in his hole. Snow lay on top of the mammoth's head and stuck to its hairy trunk, ears, face, and eyelashes. An eye peered down into the hole, and both ears reached out to listen, but Toq's attention was focused on the tusk and trunk. Busted Tusk swung a tusk over the top of the shelter, just brushing the snow piled on top. The broken tusk came into view, and the end of the trunk explored the long, narrow opening where Toq hid. He was only an arm's length from the sniffing, wet, fingerlike nostril that probed the outside of the hole, not reaching inside, showing the beast's cautious nature.

Toq remained still and calm, watching Old Busted Tusk. He knew those tusks could easily wipe away his shelter, the trunk could pick him up and toss him into the air, the feet could trample and crush him, and there would be nothing he could do about it. His fate was completely in the mind of this gigantic animal. But Toq had the feeling that the mammoth was simply curious about this little man in the hole in the snow. The proboscis swept left and right along the opening a couple times, then the long tusk swung back over the lean-to, and Busted Tusk, momentarily satisfied, proceeded past the camp and up the coulee. Toq looked out to watch him go. With snow accumulating on the mammoth's sloped back, he appeared all the more magnificent. Old Busted Tusk stopped a short distance away, lifted his tail, and dumped a huge mass of feces into the snow.

Toq chuckled, "Oh, well, shit, there goes your magnificence. Are you leaving me a gift or a message?"

Old Busted Tusk disappeared in the falling snow, and Toq forced himself to get up. His knee and back were a bit better, but even with the snow letting up, he knew he would be going nowhere. He put on his one moccasin and wrapped his other foot in a piece of horse hide, then he cleared the snow off his lean-to and tightened up the supports. The snowstorm ended, and Toq looked up the coulee to see Busted Tusk sweeping snow away with his tusks to get at the grass underneath.

Toq turned to his tasks for the day, which entailed making a new moccasin, making snow goggles, and perhaps making a fire. The ground beneath the snow was warm, creating a slushy bottom layer.

He complained mightily about the weather. "Hot and sweaty yesterday. And now winter, in the middle of summer."

Despite this storm, he was certain warm days would follow, but he wondered if summer snowstorms might be common near these huge glaciers.

Turning optimistic, he told himself, "You needed the rest and recovery, anyway, and now there are no mosquitoes."

But he knew they would return with a vengeance once the snow melted. The sun did not shine at all that day, and the snow shrank only a little.

• • • •

By the third day, Toq was impatient to leave. His knee still bothered him, and he limped a little when he walked, but he was nearly out of food, there was nothing dry to burn, and he was anxious about predators. The sun had melted most of the snow the day before, so the unbelievably white landscape was once again turning into green grass and mud. He hadn't seen Old Busted Tusk in a couple of days.

Toq had too much time to think while he was confined to camp. He'd known the risks he was taking when he set out upon this journey, but the abstract was now reality. Close calls and what-ifs plagued him. If he *had* broken a leg, he probably would have died. If he had found a way to survive, alone, how long could he go? He would get old, probably crippled, with nobody to help him. And if he lived alone for years, then showed up at some village, hoping they would take him in, when he had contributed nothing to their survival, well, they might just consider him a burden.

"That probably wouldn't work," Toq guessed. "And even if they did graciously bring me in, it wouldn't be fair to them."

He liked the life he was living, but he believed he would need to find people again, one day, while he was still young enough to hunt.

He packed up and hiked through a wet, muddy land. Old Busted Tusk's footprints showed he was going south toward the mountains. Toq felt drawn to the big mammoth—he wanted to be around him, to watch him, to study him—but the river pulled him east along the valley and its accompanying ice fields. A brilliant and pure-white layer of fresh snow covered the dirt and rocks blemishing the glacier. Today, the man's emotions were high, but two days ago, they'd been low; most of the time he loved this place, this journey, but other times, he hated it—the weather, the wind, the bugs, the dangers.

"Seems my happiness has a lot to do with the weather. Sun's out, I'm happy. Sun's gone, it's dreary, dark, cold, not so happy." This fact bothered him.

His knee grew more sore as the day wore on, so he stopped well before he normally would have. Along the way, a rabbit and a grouse—common fare—unwittingly gave themselves to the man.

• • • •

A warm, sunny morning greeted Toq and the prairie. Most of the snow had disappeared into the earth and streams, leaving only a few snowdrifts on hillsides. The mountain-hills, now to the southwest (East Butte of the Sweet Grass Hills), were still white, but melting off quickly, while the glaciers remained blanketed in the fresh snow. Toq hiked into the sun, arriving at the top of a hill, where he looked across a wide, shallow valley full of caribou. White and tan animals of all sizes—males, females, and this year's young—amassed in a large herd, grazing, slowly moving north, occasionally bellowing.

"Wow," Toq exclaimed, sweeping his gaze right and left, stopping on a small pack of wolves down toward the river. The five wolves casually trotted along the perimeter of the herd, causing a wave of caribou to move away. The herd—extending all the way to the river—was as far north as they could go, their passage blocked by the great ice sheet. Toq looked for other large predators, but seeing none, he began walking straight through the heart of the herd to the east. The wolves were going north. Toq moved slowly and steadily, thinking that if an animal presented an easy kill, he would take it. But the nearest caribou scattered, and an empty space formed around him as he moved. Toq sat down on a boulder for a while to see what they would do. They watched him and resumed eating but remained a long spear throw away. Females and their calves moved farther away. The females' antlers were small and still growing, while the males' were nearly full size and covered in velvet. The animals showed no aggression toward him. Eventually, Toq stood up and continued on.

"I'd sure like to eat one of you. If I didn't have a bad knee, I think I could get you," he said, pointing with his spear. "Or you, or you."

One bull snorted at him, and Toq stopped talking.

He crossed through the herd, scaled a hill, and looked back to where the wolves were harassing a group of caribou. To his surprise, a large turquoise-blue-gray lake filled the river valley to the north and east, bounded by glacial ice. The glacier dammed up the river downstream. Water filled the coulee coming from the south like a miniature fjord. A few waterbirds floated on the lake, but not many. Toq walked around the bay and stood on a hill looking over the lake dotted by numerous little icebergs. The glacier reached almost to his hill. The river raged through a deep channel between the hill and the glacier, and chunks of dirt rolled off into it from one side while chunks of ice broke off on the other. Toq easily tossed a rock across the chasm, watching it land on the ice. Just downstream, a waterfall, pure and clean and clear, poured off the top of the wall of ice and into a misty cloud hovering over the rushing, muddy river.

Toq marveled at the sight, and staring off downstream, it appeared that the glacial ice filled the river valley for as far as he could see, with the river cutting its path around the southern edge, making its escape.

Toq looked north across the never-ending white expanse and wondered, "What's up there? Does the ice go on forever? Is there anything on the other side?"

It bothered him that he would never know. Seeing no animals on the ice, he figured it was probably the safest place to camp—but he wasn't about to repeat his last mistake.

He continued east, where gradually, the ice sheet pulled back from the river valley, leaving room for the water to wind and divide itself into multiple channels. The valley began to angle to the southeast until, by the end of his day, upon reaching a fairly large coulee (Kennedy Coulee), Toq could see that, in spots, the glacier retreated from the valley completely. His knee, feeling less sore, allowed him to hike for nearly the entire day. Plenty of daylight remained, but he decided to find a place to camp early at the edge of the coulee, and he hunted small game.

• • • •

The next morning, Toq walked down into the steep-walled coulee, spying more of the stone-bones embedded in the ground. It was an interesting badland area with brown sandstone formations, steep gray hillsides with no vegetation, deep side coulees, and lots of rocks. Numerous tracks revealed places where even the surest-footed animals had slid on the slick mud. Toq stepped carefully, knowing he couldn't afford to reinjure his knee.

Although they left scat and tracks and shed antlers, bones, feathers, and hair, there were no animals around. Toq looked in every direction and saw nothing alive, nothing moving.

"A beautiful but dead landscape without the animals," he said, knowing they weren't far. "It's so unusual to not see anything. It's empty and lonely without them."

He proceeded east, and the serpentine river half-filled the valley bottom, flooding large swaths in shallow wetland marshes. Crossing the river and valley appeared to be impossible, and Toq saw no sign of animal crossings. He moved on, hiking across flat plains, dropping into coulees, rising back up onto hills, and seeing large animals again.

"Good to see you!" he said to some massive and menacing long-horned bison, which grunted in irritation. He felt comforted by the belief that these—and all the other superb animals—would always be around, somewhere.

As he moved farther southeast with the river, making a greater separation from the ice sheet and leaving it behind, he came to place where, for the first time, Toq saw big animals, bison, pronghorns, and horses on the other side of the river. He stopped to camp on an open plain above the river, and in the distance, a line of blue mountains stood on the horizon (Bears Paw Mountains), and the river looked to be headed for them.

• • • •

The warm, dry, and sunny day inspired Toq to rise early. Wildlife was abundant on both sides of the river. After the latest snow, the grasses seemed greener than ever. Toq felt a little sad as the prairie glaciers faded from view.

He was just thinking about how he hadn't seen any lions or bears recently when he glanced up to see a bear's massive head looking down at him from the hill he himself was walking up. Toq froze, and the two looked at each other in surprise and uncertainty. Convinced the bear would attack, he said nothing, looked away briefly, and took a step back. Then the bear turned aside and vanished behind the hill. Toq quickly moved along the hillside away from the bear, fearing it was stalking him. He gradually came up on top of a bench and looked around—no bear. He angled around to where he could see into the river valley and spotted the bear halfway down the hill.

"Itshla! Too close!"

The bear looked back at the man, turned, and stood on its hind legs to get a better view. Toq couldn't help but be impressed by the size of this fearsome beast. The bear sniffed the air, dropped back onto all fours, and walked slowly away down the hill. Toq relaxed, sat on the hill, and watched the bear amble up the valley, sniffing the ground and looking around. It looked back once but without any interest in the man.

"Huh," said Toq. "I guess not all bears are obsessed with eating me. That was a good bear; at least he was good today. Thankfully."

Toq hiked across beautiful green prairies, where the wet snow and warm sun combined to give the land a second spring. Flowers—different from the bloomers a full moon ago—decorated the land. The walking was easy, he felt nearly completely healed from his fall off the glacier, and he covered a lot of ground quickly.

Wildlife grew more abundant, too, as the rich lands fed many thousands of bellies. As a general rule, grazers and browsers consumed grass, forbs, and brush, while carnivores ate grazers and browsers. But Toq had seen the occasional herbivore eating another dead animal, and he had seen carnivores eating plants and berries. Humans are omnivores, eating both plants and animals, but on this trip, Toq had eaten almost exclusively meat. He gathered a few plants or roots here and there, thinking that variety was good for him and that this was the best time of year to harvest certain plants, but he looked forward to the season of berries the most—especially the sweet blueberries growing in the low brush.

He marched until he came upon a very wide, slow spot in the river. It split into multiple channels, going around little hills and ridges in the valley bottom, forming islands. Birds ruled these islands, finding safety from most predators—except those that were strong swimmers or could fly. A hawk, a falcon, or an eagle occasionally swept in to pick off an unfortunate duck, gull, or gosling, sending flocks fleeing in great commotion, and then, gradually, the little islands would return to a less frenetic chatter. A group of about ten mammoths grazed near the river in a flat spot at the opening of a coulee. The coulee's sloped, green hillsides were speckled with wildflowers and were interspersed with steep, barren ground and dark-brown sandstone. Red, pink, black, gray, and white boulders, left behind by the glaciers, bright-green mosses, and yellow, orange, and green lichen added to the mosaic. Grass on the hillsides and atop the prairie had been grazed down in most places. But the mammoths stood in thick grass up to their bellies.

These were the first mammoths Toq had seen since Old Busted Tusk. It was a group of females with two young bulls and one very small calf. The little calf nearly vanished in the deep grass, but the whole herd either checked on her regularly or stood right by her side. Tusks gently nudged the little one, and sometimes she protested. Trunks wrapped around large bundles of grass and ripped them up out of the mud, swishing them around a little, and then swinging them into the mouth. Toq thought the beasts manipulated the mass in such a way that the muddy ends were discarded or spat out—although it looked like some simply ate the whole thing, mud and all.

Toq arrived at a place where the river went around the east side of a prominent hilly point while water flooded a low valley on the west side with a large lakelike bay. Sunlight glistened off the water with little waves sparkling and flashing.

"Beautiful," Toq said as he passed by.

After reaching the south end of the bay, he continued over a low divide and into what appeared to be a shallow secondary valley full of a series of small lakes (Chain of Lakes). The water here was clearer than the gray, silty river water, and as a result, there were more animals here.

"Too much activity," Toq said, and he camped out on the flat prairie, far from hills and valleys, rivers and lakes.

The cloudless sky showed no sign of coming storms, so Toq didn't bother to set up his lean-to. He made no fire, either. He watched the sky and surroundings until it was too dark to see well. No moon lit the night sky. The wind died, and in the calm and quiet, Toq lay on his back and stared up into a sky thick with stars. The sky had always been an endless source of wonderment and speculation for Toq and his people. His mind wandered to his people, to the mammoths, to Old Busted Tusk, to his wolf, to the Traveler, to the assholes . . . until the whine of a mosquito broke his thoughts.

He rolled onto his side and pulled the robe over his head, thinking, *It's magical lying out here on the prairie in the middle of summer. I love it.*

As long as no animals find me. I'm not hiding in a hole or a coulee or next to a cliff. I'm out in the open, hiding in empty space with no place to run to, no defensible position, no tree or cliff to climb. Ironic that this might be the best place to be.

Animals called occasionally, far off in the distance, but he no longer heard them.

CHAPTER 14

Going South

Four black vultures soared over the sprawling prairie. From high above, they could see mountains and glaciers, but they were searching the land below for feeding predators or carcasses. They saw every animal on the prairie, and sometimes the smell of rotting flesh guided them to a meal. An anomaly—a strange brown bump on the flatland—caught one vulture's eye, and it began to circle over to it, dropping slowly in elevation. A large gray stork already stood near the thing. The other vultures followed.

Toq lay completely covered up with only his mouth and nose peeking out. He heard and saw nothing but his dreams until the loud and large wingbeats snapped him awake. Instantly, he felt a couple of hard jabs on his shoulder beneath the thick fur robe. He threw off the robe, seized his spear, and whirled around to see the bill and outstretched wings of the stork. It beat its wings and flew off without squawking. Then, two vultures that had landed nearby also took to the air, while two more circling overhead flapped away from the obviously not dead creature.

Toq looked in all directions, worried that carnivores may have been watching the vultures, and while he saw none, he quickly packed up and left.

"Damn buzzards."

The sun was warm, the sky was clear, the breeze was light, and the biting bugs loved it. Every step he took stirred up more bugs. He could not stop moving lest he be swarmed, and he begged the wind to blow harder. He wore his long pants and long-sleeved shirt for protection, but he suffered in the heat, soaking with sweat. He stopped only to relieve himself, trying to wave bugs off his private parts.

He ate on the move, complaining, "How can such a beautiful land and pretty day produce such miserable creatures?"

He hiked south, keeping a huge, flat prairie on his right and the long series of lakes and wetlands on his left. The lakes and ponds attracted animals of all kinds, and birds were abundant. Toq plainly saw the effects of trampled and overeaten vegetation around the lakes, as well as the deep hoof and paw prints in the soft mud and clay. He could sometimes reach the water from a nice grassy spot, but more often, mud prevented easy access. Some more heavily used shores reeked of dung and decaying vegetation. For all the life surrounding these lakes, he only saw one small pack of wolves lying about on a hill.

By the time the sun reached its zenith, Toq had arrived at the mouth of a valley feeding into the familiar, silty river. The river valley was especially wide and flat, and the river divided itself into multiple separate channels. Toq spotted numerous crossings, but he felt no urge to explore the other side. The valley—a mixture of water, marshes, grasses, mud, and sands—went south, then rounded a hill and ran off to the east. The wind picked up, but it remained hot and buggy. Toq wore yarrow and mud on his hands, face, and neck. He hated the mud, but it was better than the bugs. Large, fluffy clouds appeared in the sky.

Toq stayed on the hilltops, and approaching a deep, wide coulee, he heard mammoths calling out, but he couldn't tell if they were calls of aggression or fear. The roar of a lion followed, which caused Toq to hold his breath and listen, but all was quiet. He cautiously moved to the edge of the hill, where it sloped down to some intriguing sandstone formations, but his attention was focused elsewhere. He walked slowly, dipping into little valleys and rising up on barren knolls, until he came to where he could see into the coulee. He crouched down, then crawled on hands and knees, then on his belly, until he looked out from the top of a cliff above the coulee.

A herd of ten to twenty mammoths milled about the bottom of the coulee. Clearly agitated, none were feeding, and half looked toward sandstone formations on the opposite side—where three, four, five lions moved away. The other mammoths watched a lone mother nudging her calf, lying still on the ground, with first her foot, then her trunk, then her tusk, trying to get the young elephant to stand. But Toq saw the blood from his position above and could tell the youngest member of the herd was dead.

The human watched the mother standing over her dead calf, trying to bring life back to its little body, and thought, *That animal is heartbroken.*

"I would never wish to hunt and kill these animals," he said softly.

He checked on the lions, seeing all but one had disappeared into the hill. The remaining one sat on a capstone, staring down at the mammoths. Toq figured they would simply wait for the mammoths to leave, then reclaim their kill. Suddenly, the big mother cried out in rage, and—leaving the calf—charged into some tall grass, where she dipped her tusks and lifted and threw the body of a lioness through the air. The way it flew limply and landed on its head, it was obvious the lion was already dead. Every bone had been crushed, and it no longer held its form—its legs and body crumpling over its head. Toq hadn't noticed the big cat before, and the mother wasn't done with it yet. She repeatedly attacked the carcass, kicking, stomping, and crushing it with her head and tusks, turning the once beautiful lioness into an unrecognizable, bloody mess.

The anguish and rage of this mother was frightful, and Toq said, "It's no wonder those other lions kept their distance. They don't always win. A bad day for both groups."

The lions—powerful, huge, and smart—had taken a chance and paid for it. The mother returned to her dead calf. Toq guessed that she would remain there for some time. The herd stayed and watched her, the lion acting as lookout did not move, and Toq slipped away, out of sight.

He hiked a long way around the lions and back to the river valley. He knew he would be thinking of that scene for a while, but as always, he needed to remain alert. He made his way along the river, with the southern mountains coming nearer. A small dark butte appeared, and farther away, a long butte stood prominently on the eastern horizon (Black Butte and Saddle Butte).

Thunderclouds floated off and away from the southern mountains, while the clouds in the west grew in size and power before traveling north. He watched the rain and lightning safely in the distance.

"Storms north and south, yet I'm dry," he said, feeling lucky again.

This time, when he set up camp in the evening, he put up his lean-to and built a fire of dried dung. He ate and wondered when he might see people. He wasn't sure if he missed people; most of the time, he didn't feel lonely. He worked on making stone points before going to sleep. Although the land had plenty of rocks and a wide variety of them, he hadn't found many that were easy to knap. He hadn't seen a tree in a long time.

••••

Early in the morning, Toq ventured down into the river valley—which was mostly clear of big game—wishing to hike along the bottom for a ways. There, he found large blocks of hard brown and tan stone densely packed with shells of various shapes and sizes: snail shells, clam shells, and mussel shells, as well as impressions of shells. He picked up a fist-sized rock with a mass of white shells, turning it over in his hands.

"Now, how did these get into the stone? Or . . ." He paused, thinking. "How did the mud turn to stone?"

He came upon a steep hillside, devoid of vegetation, where different colors and layers of earth could clearly be seen. A layer of small white shells formed a straight horizontal line two or three fingers thick. The shells crumbled from the hill, littering the ground with broken pieces.

"And how does a layer of shells get buried so deep below the surface?" he asked. Another mystery he would never know the answer to, but he refused to make up a story to explain it.

Rocks constantly grabbed his attention—from huge boulders lying on the prairie to tiny pebbles of all shapes and colors. Some were white marble, the color of snow, and others were all black, all gray, or all brown. There were granites. There were white-and-black-streaked marbles, and gray and pink ones. There were agates, there were blood-red, orange, and yellow rocks, as well as green rocks. Some were round and smooth, while others were jagged and broken. Toq occasionally spotted the flash of sunlight coming from flat, glass-like, easily broken sheet minerals. Some large rocks with a flat side had a series of straight-line scrape marks. Bigger boulders were smoothed around the edges from animals rubbing against them, scratching an itch or removing last winter's coat. There was always something new and interesting to look at—something to wonder about. Perhaps these interesting distractions would serve him well one day.

He came to a wide coulee and a muddy creek (Big Sandy Creek), which he easily crossed. He climbed back up on top of the hills above the river. The little black butte stood immediately to the southeast, barely rising above its neighboring hills. On the opposite side of the river, a bright-orange and red hill stood out from the barren stretch of badlands, and he wished he could see what made it so red, but he had no desire to venture across here. Toq followed a herd of twenty or thirty horses along a ridge that separated the river from a couple of hidden valleys. The horses vanished down the slope, and by the time Toq reached the end of the ridge, the horses were in the bottom of another valley with a creek running through it (Beaver Creek).

Toq took a good look around before going down after them. Along the way, lying near the bottom of the hill, an old tree trunk lay half-buried in a shallow depression. It was almost as big around as a man's body. This was the first sign of a tree Toq had seen in quite some time, but this was a tree of stone. He had seen and collected stone wood before, but he had never seen a nearly whole tree trunk. In several places, the stone trunk was broken cleanly through, as if it had been cut, and Toq could see tree rings, the old grain of the wood, and old knots where branches had once connected. He lifted a small piece and was surprised at its weight and density. He examined the tree from all angles.

"Same as the stone bones, same as the shells in the rock. Stone wood . . . where there are no trees anywhere around."

He tried to work through how such things could be created, but he came up with no satisfactory, nonmythical explanation.

He moved down to the clear creek with a healthy flow. Brush grew in the bottom of this valley—albeit only knee-high. Still, this was a good sign that he would find berries as well as woody material to burn. He drank deeply from the stream, flowing with the best water he had tasted since leaving the western mountains.

The horses remained ahead of him, going up the hill on the east side of the valley, pausing now and then to watch the man following behind. Aside from a few deer, Toq was surprised that there were not more animals.

"Lead the way, ladies," Toq said to the herd that was too far away to hear him. "Don't mean to bother you, but we appear to be going the same direction."

Five colts ran with the herd, having no trouble keeping up. The horses disappeared over the top of the hill, and when Toq crested it, he found the herd waiting for him.

"I'm coming," he said.

It was still early morning, but the air warmed quickly, and the clouds thickened as they steadily pushed into the blue sky, and Toq took note. He walked toward the horses—brown and tan with some white and black patches and stripes. The wind blew their tails and manes to the side as they watched him. He stopped a little ways away, and a couple of the bigger horses surprised him by approaching. It occurred to him that they might get close enough for him to spear one, but he didn't need the meat and quickly dismissed the thought. The curiosity of these animals, their shaggy, rough hair and rippling muscles, as well as their gracefulness, impressed him.

"You are such beautiful creatures," he said.

The two nearest horses stopped a short distance away. Toq took a step toward them, and they skittishly jumped back and trotted to the herd. The herd, now a bit more excited, turned and began running, one animal's excitement quickly passing to another until they raced headlong away across the flat, a cloud of dust trailing behind. They moved fast.

"That'll keep you alive," Toq said as he watched them go.

He walked a little ways east to where a huge, lush, and marshy valley, coming from the south, merged with the main river valley. Here, the river slowed, meandered, and flooded the valley, and a small group of male mammoths gobbled up vegetation. Toq worked his way south and east along the hilltops around the broad, tributary valley, crossed a coulee, climbed a hill, and looked into the valley. A sow bear with two cubs ran alongside a small, winding creek (Bullhook Creek). They crossed the stream and ran west. The mother stopped to look behind, then fled up into the coulee that Toq had just crossed. The cubs struggled to keep up with her, running with all their might.

Toq watched to make sure they didn't come his direction. Some bison galloped out of her path, but she ignored them. Toq looked back into the valley, where—a bit upstream—a pack of wolves were assailing a large, dark-brown bear. The giant male bear swiped at the much smaller wolves as they darted in from behind, nipped, and then sped away. The bear wasn't quick enough and couldn't protect all his sides from the surrounding pack. He chased one wolf but was bitten in the behind, causing him to spin around—only to find the biter was out of reach. He stood up on his hind legs, towering above the wolves, but they did not scare off. He roared while they growled and snarled. Toq noticed a large, dead animal near the combatants, either the bear's or the wolves' kill. Both the bear and the wolves wanted it. The sow with cubs could have been scared off by either of them.

"Maybe it was her kill," Toq said.

The commotion carried on until the giant had had enough. The bear sped off across the creek and down the valley toward the river, with the wolves chasing for some distance. Finally satisfied that he was gone, they returned to the kill and set in to eating, occasionally snarling and snapping at each other.

Toq walked along the hilltops until he was straight west of the big, somewhat rocky butte (Saddle Butte). Here, the broad valley narrowed to a wide coulee. Toq looked across it toward the gently curved hills, which reminded him of the curves of a woman's body.

He laughed at himself, "Ha! You've been away from people for too long."

Still, he admired the smooth and perfectly rounded hills. Behind them, the butte stood tall with red-brown rock jutting out from the west face. The north end sloped gently up to a peak, then dove into a deep gap in the middle of the long butte, making it look as if a chunk had been gouged or bitten out. The south half of the butte rose up into a hump, before stepping down into the coulees and lower hills. It was rugged, with rocky cliffs, and Toq was tempted to climb it to get a good look around. He might take refuge there, but he knew that big cats also utilized these high points. He strained to see if he could spot anything on the cliffs, but instead he saw five lions descending from one of the rounded hills and advancing toward the wolves, still working over their meal.

The lions didn't attempt to conceal their presence or their intentions, and they began to gallop and then sprint toward the wolves. Even though they outnumbered the lions, the wolves scattered. Some lions pounced on the half-eaten carcass, while one large male chased first the wolves, then a female from her spot at the carcass. She growled and snapped, raised a paw, but backed away to find another place to feed. The valley and its animals belonged to the lions. They drove away bears, they tried to kill wolves, and they ran off coyotes and foxes. A family of cheetah-cats had lived on the butte, but the lions moved in, killed one, and the family abandoned the area.

Toq watched as the wolves ran up onto a hill, turned to look down at the lions, then moved away one by one. This was no place to linger; the butte would not be safe, and with the southern mountains calling to him, he left the river behind. Another lone butte (Indian Woman Butte)—a bit smaller—rose to the west, on the north side of a dominant, sprawling, plateau-like hill. Toq hiked away from the drainage and up a ridge onto a plain rising to the plateau.

He pondered the potential battle between lion and bear, thinking out loud, "They probably avoid each other. But a lion pride would put a bear on the run, I'm certain. On the other hand, if a bear faced a lone lion, surely the bear would win."

Now, upon reaching the top of the plateau, he entered the foothills of the extensive and sprawling southern mountain range. One large, rounded lone mountain in the middle appeared to dominate (Baldy Mountain), and neither glaciers nor snow could be seen. Thunder rumbled as a dark storm rolled toward him. Glancing down, he spotted a beautiful, orange and white fist-sized rock. He picked it up, looked it over, then placed it back the way he had found it. He looked north, then turned south, picking up his pace across the plateau.

A few big animals shared the plateau with him, but he saw no carnivores. He didn't dawdle, keeping one eye on the quickly advancing storm and the other on everything else. The sun disappeared behind the ominous thundercloud. Lightning flashed high in the cloud, while thunder rumbled almost constantly. Toq spotted a large boulder in the middle of a field, and he jogged straight for it. When he reached it, the wall of cloud was almost overhead. The large rock, not as high as his waist, offered scant protection. He sat down behind it, pulled out his lean-to, and held it over his head, peeking over the boulder at the storm.

Toq smelled the rain—that fresh, wet smell. A blinding bolt of lightning shot through the sky, one branch clearly connecting with a single bison, while the main artery hit the ground and dropped a second one. Instinctively, Toq covered his ears, and in a split second, the thunderclap shook the earth and rattled his bones. Even though he was ready for it, it was still frightfully loud. The wind struck hard, and the hot day turned frigid. One of the bison stood up on shaky legs, then stumbled; it knelt, unsteadily. The other bison lay still on the grass, while a few nearby turned their heads and bodies to face the wind.

Toq pulled his bags in close and covered up under his lean-to hide. An unimaginably strong wind shook the boulder and pulled at his covering. Hail began to fall—first small, then large—slamming into the rock, shattering, and pelting Toq. He saw the bison running helter-skelter, vanishing into the rain and hail, while the two injured bison stayed where they were. The hail stopped, but the wind carried on, and the waterfall from the sky filled depressions in the prairie. Streams flowed in torrents across what had been dry ground only a moment ago. A pond formed around Toq's boulder, soaking him from below more than from above.

The barrage went on and on, until, finally, the lightning and thunder faded away. The wind let up, and the sun shone through to light the remaining drizzle. At last, Toq removed his cover and looked up at the double rainbow following the storm. Hail covered the soaked ground, and the sound of running water replaced that of the wind. Toq pulled his drenched belongings away from the boulder and plopped them on the piles of hail.

The sun brought some warmth back. Toq picked up his stuff and walked over to the kneeling bison. He knew he too could have been a victim of the lightning strike.

"A spear thrust from the gods," he said. "Another different possibility . . . a different fate."

He stood well back, watching and listening to it breathe. He walked around to the side; the beast's eyes were closed, a little blood dripped from its nose, and the end of one horn looked like it had been singed. Toq whistled softly, but the animal did not move.

He spoke to it, "Hey, brother. You okay?"

One ear moved only a little.

"Shit. You are jumbled up."

This animal, in this state, could easily be killed. If it didn't recover its senses, it would not last for long.

He said, "I hope you make it, big guy," and he moved over to the one lying down.

One horn stuck into the ground and one poked up into the air. He approached cautiously, touching its back with his spear, then touching its opened eyes to see if it blinked, but it did not.

"I believe you are dead."

He walked around it and didn't see any visible injuries except for a blackened, burned spot on the bottom of one front hoof. He glanced around and determined they were not being watched or approached. He took out his stone blade and cut the bison's throat. Blood flowed down and pooled in the grass and hail.

The beast, from nose to tail, was longer than two men stretched out, and the size and weight of this animal made it impossible for one man to turn it over. In a hurry, Toq began to skin the top side of the bison. He was determined to get as much of the hide as he could in one piece. This would rejuvenate his worn gear. The task wasn't easy. He moved around the bison, climbed on top, peeled and pulled at the hide while cutting it loose, but the further he got, the heavier the burden. He sweated profusely. He pulled off his shirt but then swatted at biting flies with bloody hands. As he worked, he wondered how the lightning killed. He still couldn't see any sign of injury.

He pulled the last bit of skin that he could free from the carcass and dragged it away. It was too heavy to carry and almost too heavy to drag across the shrinking piles of hail. Toq wanted to rest, but with the sun going down, he had no time to waste. He looked at the partially skinned, pink and white carcass, thinking the once noble animal now looked ridiculous with its head, neck, legs, and butt covered in fur, but the body, on this one side, stripped and hairless. Toq looked at the other bison a little ways off, not moving from its position.

He looked back at his work and apologized to the dead bison, saying, "Sorry for making you look so bad. But you will look even worse pretty soon, when the wolves find you."

He cut into the back and hindquarter and took a bit out of the shoulder, stopping occasionally to flake his stone to give it a sharp, new edge. He piled the meat onto the hide. So far, no vultures, scavengers, or carnivores had appeared, but it was time to go. He walked with his spear over to the other bison, feeling sorry for it.

"If you don't recover, you're going to be torn up."

He wondered if he should put it out of its misery. Its eyes were now open, and its breathing seemed better. The beast suddenly sprang to its feet, lunged at Toq, then sprinted away.

Toq fell back in surprise at this miraculous recovery, laughing, "Oh, you shit! I guess you're just fine. Thanks for not killing me."

He dragged the hide and meat as far as he could before dark, trying to put distance between himself and the dead bison. Eventually, he folded the hide over the meat and covered it with grass, soil, and rocks. Then, he moved off a far way to camp. Coyotes called and thunder rumbled in the distance, but he slept undisturbed through the night.

• • • •

Up early, Toq was happy to find that nothing had discovered his cache. He needed to get to work on it before it all spoiled. He didn't like the location of his camp, but he had few choices. For three days, he cooked and dried meat over grass, brush, and dung fires. He scraped, tanned, and worked the hide, cutting it into smaller pieces, making new bedding and a fresh lean-to, and saving what little remained. He used his old lean-to and bedding to patch up his clothes and bags and to make new moccasins. Every day and every night, thunderstorms rolled over the land. The wind and sun dried things out, and then the storms soaked everything again.

Despite his trepidation, Toq received no unwelcome visitors—only a mildly curious group of camels passing by on their way to the hills.

••••

A crystal-clear morning lifted Toq's spirits as he packed up his gear. The last three days, he'd worried about rotting meat, carnivores, and lightning, but today, his food was done, the sky was blue, and he would be traveling. He headed south, following the path of the camels. A herd of fifty or so pronghorns trotted away. The plateau dropped off into a valley with a creek (Beaver Creek) and a sublime view. It had lavishly green hills and abundant yellow, pink, and blue wildflowers. Brush lay scattered about in the valley bottom.

Animals spread across the hills and into the valley, but not so many as to overwhelm the land. Toq started down toward the valley until he spotted a bear, causing him to turn back up to follow along the ridges. Down into a coulee, up the other side, follow a ridge, go around another coulee, climb a hill—the hiking wasn't as easy and straight as it had been on the plains. He loved the change. He stood on a sort of butte where the east side sloped off to a plain, and the west side fell down a rocky cliff to the creek below. A couple of eagles circled on the wind. The rock here was different; it was brown, red, purple, and gray igneous, but here and there were rocks of the same variety as what he had seen near the glacier, in the glacier, and everywhere between here and the glacier.

"No ice, no snow, no glaciers," he said, surveying the landscape in every direction. Most of his journey, he had been accompanied by either mountain or continental glaciers, but there were none in these hills.

He spooked half a dozen bighorns on his way down the hill, and he wandered into the valley bottom, where the brush held a treat—some kind of blue berry. Although they were not quite ripe, Toq ate a handful of the sour berries anyway. He drank good, clear water from the creek, then hiked back up onto the hilltops and proceeded south. The creek cut through a fairly deep, narrow, little canyon, from which a cheetah-cat led three youngsters. She spotted Toq, stared for a moment, then hurried her young up, away, and out of sight.

Ahead, a somewhat flat area stretched south, bounded by hills and distant mountains. It was a treeless, mountain and hill country, but the grasses and wildflowers were thick and lush. Wildlife filled the land—everywhere the eye looked. The vegetation was chewed down to the ground in only a few places. Mounds of freshly dug soil, winding tunnel tubes on the surface, and holes, marked the work of moles, gophers, and ground squirrels. Dirt flew out of a mound, and a badger popped its head up to look around, then resumed digging. A hawk glided over a field of ground squirrel holes, making the squirrels squeak out a warning. A few little, tan bodies raced across the surface, diving into the ground. Toq walked over to the badger hole, and the badger, seeing him coming, watched for a moment, then vanished into its hole.

Toq wandered up the valley, staying with the stream, moving south toward the round mountain. A group of camels sauntered along a ridge. The valley narrowed and the hills grew higher. The sun was hot, the wind was calm, and no clouds broke up the pure blue sky. Toq went to the creek for another drink and found it cloudy and dirty, which surprised him, but he drank from it anyway. He moved up onto a hill, where he saw the cause of the dirty water: A bear wallowed around in a deep pool, with only its head above the water. It seemed to be enjoying itself, cooling off, slapping the water, submerging its face. Toq smiled. He hadn't seen this carefree, comical side of the great predator before. The bear left the watering hole and walked down the middle of the creek, while Toq moved the other direction up onto hilltops.

Toq crossed another flat bench before getting into the higher hills. Hillsides were too steep to walk across for any distance, so he either needed to be in the valley bottom—a dangerous place—or up on the ridgetops. A pair of wolves, sitting on a ridge, looking into the valley, watched the man climb up. Toq continued toward them, telling himself to "be bold" and hoping they would get out of his way. They obliged and trotted off without any trouble.

The sound of the rushing creek echoed off the rock walls and carried up to the man on the hill, looking down upon the largest herd of mammoths he had ever seen. They filled the valley bottom; the creek downstream of them ran muddy, and the ground and vegetation around them were eaten and trampled down. And yet, the mammoths made no sound. Tusks and trunks conspicuously protruded from the herd. Large adults, midsized adolescents, and small calves made up this group. There were spots where the mammoths bunched up so closely that Toq imagined he could step across the valley upon their backs.

Elephant calls suddenly carried down the valley, and Toq saw a second, much smaller herd approaching. The group below grew uneasy, and as they moved down the valley, they began to vocalize, as if shouting commands. The smaller herd of young males moved fast, pushing against each other, trying to get in front. The larger herd now flowed like a river of flesh. The two wolves had reappeared on a hill below Toq and were now also watching the flowing mass of mammoths.

The valley below cleared out, and the bulls filled the space in a frantic, excited run. Toq saw a few with enormous, dangling, bouncing penises, ready to go.

"Gods! The size of those things," he said.

The bulls were out of their minds, chasing the larger herd to get to the females. Two bulls squared off against each other, wrapping trunks over tusks, and pushing tusk-to-tusk, head-to-head. Grass and soil flew, but the battle was short-lived, as they broke away from each other and resumed the chase.

Toq watched as the two herds faded away, the wolves following.

"Wow," he said.

The calls of bulls and cows and calves became more distant. Shadows grew in the valley, and Toq knew he needed to find a place to camp. Eventually, he came to a gently sloping side coulee where a small group of mammoths grazed peacefully on tall grass—undetected and undisturbed by the frenzy in the valley.

He camped among some old volcanic outcroppings, saying, "I wish the Traveler could've seen that."

••••

A yipping coyote woke Toq from a deep sleep just as the sun was about to break over the hills, following a night that had been profoundly quiet. Large drops of dew bent the grasses and flowers. The mammoths had barely moved.

"Why go anywhere? You have all you can eat here," Toq said to them.

He ate while watching a doe and a fawn make their way through deep grass on the hillside opposite, their light tan color failing to hide them against the green hill. Dew-saturated vegetation soaked their fur, making them look as though they had just crossed a river.

The sun warmed the morning quickly, and with no bugs to bother him, Toq packed his garments in his bags and wore only a leather flap to protect his private parts from any prickly or rash-producing plants. If the bugs were bad, he would put his clothes back on, but for now, he saw no sense in getting them wet as he trekked through the tall grass. He walked barefoot down into the coulee, well below the mammoths, which turned slightly to observe this alien creature.

Toq watched them closely as he moved along, softly saying, "Just stay there. I'm no threat."

His feet, legs, and loincloth soon dripped with dew as he plowed through a patch of chest-deep grass; it was impossible to see where he stepped. Moving up the hill, he followed the deer path onto easier terrain. Looking back, it was easy to see his route through the grass.

Toq took one last look at the mammoths in the coulee and yelled, "So long, ladies!"

They looked up at him, then went back to eating. Toq, as was often the case now, was a bit startled at the sound of his own shouting voice—so loud, so unusual. His was the only human voice he had heard for a few lunar cycles. He wondered if he might go insane after spending so much time alone.

"Maybe. Maybe not. Nah, I'll be fine."

He walked along the ridgeline and said, "Shit, I think I'm better than ever. It's having too many people around that makes me insane."

He dropped into a steep coulee, crossed a small stream, and climbed up onto a ridge that ran parallel to the main creek valley.

The views here were grand, and with the sound of the creek below, the smell of the meadows, the light breeze, the excitement and anticipation for what lay ahead, Toq said, "What a perfect day. That's happiness. Finding the perfect day."

Animal sign was everywhere, but he did not see the animals themselves. He reached a high point, where he stopped to look over the tops of the hill country he had just spent the last day passing through. He looked past the hills out to the plains, those vast flatlands. Out west, on the horizon, the lonely blue mountains stood (Sweet Grass Hills). They had been in view for a long time. One small peak, separate, to the left, showed itself. Toq was certain that was the one he'd climbed.

He squinted at the perfectly flat northern horizon, where the pull of the great ice sheet remained. The atmosphere—clear and free of haze—allowed for sharp viewing over long distances.

"Sure enough, there it is," Toq said of a thin white line. "That must be it. I think that's it. It has to be the ice." But he couldn't be certain. "It could be an illusion."

He turned back south, climbing up a steeper section, walking along another high ridge, then up the north face of a mountain. From the top, the views kept getting better. He no longer heard the creek—only his breathing and the breeze. Still, there were no biting bugs—just hundreds of butterflies, flying defiantly against the breeze, chasing each other. He followed the ridge around to the southwest. A small, scattered bunch of llamas were bedded down in a wide bowl on the side of the next mountain. Toq wondered if he would forever be going up, topping one point only to find another higher peak waiting beyond. He hiked up the steep side of the next mountain, scrambled onto an outcrop on top, and took a good look around at the surrounding hills, mountains, and valleys. He walked along a ridge going south, with a grand view of the massive, dominating, round mountain (Baldy Mountain).

He went down into a little pass, then up onto another peak. Now, only a wide valley separated him from the big mountain. There were other high mountains nearby, but this one colossus, standing by itself, ruled over all the others. He looked over the country carefully, mapping out a route. He deliberated whether he should climb the mountain or not. He wanted to. The top pulled at him, he felt good, the weather remained clear, and the day was only half over.

"Go for it, Toq. You may never be here again."

He hiked down, following ridges as often as he could. Bison and a few caribou grazed in the valley bottom. He drank from a small, clear stream and filled a bladder with water. He ate a bit and put on his moccasins. A small pack of wolves lay in the shade of a rock formation. They paid him little attention, mostly sleeping and panting, trying to stay out of the sun. He curved well out of the way around them. He went up a few foothills before reaching the true base of the round mountain. He looked up at a steep slope covered in loose rock, with only a few grassy patches, flexed his old, injured knee a few times, and started up.

He stopped to stuff grass into the bottom of his moccasins to lessen the pounding and bruising his feet would take. He knew the rocks would destroy his moccasins, but he had an extra pair plus hide for patching. He tied his bags together so they would ride better on his back and keep them from swinging as much. Climbing up, he was surprised to find a faint trail worn into the rocks by bighorn sheep, and he followed it. This trail was significantly easier to walk on, but still, sliding rock made some spots difficult.

When the trail no longer went upward, Toq left it. The sun was hot, and though a light breeze cooled his sweating body, the water he carried would not last long. He rested once to cool down. He sat and gazed upon the country north of the mountain. Despite the rains, those wonderful, treeless hills below were beginning to turn yellow and brown in the sun. The clear air of the morning had been replaced by a bit of haze, and a few small clouds floated through the sky.

He climbed up, using his spears as walking sticks. Upon reaching a grassy slope, he spotted the heads and fully curled horns of a couple of bighorns bedded down. They watched him without moving, and Toq climbed on.

By late afternoon, he'd left the steep slope behind and walked onto a gently rounded summit with a feeling of elation and thirst. He took a quick look around and drank some water. The summit was rocky, but there was a bit of grass, and Toq lay back on it and looked into the deep blue sky. He closed his eyes and breathed the cool mountaintop air. He dozed off, and immediately, fleeting dreams of the flood, his people, and the Traveler appeared in his head. He didn't nap for long, slowly opening his eyes to a sky that now seemed too bright. He sat up. Thinking about the flood depressed him, forming a knot in his stomach, and making him anxious, even fearful.

He looked south, where a large assembly of billowing white thunderheads loomed far away. Little mountain ranges stood off to the southwest (Highwood Mountains), south (Judith Mountains), and east (Little Rocky Mountains), each separated by a great expanse of prairie. Far off, straight south, a large plume of smoke rose and drifted to the east.

"Hmm, fire," Toq mumbled, wondering if it could be man-made, but acknowledging that lightning had been frequent the past few days.

Everything but the sky and the sun lay below him. While a couple of good-sized mountains were to the west and southwest, it appeared that he had already come through the bulk of this range. South of his mountain, a shorter area of foothills trailed off into a broken, rolling prairie.

No storms threatened this mountain yet, and the sun had a ways to go before dark. Toq circled the mountaintop and pondered staying overnight. A large outcrop formed the perfect windbreak, and a little patch of snow remained in its shadow. Toq finished his water, then shoveled snow into his water bladder. Ultimately, he couldn't resist the idea of spending the night here, especially when the weather looked to be good. He stared over at the northwest mountains, far away and hazy, and thought about the mountain he had climbed there, right after the full moon.

He set up camp, ate, drank, and watched the world. The clouds moved, and shadows grew on the hills and prairie. The earth darkened, while he remained in the sun. He felt the long whiskers growing on his chin and the ever-lengthening hair on his head. He wore down his finger- and toenails with coarse stones and picked at his teeth with a small, sharp sliver of broken bone. He knew he needed a proper cleaning; he rarely took the time while hiking, and here, he had the time, but no water. He looked over his moccasins, and since they were too holey to be any good, he threw them away down the side of the mountain.

Sitting on the outcrop, he watched the sun turn a deep red as it fell to the horizon. The bighorn rams came up onto the summit to graze, and Toq remained still, watching them. The sun set, and a thin cut of a crescent moon took its place in the western sky. Darkness concealed the world below, light faded from the horizon, and only dim shadows gave away the positions of the bighorns. Toq's butt grew sore, and the temperature dropped, so he slipped off his perch, unseen by the rams, and stood behind the outcrop, looking at the distant glow of fire.

Stars filled the sky. The rams were almost impossible to see now.

He went to bed saying, "That's it. That's the day. And a good day it was."

• • • •

Daylight arrived with utter quiet—no wind, no birds, no insects, no animal calls. Toq got up to see if "his kingdom" below was still there.

"It would be nice to rest here all day," he said.

The sun hovered just over the horizon, and already he could feel the heat.

"Going to be a hot day."

The bighorns were gone. The only signs of life were a ladybug and a couple of little blue butterflies. The smoke from the fire down south was now just a wisp. Big thunderclouds hung over the landscape in the southeast, while the rest of the sky was cloudless.

Toq soaked up the sun, ate, and relaxed.

"Chiefdom," he said, smiling and looking down from the mountaintop. "Nobody even knows you're here and that you're their chief. But I'll pretend that this is all mine. Huh. I am like the gods—except I will go down and make myself known. *Ha!* I'm *better* than the gods!"

He chuckled nervously. Though he didn't believe in gods or the spiritual realm, he did feel some trepidation about his blasphemy. He would never dare say what he truly believed around anyone else—except the Traveler.

The sun climbed into the sky too quickly. Toq decided to get moving. A ridge ran down off the southwest side, and Toq followed it around large rock formations as he went. He left one ridge to follow another down off the mountain and into a little drainage full of animals. He followed the drainage south through hill and valley country, his mountain shrinking behind the further he went. The day was hot, the biting bugs multiplied, and the drainage contained only sporadic spots of water, which the beasts had turned into muddy messes. Though he tried to find clear running water, he often had no choice but to drink from stagnant holes that reeked of excrement. He paid the price with dysentery, which slowed him down, dehydrated him, and weakened him. But he kept moving until he finally came to a side coulee with a clear spring coming out of the ground. He camped nearby, hoping for a quick recovery.

Toq felt overheated, thirsty, and nauseated; his head pounded, his legs were weak, and he was no longer alert enough in his surroundings. He drank from the spring, then rested in the grass—the sun beating down on the shadeless coulee—and hoped he would not have to run off to shit anymore. Though day's end approached, the heat remained. The rest revived him somewhat, and with his gut still in turmoil, he gathered fuel and made a fire, then dug a shallow hole, lined it with a spare skin, and filled it with water. He heated some stones in the fire, which he then plopped into the water along with some berry leaves and brewed some tea. The work exhausted him, and in the middle of it all, he had to frantically dash off to evacuate his bowels. He leapt onto a layered sandstone rock, pulling at his trousers, intending to spring gracefully to the other side, but the sandstone collapsed, pitching him forward. He somersaulted across the grass, and in one smooth motion, regained his feet and kept running—as if it had all been planned. He laughed at the absurdity. Afterward, he cleaned himself with grass and leaves and a splash of water from downstream.

He walked back to his fire, exasperated. "Son of a bitch! How long is this going to last?" He scooped some ash out of the fire and added it to the tea, saying, "I hope this helps."

The water heated quickly, and Toq let his brew cook awhile. He removed the stones and drank directly from the hole in the ground since he had neither a cup nor a straw-like plant stem. Once the brew cooled down, he fished out some leaves and chewed them, then scooped out the muddy ash and ate it.

He set up his lean-to and lay down to wait for the end of the day. He ate no food that evening. Only a couple of pronghorn bucks wandered by, and no storms attacked.

• • • •

Two days later, eating well in the morning and feeling good, he marched south with renewed vigor, eager to get to wherever it was he was going. The creek valley (Birch Creek) quickly deepened with steep, bare hillsides, cutting deep into a badland-breaks country, a rupture in the prairie. Some hills were too steep to climb, so Toq stayed above the deep coulee and the mostly dried-up creek. He did not drink from the muddy yellow watering holes.

He crossed numerous small coulees and a large, deep one with decent water. He passed through a coulee with massive black sinkholes—deep enough to swallow a mammoth. He stepped carefully around them so he wouldn't collapse a portion of earth and end up in a hole he could never get out of.

"Good animal traps," he said, thinking about using them for hunting.

He camped on a bluff overlooking the canyon-like coulee, hoping for no rain.

• • • •

Toq crossed another large, deep coulee first thing on the unusually cloudy morning. He moved east, then south across a high bench, while a herd of musk oxen moved north.

"Heading for the hills, eh, boys? Better hurry, the grass is turning."

The sleek brown musk oxen carried no remnants of their old winter coats—the long, thick, dark hairs having been shed. They paused to look at the human, wary of his intentions, then quickly resumed their trek north.

Before midday, Toq stood on a point at the end of the benchland, looking down into a chasm created by two equally large coulees converging.

"Wild, rough country," he said, gazing into one impressive canyon after another. "Like upside-down mountains."

A few mammoths stood out in the main valley, while a small group of bison grazed in the coulee bottom to his left. He went east, where he found the musk oxen's trail emerging from the coulee. He followed their tracks to the opposite side, which he scaled, putting him on a ridge running west. He walked to where a deep valley opened up. A large brown-gray river filled the bottom (Missouri River). River breaks country dominated the landscape, forming impossible cliffs and unusual sandstone formations, steep walls, flat benches, uncountable side coulees and tributaries, as well as this one large river and its valley.

Across the river, in the southwest, a flat-topped mount (Square Butte) ruled over the plains. Toq had seen it before, earlier that summer. Sunlight spilled down from a sky that broke free of the clouds. Rising from behind the southern hills, a large cloud of smoke blew with the wind. A few small trees grew here and there on the north side of the river valley, but on the south side grew many large, mature conifers.

Toq continued along the ridge, knowing the river below was the same one he and the wolf had followed out of the mountains. Looking west, he had a good idea of where it came from and the lands it passed through, but looking east, he had no idea where it was going. These were the first trees he had seen in a long time, and he rejoiced, once again entertaining the thought of finding humans.

He wanted to go south, but the river posed a major obstacle.

"No point in going back west," he said, while turning to look east along the river. "No idea if that country gets tougher or if the river turns north. You might be stuck here until the river freezes over." The thought of wintering here was fleeting. "There's too much summer left to stop here. Let's go down and see. Maybe there's a crossing."

He walked along the ridge while looking out for wildlife. Just where the end of the ridge dropped off into the drainage, Toq spotted a wolf's head seemingly sticking up out of the ground. Startled, he stopped and stared into the wolf's eyes.

"This can't be," he said, recognition dawning on him. "Wolf!" he cried.

The wolf glanced backwards, then bounded ecstatically up the slope to his old hunting partner. Toq held his arms out wide, dropping to his knees and grinning with delight.

"Wolf! How you doing? What are you doing here?"

The wolf stopped short of making contact, bowing playfully and half-yipping, half-barking. His mate appeared behind him, eyeing Toq guardedly.

"Oh, it's you." A bit deflated, Toq rose to his feet.

The wolf ran to her then back to Toq.

"You're still with her?" Toq asked sardonically. Once certain that she wouldn't attack, he laughed and said, "You have any pups? No, not this year. You guys were too late for this year. Maybe next year. But you've probably been doin' it, yes? Oh, sorry for being so crude. But you're the one without shame!"

Laughing again, his happiness at seeing these familiar faces he'd thought he would never see again could not be hidden. He sat down and began to tell his wolf where he had been and what he had seen. He laughed at himself for having such a long conversation with an animal. The wolf settled down, sniffed around, then lay near him, still out of reach, but undoubtedly listening.

With no shade and increasingly scant cloud cover, they began to cook in the sun. The female, panting heavily, went back down the hill toward water. She didn't understand her mate's interest in this apparently inedible thing on two legs that wouldn't stop talking. His wolf watched her go, then suddenly jumped up and followed her.

"Oh! Are we leaving? Yeah, I'm getting hot, too. Don't worry, I can finish my story later." He stood and gathered his stuff. "You know, it's rude to just leave in the middle of a story," he called out, but they didn't look back.

He followed them into the river valley, zigzagging down steep slopes. The rushing water echoed loudly off canyon walls. The nearer he came to the river, the more ominous it grew. It flooded the valley bottom almost completely. He arrived at the outlet of the large coulee coming from the north, where it opened wide into the river valley. The river flooded a good portion of the mouth of the coulee, and a few small spruces had established themselves along the bottom. A good-sized island survived here, a little too far from the main rushing current to be eroded away. Brush, grass, and a patch of small birch trees grew on it, and birds, numerous and diverse, took advantage of this sanctuary.

Toq watched the two wolves trotting across a plain at the bottom of the hill. They waded belly-deep into the water, lapping at it as they went. He saw no other large mammals and so proceeded to the river's edge.

"Tough country. Too steep for a lot of animals," he said, but then spied a steep hill with numerous bighorns on it. "Except them."

He frowned at the muddy, silty water. With nothing draining down from the coulee, this river water would be all he had, so he drank from it and hoped he would not get sick again. Looking at the river up close, it truly was an intimidating sight. The water out in the middle rushed by in a hurry, forming waves as it went.

"Impossible. Can't swim that. You'd be swept away, or you'd freeze to death before you got across." Old anxiety and memories of the flood overwhelmed him. "Can't think right now," he said.

He looked to the east, but with the hills blocking his view, he could not see far down the valley. He looked west, where the north side appeared to be more open. The wolf and his mate both came running up to Toq, looking refreshed.

The wolf shook the water off onto the man, and Toq burst out laughing. Surprisingly, the female seemed a bit friendlier. The two animals briefly play-fought, then retreated to lie in the shade of some brush. Watching them calmed Toq's anxiety.

But he couldn't stay here. He had to find out what his options were. So, he hiked west.

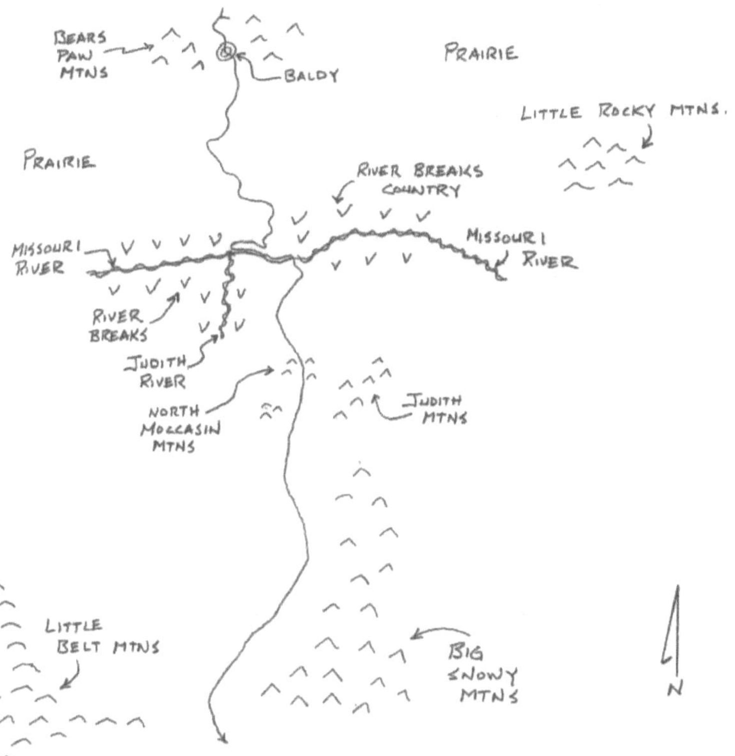

BEARS PAW MTNS
BALDY
PRAIRIE
LITTLE ROCKY MTNS.
PRAIRIE
RIVER BREAKS COUNTRY
MISSOURI RIVER
MISSOURI RIVER
RIVER BREAKS
JUDITH RIVER
NORTH MOCCASIN MTNS
JUDITH MTNS
LITTLE BELT MTNS
BIG SNOWY MTNS
N
TOQUUXLA'S ROUTE
RIVERS

CHAPTER 15

River Crossing

Toq watched a bear scale a steep hillside on the south side of the river and vanish over the top. The man struggled with what to do, where to go. East looked difficult; if the river turned south, he would be good, but if it didn't, he could be stuck in a winter with little to no wood. He could go west, back up the river from where he had come, but he had no knowledge of any place to cross. Timber around the great waterfalls area was plentiful, but so were the bears. To cross the river, he needed a good raft or boat. But with the trees being too small and too few, his only real option was to make a skin boat, and the simplest boat to make would be a round bullboat. Even in this, crossing the river would be dangerous and risky. He could stay here and wait for winter to slow down and freeze the river over, but this too would depend upon finding enough fuel to burn.

He spent a day exploring the area, seeing if there were enough resources around for shelter, food, and fuel. Game was abundant, but fuel was meager. In the afternoon, he stood on a hill looking south across the river into a wide valley with a good-sized stream (Judith River) flowing into the main river. Trees adorned the valley, going south and away, many more than on his side, and bigger.

"Damn, I wish those trees were over here," he mumbled.

He looked around for the wolves, but they were nowhere to be seen. Toq sometimes wished he was a wolf; their lives seemed easier, simpler, than a human's. "Until you get into another pack's territory, or you get old or sick. Oh well, they have it tough, too, I guess. Everything has it tough."

Toq hunted and began collecting material for a boat, thinking about all those melting glaciers feeding water into this river.

••••

The morning sky—dull, dark, and gray—reflected the man's mood. A hard, cool wind rattled his lean-to and pushed big waves, with white caps and foam, down the river. The air was dramatically colder, and Toq smelled rain. He busied himself with gathering material and hunting before the rain, or snow, came. By midmorning, the rain fell—light at first, but then heavy. Toq moved his lean-to onto a bit of higher ground with good grass, facing to the east. He settled in, wanting to complain about the miserable day but having to acknowledge that he'd had excellent traveling weather since the last snowstorm.

Wind and rain drowned out all other sounds, so he was taken completely by surprise when suddenly two large, hairy beasts burst out in front of him. Toq jerked up, his eyes flashed, and he instinctively reached for his spear. The wolves tussled in the grass and rain in front of the shelter.

"Itshla! You sons'a bitches! You scared the shit out of me!" Toq chuckled with relief while watching the two tear off. "You guys seem to be enjoying this weather."

It bothered him that he couldn't see what might be coming behind his shelter, but he had to trust that he'd chosen a good spot.

The wolves disappeared to hunt, and Toq watched the weather, wishing he had a larger shelter. Through the driving rain, on the other side of the river, he saw a herd of about ten mammoths walk down to the river's edge, impervious to what the sky brought down upon them. They lingered there for a while, and Toq wondered if they were considering trying to cross. "That would be a mistake, even for them."

Without a sound, one, then two, then the whole group turned and moved south up the valley, vanishing into the rain. Toq stuck his head out of the side of his lean-to into the wind and rain and looked along the river. To his surprise, another small herd of mammoths stood at the water's edge on his side of the river.

He pulled his rain-splattered head back under the shelter but, after some time, looked back out to see the mammoths spread out along the flat part of the valley, feeding.

"Now, don't wander too close over here." He wondered if he could scare them away or if they would just charge him. A large animal appeared across the river, but Toq could not tell what it was.

$$\bullet\;\bullet\;\bullet\;\bullet$$

The next day, with clearing skies, Toq attempted to hunt, but the mud limited his movements. He had decided to make a boat out of wood and large rib bones. Although he didn't know what lay across the river, he felt it held the most promise. Now, he needed a large hide, but killing a large beast by himself would be difficult. He cut down a small spruce and fashioned a second stone-pointed spear. He spent the rest of the windy day scouting canyons and arroyos, figuring his best chance would be surprising something from above. Though, admittedly, most large animals knew not to get themselves trapped in tight spots.

A deer or a bighorn skin would not be large enough. He needed a bison or a camel or a musk ox or a mammoth—although he would have to find a freshly deceased mammoth.

"I need some luck," he said, surveying the valley.

He hated the thought of killing a large animal just for its skin. He would take as much meat as he could, of course, but it would still be such a waste.

Sewing together and sealing multiple smaller skins would take time, but it could be done. Trying to drive an ill-tempered bison or musk ox over a cliff or into an arroyo, by himself, would be next to impossible.

The mammoths left, mud sticking to their feet. Toq saw one slip in the muck, falling to its knee and catching itself, but even with that, the herd sauntered off, much more easily than the man. While exploring the wider valley, he had seen bison, bighorns, pronghorns, horses, and a few caribou. He tried to approach some bison, but they were out on a flat, and the nearer he came to them, the more menacing they looked. Bulls were aggressive, and cows with calves were defensive, either charging him or fleeing. He had to run a couple of times.

After one such charge, breathing heavily, Toq noticed the two wolves had come to join him in this back and forth, but it didn't faze the bison, having little to fear from two wolves and a single human.

Toq gave up and called to the wolves, "They're too much, guys. Gotta find something easier."

He walked away, while the wolves kept at the game for a bit.

The wind blew hard all day, helping to dry out the earth. By sunset, the sky was free of clouds, and the fire south of the river appeared to be out, and the air was clear.

• • • •

Going on his fourth day in this spot made him question what he was doing.

He calmed himself, saying, "Don't worry about it, Toq. No need to hurry. It'll work out." But he had doubts. "Maybe you should give this adventure up. I could probably get back to that village before winter." He thought some more. "I'm not going back there. Maybe I should go east instead. Maybe I should just wait here for winter. Maybe I should be killed and eaten by a bear. Nothing to worry about, then." This second-guessing fortified his resolve to get across the river.

He had observed animal trails running from the valley bottom up a narrow coulee to a higher benchland. Most of the tracks belonged to deer or bighorn, but there were also some large bison tracks and a couple of wolf tracks—his wolves. Toq followed the trail to a sandstone column capped by a large, brown, flat-topped rock, connected to a hill by a whitish-gray sandstone ridge. He climbed onto the capstone and looked down upon the trail. He could lie on top of it or hide on either side of the ridge, below the capstone. He explored the area, trying to determine the potential for prey to walk by while he lay in wait, not wanting to waste time if an animal only walked by once every three days.

Nearing the end of the day, he returned to the sandstone column and hid on one side, near the top, knowing he would be too easily seen if he lay directly on top of the cap. Wondering if his scent or that of the wolves would scare animals away, he watched the trail coming down from above, while peeking over the ridge to see what might be coming from below.

"The wolves," he wondered, "how could I use them? If I get something, they could take my kill away."

"One problem at a time. First . . . get something."

The sun hung low over the hills. Toq tried to get into a comfortable position. Two spears and his water bladder lay by his side. Having no vegetative cover, he considered hiding in some brush below. "Nah, this is a better spot."

Shadows lengthened in the river valley, and Toq figured if he didn't get anything this evening, he would come back before sunrise. He had resolved to take whatever came along, so if he had to, he would sew together some smaller skins for a boat. The sun set, the wind died, a few animals called out in the distance, and a cricket chirped.

Toq looked over the top. Nothing approached from below.

He thought about getting something with darkness coming. "Not good timing." Visibility was still good, but not for long. "Just a little while longer," Toq mumbled. He sat up and stared up the trail, trying to look like a rock.

Movement above caught his eye, and he looked intently, trying to identify the lone animal. He immediately thought, *Don't be a bear*. It moved down into a depression out of sight. Toq didn't move, and he wondered where the wolves were. *This beast doesn't move like a wolf.* He watched the trail where the animal would rise out of the depression. The cricket chirped, a mouse scurried by below Toq's feet, and a redheaded male lion appeared above the trail in the twilight. It stopped and scanned the area below, its massive head moving left to right, before proceeding down the trail, much as Toq himself would have done. The lion saw the sandstone column, but it didn't see or smell the man.

Toq froze. Barely breathing, he did not reach for a spear, not knowing if the lion knew he was there. It was too late to slip away, as the lion would spot any movement. The beast, apparently alone, moved cautiously down the trail. Toq felt a very gentle breeze carrying his scent away from the lion. The big carnivore moved along the trail closer to the sandstone, peeking up at the perch above the trail, seemingly looking right at Toq, but it kept walking. Toq slowly turned his head, gaze following the lion, which now passed nearly directly beneath him; Toq could've spat on the creature. Just before disappearing around the sandstone corner, Toq noticed a very quick, subtle look the lion gave in his direction. He knew the lion had seen him silhouetted against the still-light sky.

This is it. Keep your head.

He whispered, "He's coming."

He'd always known a confrontation with a lion would come. His heart beat fast in his chest. He took a couple of deep breaths and reached for a spear, his hand shaking a little until he gripped the wood shaft. Toq turned slowly around to look over the top of the sandstone ridge, hoping to see the lion walking away. Instead, he heard the large animal bounding up the slope on the other side. It occurred to Toq that perhaps the lion wished to use the perch as its own launch point for an ambush, but regardless, Toq was in a bad place.

Toq quickly slid back down, reaching for his other spear, eyes fixed on the top of the sandstone ridge, hands, feet, and knees touching the steep slope. He was halfway down when the lion's outline showed at the top against the sky. The lion didn't pause there. He knew the man was on the other side, and though he didn't know what the man was, he knew he was bigger, and the lion didn't fear anything smaller than himself. The beast rushed over the top and poured down the other side onto the very slow man.

Toq had little time to react. He heard a low growl erupting from the lion on its way down as he tossed the spear in his weak hand lamely at the beast—the wooden shaft bouncing off its head—and then quickly gripped the other spear with both hands. He faced the lion, and in the dim light, Toq saw the eyes, the open mouth with enormous fangs, the giant head, and the outstretched front paws with toes and claws splayed out.

Because he stood downhill, Toq's face would be struck first. His instinct was to duck or put up his hands to shield his head, but his hands were full. His next instinct was to push the point of the spear out in front of him, hoping the lion would run into it, but Toq knew the lion would just bat it away, so he held the spear low by his side with both hands on it. He wondered if the lion would strike with its paws first or if it would bite his head directly.

The lion had this slow, little human. He had the high ground, and it could crush the man under its weight alone, even without fangs and claws. The little man's timing had to be perfect. The lion reached out and forward to catch the man if he tried to dodge. For a moment, the lion's chest was exposed, and Toq thrust his spear up into it as the lion came crashing down on top of him. He felt a large paw wrap around his back, claws digging into his skin. He saw, briefly, the massive teeth about to clamp down on his face. He turned his head to the side in time to just miss the teeth, but the momentum of the gigantic beast smashing into him carried them both down off the sandstone ridge.

Toq somersaulted helplessly backwards under the lion, which stayed on its feet, maintaining control, and attempted to sink its claws and teeth into the man. When they reached level ground, Toq expected one bite to the neck and that would be it, but no bite came. He looked at the lion standing off to the side, a body length away, struggling to breathe. It walked away and stopped, its sides heaving, a gurgling sound coming from its throat. The beast hung its head and blood flowed out of its mouth. Toq saw blood dripping from the wound where his spear had pierced the lion's chest.

He stood and limped up the slope to find his first spear, then turned to watch the great beast. The lion quietly lay down and died. Toquuxla could not believe it.

He raised his arms, and cried out with all his might, "*Aaahhh!*" The stress, the adrenaline, poured out through his voice and echoed down the valley.

The big cat, with murder in its eyes, lay silent and still. Toq walked down toward it, asking, "Was this a dream?"

Blood pooled around the front of the animal. Toq touched his spearpoint to an open eye, and it did not blink. He startled briefly when he heard something in the brush. "Ground squirrel?"

Fearing a lion pride could be around, he said, "Too dark. I'm getting out of here."

He limped back to his camp with one spear. His bad knee was hurting again, his neck was stiff and sore, and he had a knot on his head and bloody claw marks on his back.

He lay down to sleep and said, "I wonder where those wolves are."

••••

Toq didn't want to move, but he needed to get up. The valley was filled with morning sunlight. Aching and bruised, he hobbled down to the river. The wolves were nowhere to be seen. He pulled off his shirt, tearing at the dried blood on his back. Four holes marked the spots where the lion's claws had gripped him, and they burned and stung, but with his whole body sore, he hardly noticed. He washed the blood out of his shirt, then tried to touch his wounds but could only reach two. One was a puncture, the other had torn skin hanging loosely. Toq knew well that some people died from wounds like these, and he used his shirt to try to scrub the wounds clean with muddy water. He gathered some yarrow—his favorite remedy—crushed it, and tried to apply it to his back with limited success. So, he put some on a flat stone and laid back upon it, trying to work it in.

He felt the knot on the side of his head where he thought the head or jaws of the lion had crashed into him. Sore as he was, he felt powerful and confident—the conqueror. Looking around, he saw only birds, so he limped cautiously back to the sandstone column, his confidence fading quickly. Slowly looking around the edge of the column, he saw the lion laying in the sun, untouched by scavengers. Toq walked up to it and took a good long look. Much of the blood had soaked into the ground, but some remained pooled, not yet dried.

The lion was large but thin, with ribs and hipbones noticeably visible beneath its skin. Old scars marked its face and sides. Two fresh wounds across its nose and one on its tail were signs that this male had recently been in a different fight. Now, Toq didn't feel so tough. It was only with a good dose of luck that he'd been victorious over a poor, old, starving, beat-up male. There it was again, that strange thing about Toq, feeling pity for this great carnivore that had nearly had him for a meal.

"I am sorry that we met this way and that you are dead. I'm really sorry for you."

He pulled back a lip to reveal a huge yellowed and bloodied fang—the last good tooth in a mouth full of broken, worn, and lost teeth. He examined a claw on a bloody front paw. It was tradition to take a tooth or claw, but Toq wasn't sure if he would.

He lifted the leg to see where his spear had entered, pushed his finger into the hole, and felt the end of the broken shaft. He found the rest of the spear shaft in the brush.

"I'm sorry, but I'm glad you're dead instead of me."

Toq gutted the lion and skinned it from neck to tail in one piece. He took some meat, a claw, some long red hair from the mane, and the hide back to his camp. There was no fat on the lion. He went back to collect some of the guts for tanning and the heart to eat. He left the stripped-down carcass for the flies and magpies.

Walking back to camp, he said, "I wonder how old he was. How many animals did he kill and eat in his lifetime?"

• • • •

Toq spent a few days scraping, tanning, and stretching the lion skin, and cooking, eating, healing, and hunting. He retrieved his spearpoint from the lion and made a new spear. He ambushed a deer and over another three days skinned it, tanned it, rolled a seam in with the lion skin, sewed the skins together, and used deer fat to seal the seams. He stretched the hides over the bowl-shaped frame he had fashioned out of wood and bone, sewed them on at the top edge of the frame, and attempted to seal any other questionable seams.

He ate lion and deer meat and healed up well. No animals or predators bothered him. The wolves had not been seen in seven or eight days.

"I do believe they've left me. I wonder where they went."

He looked over his boat and said, "Now I need a paddle."

He searched the valley until he found an animal scapula. He cut and ground down the bone until he had a good surface to attach a whittled wooden handle. He lashed the two together using sinew and tree resin. Raw material was not plentiful on this side of the river, but Toq found what he needed. He was ready to go.

• • • •

Early in the morning, Toq took the paddle to the river, dipped it in the water, and pulled it through, watching the joint flex, causing him to worry if it would hold together.

"Wish I had one good, solid piece of wood," he said.

He looked at the water rushing by, an unstoppable, never-ending force. In a calm pool of water, out of the main current, Toq tested his little bull-boat. It was tippy and tricky to get into, but once in, it was stable and did not leak.

He climbed a hill to see if he could spot the wolves. He hated to leave them again, but they were probably gone anyway. From the hill, he saw a bunch of horses, but that was all, as if he, in moving in, had caused all other animals to move out. He went back, packed up his camp, and took a last look around. This was the longest he had stayed in one place since leaving the village, and he saw the effect he'd had: small trees he had cut, wood and rock chips, ash from his fires, trampled grass, trails and footprints, hair and bones.

"I guess somebody would know I was here," he said.

He whistled to see if the wolves might come, then he shouldered his bags, picked up the boat, and swung it up over his head. His hands were full with his spears and paddle, but his chosen launch point wasn't far.

"Eleven days here," he said while eyeing the river.

He walked carefully along the shoreline—the ground uneven due to mammoth footprints in now-hardened mud. Reaching a spot where a shallow channel separated the bank from an island, he left his burden on the bank and waded into the channel, finding a good point to cross. He made two trips, carrying his stuff across to the island. Though the sun was warm, he still shivered from the cold water and perhaps apprehension. He stood on the downstream side of the island, looking out at the river. In this location, the river was wider and a bit slower, and Toq hoped he could cross without being carried too far downstream into "who knows what kind of trouble."

He put his bags over his shoulders—not wanting to lose them if he got dumped in the water but also not wanting to be dragged under by them. This way, he could easily slip them off if need be. He pushed his spears through two holes at the top rim of his boat and lashed them securely so they rode horizontally, out of his way. He pushed his boat into nearly knee-deep water, tipped the near edge toward him, and stepped one foot inside. He shifted his weight to the bottom, sinking the boat down into the water.

"Now the hard part," he said.

Bracing himself with the end of the paddle stuck firmly in the riverbed, he slowly transferred all his weight to the leg inside the boat, causing the bottom to touch ground, stabilizing his position, and he climbed the rest of the way in.

Getting down on his knees, he pushed the end of his paddle against the sandy river bottom, hopping and wiggling his bowl-shaped boat out into deeper water until he floated free—the top edge of the boat about a fore-arm's length above the water. The boat drifted slowly downstream.

"No leaks! This'll work," he said, pleased with himself.

He paddled out into the main channel, where the current spun his boat, and Toq struggled to keep a straight line, trying to make progress to the far shore. The water was faster than he'd anticipated, and it rushed the boat downstream—already sweeping him past his old camp. He paddled harder, but the round boat was difficult to steer. Halfway across, where the current was strongest, a couple of waves bounced Toq, sloshing water into the boat.

"Crap!" he said, as he spun around to face north. "Wrong way!"

Still, he felt secure, his boat and paddle holding together. The river pushed him back to the north side, where it slowed, and he drifted by the bird-covered island and the ridge he'd come down with the wolves. He re-laxed and looked up at the high hills and ridges on either side.

Watching the land speed by, he said, "This is the way to travel. No work. And look at me go!"

A large eagle flew overhead to see what he was. Toq paddled back into the center of the river, passing hills and coulees, sandstone and rock formations, and cliffs.

He spotted two wolves sniffing along the water's edge below some steep hills.

"Hey! Wolf!" he called out.

The wolves looked at the man in the boat, in the river, racing by.

"I guess I'm leaving! I'll see ya later, okay? Stay alive! Have some pups!"

His wolf ran along the bank for a ways, obviously excited, but soon turned back to his mate. Toq smiled at his old friend as he drifted away.

He passed numerous animals on both sides of the river—bears, mammoths, bighorns, bison, hawks and eagles, waterbirds, and a pack of wolves on the south side to which Toq said, "Stay there. Leave my wolf alone."

The wildlife didn't know what to make of this thing floating by, and while Toq talked to most of them, they were not alarmed. He went by several islands but no major tributaries. Seeing and hearing some rapids downstream, he pulled on the paddle, aiming for a flat, open spot, and with the current's help, it didn't take too much effort.

"Good thing," he mumbled. Water slowly filled the bottom of his boat.

He pulled a little too hard on the paddle, and it broke at the joint. He threw the shaft into the water and, holding the scapula with both hands, paddled hard. The closer he came to the river's edge, the greater his awareness of just how fast he was traveling. A small herd of horses, drinking from the river, were in line with his landing point. He tried to paddle upstream to slow his speed—but it wasn't enough. Watching him, the horses backed up. The boat hit a sandbar hidden in the cloudy water, wrenching it to a sudden stop and sending Toq rolling over into the water.

"Oh!" Toq said as if he'd caused the accident.

He flailed about, trying to get to his feet, grabbing his boat so it wouldn't float away with his spears. The water, thigh deep, pushed hard against him as he struggled to pull his spears free. Once he got them, he let the river take the boat, floating on its side, mostly submerged.

Toq said to the horses, "Don't just stand there! Go get help!"

He threw two of his spears onto the bank and used the third as support against the current. The sandbar ran out, and a deep channel separated him from the shore. He threw the last spear to shore, but it was too far to try to throw his bags. Pushing into the deep, cold water, he swam with all his might until his hands hit mud. He struggled to his feet and pulled his heavy, wet load out of the river. Breathing heavily and shivering, he looked to see his boat caught up by the bank downstream. He could retrieve it, but he no longer needed it.

He waved and said, "Thank you, boat. Thank you, lion."

The horses had moved off a safe distance. Finding a place to camp, Toq spent what remained of the day drying out his clothing and gear, thankful for the sun.

CHAPTER 16

On South

At times, Toq's mind would get stuck on some gloomy memory, and this morning was one of those times. He lay awake obsessing about the assholes from the village, thinking, *How unfortunate that those idiots are the last humans I've seen.* Vengeance and anger consumed him, and he struggled to move on to more pleasant or more pertinent thoughts.

"Kindness, understanding, forgiveness," he muttered as he rose from his bed to check on the morning. "Get busy. Get going. That's the best cure for negative thoughts."

So, while breaking down his camp, he began to wonder if he would ever have any children.

"Not if you don't find another human being, you won't," he laughed.

If he had none, he would be the end of the line. A sobering thought in some ways, but then, on the other hand, *So what?* He wasn't certain it would make any difference to him. If not children, what would he leave behind? What would be permanent?

"Back to leaving your mark, huh?" A concept he rejected in theory, but he found that rejection hard to live up to in reality. What would people say about him? Would they tell stories about him? Would he be a bad guy or a hero? Would they make up lies to diminish his life, or perhaps exaggerate his accomplishments?

He laughed at himself again, saying, "Nobody will ever know what I've done, where I've been, or what I've seen, except that I would tell them, and then they'll say 'big deal' or else they won't believe me. Will I tell them I killed an old, sickly lion or a massive, powerful male in his prime? Some will believe me; others won't, no matter if I tell the truth or not. Most will never know that I even existed. And that's just fine. I don't know about most of humanity, so why should they know about me?"

After packing his bags, he started up a steep hill going south away from the river. He thought about the stories his people told of their nobler ancestors, bravely fighting the elements and marauding beasts, enduring arduous journeys, outsmarting and overpowering human enemies, vanquishing evil spirits, being loved and favored by gods, and either valiantly facing death or else rising up from death to live again. He stopped halfway up the hill to look around, behind, and below.

"Yup, that's me," he said sarcastically, posing as a hero.

He knew that his ancestors had been just like him—just trying to survive. While their stories certainly bore some truth, he didn't believe all those fantastic exploits actually happened. Most people believed these stories to be absolutely true, or at least they said they were.

"So, Toq, you don't believe all those tales, why should you expect anyone to believe yours?" He began climbing again. "I guess I shouldn't. Who really knows what happened in the past? Nobody. Only the person who was there—and even then, they probably misperceive what took place, and they most likely misremember the details. When they die, their life's experiences and memories go with them. I can tell my story, but only I know what I saw and how it felt. I can't pass the entirety of that on to anyone else. My own recollection of anything in my life becomes cloudy with time anyway. Do you really want stories, legends, and myths told about you? It's best to remain unknown. That way, people don't get stupid ideas or some stupid inspiration."

He reached the top of the hill, hardly winded from the steep climb. He looked around without actually seeing. "So, it doesn't really matter what people say about me in the future—if they say or remember me at all." He consciously brought to mind his deceased relatives and friends, saying, "I may be forgotten, but I must remember them."

Toq sat down and thought for a while about his family and his people, living and dead. "Who will come after us? What will people of the future be like?"

He left his reverie and paid more attention to the present time and place. He felt like it did him good to ponder these things once in a while—but now he needed to return to the world and the task at hand.

"Who knows the future anyway? No one." His mind didn't stop, and he pointed his spears in emphasis. "We don't know the future. We can't really know the past. We probably barely know the present. We get bits and pieces of the past, present, and future right, but that's probably about it."

He looked more intently down upon the river below, his gaze following the valley downstream, where it disappeared into canyons and breaks that spread as far as he could see. From this high point, he could once again see far off mountain ranges. Where some would feel overwhelmed or despondent, the resplendent morning with shining mountains and rough country energized him. Toq often felt that the only thing that could stop him or kill his spirit would be an empty stomach. "Or no water, or bad water, or a lion or bear, or a cliff, or a mean river, or a glacier, or bad weather, or an injury . . . or death. Yeah, that could ruin my day. In reality, there are a lot of things that could stop me."

"But this is such a magnificent place," he said, admiring his surroundings. "I wonder what this world will look like after more people come."

Five large mammoths approached the river below. They paused at the bank, where they seemed to be in discussion, and then to Toq's surprise, they waded into the water, wakes flowing out from them in a V pattern. They moved forward—knee-deep, then belly-deep, and then their backsides disappeared underwater, until they swam. Tusks and trunks stuck up out of the water, while their heads bobbed up and down, sometimes going completely under. The mighty river pushed the giants well downstream before their feet touched bottom, and all five, one by one, rose up and out onto the opposite bank.

"Amazing," said Toq, never thinking such a swim was possible.

The mammoths paused for a while. "Probably catching their breath." Then, they moved up into a canyon and out of sight.

"How many people have seen that?" he exclaimed. "How many in the future will ever see it?"

He knew people would come, and some would see it, but he didn't know sights like that would not last forever.

"Well, goodbye, river. Goodbye, wolf. Hope to see you again."

He hiked south across a ridge (Whiskey Ridge) and down into and out of a deep, wide coulee (Dog Creek). He walked across a prairie upland area parallel to a large river valley to his west (Judith River valley). Spindly spruce trees, scattered here and there, became taller and more numerous. He reached the burn area—a blackened zone with smoke still rising in a few places. Some spruce trees were only black poles sticking up into the air; some had retained a few green needles high in the treetops. Many whole trees had fallen, bringing up roots from the ground, while others had snapped in half, leaving only broken trunks standing. Most of the brush and grass had burned, but patches of green and yellow showed where the fire had not reached. Toq walked across the charred earth, his moccasins turning black with ash. The burned-off cover revealed soil and rocks and bones and antlers, things normally hidden beneath vegetation.

The burn area was long and narrow. He came over a rise and surprised a herd of flat-headed peccaries—the first he'd seen since leaving his homeland. Their brown-gray bodies stood out against the black landscape, and when they saw Toq, they ran with impressive speed up over the next ridge, a cloud of dust trailing behind. Toq followed them through the burned grass. The burn zone ended at the next ridge, and Toq stood looking into a land of yellow grasses, green brush, and scattered spruce. The peccaries had disappeared into the vegetation, and while Toq could track them, today, he had no need to hunt.

He trekked south, into a greener, more wooded land with more brush and abundant ripe berries, which he ate by the handful.

"So good. So sweet. Don't eat too much," he warned himself, but the treat provided a welcome change from his diet of flesh.

He wandered through a parkland with open, grassy meadows and more spruce, as well as alders, willows, aspen, and birch. Bogs of clear water filled some depressions. He progressed into a mature forest. As the planet warmed, the ice sheets retreated, and the woods advanced north.

Toq enjoyed the change of scenery, but the forest obstructed his view of his surroundings, making it difficult to spot predators. Also, his pace slowed, as he had to zigzag around marshes and thick stands of trees and brush. He felt that after days of this, he would be walking blindly, with no good sense of where he was going. He followed animal trails, which sped his progress, but predator tracks in the mud made him nervous, so he often forged his own path instead. On the positive side, he could camp and hide in thick brush, and the wood provided material for lean-tos and spears and fires.

The birds of the woods were different—some of them anyway. He seemed to be seeing more crows, ravens, jays, magpies, woodpeckers, and chickadees, and he even saw a couple of owls. But there were fewer prairie songbirds, swans, geese, and ducks. The furry critters changed, as well. Ground squirrels and prairie dogs were replaced by tree squirrels; pronghorns and horses were gone, while whitetail deer and elk began showing up. Toq did not recognize some animal tracks. Other beasts were very familiar to him: wolves, caribou, some bison, and a small group of mammoths—one pressing all her weight against a tall spruce until it toppled over. Brilliant blue birds danced in the air over the mammoths.

He nearly stepped on a porcupine and said, "Well, I haven't seen one of you in a long time."

He watched the sky. The warm days were churning up thunderstorms again. The woods crackled with dryness—even after the rain. Grass crunched under his feet, and he could only hope that lightning wouldn't cause a fire. The woods and shade felt cooler than the plains, and although Toq heard the breeze flowing through the pine needles and leaves, swaying the tops gently back and forth, he felt only a whisper on the ground.

"No lions, no bears," he said at the end of the day, though he'd seen lion tracks and bear poop, as well as deep claw marks in a tree well above his head.

Thunder rumbled as he set up camp and made three healthy fires in a triangle around his shelter. He felt suddenly rich with so much wood available, but he also took great care to contain his fires. Relaxing and enjoying his first night in the woodlands, he remained vigilant.

• • • •

No rain and no forest fires, but at night, the woods were darker than the prairie, and when animals moved, they stepped on dead branches, which cracked and snapped loudly, causing Toq to lie still and listen or to peer into the blackness to identify the intruder. He got up often to add wood to the fires. It was another change—a new world for him to adjust to. One continuous episode of movement and crunching wood told him a giant was passing by, perhaps more than one. He heard snorting and low growls, as well as horns or antlers or tusks whacking against wood. Deer pawed in the leaf litter around his camp, undeterred by the fires. He chased them off, but one kept coming back, and he finally gave in, just lying there, listening to the creature paw the ground and chew only a couple of steps from his head. Any little sound or movement caused it to jump or leap away. Still, Toq loved these animals. They made him feel alive and not alone.

Now that the sun was up, the forest seemed quieter. He stood at the edge of a coulee, where a clearing gave him a good view into the wooded valley bottom to the west. He saw a little river through the trees (Judith River). A few large beasts moved slowly in the brush and the shade of the trees, but he couldn't tell what they were. He was tempted to go into the valley and follow the stream south, but the brush looked much too thick, making the route slow and dangerous.

He stayed above the valley and continued southward, walking through a land of scattered woods and open meadows. The prairie clung tenaciously to a few places, but woodlands were replacing grass. Toq was leaving his beloved plains far behind. He made his way to the base of some higher hills and treeless mountains (North Moccasin Mountains), where he camped and, the next day, climbed to the top to get a good look around.

From the summit, he looked down upon lands that appeared to be equally divided between trees and meadows—although off in the distance, it looked like a sea of woods across the rolling lowlands. New mountain ranges came into view (Big Snowy Mountains and Little Belt Mountains).

"Where now, Toq?"

The summer days were coming to a close, and even though he was certain to have plenty of good fall weather, he needed to find either people or a good place to overwinter with plenty of time to make preparations. He searched for the telltale sign of smoke from campfires rising above the trees.

"There's nobody there," he said. "Don't worry about it. You are going to be on your own. But which way to go?"

He looked east, thinking of going around the mountains in the southeast, or continuing south toward the distant, flat-looking mountains. He had no way of knowing if he would run into impassable mountains, canyons, or rivers.

"Well, let's go see." He walked south down a ridge and up another to a different peak. He followed more ridges down off the mountains into a valley of trees. He went around the east side of the next mound of high hills and continued south, stopping whenever there was a clearing, so he could see farther out. He seriously considered a possible route east, but he felt the pull to go south and that pull won out.

Toq wandered for three days through thin birch and spruce forests. He followed along the foothills of an extensive range of domed mountains (Big Snowy Mountains), meeting them on the northwest side and walking the line where the woods gave way to the higher, treeless slopes. He moved in and out of treed zones with views north and west showing lower, hilly, semi-forested lands, prairies, and squat mountains. The open slopes fed bighorns, deer, and the occasional bison. Toq saw a few separate groups of long-legged llamas on the grass and brush–covered foothills. He crossed paths with a cougar, a lynx, and a big wolverine with a kit—animals he rarely saw outside the woods. Showing no fear, the wolverine approached to see what he was. Toq stood still, his spear pointed at the creature that looked like a little bear. She could be dangerous if she attacked.

Toq spoke softly to her, "Easy, girl. That's close enough. We don't want any trouble here."

The young one held back. Both animals moved quickly, looking, sniffing, their heads bobbing up and down. The mother growled a little, and then they scampered off.

He came off the foothills of the west side of the mountains and made his way across a wide gap between mountain ranges opening to the south. Nearly treeless, the gap held brush and grass intermixed, and Toq saw bison and musk oxen here.

He left the gap and followed a small herd of mammoths back into the trees and brush, staying well back so as not to disturb them and stepping around large piles of dung. The mammoths paused in the trees. Toq moved around and away from them, wary of what might be impeding them. He stood on a small rise, looking down into the trees, hiding himself in the foliage.

Trees and shadow created dark spots in the wooded area below. Dust floated in the sunlight around the mammoths, standing silently, every one of them with a raised trunk, sniffing the air. Toq couldn't see or smell anything. Then, the big female in front emitted a low, faint rumble as she rocked from side to side, stepped back, and then turned around. The others did the same, snapping the surrounding branches and shaking the birch leaves. Toq didn't see any little calves in this group, which was good, since the herd began to panic. The big female—now in back—bellowed a high-pitched call to get the herd moving, and she pushed the mammoth in front of her. Every one of the elephants filed back out of the woods, almost running in their funny, awkward way.

Nothing chased after them, though. Toq remained still, peering into the now quiet forest. From the corner of his eye, he saw movement and turned to focus on something—big, brown and black, and superbly camouflaged—that rose up from behind a bush.

Not a bear, thought Toq.

It hoisted its body up into the air so that it stood upright, on two legs, and turned to look in the direction of the long-gone mammoths. Toq didn't move. *What is that?* He didn't know if it was a predator or not. The beast raised an arm overhead and scratched its side with massive claws. Toq couldn't see its eyes, but it had a large, smooth head with tiny ears. It looked left and right, and the rounded front of its face opened up in a giant yawn, revealing no fangs. Its teeth looked more like those of a plant-eater than a man-eater.

Toq relaxed. The big animal walked on all fours to a birch tree, where it rose up, hooked a branch with its front claws, and stripped off the leaves, twigs, and soft bark. It wrapped a long tongue around the bundle and put it in its mouth. Upright on its hind legs, it would tower over a man. It moved slowly and deliberately, and while he was certain it must be able to defend itself with those huge claws and long, muscular front legs, he couldn't see how it would not be easily taken down by a bear, lions, or wolves.

"You have to run fast, fight, or hide. So, what do you do?" he whispered to the giant sloth. "And you're alone?"

He moved slowly through the brush to get a closer look, careful not to step on any dead branches. Toq wondered why the mammoths were so wary of this animal, concluding that they probably didn't know what it was. The closer he came, the more he saw that the beast had been here for some time. The lower branches of several birch trees had been stripped clean or broken off, new growth on the spruce trees had been nibbled, some brush was chewed up, and clearly the giant had been digging up roots. Toq got close enough to see scars on its back. A spot where the fur was mostly worn off revealed a thick, hard skin beneath.

"Ah. Skin too hard to bite through," he mumbled.

Suddenly, the ground sloth stopped feeding, dropped on all fours, and turned to face the man. It made a loud, croaking call, causing Toq to move slowly away. The brush to his left rustled, and two more huge sloths stood up. Toq had no inkling the brush had hid two other slumbering sloths, and now he realized he was in danger. They surprised him with how quickly they moved. First, one stood tall to measure him, while the other two charged. The nearest one lunged at him and swung a long, claw-tipped arm at Toq, who ducked and leaped away, clinging to his bags and spears as he sprinted through the brush. He ran a little way past some trees, then glanced back to see that they were not pursuing him. A trickle of blood ran down his cheek from where a thorn had raked his face.

"I guess I won't mess around with you guys!" he said, breathing hard.

The three sloths watched the man, and he looked back at them, and then noticed a fourth giant moving toward the other three. Wondering if there were even more, out of sight, Toq decided to get out of there.

"That's why the mammoths turned around . . . bad-tempered sons of bitches." Toq felt like a fool. "You're a lucky dumbass, Toq."

The encounter reinforced his awareness of the dangers hiding in the brush, and he lamented his inability to smell or hear things that other animals could. As he walked on, his mind wandered into a more nightmarish outcome: The claw of that huge arm could have connected with his head, sending it flying off into the brush without the rest of his body. In another scene, he saw his feet get tangled in the brush, tripping him. The sloth would pounce on him, forcing the air out of his lungs and squashing his body, and Toq would hear his bones breaking. The jaws, well adapted to crunching branches, would bite down on a leg, crushing bone and tearing open an artery. In his mind, he watched the sloths play tug-of-war with his body, pulling him into two, then sitting on their tails and throwing their heads back in laughter at how easily the soft man had come apart.

"Well, now we're getting a little ridiculous." Toq chuckled at the stupidity of that last image. "Giant, laughing ground sloths!"

But it was clear those beasts were formidable.

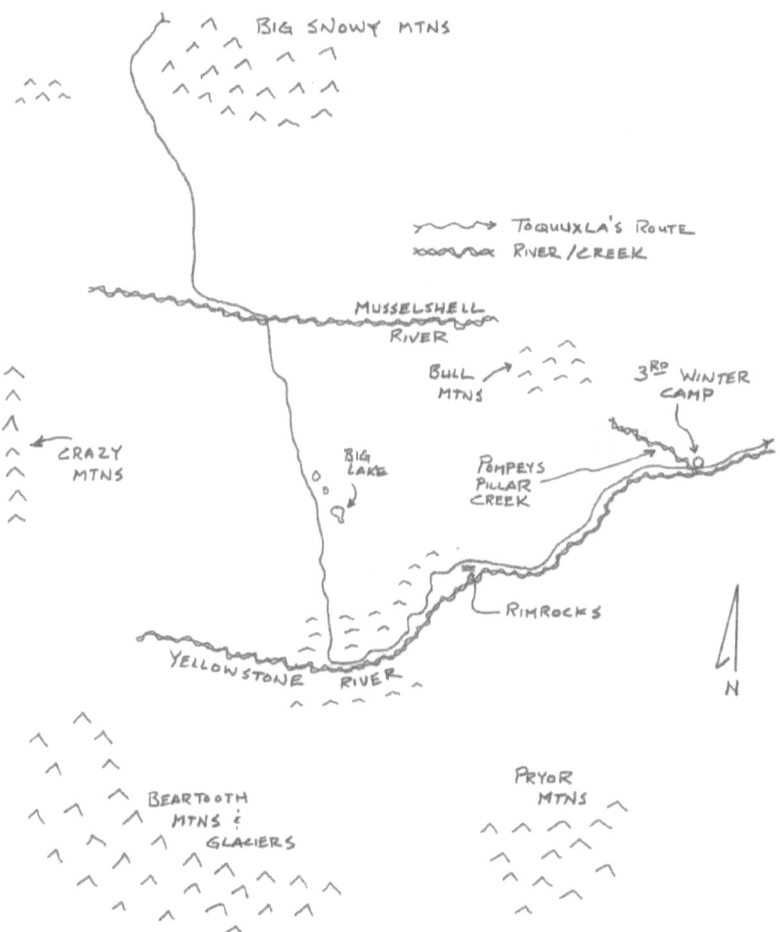
BIG SNOWY MTNS
TŌQUUXLA'S ROUTE
RIVER /CREEK
MUSSELSHELL RIVER
BULL MTNS
3RD WINTER CAMP
CRAZY MTNS
BIG LAKE
POMPEYS PILLAR CREEK
RIMROCKS
YELLOWSTONE RIVER
N
BEARTOOTH MTNS & GLACIERS
PRYOR MTNS

The next morning, Toq continued trekking south through lands that alternated between open prairie, sparse tree and brush, and thick patches of woods. He liked the variety of landscapes and ecological zones, as well as the diversity of wildlife. The giant sloths dominated his thoughts the same way the mammoths had when he'd first encountered them. He hoped to find more so he could observe them and learn about them.

He walked onto a treeless hill, where he saw the high, rugged, glaciated peaks of a mountain range to the southwest (Crazy Mountains). Large, puffy thunderclouds grew over those mountains, and big clouds formed above the horizon straight south as well.

Near the end of the second day, he reached a valley with numerous sandstone formations and cliffs above a river flowing east (Musselshell River). The valley was busy with wildlife, and after carefully selecting a safe campsite away from the valley, he spent a night listening to the roars of lions—the first ones in quite some time.

The next day, he followed the north side of the river valley, spotting the pride of lions along the way, and steering clear. He walked half a day east, then dropped into the valley bottom to drink from the river. The silty gray water, partially fed by glaciers, was not as bad as some, not as good as others. He thought about all the rivers he had followed and crossed and that he had not named any of them.

"They don't need names. I know them. Things only need names when there are other people around," he said.

This river ran strong, but he would not need a boat to cross it—probably not even a raft.

He happened upon a wetland area adjacent to the river, with cattails lining the perimeter. A pond appeared in the middle, glassy smooth and reflecting the trees and blue sky. The clear water and nearly unblemished surface was disturbed by only a few bugs and the circular ripples of a couple of rising fish. A beaver pushed into the water across the way, trailing small waves. This was the first beaver Toq had seen on his trip. Beavers had followed the rivers and streams and trees as they expanded into new lands opened up to them by a world getting warmer. As usual, Toq was delighted to see a new but familiar friend—and not just because they provided fur and food.

He walked around the pond and crossed atop a dam of sticks, reeds, and mud that was as tall as he was. The beaver slapped its tail on the surface and dove beneath, vanishing from sight. A large beaver lodge rose above the water on one side of the pond. Toq stood in awe of everything these water mammals had built—one stick and one scoop of mud at a time. They made him think. A couple of ducks and a brood of nearly full-grown ducklings paddled away from him. The scene was so peaceful, it filled him with a great sense of contentment and a desire to dwell there for a while to allow it all to saturate his being. He breathed deeply the fresh cool air permeated with the aromas of pine, spruce, grass, and clean water. An osprey landed on a treetop, and dragonflies and damselflies darted around the edges of the pond. Little yellow birds, blue birds, and orange birds flew across the pond into the trees or brush, sometimes in a straight line, sometimes flitting to nab a bug out of the air.

"No wind, no bug bites, perfect temperature. It's flawless, undamaged, unsullied," he said.

Toq wished the world could be peaceful like this all the time, but he knew in just a couple full moons, the wind would blow, the cold and snow would come, the pond would freeze, the plants would turn yellow and brown, the birds would leave, the bugs would die, and this perfection would be changed. And even within this period of calm, violence *was* being done—mostly to bugs, and by fish, birds, and dragonflies. And once that osprey spied a fish, she would dive in to grab it and tear it apart. Any number of large beasts might suddenly invade the picture, breaking the peace. He reveled in it for a few moments longer, just to see if the osprey would strike, and then he moved on.

He continued east, looking for a place to cross the river. He came upon another small group of giant ground sloths just inside a line of birch and spruce trees and watched them. He estimated that they were about the same size as the short-faced bear but not as large as the bison. This time, he kept his distance.

By midafternoon, he arrived at a wide, shallow animal crossing. A large bull moose crossed the river ahead of Toq, who waited in the trees until the bull disappeared into the woods. No predators gave chase, and none could be seen. At its deepest, the stream had come to the bottom of the moose's body, so Toq guessed he could cross fairly easily, though he might have to swim if the current was strong.

He stuffed his clothes into a bag and ventured across the shallows to a rocky, muddy island in the middle of the river. The next part of the river was deeper, so Toq left a spear and a bag on the island and carried the other bag and two spears above his head into cold, chest-deep water. He struggled to keep his feet.

"Damn it! It wasn't this deep on the moose." He rose out of the river and deposited his belongings on the bank, saying, "One done."

He took a moment to catch his breath, and then he plunged back in. He retrieved his remaining spear and bag from the island and pushed back across the current. Once out of the water, he shivered for a while, then dressed, and counted himself lucky that he didn't have to dry out any of his stuff.

Toq walked up a hill and out of the valley. As far as he could tell through the trees, the river continued east. His mind was set on going south, so he hiked the rest of the day over a highland and down into a nice little valley with a clear-water creek running to the east (Fish Creek). He crossed it and set up camp on a small rise in a stand of birch trees.

In the dusky light, he saw a cougar making its way casually through the brush straight toward him. Toq had yet to make a fire and felt a bit irritated that he might have to deal with this cat. The cougar didn't seem to be hunting him; in fact, it seemed oblivious. Toq picked up his two big spears and moved directly toward the animal. The cougar stopped. Toq had no desire to kill it, but he did want to squelch any thought the beast might have of attacking him.

Toq yelled, "*Hiyahh*!" and ran at the cougar. It crouched, ears back, then panicking, swapped its head for its tail and bolted away at lightning speed, except instead of running off, it leaped up into a spruce tree, crashing through branches and twigs until it was nearly at the top, well above and away from this dangerous man-thing. Toq looked up at it, its bulk causing the top to sway a bit.

"Huh," said Toq. "You didn't exactly leave the area, like I'd hoped."

But he figured the cat wouldn't trouble him, so he headed back to camp. Halfway there, he looked in time to see the cougar jump an unbelievable distance from high in the tree. The spruce rocked, the cat landed with a graceful thud, and it sprinted away into the brush. It was gone, and Toq returned to build his fire.

• • • •

Toquuxla may have felt vexed that he lacked the superior sense of smell or hearing of some of his fellow animals, but spending many moons alone, camped out in the open, had sharpened even his unconscious brain. Most nights, he slept through the distant calls of wolves or coyotes or bison, but not lions and not mammoths. A snapping twig would wake him immediately. With his ear against a fur pillow, he could often hear or feel footfalls transmitted through the ground.

Now, something woke Toq in the middle of this deeply dark night. He couldn't even discern what had done it: a broken branch or twig, a smell, footsteps, breathing, digging? He silently rolled over to look at his fire, now just a dim pile of coals. Since entering the semi-wooded lands, he'd made a habit of camping in thick brush or right next to a good climbing tree. He wondered if thunder had woken him. Perhaps that cougar had returned. He looked out into the blackness, seeing and hearing nothing. Then, sound erupted from the silence, branches broke in the dark, and Toq scrambled to his feet. He had not set up his shelter on this night, so he stood straight up and briefly considered reaching for his spear. The beast moved toward him. Toq left the spear and reached up in the dark for the first branch of the birch tree above his head.

The evening before, he had chosen this spot and this tree for this reason. He pulled himself up into the tree. The cougar would have no trouble coming after him, but somehow, he was certain this was not the cat. Whatever it was, the beast did not charge headlong into his camp. Toq moved quickly but carefully, gripping the trunk and a branch, getting a foot- or toehold, until he soon was high and safe enough to look down. The earth below was dark, and a large black shadow moved into his camp, momentarily obscuring the glowing coals of his fire.

From the way the shadow moved, Toq knew it was a bear. The massive bruin walked to the base of the birch and looked up. Toq heard it sniffing.

It stood on its hind limbs and reached high, but Toq was out of reach. He didn't know if this bear could climb, so he went higher. The beast did attempt to climb, digging into the trunk with front and back claws, but there was no way he was going to get his mass up that tree. He tried, but only briefly, then bellowed at the man, raking his claws down the tree trunk and pushing on it a few times to see if he could topple it. The birch moved, and Toq feared the bear would succeed, but the bear wasn't sure the man was worth the effort, so he sniffed around the camp, found the bag that held the dried meat, ripped it open, and devoured all the man's food.

Toq couldn't see what was going on below, but he could hear it. "Ahh, shit. Bad bear!" He wished he'd thought to carry that bag into the tree with him. He listened to the bear ransack the rest of his stuff, hearing a spear shaft snap under its bulk, teeth gnawing on leather and wood, and fur bedding tossed to the side into the coals, briefly flaring up, startling the bear. But the bear kept on searching for something to eat. Once satisfied that he had eaten or destroyed all that he could, he reached back up into the tree, exhaled loudly in frustration, and then wandered off into the night.

An owl hooted in a distant tree, but otherwise the night was still once again. He had no intention of getting down, and he tried to find a comfortable position among the branches, but they angled upward, making for an awkward perch. After a period of quiet, Toq finally slipped to the ground, grabbed his sleeping fur, and climbed back up into the tree. He wrapped the robe around himself for warmth, but still, he couldn't sleep. He sat in the V of a branch and leaned against the trunk, waiting for daylight. The bear did not return. The man and his stuff provided slim pickings for the giant. Toq waited for what seemed like forever for light to appear in the east. He then waited for another long period before the land below reflected enough light to reveal what may or may not be lurking in the remaining shadows.

Sunlight hit the treetops before Toq came down. He was tired and sore, and he wanted to lie down to sleep, but that was not an option. Thankfully, only a small spot on his bedding had actually burned in the embers, but both bags were ripped up, one spear shaft and point were busted, his rolled-up lean-to had been chewed, and all his food was gone. Toq quickly gathered his scattered belongings atop his fur sleeping skin and rolled them up together, then he picked up his two remaining spears and skedaddled. He hiked south far and fast on an empty stomach, believing the bear had gone north.

He finally stopped around midmorning, hungry, tired, and thirsty. He lay in the shade of a few spruce trees and slept until past midday. Then, he rose and hiked to a wide and deep coulee (Big Coulee), where he found water and set up camp. He hunted for food and tried to patch up the damage the bear had done.

Toq spent the next day in this coulee, hunting, eating, rehabilitating his gear, and searching for stones for a new spearpoint. One little bear encounter had thrown him completely out of whack. He was lucky he hadn't had any nights like that on the prairie.

"No blood, no scars. Not too bad," he said.

●●●●

Toq trekked south crossing open, flat prairie, sandstone-walled coulees, spruce and birch woodlands, and a wide expanse of land that had burned a year or two before. Blackened, dead trees, standing and fallen, spread across the land, but new grass, fireweed, and brush pushed up out of the earth, concealing most of the charred remains of their kin. The ground beneath an old, burned-out stand of trees was ankle- to knee-deep in a thick covering of birch seedlings. In fact, the burned area was greener than its surroundings, and all of this new growth showed plenty of signs of being eaten by a wide variety of creatures.

He walked around groups of bison, horses, musk oxen, and mammoths—by far a higher concentration than what he'd seen in the unburned zones. The bear encounter left him acutely on edge. Indeed, he knew he was too tense, too nervous—jumping at the sight of every animal.

"Snap out of it, Toq. You're going to make yourself crazy."

He camped in a large area of wetlands and lakes (Lake Basin: Hailstone and Halfbreed Lakes), which was more thickly wooded and overrun by mosquitoes. With the forest blocking the wind, there was no relief from the flying demons. Toq dealt with them the best he could, but they made him wish for a killing frost to knock them down.

• • • •

Thunderstorms rolled over the land throughout the night, lightning illuminating sky and earth in blinding flashes, thunder shaking the ground, and rain pouring down, stopping, and then pouring again. By daybreak, the violent storms had gone, leaving a dull, cloudy sky behind. A cold breeze from the north kept Toq lingering in bed. He gazed at the bottom of the lean-to, where a spider slowly made its way toward an outer edge, clearly sluggish in the colder air. Toq flicked it away with a finger.

The quiet, cool morning was suddenly interrupted by the nearby smashing of wood.

Figuring it to be mammoths or bison, he decided it was time to get up. "Let's see what's out there."

After relieving his bladder, he picked up his spear and listened intently. All was quiet—the only sound that of the breeze forcing its way through the trees. Toq looked into the woods where he believed the activity had come from. He moved slowly and silently, stopping often to look and listen. A clearing on his left was empty. He checked the trees as he proceeded in case he needed to escape up one.

More sticks snapped ahead. Toq peered into the dark forest gloom, missing the bright light of the sun. He snuck forward. Branches broke continuously now.

"Maybe it's ground sloths," he whispered.

Movement caught his eye. An elephant trunk reached out from behind a tree, as did a couple of stained ivory tusks.

"Mammoths."

He never tired of seeing them, and so he moved closer to see how many there were. What were they doing? What were they eating? He imagined a group of hunters attacking the giants in the woods. How would they do it? How dangerous would it be? How many people would one mammoth feed? He knew people would come, and the mammoths would be hunted. Even if there were other animals to be had, there were always people who had to prove they were the greatest, the strongest, the bravest, the smartest hunters.

"Idiots," Toq said. "The human horde is often the lowest of creatures."

He moved downwind of the giants, then slowly advanced until he could see the whole lot of them, keeping in mind his close call with the sloths. Seven large animals browsed on the trees and brush, but these were strange-looking mammoths. Puzzled, Toq moved to get a better look. They were shaggier with darker hair.

"They might be wet." One of the animals turned so Toq could see it more clearly. "What are you? That's no mammoth," he whispered.

While still giants, these were not as big as the mammoths Toq was used to seeing. They were shorter, longer, stouter; their tusks were straighter, their heads were flatter without the dome, and their shoulders lacked the hump.

"They're not young mammoths, either. It's a different kind of animal."

Now deeply curious, he wondered how many kinds of elephants there might be. He watched the mastodons for some time—the way they moved, what they ate, and how they interacted.

"Always something new to see," he said quietly. "Different kinds of cats, canines, horses, deer, fish, birds, bugs . . . and elephants." The more he thought about it, the more he wondered. "It is an incredible world."

He slipped quietly away without ever alerting the mastodons, and he wondered if a mammoth could mate with a mastodon. He packed up his camp and walked on south, happy to have seen something new and unusual to begin his day.

After the night's rain, it was a sloppy and slow day of hiking through mud and puddles. Not Toq's favorite kind of day, it was a tedious, laborious slog with no sun, no blue skies, and no views. Occasional spatters of rain kept everything wet, but it never developed into a downpour. Toq set up camp in the trees earlier than normal so he could build a couple of fires and dry out. He saw elephant footprints in the mud and wondered if they were mammoth or mastodon.

•••

The morning was cold and damp, the air still and silent. A thick fog turned the nearby trees into ghosts. Toq took his time breaking camp and walked slowly south. By midmorning, the fog began to clear, and sunlight tried to seep through. He followed large, wide animal trails through the woods and across meadows, clearings, and hills, always on the lookout for the prints of predators in the mud. Before midday, he followed a wandering ridge out to a point, clear of trees, and stood in the sun, looking down into a fog-enshrouded valley. A few openings in the fog revealed a forested valley floor with a substantial river flowing through it (Yellowstone River). Above the fog, south to southwest, a distant, high range of mountains wrestled with scattered clouds for dominance (Beartooth Mountains). Thick glaciers glistened in the sunlight, often capping the peaks and mountain plateaus. Massive ice floes crept slowly off the mountains, converging in the main valleys where they pushed down into the foothills.

To the southeast, he could see a lower, flatter mountain range without glaciers (Pryor Mountains). Toq waved away the flies in front of his face and sat on the edge of the bluff to watch the valley below. The fog persisted for some time, resisting the warming sun and a nearly nonexistent breeze. Large beasts easily stood out in the brush and even among willows and trees, but despite their size, bears and lions could easily hide in the growth. He pondered the absence of the long-fanged cats (saber-tooths); he had not seen any in this new land and hoped he would not see any here.

"You never know where one might turn up," he said.

The river ran east, and in places, it flooded the entire bottom from the hills on the north to the hills on the south. In most stretches, the river divided itself into multiple channels, forming islands, sweeping crescent-shaped bows, and marshes. From the bluff, Toq could see clearly where mammoths or mastodons or ground sloths had been gorging on willows, brush, birch, and spruce. The ever-changing path of the river made life difficult for trees, but despite that, they grew well in places that the water had not ravaged for years. The large animals knew of these places and did their own ravaging.

Toq walked down into the valley, having seen only one bear and a cub far upstream. He made his way along animal trails through the woody vegetation to the riverbank. The silty gray water ran fast and rough and deep.

"Another river needing a boat."

This place had many trees, but none were large enough to make a dug-out canoe. Once again, Toq had to weigh his options. The summer days were running out. Surprisingly, there was no sign of people here, either, although he knew they might be somewhere up- or downstream. Finding people would make his decisions easier. Not finding anyone, and not finding a good crossing, would leave him settling on this side somewhere, since he didn't wish to take the time to build a reliable boat.

He looked west, talking to himself, "I could go upstream. Maybe the river will be smaller that way. But that would probably mean going into those glaciated mountains, leaving wooded lowlands." He made up his mind pretty quickly, saying, "Go downstream. You might find people. If you don't, this seems like a good valley to stay through winter. Find a shelter, make shelter, maybe more than one. Yeah, let's do it."

Feeling good about making up his mind so quickly, he left the valley bottom to hike the northern hilltops. He crossed a small, clear creek late in the afternoon and decided to camp a short distance up the hill from it. He hunted the rest of the day, and as the darkness grew, he settled under his lean-to, considering the possibility of finding people. The thought of it excited him, believing he would find safety with others in addition to human interaction. That is, if they were friendly and welcomed him in. The anticipation left him restless, and he found it difficult to fall asleep.

CHAPTER 17

Settling in One Spot

Toq wandered east over hills, into coulees, across benches, and through valleys. He reached places where the river, less confined by valley walls, spread wide with braided channels and islands. During the afternoon of his second day, he sat on the edge of a long sandstone cliff wall (Rimrocks), looking into a sprawling valley of water and woodland. The only clearings in the bottom lands were the ones created by large herbivores. A herd of mammoths filled a marshland, eating and trampling water plants, rolling in muddy water, and spraying their heads and backs. Toq didn't see any of those new mastodons.

Gigantic boulders and slabs fallen from the cliff littered the slope below, where a pride of lions wove around them. The predators vanished into a thick stand of trees, and Toq could not see what they were after. Two big males appeared, trailing the females, moving as if they were being dragged along reluctantly by the females. The valley was quiet, except for a few late summer birds, but even these had slowed their chatter. Toq scrambled out to a spot where he could see where the lions had come from. Down below, at the base of the cliffs, two lionesses lay in the shade, patiently tolerating the running and wrestling of a bunch of cubs. The cubs were three or four full moons old, growing bigger and more agile, and full of energy and carefree play. From his safe perch, the cubs were fun to watch, and Toq grinned at their antics.

He looked back into the valley, catching a glimpse of the roving pride in the distance. "This would be a great place to winter, but I'm afraid it belongs to these lions. It's not for me."

Deer sprang from the woods in front of the lions and hopped away, but the lions did not give chase, and Toq moved on.

He trekked along the river for two more days, growing concerned that the general northeast direction he was taking might lead him out of the wooded country he wished to winter in. He told himself he would settle in the next suitable, lion-free place he came across. He entered a wide and flat coulee coming from the northwest with a small stream snaking back and forth (Pompeys Pillar Creek). Beaver dams created a series of ponds stepping up the coulee. Toq searched the area—every hill and gully—looking for signs of predators.

"No poop, no big cat tracks, no claw marks, good water. I think this is it. I'm moving in."

He chose a location well away from and well above the river, in a side coulee, over a hill from the beaver-dammed creek. Using a flat, spade-shaped stone large enough for two hands, Toq dug into a hillside below a sandstone cliff outcrop, leveling out a spot for his winter home. Here, he'd be out of the usual animal travel corridors but still close to water. The cliff faced south— not the best for keeping out of the wind, but he hoped it would minimize the buildup of snowdrifts.

"I have no idea how much it snows here. It's probably different every year, anyway," he told himself.

Toq divided his time between hunting, gathering material, and exploring. He found some cliff overhangs but no caves. He didn't want to try to settle in a cave, anyway, since they were harder to heat and all too often used by larger and dangerous animals. He dragged six long mammoth tusks back to his campsite, along with some large leg bones. He dug holes for the ends of the tusks, which served as the framework for his shelter, and then piled rocks around the base of each tusk to help hold them up. He tied the tusks together at the top, where they met at the apex of his shelter, using sinew and hide. The shelter would be just a little taller than his full height. Toq stood back to critique his work. A strong gust of wind blew by, pushing against the tusks, but they did not budge.

"Ah, good! Glad that wind didn't blow when I was setting it all up," he said.

The tusks created a shape that was far from symmetrical, as they were of different lengths and curves. He had not yet made any tools that could saw, cut, or chop away at the tusks, but he didn't think he needed to cut them. One tusk rose straight up, then curved over to the top; one bowed out then over; one bowed in then over; one was straight; one was perfect; and one was too long, with the tip projecting up and out above all the others. Toq chuckled at the chaotic arrangement. He'd tried to imitate the beaver lodges, but their round homes looked much better than his.

"Well, I'm not done with it yet!" he reminded himself.

He stacked bones and stones up around the base. He added slender tree trunks and long branches to the vertical frame, sticking the ends into holes, braced with rocks, and bending them up near the top to be tied in with the tusks. He dug a small ditch around the base and built up a berm of dirt and clay over the rocks and bones. He mashed plant materials and sod into the berm to help hold it together.

Next, he needed a covering. Birch bark, long bundles of grasses, reeds, or cattails for thatching would work, but they could also catch fire in his small shelter. "Hides would be best," he mumbled, but skins were hard to come by, because they were usually consumed, torn up, or shriveled and dried.

In his gathering trips, he stumbled upon a dead caribou, surprisingly untouched by scavengers. He skinned it and brought the hide back to camp.

"That's one. Need more," he said. He didn't need the meat, but he brought some back to camp anyway, saying, "Can't let the scavengers have it all."

He couldn't imagine killing all the animals he would need to cover his shelter, nor eating that much meat, even with a long winter. He decided to save the caribou fur for winter clothing and instead began to weave thatch walls onto his shelter. He searched the area for days, hoping to find good skins, and he finally found a mastodon carcass. Bear and wolf tracks covered the ground around it, and the belly and neck had been eaten out, as well as an area around the tail. Bird poop covered the carcass, and it smelled putrid. Toq looked all around for the carnivores, but finding none nearby, he took a chance at trying to remove the hide on the top side of the beast. It seemed okay to use, but it stunk, and it was thick, tough, and heavy. He worked only a short time, then left without taking anything, not wishing to press his luck. He walked to the nearest stream to wash off, deciding to return over the coming days to see if he could get at least one side of the skin off.

Over the next two days, he kept going back to the mastodon. He never saw the bear, or bears, but he saw that they had returned and fed on meat exposed when Toq cut the hide back. He eventually freed the skin from the carcass, but it was too heavy to drag very far. So, he split it in two and dragged them, one at a time, to a place not too near his camp, where he scraped the fleshy sides clean. He brought them to his hut and tied them onto the top, where they could dry in place.

"That helps. We're getting there," Toq said, looking over his home, partially covered with skins at the top and thatching at the bottom. He attached a long rib bone to a separate flap of mastodon skin, so he could open and close a smoke venthole from inside. The skins smelled better after scraping, drying, and getting smoked from the fire.

Toq placed the firepit a bit closer to the doorway in order to discourage animal visitors, leaving him with more room along the back of the circular shelter.

A cold wind blew in, and it rained off and on for six days straight. Toq was miserable and cold when the wind shifted, and without a completed covering, rain and wind now poured inside, and he had to dig a ditch to drain water out through his front door. He set up his old lean-to inside the hut to provide an extra layer of protection. On the last day of the storm, a heavy, wet, wind-driven snow bent trees and broke branches, adding to the difficulties of man and beast alike.

The day after the big snow, the sun came out and immediately began melting snow. Relieved of their burden, tree branches and leaves bounced back. Toq made a hand ax, cutting blades, awls, and several new spearpoints. He hunted, searched for good rocks to work with, and worked to complete his hut. At the end of one day, he examined his cut, bruised, and swollen hands, aching from all the work, and he opened and closed them repeatedly to try to loosen them. He wanted a break, but the storm had left him feeling the urgency to get done and be ready.

He hunted more and gathered wood for winter. He piled wood and dung outside his hut. He dug a hole and made a lid of birch, bone, and sod to cache meat, and he gathered, dried, and stored berries. He collected the long hairs that beasts had shed for padding, sleeping upon, and braiding into cordage, but with too much to do, rope-making would have to wait.

Toq decided the caribou skin would be better on his roof than on his back, since the creature had not yet developed a good winter coat when it died. He finally completed his shelter's roof using multiple smaller animal skins to fill in the gaps and stitching on his old lean-to. It was early afternoon, and he stood on the cliff looking down upon his winter home—a mostly round, imperfect, domed lodge cobbled together with a menagerie of animal parts and skins, earth, bark, plants, tusks, and poles.

Toq chuckled at the sight, knowing it was not the best a human could do, but he was confident it would hold up through the winter. He had enough room to stand tall inside, and it could sleep three people, if needed.

He sat on the cliff, soaking up the warm sunshine. The snow was gone, and birch, aspen, and willow leaves had just begun to change from summer green to a faint yellow. He considered all the preparations he still had to do: more firewood and dung, more spear shafts, more food, more furs. The sun was not as high in the sky, and the days grew noticeably shorter and the mornings much colder, with frost on the grass rather than dew.

Fifteen days later, Toq stood again on the cliff on a clear sunny day and marveled at the sight of a land of brilliant golden birch and aspen and red and orange brush amid tan grasses and dark-green spruce, as far as the eye could see. On his daily excursions, he stopped often to gaze up through sunlit yellow leaves with a background of pure blue sky.

He hunted white-tailed deer and caribou, as well as beaver, raccoon, muskrat, and porcupine. There were few horses around and no pronghorns. He had not seen any camels or llamas. He knew a few groups of bighorns and musk oxen were scattered about, but bison seemed to be the most numerous large animal. The occasional moose and elk made appearances, too. He saw lynxes, wolverines, red foxes, coyotes, badgers, weasels, prairie dogs, marmots, squirrels (tree and ground), jackrabbits, cottontails, lemmings, wolves, bears, mammoths, a couple of giant ground sloths, mastodons, and one cheetah, but no lions or cougars. Peccaries were around, too, but they were wary and fast. Plus, there were fish in the streams and countless species of birds. But only one human.

The cooler weather brought more animal activity—more movement, more howls, barks, grunts, growls, challenges, and screeches. Males fought for mating privileges, some animals herded up, all tried to fatten up, and birds began to either disappear to the south or flock together in anticipation of their migration.

It felt different, settling in one place rather than traveling through the land, but he welcomed the opportunity to gain a more thorough knowledge of an area and its inhabitants.

The Traveler had once told him, "The downside to travel is that it's like hopping from woman to woman, which is fun and exciting, but you never really get to know them. When traveling, you pass through a land, it's fun and exciting, but you never get the chance to really know it. But then, on the other hand, if you settle in a land and stay too long, you can wear it out. Hmph, I wonder if that applies to women. You know, maybe we do wear them out if we stay too long. Ah, shit! My comparison is falling apart."

Toq smiled at the memory of his friend and his often reckless, sometimes wise, approach to life.

CHAPTER 18

Winter

On an early winter's day, with only a light covering of snow on the ground and the sun peeking in and out of clouds, the fur-covered man walked to the icy edge of the river. Clouds of frozen breath blew out from beneath his hood. Toq was amazed at how cold it was—the first real cold to strike. He dipped a water bag in the river, careful not to get his leathers wet. The river had slowed considerably since summer, now that there was less glacial ice melting, and he figured it would not take long to freeze over.

Downstream, something stuck out of the water near the shore. He walked toward it along the rocky shoreline and climbed onto a logjam for a closer look. It was the remains of a giant sloth. It was mostly bones—big, heavy bones—held together by pieces of tendon and hide. The skull was gone. Water washed up around the rib cage and had frozen on the portions exposed to the frigid air. He could see a large patch of hide and hair, still attached to the back, beneath the water's surface. He poked the end of his spear into the water until it jabbed the skin. Even soaked in water, the hard, rough skin did not give way.

"Wow, it's like a rock!" he said with surprise. "I don't think a lion could bite through the back of this creature."

The animals of the land filled him with endless wonder and excitement. He followed tracks, large and small, through the snow. Many of the species had vanished for the winter, and he wondered where they had gone. With the leaves gone, it was easier to see into the woods. A group of mammoths stayed in one place in the woods for days before moving on, and after they left, Toq checked out the spot, carefully stepping around large piles of dung. They had cleared the area of its brush, grass, smaller tree branches, and spruce needles. Tusks had rubbed the bark off some trees, while others had simply been knocked down. Some of the roots had even been eaten.

By winter's solstice, Toq had seen no sign of ground sloths or bears. Certain that one day a bear would tear into his lodge or discover his food cache, he was relieved to think they had either left the area or were hibernating. A pack of wolves began to snoop around his camp, and although he was wary and watchful with them around, they never really bothered him. Magpies, ravens, crows, and chickadees kept him company. A couple of cheetah-cats visited, their coats much thicker and longer than in the summer, but the wolves chased them away.

Toq hated the cold, gray, windy days that kept him inside, but most days were fine, and in some ways, he even preferred the winter.

"No bugs, no sweat, easy hunting."

He had little trouble staying warm in his lodge, and when he was out on the coldest days, he only needed to keep moving—to keep his heart thumping—to keep warm. And there *were* some incredibly cold days and weeks—much colder than anything he had ever experienced before. The snow cover remained light. He made snowshoes but had no need for them, at least not yet.

He watched how most predators hunted using speed, power, or a pack, but he had none of those. The cougars and long-fang cats used stealth and ambush, and so did Toq. He learned the habits and trails of deer and caribou and waited in trees or on rocks or cliffs with two spears, one long, thrusting spear and one shorter, throwing spear. He only hunted when he knew the wolves were gone. So far, his success rate was high, and he had plenty of meat.

The long, dark nights were the toughest for him. He slept more and kept busy working on things inside by firelight, but he missed the games, stories, laughter, and companionship of people. He did not miss the fighting and jealousy that came with people, though.

"Is it possible to find people who *don't* become irritated with each other?" he asked.

He continued to be amazed that he had seen no other people on this river that had everything a person could need.

On clear, calm nights, he frequently went out to look at the stars, different from the summer patterns and seemingly more brilliant. "Fantastic," he would say, every time. The moonshine on the snowy landscape was enchanting, casting shadows and revealing animals on the light reflecting snow. He nearly expected to see ghosts or fairies. Some animals bedded down for the night, while others were active. Toq didn't wander far from his hut in the dark, knowing some cats hunted at night.

It endlessly baffled him how birds and beasts survived the cold without a fire and shelter, and he wondered how long he could last with only his furs. They were so warm, though, and he knew he could survive.

"But my feet and fingers would be the problem," he said.

On a relatively mild morning, after a long stretch of fierce cold, Toq walked to the river, now completely frozen over. He had explored everything within a day's hike of his camp but not the opposite side of the river. Some days before, a small group of caribou had safely crossed the ice. Shortly thereafter, mammoths approached the frozen river but turned back, experience telling them it was too dangerous. This morning, half a dozen bison— giants and much heavier than the caribou—were crossing just ahead of Toq.

The bison walked single file, slipping on uneven surfaces. Nearly at an island, one in the middle lost its footing, and with its feet flying out, it fell hard onto the ice. Toq heard the crack. When the bison behind tried to rush by, the added weight caused the weakened ice to give way. The fallen beast broke through and sank into the water, and then a second one fell through. It managed to get its front legs up on top of the ice—but only for a moment, before it slipped backwards, tipping a thick slab up into the air. The bison behind it panicked and leaped forward, slipping and landing on its companion in the water. It used the other bison as a stepping stone to get onto the ice on the other side of the hole, further sinking the victim under its weight. The bison in the rear wisely turned upstream and moved around the hole. The two in the river struggled, and one soon disappeared under the ice, carried downstream to be consumed in the spring by scavengers as it lay jammed against logs.

Four bison made it safely to the island, where they turned to look at the one still struggling in the water. Toq watched the huge head and sprawling horns lunge up and forward, but the animal couldn't get its feet up on the ice. It bellowed loudly, and Toq felt sorry for the beast, while the others turned away and continued on without it. Its head, resting on the ice, grew still, and it stopped crying out. The exhausted animal's frozen breath rushed into the cold air. The wolf pack appeared and ran toward the bison's head sticking up out of the water. They stopped short of the broken ice and the bison—so close but impossible to get to.

Toq walked away from the river, feeling a little too close to the wolves. The wolves surrounded the hole in the ice, and the bison silently gave up, sinking beneath the surface, leaving the wolves staring at the empty water.

Toq mumbled, "Maybe I'll try crossing tomorrow."

• • • •

For two days, Toq waited for a snowstorm to pass. On the third day, he stuck his head out of the shelter's door flap into air so cold the first breath caught in his throat. He coughed a little and looked around. The sky was clear, bright, and blue. The sun had just come up over a light, fluffy layer of snow covering all the imperfections and blemishes of the land.

"Beautiful," Toq said.

He was excited to get out, and so, without knowing how long the good weather might last, he layered on his furs with his food bag and water underneath, picked up two spears, and headed out into the snow.

He first climbed onto the cliff above his shelter to have a look around. He wore his eye-slit snow goggles, but he frequently slid them up or down off his eyes to get a better view.

"No clouds anywhere," he said.

Completely white mountains (Pryor Mountains) stood on the southwest skyline. The air was still, and the world made no sound. Toq pulled back his hood to listen, but there was nothing—no wind or rustling leaves, no rushing river or trickling streams, no birds, no bugs, and no footsteps or calls from wild beasts. He heard his own breathing, so he held his breath, and then he heard only a faint ringing in his ears. He had the urge to shout, to make a noise, to pierce the silence, but he resisted, knowing that would pollute the purity of the calm.

Stepping along the cliff top, he listened to the creaking snow beneath his feet. He pulled his hood back over his head and gazed down upon his camp. The pristine snow covered the dirt, the mud, the worn paths, and half of his lodge—making it look as if nobody lived there. A few clouds of blue-gray smoke puffed out of the hole in the lodge right next to the giant, protruding tusk, gradually turning it brown and black. Snow piled onto the spruce trees, but the next good wind would blow it all off.

In the distance, large animals cleared away the new snow in search of food. He turned to leave and was startled to see a coyote just sitting there, silently watching him. Toq lifted his goggles and admired the beautiful animal in its perfect winter coat. Toq had enough furs for now, but the thought crossed his mind that he should try to get this coyote.

"Nah, your coat looks better on you. Now, you're wondering if you could eat me. Well, you can't, and I'm not sharing my food with you."

He walked directly toward the coyote until it jumped out of the way, and Toq walked on by, eyeing it as he passed. He didn't think about the critter anymore, and he didn't look back, so he was surprised when he felt a sharp, hard bite on the back of his leg. He quickly spun around, throwing the coyote off a little. It snarled and showed its fangs as it circled around.

"Why you little son of a bitch!" Toq said to him.

The coyote sped around behind him and dove in for another bite, but Toq whacked it with the butt end of one of his spears. The coyote yipped and backed away.

"Stay away from me or you'll be dead!" Toq said, pointing at it with a spear.

He lunged at the coyote to run it off, then he pulled off a mitten to feel the hole in his pant leg.

He looked at the coyote, still watching him, and said, "You shit. Don't try that again."

Toq descended the hill, turning to look back often, with the coyote following at a distance. The fangs did not tear or pierce his skin, but the bite did leave him sore and bruised. Toq headed for the river with the coyote trailing him. Spotting a pair of caribou antlers sticking up out of the snow, he went to investigate. Under the fresh snow, a frozen carcass waited to feed something.

Toq would gladly have taken it, but he had all he needed, so he brushed off the snow, looked at the coyote, and said, "Here. Eat this and leave me alone." He walked away and looked back to see the coyote sniffing the carcass. "That oughta keep him busy," he said.

He reached the river and saw no animal tracks across the fresh snow. His would be the first. He lifted his goggles and looked west up the river valley when something in the sky caught his attention. A bright, glowing object, shining like the sun, sped through the deep blue sky, making no sound but leaving a trail of smoke and flying to the north.

"What is that?" Toq said slowly.

The fireball moved fast and steady, in a perfectly straight line, but it wasn't as fast as lightning or a meteor. He stared after it until it disappeared behind the northern hills.

"Wow!" he said, thrilled. He looked around, wishing someone else had seen it. This was another one of those mysterious phenomena of nature that people would say was a god or a sign from the spirits. "Wow!" he said again, pulling his goggles back over his eyes. He looked into the sky several more times—now an empty blue streaked with white vapor.

He turned to walk across the river, wiping the condensation and snot from below his nose with the back of his mitten, but the mitten only slid across the surface of the ice between his upper lip and nostrils. He searched for the place where the bison had fallen through and found it mostly frozen over again except for one small patch of open, moving water. He went far upstream of that spot and crossed to the island, then crossed a narrower stretch of frozen river, testing the ice in front with the butt of one of his spears. He climbed the bank and explored these new hills and coulees. Looking back, he could see only the faint cloud of smoke from his lodge.

He did a big loop south, then east, and then by midday began following a coulee back toward the river, with the winter sun behind him. The low sun felt like it was always nearing sunset; his own long shadow, the shadows of trees on the snow, and the sun glinting through the trees, gave a comforting, sublime feel to these short winter days. He walked across and down some hills into a different coulee, disturbing a small herd of musk oxen with icicles hanging off their long, hairy coats and faces. He followed the coulee, checking animal tracks along the way. The new snow left stories about where the critters had been and where they were going.

Spruce trees swayed, and snow flew off the branches as the wind picked up. The sun, gliding lower over the horizon, lengthened the shadows. He followed bison tracks down the coulee to a large pond created by a beaver dam. The pond was frozen solid, perfectly flat, covered with snow, and had a single set of tracks that crossed from one side to the other. They were unusual tracks, compelling Toq to take a closer look.

He walked onto the ice. Snowflakes, blown by the wind, were already filling in the tracks. Toq stood dumbfounded, looking at the unmistakable pattern of human footprints. He lifted his goggles off—not needing them anymore anyway—and he turned in every direction to see if he might spot someone.

His mind raced. Were they watching him? Would they be friendly? Was the person alone or with a group?

He ran across the pond and followed the tracks up a treeless hill to the east. The wind blew the tracks away at the top of the hill and on the other side it covered them up. Toq looked off into the distance—north, south, and east—but saw nothing. He moved about in wide semicircles, trying to pick up the tracks again, until finally he found them, going east. The sun dipped behind the trees, and the temperature dove quickly with it.

"No time," he murmured.

He turned away and began trekking back toward the river and home as the sun set. He crossed the river near the small, prominent, rocky island with vertical walls sticking out from the ice (Pompeys Pillar). He stopped at the caribou carcass; the coyote and ravens had been working on the frozen meat. He reached his lodge with only a hint of light left on the horizon. Rekindling his fire, he wondered who was out there. He was not alone here anymore, but he felt apprehensive about it, which surprised him. Life was simple without people. This human—or humans—could be good, but they could just as easily be bad. Like the lion, the bear, or the wolf, whose greatest threats were their own kind, Toq knew people could be dangerous.

He sat staring into the yellow flames, warming his hands and feet, and thinking.

"What a day. Bitten by a coyote. Fireball through the sky. Human footprints. Signs? Is there a message here I'm supposed to be getting? Naw . . . it's all just by chance," he said. He thought for a while, then added, "Chance or not, this was a pretty incredible day. You may not see that coyote again, you'll probably never see another fireball in the sky, and you may never see that human. Shit! Maybe you're losing your mind. Maybe those weren't even a man's tracks. Maybe I got lost. Could they have been *my* tracks?" He lay back and covered himself in furs. "I'm not crazy. There is somebody else out there. I wonder if they know I'm here. I wonder if they're watching my camp."

• • • •

A powerful wind shook the shelter throughout the night. The noise of it rushing through trees and flapping the skins on the roof kept Toq awake. At times, he worried the wind would lift his lodge and blow it away or perhaps flatten it. He listened to windblown snow and ice crystals crashing into his shelter like grains of sand. The wind blew hard for two days from the southwest, and it did not take long to scour the cold air out of the valley, bringing unusual winter warmth and melting snow.

Toq ventured out to check the ice on the river and to look for more signs of humans. Staying on his side of the river, he wandered east, but the warm winds created slick ice and mud, preventing him from wandering too far. Knowing that most beasts would be sheltering in areas out of the wind, he kept an eye out for opportunities to surprise an animal, but he didn't hunt too hard, since his food cache was still half full. A small herd of caribou fed in a coulee, mostly out of the wind, taking advantage of vegetation and lichen exposed by the melting snow. Toq did not stalk them. Instead, he climbed the hill west of them and sat behind a sandstone outcrop out of the wind.

The caribou moved slowly in and out of trees and brush and clearings. Most of their heads were down to the ground, feeding. Toq had not seen the wolves in some time, and he figured they were roaming another section of their territory. The sun broke out momentarily from its cloud cover, and Toq pulled back his hood and soaked in the light and warmth. The moment did not last long as the sun vanished behind a cloud, and Toq pulled his hood back over his head, lay on his side, closed his eyes, and napped.

A calling magpie woke him. The caribou had moved a little way up the valley. Toq heard a grunt, and the entire herd looked east into a stand of spruce, then took off running up the coulee. Toq guessed the wolves must be back, and so he was surprised and disheartened to see two large, but fairly young, male lions burst from the spruce trees. The caribou had a substantial head start and easily left the lions far behind. The two slowed to a trot, then stopped to watch the herd fade away up the coulee.

Splattered with mud, the lions glanced at each other and started looking carefully around. Toq didn't like this position, and the moment the lions looked away, he slipped behind some trees and brush and climbed up the hill to where he thought he could watch them safely. They sniffed the ground and the air. One rubbed his head against the other's neck, and they turned and moved down toward the river. Toq pulled his hood back off so he could hear better, and he followed their movements from the ridge.

The lions left the valley before reaching the river, climbed the hill, and moved west toward Toq's camp, causing him to say, "Damn it, damn it, damn it!"

He worried they might settle in the vicinity or find his meat cache or ransack his lodge. Keeping his distance, he followed them, wondering what he could do. They appeared to be going somewhere with a purpose, with some unknown scent leading them on. Their long manes billowed in the wind. They didn't know they were being followed.

The two crossed a partially wooded flat, then down into another coulee, then up and over into the next coulee. Toq's camp was next. He ran north up one coulee and up onto a hill, looking. No lions. He moved quickly down into the next coulee. No lions. He climbed out of it and moved cautiously south along the ridges and hilltops, but he saw no lions. He crouched low as he approached the edge of the cliff over his camp. On hands and knees, he ever so slowly peered down at his camp. To his surprise, the coyote was sniffing around his lodge. Toq looked down into the trees where he thought the lions might emerge.

Sure enough, they appeared a short distance down the slope from his camp. They stopped, looking intently up at the lodge, trying to smell the air. The coyote, upwind of the lions, was unaware of their presence. The coyote came around the front of the lodge, and the head of one lion lifted slightly when he spotted it. The two were wary of the camp's strange smells, but they now focused all their attention on the coyote. They looked around for danger, then proceeded to stalk the coyote. Toq had cleared most of the brush and small trees around his lodge, so the lions had little cover. They crouched low and slowly advanced toward the little canid.

Out of the corner of his eye, Toq spotted movement on the hill to the east. The wolf pack came running along the route the lions had taken. Against the wind, he heard a brief yip and yowl from the pack, and the coyote and the lions all looked toward it. Then, the coyote flew out of the camp in the opposite direction. The two lions, on the other hand, faced east with great attention, not moving. The first wolves rushed from the trees straight for the lions. The two stood their ground, and both let out thunderous roars. But the pack of fifteen or twenty wolves did not scare off; the lions had invaded their territory. Toq watched and suddenly wondered why they tolerated *him* in their territory.

The pack swarmed around the two lions but kept their distance. Toq had seen this before, and it did not end well for the wolves. The two brothers crouched low and tried to face their attackers, growling, showing fangs, taking big swipes with their paws. The pack snarled back, acting amazingly aggressive, jumping in to bite an exposed backside or tail, but quickly letting go and leaping out of reach. They were bold, bordering on overzealous, yet they remained smart, nimble, and cautious. One lion charged, and the wolves scattered. Toq saw blood on one lion's hind end and tail. The animals moved so fast it was a blur, and mud and snow flew into the air. The lions began to show extreme agitation and fear. One lunged at a wolf, clobbering it with a swift paw. The wolf rolled and yipped, but it was fast on its feet again, appearing unhurt, and in response, the lion received a sharp bite on its back leg from a different wolf.

Shortly, the lions had had enough. Finding an opening, they sprinted past the wolves, who allowed them to go, before giving chase. One excited wolf gave the rear lion a last bite on the tail. The lion whirled around, and the wolf backed away. The lion turned again to run after its brother, and Toq stood, then sat and watched them flee. All the fighters disappeared into the next coulee and trees. He listened, but he heard neither lions nor wolves, only the wind.

"Wolves win this one," he said.

Toq waited on the cliff for a while, the sounds and the sight of the fight playing back in his mind. Any feeling of security he'd had in his lodge was gone. How small, how fragile, he and his camp were in the face of such massive and powerful animals. Far off to the west he heard a wolf howl, carried down to him on the wind. He grew chilled, sitting there on the cliff in the wind.

He pulled his hood back on, shrugged, and said, "I guess that's it for excitement today." He walked down to his lodge, looking around before going in. "It may be small and fragile, but it's all I've got, and it's my home, for now," he said.

••••

Only a few days later, the wind died, then changed direction, dropping the temperature sharply and bringing a light snowfall. Snowdrifts, water, and mud hardened with the cold, forcing Toq to avoid steep slopes with their dangerously slick coatings. Fresh snow concealed the ice, causing Toq to slip and fall a few times even on short trips outside. He saw tell-tale signs in the snow where his surefooted, four-legged friends had also slipped in the treacherous conditions. Toq knew the grazers would have a difficult time getting to food. Brush and tree branches were being eaten by multiple species. As the winter wore on, the herbivores were going to struggle, many weakening and starving or freezing to death. The meat-eaters, including the man, would feast upon the dead and dying. Toq grew a bit heavier.

The two lions never returned. The wolves came into Toq's camp only once afterward, cautiously sniffing around. Toq was inside his lodge when he heard them. He peeked out through a slit in his door flap, then stepped back and readied his spear for any brave wolf who might try to enter, but none attempted the suicidal intrusion. Once their curiosity was satisfied, they ran off to find their next victim.

Cold air engulfed the river valley, and many flat, gray, cloudy days passed, with the occasional light snowfall followed by several brilliant, cold, sunny days. Toq wandered far from his lodge, back across the river, searching for signs of the human, but he found nothing. He began to doubt whether he'd even seen a person's footprints at all.

He watched two full moons go by since the winter solstice. The sun rose and set in spots on the horizon closer to the north. He figured that with one more full moon he should begin to see signs of winter's end. But winter grew long, and Toq grew increasingly restless, wanting to travel again and to put the longest, coldest winter he'd ever known behind him.

More time passed. Some days, the coyote followed Toq out of camp. The critter never again tried to bite him, and Toq never fed the animal as he had the wolf, so he figured the coyote simply hoped to take advantage of whatever he found or killed. Perhaps he felt safe from the wolves while around Toq. Toq liked the company most of the time, although the coyote never came as near as the wolf had.

On one of Toq's trips east along his side of the river, with calm winds, partly sunny skies, and slightly warmer temperatures, he walked through a sparse, open woodland area. The coyote followed him, while he followed the footprints of a group of mammoths. He found them in a patch of shrubs and willows, feeding on woody plants. He kept going, following their tracks, and soon noticed a second set of mammoth tracks. These mammoths had crossed the river to join the first group. Spots of red in the snow told of a bleeding mammoth.

Toq followed the trail to the little herd, trying to see who bled and from what kind of wound. He quietly shooed the coyote away with sticks and snowballs, and wove downwind through trees to get closer, grimacing with each crunching step. Two mammoths paid special attention to a third, vocalizing in a low, gentle rumble. The third one did not move, holding its head and tusks low while it barely sniffed at the shrubs. Large puffs of breath—exhaled into the cold air from huge lungs, through nostrils at the end of the trunk—formed clouds that faded as they rose into the air over the mammoths. Toq admired their beautiful, long, reddish-blond winter fur.

One's long, muscular trunk moved like an arm and hand, but with more strength, flexibility, and dexterity as it smelled and gently felt around the back quarter of the third animal, until the listless one bellowed in protest, tossed its head, and shifted its weight. This revealed a spear shaft stuck in and dangling from the meaty upper part of the beast's back leg, just behind the belly. Toq's mouth hung open as he pulled off his hood and goggles.

Shocked, he whispered, "Is that a spear?"

The mammoth felt the pain, while the other continued to probe with its trunk. Toq wished he could run up and pull out the spear—an impossible proposition.

He said under his breath, "We shall see how tough you are, whether or not you can survive that."

He wondered if it might come out on its own, since the wound did not appear to be bleeding a great deal. He guessed the hunter had aimed for the belly—not a quick and easy death for the animal—and missed.

"If he was trying to hit the heart and lungs, he wasn't even close," he muttered. "Idiots." He thought there had to be more than one hunter.

Toq remained behind the tree but looked back along the route the mammoths had come, thinking the hunters might be following the blood trail. No one was there, only the coyote, sitting, watching the man and the herd. He turned back to the mammoths. The wounded one was big but not the biggest in the group. She might not be able to run or defend herself, and she might attract wolves or lions, if any were around.

"Wolves couldn't bring her down, I don't think. A pride of lions probably could. I wonder if the herd would defend her. She may just slowly die from the wound, the stress, the cold, the lousy winter feed. A crappy way to die," Toq said.

He could see the giant's suffering and the concern, sympathy, and comfort her companions showed.

"Just stupid animals, huh?" he mumbled, thinking about the comments his fellow humans often made. He felt indignant at what people had done to this animal, but he didn't know if he was justified in feeling this way. After all, "You kill and eat animals, too, Toq. You can't have it both ways. Those people have to eat, and there's a lot of meat on a mammoth. Death is nature's way; it gives, and it takes. It's cruel and merciless. The universe is indifferent and disinterested in any suffering in this world."

He thought and watched the herd.

"This is different." But he couldn't explain how, not even to himself.

The herd appeared to be staying put, at least for now, so Toq decided to leave and check on them in the coming days. He decided to follow the blood trail back across the river and slowly made his way out of the trees, taking care to step into his previous footprints to minimize the sound, while keeping a close eye on the mammoths. He was nearly out of what he considered to be the danger zone when he heard an elephant call. His head snapped around, eyes wide, seeing three big females charging through the brush. He'd wondered if they might run from humans now—but here was his answer. Without saying a word, he sprinted across the snow, hoping he wouldn't slip on the ice and get crushed.

The mammoths were faster, but Toq had a significant head start. Two quit early, but one persisted. Toq ran along the blood trail, and when he got to the river, he looked back and saw the lone pursuer had stopped. But when she saw him stop, too, she sprinted forward again. Snow flew into the air, and she charged through a cloud of her breath. Frozen, dead branches snapped off and spun through the air as she crashed through trees and brush. Toq saw a massive head with ears out, a trunk held high, and those two huge, unbroken tusks. He ran onto the frozen river, knowing that if the mammoths had crossed, it was safe. His pace slowed on the ice, and when he reached the other side, he looked back again and saw the mammoth had finally ended her chase. The coyote was gone.

Still winded, Toq went back to retracing the blood trail, continuing on for quite a ways east. The farther he went, the heavier the blood flow, which told him the wound was healing. By early afternoon, he still had not reached the site of the attack, and he had to turn back in order to get home before dark. While walking, he realized how much he wished to meet these people, though he remained apprehensive about how they would receive him.

"They must be quite a distance from here if they didn't pursue the wounded mammoth. Or they killed one and let this one go. Or maybe the mammoths killed one of them."

Many possible scenarios ran through his head.

He crossed the river in the same spot, moving slowly, cautiously, but the mammoth herd had moved to the mouth of a frozen creek that joined the river. They had broken through a layer of ice and were sucking up water. Ice-cold water was painful for Toq to touch or drink, and he figured most animals ate snow when all the streams froze, but he wondered about these large animals. Could they get enough water from eating snow?

They drank little bits at a time, pausing in order to give the insides of their snouts a chance to warm up. After dipping their trunks three or four times, they were done, and did not linger as they would in summer.

The herd moved into a grove of spruce, where they would spend the night somewhat sheltered from any cold winds. Toq went around them and, from a hill, tried to spot the wounded one. She was still with the herd and now appeared to be eating. Toq was glad about that and headed for home.

• • • •

Some weeks passed with Toq watching the mammoths and searching for people. He rarely saw the wolves. The coyote showed up once in a while, and a pair of magpies decided they liked his camp. They perched on the tip of the tusk above his lodge and made a racket until he tossed them some morsels of meat. Normally, he'd be concerned they would attract carnivores, but he put up with these two beautiful, black and white, iridescent, intelligent birds. He lay in his lodge later than usual one morning, and the magpies called out to him, but he did not move. He heard their wings flapping down to the front of the lodge, and the next thing he saw was a sliver of light pouring in from the door flap. One magpie used all its might to pull back the flap, while the other peeked inside, cocking its head left and right, back and forth. The magpie saw only the glowing coals of a fire in a dark room.

A voice in the dark said, "What do you think you're doing?"

The bird holding the flap lost its grip, and the flap flew shut, knocking the other one out of the way. Toq heard them squawking as they flew off, and he chuckled at their antics. They made his camp feel more alive, more fun.

The days were longer, the sun warmer, and snow and ice melted in the afternoon sun, but this could be a dreary time. The disappearing snow cover left a dull, muddy land with no sign yet of new life. It took time for green grass and leaf buds and flowers to appear. Many beasts looked haggard, thin, and weak—though the predators looked strong and healthy. Toq found the herd of mammoths one morning not far from his camp. They looked better than most herbivores but not as fat as last fall. Even though the herd knew he was there, they did not attack. They had come to tolerate this one man as long as he kept his distance.

The speared mammoth still lived, moving with the herd, albeit with a limp. It amazed Toq to see the spear shaft still hanging from the wound, and he thought it would never heal if it didn't come out.

With time, he became very familiar with the herd. There were fourteen animals—mothers, daughters, sons, but no big males. One large female, seemingly in charge, was the one who had attacked Toq, and he was always aware of where she was. He named the individual mammoths—a rare thing for him to do. He learned a lot about mammoths in those late winter days, more than he ever had during his travels. He began to feel like the mammoths, the magpies, the coyote, and the wolves were part of his family. They were his only relationships with living beings.

"I suppose that's what happens without people," he said.

On a warm, sunny day, he gathered, chopped, busted, and sawed firewood, all the while wondering what his people were doing—people he hadn't seen in two years. He wondered if they ever thought about him.

CHAPTER 19

Humans

Another full moon came and went. Toq spent his spare time preparing to leave his home, constructing new bags, a new lean-to, new moccasins, and clothing. Grass began to turn green, snow and ice melted away, a few early flowers appeared, and the river ran nearly free of ice. If he wished to travel south, he would need a boat. He hoped he hadn't made a mistake in not moving across the river while it was still frozen, but the thought of moving his lodge by himself was daunting, if not impossible. He guessed this was about the same time he'd left the village last year, but he would wait before going this year. A strong spring snowstorm would be sure to come, and his lodge was a good place to be. He did not intend to dismantle the lodge, since he thought it possible he might return in the fall.

The coyote had not shown itself in a while, and the magpies left him. The mammoths finally moved north out of the river valley. Before they left,

Toq saw the speared mammoth at the back of the herd, still limping, but now, the spear was gone.

"Good for you, my friend! I hope you live a long life," the man said, watching them walk away. Sadly, he knew the animal would be a target for lions . . . or humans.

For two weeks, a cold wind blew, and it rained and snowed off and on. Toq was glad he hadn't left his lodge yet. A large male bear—the first he'd seen since the beginning of winter—wandered down the valley on the other side of the river.

Oh, great, thought Toq, *now they're moving around.*

He revered them, and he feared them, and he knew his lodge would not protect him from them.

After the rain and snow and some drying winds, Toq packed up his bags and left his lodge to venture farther downstream to see if he might catch sight of humans. By midday, he passed the imaginary boundary of his territory—half a day's walk from his lodge. By late afternoon, he stood on a bluff looking across the river valley to the southeast. Below him: dark-green spruce, budding birch, alder, aspen, and shrubs, greening grassy meadows, and a freely flowing river with giant blocks of melting ice pushed high onto both banks. On a rather low, flat bench on the other side of the river, nestled among the trees, Toq saw a couple of dome-shaped lodges very similar to his own. A puff of smoke occasionally rose up and blew away on the breeze.

"There they are," he said.

He thought it likely there were more lodges in the trees, and he strained to see movement. He searched below, on his side of the river, for people and wildlife, and seeing neither, he walked off the bluff into the valley toward the river. The pleasant and calming singing of the birds that had returned from the south serenaded him as he passed by two blinds constructed from bones and tree limbs, made and used during the winter when the river could be crossed. He found it almost unbelievable that these people were here— within just a single day's walk from his camp.

He thought he heard voices, but his ears had played tricks on him so many times over the past year he no longer trusted them. He walked slowly through the trees, stopping frequently to listen and look, hearing only birds and the rushing river. The sky opened before him over the river, but Toq stayed in the trees where he could watch, unseen. But then he worried they might interpret his cautious and surreptitious approach as maliciousness. The Traveler would have broken from the trees, waving his arms and hollering a greeting, but Toq did not have the Traveler's temperament or charm.

A footpath led from the bench down to the river. The bench was mostly open, clear of trees, except where the lodges were located, and the path wound across a meadow and through some brush. Although Toq didn't have a clear view of the encampment, he removed his bags, sat behind a bush, and waited and watched. A human figure moved between two lodges.

Toq's eyes fixed upon the person, as if they were a phantom, and he thought, *It's so strange to see people, so unlike any other animal, these upright-walking creatures.*

He faintly heard the shouts and laughter of children, then three men walked down the path from the lodges. They stopped at the edge of the bench and looked in every direction for game and danger. Toq remained hidden.

He was far enough away that it was difficult to see details or hear clearly, but the people on the other side of the river appeared well-dressed and clean, decorated with bone or shell or claw or tooth, and leather headbands. Each man carried a long, stout spear. Seeing no danger, one taller man turned and whistled loudly toward the camp. Five kids of all different ages came running and laughing down the path, with one knee-high tyke bringing up the rear, trying to keep up. A group of women followed close behind, each one carrying two bags—bladders or stomachs—for water. They were also clean, well-dressed, and decorated, and a couple of them carried spears, as well. Toq became very self-conscious of how he must look, with his scraggly whiskers, long, unkempt hair, old, dirty leathers and furs, and no necklaces or adornments of any kind.

All the more reason to remain out of sight, he thought.

The children ran past the men down to the riverbank. One man held back the littlest boy, who screamed in protest. His mother picked him up and carried him down to where the other children threw rocks out into the water. Toq smiled at their exuberance and carefree spirits. He missed that part of village life—the fun and the joy.

The women filled their bags with water and sat for a while by the river. The men turned their attention downstream, but Toq couldn't see what they were looking at. He heard a man's voice, and one of them waved at the children, who gave up their game and ran back to camp, hopping and flapping their arms. The women calmly carried their loads back, the three men following close behind. One man took a bag of water from one of the women, while the other two carried only their spears. Two young guys—probably teenagers—carrying spears appeared from downstream, taking a different route to the lodges.

With the day nearing its end, Toq withdrew into a denser stand of trees to set up camp. He felt certain the villagers were not regularly crossing the river—although they might have made boats of some kind. Before lying down to sleep, Toq climbed a tree near the river to see if he could get a better view of the camp. Through the dusk, he thought he could see five lodges, perhaps six, grouped close together. By the dark figures around the fires, he guessed there might be thirty to forty people, and it seemed as though half of them were children. Toq retreated to his fireless camp, struggling with whether or not to present himself and try to join the group.

"They look okay from a distance, but that doesn't reveal what's going on inside the tribe," he said. "You may not even speak the same language." He listened to some loud grunting coming from the hills to the north. "People . . . they change everything. If you join them, you lose your freedom, and they become the focus, demanding attention and diminishing your bond with nature."

• • • •

Early in the morning, just before sunrise, Toq awoke, hearing something big in the brush. He moved slowly into a ready position, crouching beneath his lean-to, spear in hand. He raised his head to look behind his lean-to at a big, black, hairy back moving through the brush. A single, very large musk ox grazed much too close to camp. These beasts were surly and unpredictable, and Toq wanted to shoo it away, but he was too close to do so safely. The musk ox turned to look at him, stopped chewing, and stared.

Toq didn't move. The bull snorted and charged through the brush, and Toq sprinted away into some bigger trees for protection, finding it odd that he was thinking he had not yet seen a musk ox like this one. He jumped behind a tree and looked around the trunk in time to see the tremendous beast crash over his lean-to like a rolling boulder. The bull ran toward Toq—and directly into the tree, its thick, heavy, horned head colliding with the trunk with a loud crack. Its body shook, and a rain of branches and dead pine needles fell onto both man and beast.

Toq thought, *Are you stupid? Or blind?*

Man and bull looked at each other from around the tree trunk, the bull's brown eyes fixed. Snot dripped from its nose to mix with the foam from its mouth. Toq backed away and then ran behind three trees tightly packed together. The bull ran around the first tree, but this time stopped short of crashing into any others, instead weaving around the trees to chase Toq out. Toq left his spear and leaped up into the lower branches of a sturdy birch. He climbed out of the bull's reach, hoping it would give up and leave. The ox grunted, looked up at him, and then butted the tree trunk a few times, causing the birch to shudder. The tips of the horns ripped the bark, and it rubbed the sides of its face against the trunk.

Toq looked down at the animal's back, thinking, *What an easy kill this could be.*

The bull looked up one last time, then slowly wandered out of sight. Toq left the tree, retrieved his spear, and went to assess the damage to his stuff. The bull had busted a pole and ripped a large hole in the lean-to.

"Not too bad," he said. "Could've been worse."

He left everything there, taking only a bag with food and his spear, and went to the river to check on the encampment. Before he reached his hiding spot, he looked past the trees toward the lodges. He felt the blood leave his face at the sight of several men, a couple of women, and a few curious children standing at the edge of the bench looking across the river in his direction.

"They must've seen the trees and brush moving in the commotion," he mumbled. He thought he'd been far enough away, but apparently not. "Ah, well, shit. I guess, now's a good time," he said, and he walked out of the trees and into plain sight.

The two women pointed at him first. He heard voices, but the water muffled their sound. The men stood still and stared at the stranger, sizing him up.

Toq set down his spear, walked to the river's edge, raised his hands in a universal sign of peace, and loudly called across the river, "I am Toquuxla! I travel alone!"

One man held his hands behind his ears to signal that they could not hear him. A woman ran partway back to the camp and called out, returning with the whole village.

Toq thought this was a good sign. The distance between them made even hand signals difficult to see and interpret, so he brought his palms together in an exaggerated gesture and raised his joined hands over his head so they could see clearly his sign of friendship. Toq watched as one man spoke and waved his hands at two other men. Four men ran back to the lodges. The man who spoke and gave orders—the chief—turned to look at Toq. Half of the villagers watched their chief, while the rest watched Toq.

The chief yelled something at Toq and thrust his spear repeatedly into the air over his head. The whole tribe joined in, yelling, screaming, making threatening and obscene gestures. Even the children found rocks to throw. Toq's heart sank. He was not entirely surprised, just extremely disappointed. He had been rejected and cast out before even getting the opportunity to know these people, and it crushed him.

"How can they hate me without knowing me? What is their problem? They're a bad tribe. You don't want to be with people like that, anyway," he told himself.

But the reality of how alone he was hit the hardest when he was around people. He hardly ever felt lonely when he was by himself.

The people advanced to the river's edge, working themselves into a frenzy of hatred, quickly turning Toq's disappointment into anger, causing him to holler, "Piss on you, you assholes!"

He made his own obscene gestures, threw rocks at them into the river, and went back to get his spear, which he thrust into the air in defiance of the chief. The four men came running down the path, through the people, and down to the river, carrying paddles and two canoes.

Toq's eyes widened. "Itshla!"

Suddenly, he had one thing on his mind and that was fleeing. He did not wait for the canoes to get into the water. He vanished into the woods, ran to his camp, quickly packed up his belongings, and tore out of the valley, taking care to stay in the trees. He climbed up the bluff and slowed, not wanting to attract the attention of any predators. He looked back toward the river, where he could see the villagers in the distance, the two canoes still on the bank.

Toq laughed at himself. "Oh, you're so brave. Until they come after you."

He watched them, little dots running around, and wondered if they'd been bluffing. He realized he might have sent them into a panic, believing he represented another tribe, a threat. He imagined the chief must be giving commands to young fighters, women, and children. Then, a large, dark animal burst across the meadow and through some brush onto the bench.

"Oh, shit, a bear," he murmured.

The people were unaware of the rushing danger until it was too late. Suddenly, the little dots scattered. He watched in horror as one rushed to pick up a smaller figure just as the bear bore down on top of them. The two—certainly a woman and child—disappeared beneath the bear's mass.

"Oh, please let them live," Toq said, his anger turning at once to dread and pity.

The people stopped fleeing, turned, and attacked the bear. One figure—probably the woman's mate—rushed headlong at it. The bear roared—the only thing Toq could actually hear—and attacked him. More figures converged on the bear, surrounding it, at first throwing spears, but then rushing in to thrust their spears into vital organs. Turning from aggressor to defender, the bear now attacked to save its own life. It did damage to the slower humans, but the longer it fought, the more spears were stuck into its sides. Finally, the bear tried to flee, but it was too late; three spears pierced its lungs and cut arteries. It fell a short distance from the people, where it died. One man approached the downed beast and jammed a spear into its heart.

From the bluff, Toq could only imagine the terrible scene below. Small figures gathered around motionless ones, and the faint sound of wailing drifted across the river valley. He guessed that four people may have died:

the woman, the child, the woman's mate, and one other man. Others could still die from their wounds. Toq shook his head in sorrow, feeling the anguish of his "enemies."

"Nothing I can do. I am sorry for you," he said, holding up a hand in farewell, and he left the people, the village, to heal.

••••

Toq returned to his lodge to retrieve some items before leaving for the summer. But when he got there, he found it demolished. Mammoth or mastodon tracks told him who the culprits were.

"Gone one day and this is what they do. As if they were waiting for me to leave," he sighed.

He found what he needed and headed north. In less than half a day's walk, he came upon the carcass of the mammoth with the spear wound. It hadn't been dead for long, but wolves and scavenging birds had been feeding upon it. Toq was sorry the animal had not made it after all. He passed by the carcass quickly, lest a large predator catch him, too, reflecting, "Too much death, too much sadness. Dead people, dead mammoths."

He turned east, then followed a creek (Antelope Creek) to the southeast, until he met up with the river once again—now farther downstream of the tribal village. Getting the people out of his mind was impossible. They were sure to blame their misfortune on his appearance, and they might even come to believe he was a spirit.

"All this time, you'd thought you would find safety with people, but look what happened to them. I've done better by myself." He walked on, thinking, *I've been pretty lucky.*

Toq followed the river for days, walking on bluffs, hills, and benches above wide, flooded valleys and narrow canyons, through woodlands and bush country and across open meadows, prairie, and valley bottoms. As always, the wildlife accompanied him. They were everything to him; without them, his life would be far too lonely, empty, and boring.

Nearing the end of one day, he paused in the trees before crossing a clearing. He'd been thinking about the mammoth, killed by the hunter's spear, and the bear, which had probably never seen humans before, thinking they looked like easy prey and soon regretting it, "If bears have regret, that is." Toq was sure the bears and mammoths would quickly learn about people, and they would not have a passive view of them. It would not take the animals long to view humans as the enemy.

"Mammoths will avoid people or become aggressive toward them. Bears will become cautious, perhaps also avoiding them—occasionally killing and eating a loner like me. Wolves are smart, so they'll avoid 'em. Lions? I don't know. Everything fears the big pride, and the lions know it." But he thought back to the lion killed by the mammoth and the two chased away by the wolf pack, saying, "Lions can be whipped as well."

Seeing no threats, he walked around the edge of the clearing. Constantly alert, Toq checked every tree, rock, and cliff he walked by, but at times, his mind distracted him from his environment, and sometimes he suffered a surprise when something flushed or bolted from a hidden position. After such frights, he often said, "Son of a bitch!" while feeling relief and telling himself to pay better attention. So he watched diligently for cougars and those cheetah-cats whenever he neared the ubiquitous sandstone pillars and cliffs.

He approached one of those sandstone columns just inside the trees. Nothing sat on top. He thought it might be a good place to camp, so he moved slowly through the trees, keeping some distance from the sandstone until he could verify that the other side was clear. Passing by one birch while looking up at the other side of the sandstone, he stopped dead and stared up at a man sitting on a ledge, looking down at him. Immediately, his heart pounded, not knowing what to do or how to feel about this man, so close, who had obviously been watching him. Although shocked to see him, Toq did not move or show his surprise. Would he have to fight? Was the man alone? The man only looked at Toq, his own spears laid across his lap, and he did not prepare to fight. Toq had not been this close to another person in over a year, and the man looked out of place to him—like he didn't fit in with the images Toq had been living with.

The man smirked at Toq and said, "Don't worry, I'm not a ghost."

Toq leaned his spears against his shoulder and made the friendship sign without saying a word.

The man chuckled, and said, "Not a talker, huh?" He had an odd accent. He made the same sign back to Toq, then stood up, spears in hand.

"Are we okay, or are you going to attack me?" he asked.

"We're okay," Toq replied, wondering if he should let his guard down.

"You talk weird," the man said, and he scrambled down to the ground to look Toq in the eye.

Toq was wearing only pants and moccasins to avoid sweating into his shirt; the stranger, meanwhile, was fully clothed, and his hair was braided, neat, tight, and clean. His face was mostly plucked and shaved. He was about Toq's age and size, and it looked like his nose had been broken. A scar marked his forehead, and multiple smaller scars appeared on his hands. Cracked yellow, orange, and white paint and a few iridescent shells decorated his stained and tattered leathers. A fairly tight leather strap around his neck held some large fangs and claws as well as a talisman—a small animal figurine carved from ivory. Compared to this man, Toq was plain and unkempt. The man's spears had faces carved into them near the point, making Toq think he might be a spiritual man.

Confident and sure of himself, he stood a spear's length from Toq and asked, "Who are you? Who are you with?"

"I'm Toquuxla, from across the western mountains," he said, waving his hand to the west. Toq was certain the man was not alone.

The man mispronounced Toq's name, "Tococksla. Strange name. What does it mean?"

Toq grew a bit irritated but didn't show it. "One who questions or doubts, wonders and searches."

"Ahh, a doubter. You looking for something? You traveling alone? Where are your people?"

"I'm alone. What's your name?"

Toq thought perhaps he should not have told him he was alone.

"Padetmit," said the man, never taking his eyes off Toq.

Toq smiled imperceptibly and nodded at Padetmit, which in his tongue meant "one who always jokes."

Padetmit saw Toq's face relax a bit and said, "I doubt you would be so stupid as to travel alone."

Toq heard people coming through the trees behind him, and he took a quick look, seeing two young men approaching rather noisily. An older man appeared from the other side of the sandstone, moving silently. Toq had had no idea he was there or was coming. Soon, the four men surrounded Toq like a pack of wolves. His face tightened, fearing the worst.

The older man said, "No one else is there."

One of the young men said, "Same here. We saw nobody."

Padetmit smiled. He still had all his teeth. Looking at Toq, he said, "This is Tococksla, the doubter. He travels stupidly alone from the other side of the mountains. He is our friend!"

The men laughed, and the older one approached Toq, slapped him on the back and said, "Well, Tooksla, you're not alone now! You come camp with us tonight. We have fresh meat. We are your friends. You tell us your stories; we'll tell you ours. Do you speak?"

Toq relaxed a little and answered, "Yes, I speak. Thank you for inviting me."

One young guy said, "Whoa, you talk funny!"

"Yes, I know."

"That's all right. Follow us," said the older man, and they led him a short distance through the trees to their camp.

Toq thought they appeared to be good guys, although rude, but he did not intend to drop his guard completely. They all dressed like Padetmit, and they were all clean and well taken care of. As Toq followed, he noticed long strands of mammoth hair had been braided into Padetmit's hair and hung down his back. Long guard hairs and fur, left in a narrow strip on the hide, ran down the back of his leather shirt.

For the first time in a long time, Toq was with people, and he was strangely uncomfortable. He told himself, "Show some trust. Try to relax. But sleep lightly."

They entered a camp where two women—one older, one younger—and two men worked and guarded a large quantity of fresh meat. They stopped to watch the stranger—a rough, wild-looking man whose eyes darted from them to the camp and back to them. Toq had a difficult time taking his eyes off the women; the attraction was immediate but so too was his awful feeling of self-consciousness about the way he must look. Padetmit introduced him to everyone, this time with respect.

Toq threw his timidity aside, thinking, *So what? Who cares? I am what I am. They don't care what I look like.* He greeted each one openly and warmly, telling them they could call him "Toq."

The older woman said, "Toq, nice to meet you. But you look and smell like mammoth shit. There's a clear creek running over there you can clean up in, and when you get back, you can set up your camp over there."

Without cracking a smile, she pointed toward the creek and campsite and then went right back to work. Toq glanced sheepishly at the older man, who grinned and shrugged.

Toq nodded, feeling embarrassed and a little angry, and Padetmit said, "Come on now. Be nice to our new guest. He's been by himself a long time. Toq, you want food?"

"Oh, no. Thank you. I will go clean up and set up camp first. Thank you."

He washed his body and hair in the creek, but not his leathers, as he did not wish to go into the night with wet clothes. He set up his lean-to and then joined the group around the fire as twilight engulfed the hunting party. They shared freshly roasted meat as well as tender spring plants and roots.

"Your food is excellent. Thank you," Toq said.

Although it felt strange to be sitting with other humans in the dark around a fire again, the group laughed and joked—even the grouchy woman—and Toq began to feel at ease. They seemed to be good, happy people, and he enjoyed their banter. After he finished eating, they all turned their attention to him. Everyone had questions, except for one fellow who only wanted to talk about himself until Padetmit signaled for him to be quiet.

Padetmit asked, "So, Toq, where did you winter?"

"Up the river about five or six days away."

"Did you see any other people, any camps?"

Toq hesitated, believing this group must know about the first village he'd seen, and he nodded while looking into the fire. "Yes, a band on the south side of the river."

He glanced at Padetmit, who, along with everyone else, watched him intently.

The younger woman suddenly got up and moved out of the smoke.

Padetmit said, "*You're* the one they saw. They saw you, right? But you didn't meet face-to-face?"

"No, we didn't meet. But they saw me."

"They think you're an evil spirit, that you brought death to them. They sent two runners. Our village just heard this yesterday."

Toq felt as though he had just been caught in a lie. He'd predicted that they would somehow blame him for the bear attack. He was now very uncomfortable, and he looked back into the fire, thinking about how to handle this.

Padetmit said, "A bear attacked them. Three people died, including a child. Two are badly injured. Are you an evil spirit?"

Toq looked at Padetmit and the others; the fire suddenly felt too hot.

"No. I'm just a man. I am not a spirit or a ghost. I'm not evil. They did not want me, so I left. It's okay. I did not wish any harm on them. I did not put a curse on them. I did not send the bear, and I was not the bear. I am filled with sorrow that some of them died, but I really am only a man. I have no special power."

Some people might claim they did indeed have special powers so others would fear them, but that was not Toq's way. Padetmit studied his face carefully. One young guy angrily jabbed a stick into the fire. The younger woman and one man now seemed fearful, looking from Toq to Padetmit.

Padetmit said, "Tococksla, the doubter. What do you doubt? The shamans, the spirit world? Maybe you've made them angry. Maybe you're cursed."

The younger woman said, "Stop, Pad! You'll make him angry!"

Padetmit frowned and waved her off.

Toq held up his hand and said, "It's okay. Padetmit asks good questions. I will harm no one. I have never killed another human being. It is not the right way. I see that you are good people. You brought me into your camp. I will do no evil."

Padetmit asked again, "But you're the doubter?"

Toq regretted telling him that, saying, "We all have doubts, little doubts. My name . . . it really means more of the questioner or searcher, not so much the doubter. The spirits are not angry with me. I do not speak against them or the shamans."

Of course, he lied. *This is what's wrong with religious and spiritual beliefs. They turn people into insane idiots, and now I have to lie to save my own skin.* Sweat ran down his brow.

Padetmit looked at him and then around the fire at his hunting party.

He nodded slowly and a faint smile came upon his lips. "I believe you, Toq. You don't seem evil, and some people do question and search for their own answers. It is good, so long as they don't put down spiritual men or women."

Toq smiled back and said, "Yes, I agree," though, in fact, he disagreed, thinking that spiritual people put down the unbelievers all the time.

The mood lightened, and they shared a couple of laughs.

Toq asked where they'd come from, and Pad said they'd come from the south along the zone between the mountains and the plains. Their people had spread from the coast, following rivers, valleys, and plateaus to the east. With human populations growing rapidly, everyone was looking for new hunting grounds. His people, several small bands with loose ties, had reached the flatlands and turned north. They inhabited lands where they saw no one else, and they told Toq he was the first person they had seen from outside their own tribes in years.

Padetmit said, "We just came to this valley last fall, so we don't know where the river came from or where it goes."

They knew of no other bands to the north or east, but a lot of people existed to the south. Conflicts between bands were rare, since food was abundant and the open, wild country allowed everyone to move on before battles erupted. Despite taking care to keep the peace, paranoia and distrust lay just below the surface of every band.

They asked Toq where he was from, how far away was his homeland, what his tribe was like, why did he leave, why was he alone, what he had seen on his journey, how had he survived by himself, would he stay with them, where would he go next, did he want to have a family, would he wander and search forever, what did he fear the most, did he like being alone, and more. They were as starved for a new face and voice as he was. The group decided that the assholes from the village must have killed the Traveler, and though Toq himself didn't think so, he found it interesting that they'd come to that conclusion.

He told them about the huge rivers, glacier-covered mountains, and open prairies, as well as the wildlife. They were well acquainted with mountain and valley glaciers, but when Toq told them of the vast ice sheet covering the northern prairies like an ocean, it amazed them. The hunting party had plenty of their own stories to tell, too—some happy and triumphant, others sad and heartbreaking. They had driven off, and even killed, both lions and bears, but they seemed to doubt that Toq had killed a lion on his own. By the middle of the night, Toq decided to tell them the story of the great flood, and to his surprise, they believed him.

Padetmit said, "The mighty powers and spirits favor you, Toq. We would be glad to have you join our band."

Toq nodded, smiled, and said, "Thank you. I will think about that," knowing Padetmit's response could have been the exact opposite. He could have said, *Toq, you are cursed, and evil comes upon all you come in contact with. You are cursed to wander alone, and you were probably banished from your tribe.*

And of course, Toq knew he'd just been lucky. No powers or spirits or gods favored him at all.

As the night wore on, people left to go sleep until only Padetmit and Toq remained by the fire.

Finally, Padetmit said, "There is not enough time for you and I to tell all our stories. You sleep. Tomorrow we can talk more, if we wish."

So, Toq retreated to his lean-to, but his mind allowed only a restless sleep as he replayed the talk around the fire. He hoped he hadn't said anything stupid or offensive.

• • • •

A cloudy morning and a late night kept the hunting party asleep later than usual. Still, they were up before Toq. When he heard them moving about and talking, he quickly got up to lend a hand.

The older woman barked at him, "Get packed up. We're going back to the village."

"Yes, yes," Toq replied, feeling simultaneously irritated by and afraid of her. Clearly, she had no fear of him or any special powers he might have.

The group quickly and efficiently broke down the camp and loaded all their gear, meat, and hides, onto travois—one for each person. Padetmit told Toq that he would pull one while two men stayed behind to make another. With Toq's help, they could drag everything back in one trip. One by one, each person picked up the leading end of their travois, put on leather harnesses that crossed their shoulders and chests, and began pulling their loads down a widened path toward the village.

It took half the day to get there, and Toq—unaccustomed to pulling a travois—ended the trip with sore stomach, back, and leg muscles. It was much more weight than what he carried in his bags, but he never complained. The village was small, with only twenty-five people or so—including those from the hunting party. A bit more than half the village was female, plus there were a few healthy elders and eight children of various ages. The scene was busy and chaotic. Everyone was happy to see the hunters, and they ran to help pull in the loads. The children ran up to Toq to see who the stranger was.

The older woman yelled at them, "Get away from him! You're gettin' in his way! What's wrong with you kids?"

Toq laughed at the children and thought, *Man, that woman is grouchy.*

The travois loads were all brought to one central place, where the women immediately went to work on the uncooked meat. Some of it went into a cold-water bog, while they cut up and boiled, roasted, or dried the rest. With so many hands, the village accomplished a lot in a short amount of time. Toq admired the women's skill, especially since he knew how long it took him, working alone, to do the same job.

Nobody paid him any attention until one of the elders approached, accompanied by Padetmit. He was a rough-looking man with graying hair. A scarred and warped nose, a shriveled, dead ear tip, and a missing finger were signs of a past battle with frostbite. He walked as if thorns pricked the bottoms of his feet. He made the friend sign, and Toq returned the greeting.

"Toq, I am Wewacuni. Welcome to our camp. Padetmit tells me you are considering staying with us. I hope you do. We need strong men and new blood. You will find a woman here. I think you will be happy. It's better than traveling on your own. Padetmit will find a place for you. Come talk to me after you've rested."

Toq nodded respectfully, and said only, "Yes, thank you, Chief."

••••

One full moon cycle passed and Toq still lived with Wewacuni's band. They moved downriver, traveling four days before setting up camp near the confluence of another river coming from the south (Tongue River). Here, they planned to stay for the bulk of the summer as long as the hunting was good. Their language and culture were new to Toq, but he adapted quickly. Everyone seemed to accept him, except for maybe the grouchy woman, but she didn't appear to like anyone. Padetmit told him she got a lot of work done and deep inside had a big, soft heart, but that it was hard to see.

The band's sister tribe—the one that thought Toq was an evil spirit—heard that Toq was with them, making them angry and afraid.

Wewacuni told Toq, "Do not worry. With time, they will see that you are good. They will be okay."

But the sister tribe moved upriver, putting a greater distance between the two groups, effectively cutting off contact. Another band, with twice as many people as Wewacuni's, came down to the valley from the south and set up camp across the river. Padetmit did not recognize them, and the people were annoyed and apprehensive that they set up camp so near theirs.

Padetmit and two others paddled a canoe to the other side to meet this new tribe. People watched from both sides of the river. Men and women met Padetmit and his companions, and soon they all disappeared into the encampment. After some time, Padetmit and his men returned and spoke privately with Wewacuni, who listened intently, asking questions and nodding, then shaking his head. Everyone, including Toq, was anxious to hear the news, and they gathered around Padetmit at the center of their little camp.

He began by saying, "They are new people. We don't know them. They have many more people than we do, and they said that even though we got here first, they are not moving on. They like it where they are, and if we don't like it, then we should move."

The grouchy woman swore out loud.

Wewacuni spoke up, "They are too big. We cannot risk a fight with them. We do not want to kill anyone. There is no need to—doing so would be stupid and vile. We will go in peace."

One respected man asked, "How long can we go, getting pushed around by larger groups?"

Padetmit nodded and replied, "I know it is hard, but if we join with another band, then we have more mouths to feed, and the hunted beasts disappear. It is easier for us to go. There is lots of open country."

Then, to everyone's surprise, Toq said, "Please, pardon me for speaking, as I am new to your band, but I think, sooner or later, all the open country will have people in it. Then, there will be too many people in the land, chasing away the game or killing it all off, and then people will starve and fight each other for what is left. Then what?"

Padetmit chafed at Toq's question. "So what are you proposing we do? Stay and fight? Join another band? Disband? Or move on? We're not going to wander alone like you did. Besides, there is no way people can kill off all the animals—that's impossible. The spirits would never allow the people to starve. There are always going to be new lands for us to move to."

Most of the group nodded in agreement, and Toq felt like the outsider.

Padetmit softened his tone, and he said, "They know about you, Toq."

Dumbfounded, Toq asked, "How can they know about me?"

"Word traveled from our sister tribe, moving from band to band. That tribe across the river asked if we had seen you. I told them yes, but that you had moved on. They said that if they find you, they will kill you, that their spirits and spears are stronger than your power, and that they are not afraid of you, or us, if we are friends with you."

Toq listened in disbelief, glanced at Wewacuni, leaned back, and said, "Godsdamn shit! They've all lost their minds."

Padetmit shot him an angry look for his profanity, but he said nothing. Some spoke in favor of Toq, saying they would stand with him and defend him. But others voiced their fear of losing their tribal alliances or being attacked because of him.

One fellow said, "It's only a matter of time before bad things start happening to us because we took him in."

The grouchy woman said, "Shit!" She spat into the dirt between her feet and dragged her finger through the mud. She wiped her muddy finger down her chin in a sign of disgust. "You're all talking like fools. There's nothing special or magical about Toquuxla. He's an ordinary man—we've seen him, we know him. He irritates me, but most of you irritate me. He doesn't deserve to be cast out or hunted and killed. We will convince the other bands that he is not an evil spirit—"

But several raised voices interrupted her, insulting her and attacking Toq, and the grouchy woman argued loudly with them.

Wewacuni and Padetmit held up their hands to try to restore calm. A couple of people withdrew with their children from the gathering, troubled that the leaders had not taken control of the situation. Finally, Padetmit stepped between the grouchy woman and the others before they came to blows.

Angrily, he looked into everyone's eyes and said, "Stop! That's enough! You've had your say!"

They backed up and held their tongues. Padetmit looked at the frowning Wewacuni, who waved toward the band's shaman.

Padetmit said to the shaman, "What do you say?" even though Toq knew he did not think much of the man.

Toq had done his best to show respect to the shaman, but he considered him a weak, delusional spiritualist who basked in his position.

Now, the shaman showed his power, saying, "We are turning on each other and fighting. Our friends turn against us. Strangers threaten us. Trouble goes with this man. He lived alone, and he is meant to be alone—not with us. The spirits have told me he should go."

Toq met Padetmit's eyes with sadness and resignation. He knew the idiot shaman's words would sway opinion against him. He turned to Wewacuni, who looked down, deep in thought. This rejection stung, and Toq felt humiliated. A lump formed in his throat. He stood up and all eyes were on him.

Padetmit said, "We will decide tomorrow," and Wewacuni looked up and nodded at Toq.

Toq withdrew to his shelter without a single person saying a word to him; they did not dare at this point, fearing judgment would come upon themselves. He passed one young woman trying to hide her tears.

Toq gathered his traveling gear together, and spent the rest of the day reclining quietly, keeping to himself. He had no visitors, and he did not attempt to join the group for the evening meal. His thoughts were already turning to what he would do next, and he was thankful that he had only been with these people for a little while, making leaving less heartbreaking.

"The idiot was right. I am meant to be alone."

• • • •

Toq strode to where Wewacuni and Padetmit sat in the glorious morning sun, carrying his loaded bags and spears. The people watched him.

"It looks like you are leaving us," Wewacuni said.

Toq responded, "Yes, I think it's best. It's time. Thank you for your kindness and for inviting me in. You are a good and wise man. I wish you and your tribe well."

"I think it is best, too. You are good, Toq, not evil. I am sorry all this is happening, but . . ." He hesitated. "May the spirits keep you safe, and may you find your people." He waved at his wife, watching from a distance, while saying, "Here, we have extra food for you."

She approached and handed Toq a bag of pemmican.

He nodded at her and said, "Thank you."

He looked at Padetmit, saying, "The first human I'd come face-to-face with in a long while. You were good to me and fair. Be well." Toq meant it. Padetmit was fundamentally a good man, though his religious fanaticism made him a bit of a self-righteous ass.

Padetmit replied, "Peace, Toquuxla. Let the gods guide you. Don't be a doubter."

Toq smiled and nodded, and then said, "Tell me, Pad, why do people believe false things are true and true things are false?"

Padetmit replied, "I don't know, Toq. You tell me. Why do you believe true things are false?"

Toq again smiled and nodded.

He waved the friend sign and began to walk away when the grouchy woman called out to him, "Don't be lazy and stupid!"

Toq laughed. "I won't. Don't be so grouchy."

He made the friend sign to her, then again for added emphasis, and she signed it back to him. The shaman did not show himself.

Alone, Toquuxla followed the river to the northeast, through the scattered woods, over hills, across open meadows and plains of fresh grass and wildflowers, accompanied by birds, butterflies, and bees, once again meeting and greeting the wild animals of a land no other human had yet seen. He was alone, he was free, and he was happy. And he wondered about his future with people.

••••

Over the next few days, Toq's emotions swung wildly from elation to loneliness and dejection. Most of the time, he felt that he ruled his realm and was confident in his abilities, but sometimes, the reality of his smallness in this tremendous land—and how precarious his survival truly was—rattled him. Although he put what he thought was a great distance between him and his potential human enemies, he held a nagging fear of bands of people appearing suddenly over the next hill.

He hastily pressed north and east along the river for days and days. The country was hilly to flat, with thinning trees and the occasional large, beautiful badlands. The wildlife was plentiful and familiar. He saw no people. After about half a moon cycle, he reached the confluence of another large river coming from the west. He was certain it was his river from last summer. He stood on a knoll overlooking the two rivers (Missouri River and Yellowstone River) joined together, disappearing into the east. The wooded lands had petered out a couple of days ago, so now only a few trees dotted the hills and valleys. Prairie and prairie beasts dominated this landscape.

Toq gazed at the two rivers running full and fast, flooding lowland areas. The temptation to cross and go east was strong, but he wondered if he might run into more people. In fact, there were no people to the east, but he could not know that. He also felt the pull to go back west, to more familiar places—places where he knew there would be no humans out to get him.

He laughed. "Boy, you are paranoid. Maybe for good reason."

The massive amount of water pouring off faraway glaciers flooded these valleys to such an extent that it looked more like a lake than a river system. It was a long way across, and he would definitely need a boat.

He proclaimed, "I don't want to build a boat." And he replied to himself, "Yeah? So, go west."

He began to daydream about going all the way back to his own people, and the thought of seeing them again added energy to his step. His trek west along the big river began easily enough, but the farther he went, the more rugged the land became, and then he entered the rough, river breaks country. He hiked down and back up out of countless deep and steep coulees and canyons, with the summer sun beating down relentlessly, biting bugs making him miserable, and lions, bears, wolves, cheetahs, bison, and mammoths keeping him on edge.

After more than twenty days, he stopped in a coulee that looked familiar, but after crossing so many, they all looked the same to him. He proceeded around a bend and went to the riverbank. The water ran considerably higher than the year before, but he was sure that this was where he'd ditched his boat last year. A small herd of horses grazing nearby made him more certain.

"Ha! This is it. I made the loop. And those are probably the same horses." He knew they probably were not the same horses. "Wow. I can hardly believe it."

Along the way, the small, isolated mountain ranges north and south of the river had come into view. Toq knew these places, and although he'd only briefly passed through, he unconsciously thought of them as his lands.

He felt the pull to go north again, but the river ran higher and wilder than last summer and he still did not want to stop to build a boat. He worked his way west, pausing at the place where he'd last seen his wolf, wondering if he might find his old friend with his own family. But no wolves were there. He climbed up onto the tops of the breaks, away from the river, and walked west along ridges.

After skirting the upper end of a deep coulee, he started across a flat, open area. He spotted a couple of red-blond heads on the opposite side, and he stopped dead in his tracks, completely exposed. The two lionesses had been walking in his direction but only noticed him at the same time as he saw them. They stopped and stared, then two more lionesses joined them. Toq swallowed hard, and his palms began to sweat. Four lion cubs popped up behind the lionesses. Toq had nowhere to run and no tree to climb, so he stood still. Another female came up, and then a large male moved to the front—all eyes focused on the unmoving man.

Toquuxla thought, *This will be my last day. The lions will get their revenge, not too far from where I killed one of them.*

He looked for an escape route, wondering why they were not coming at him. He slowly started toward an adjacent coulee, keeping half an eye on the lions, prepared to duck into the coulee as quickly as he could. The male lion huffed, and Toq quickly looked to see if they were charging. Instead, to his surprise, he saw the lionesses and cubs running away out of sight. The male glanced at them, gave Toq a last look, then spun his massive bulk and galloped away after the females. The pride vanished into the ravines to the south.

Astonished, Toq looked around to see what scared them off.

"Nothing. There's nothing here. No bears, no wolves, no mammoths. Only me. So, what made that happen?" he asked himself.

The lions were afraid of the man, but Toq could not yet fathom that, so he continued on his way, constantly checking behind him for the pride. The faint smell of smoke loudly proclaimed fire somewhere, just before he reached the end of the ridge. He held the thought inside, hoping it was the result of lightning, but deep down, he knew it meant people. Standing on a hilltop, he looked down into the valley where two rivers met (Judith River and Missouri River). The wide valley across the big river was where he'd lived while constructing his boat. He saw no humans and no village anywhere. Plumes of smoke did not rise into the sky in the distance. No large fires burned. Still, the smell of smoke, coming and going, gave him all the more reason to believe people were there.

"Who are you?" he wondered aloud.

If they were from the south, they might have heard of him; if they were from the west, he might know them. He moved slowly down into the valley. A couple of vultures and some magpies gathered in a small coulee—not an uncommon sight, but there were no mammals there, making it a little unusual. Toq ambled down to investigate, causing the birds to fly off, protesting mightily. The strong smell of a dead carcass filled the warm summer air, but what the birds were after was not at first readily apparent.

Then, Toq noticed a spot of disturbed ground. Brush, grass, soil, and stones unnaturally covered a place in the bottom of the coulee. Bears and big cats might cover a meal, but this looked different. It looked like people had tried to bury and conceal a carcass, and the large birds had uncovered a portion of it, leaving some flesh exposed. He held his breath and threw off some brush and grass. A large gash in the soil exposed the guts, while dirt and rocks covered the rest of the body. There was no hair or fur scattered about as there would normally be at a scavenging site.

Toq took shallow, short breaths as he removed some large stones. He pulled off sheaves of grass that had been laid over the body, exposing to the sun the brown skin of a human back and neck—a single bloody hole marring the perfect skin.

His hands shook and his face turned pale. "A person."

Flies swarmed the body.

He removed the rest of the rocks and grass to reveal a woman's naked body. He slowly turned her over, fearful of all the commands not to disturb the dead. Dirt and pebbles stuck to her skin and bloody wounds. The wound on her back went through to a hole in her chest, where blood had poured from her body. Toq carefully turned her head so it faced up. Her black hair stuck to the dried blood on her face, which was bruised and had multiple cuts and gashes. She'd been so badly beaten that no one could possibly recognize her.

Toq looked upon her with shock and sadness. "You poor woman. Who did this to you?"

After sitting for a while with the woman's body, he looked around to see if any people or bears approached. Then, leaving her face up, he covered her again with grass, dirt, and rocks—doing a much better job than her murderer had, so the scavengers wouldn't get to her. He believed she'd died only a day or two before. He searched the area for footprints or drag marks and followed a faint trail of bent grass through the bottom of a depression connected to the coulee.

The killer kept hidden in the depression, out of sight of any witnesses, Toq thought.

He followed the low spot to the river and a stand of spruce, where animals had sniffed and pawed at the bloodied grasses, pine needles, and sand. He saw no one.

 This is where you died," he said to the woman's spirit. "What did he do with your clothes?"

Any clear sign of human tracks had been obliterated by the myriad of animal footprints, and the land did not tell on those who'd passed by. Toq searched upstream a little ways, then turned downstream toward the big river. The much smaller, north-flowing river ran fairly clear. It could easily be crossed, but he remained on its east side. He saw more birds converging on a spot away from the river, and he walked over, chasing the birds away. He braced himself, but only hair and scattered entrails remained on the bloody ground—no skin, no head, no paws, no bones.

"People took this animal," Toq mumbled.

He followed a clear path through the grass toward the river as the birds immediately returned to what little remained of their bloody feast. He moved cautiously, using trees for cover, wishing to see them before they saw him. The trail ran down the stream bank and across some mud, where the footprints of fifteen to twenty men dented the ground. The tracks went directly into the water, and Toq looked across to see where they'd climbed the opposite bank.

He pondered his options: Hold back, wait, and watch, or march straight into their camp, or else just leave and avoid the humans altogether. He moved north along the river, but the sparse trees and brush no longer provided adequate cover. After some distance, he saw, downriver, on the west side, within eyesight of the big river, smoke rising up and drifting over a group of women. Nobody saw him. He quietly moved up a hill to the east for a better look at the big village sprawled across a gently sloping plain near the small river. Willows, spruce, and birch separated the village of domed shelters from the river and partially surrounded the plain.

"Wow," said Toq. "There was nobody here last year."

A group of nine men came out of the village and crossed the river in Toq's direction. Four women followed. The party split into two groups going in different directions, and Toq sat behind a tree watching the groups go around him. He heard them calling out for the dead woman. Mostly, he heard the women's voices. As they spread out to search coulees and hilltops, Toq recognized the walk of the man leading one of the groups.

"Shiiiiit. It's the Asshole," he whispered.

Rage filled his heart. The Asshole pointed and waved and shouted at the people following him. They would never find the murdered woman in the direction he was leading them.

The life of freedom Toq had so enjoyed slipped away with all these people around. Already they affected him and his movements and his thinking. The sun dropped low over the western horizon, the two groups faded from view, and Toq stood up, walked to the river, crossed it, and walked into the village.

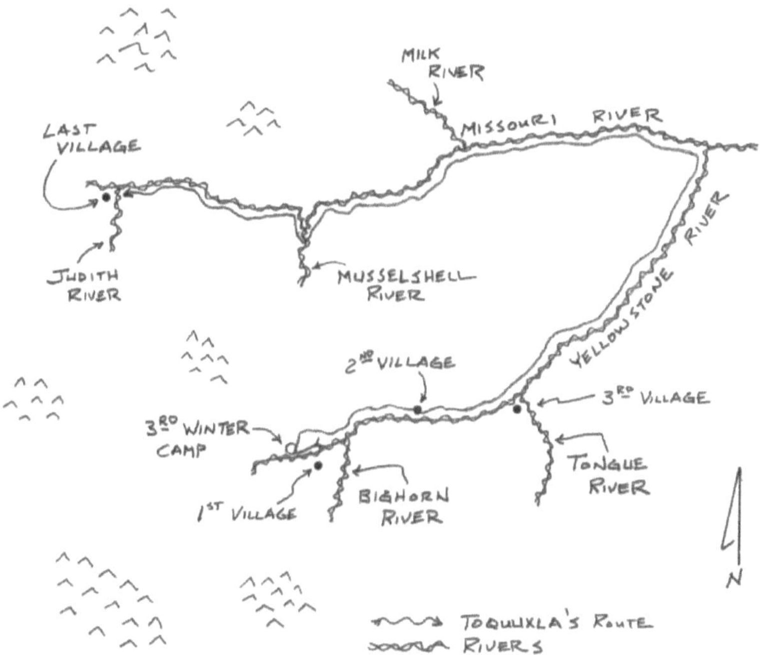

MILK RIVER
MISSOURI RIVER
LAST VILLAGE
JUDITH RIVER
MUSSELSHELL RIVER
YELLOWSTONE RIVER
2ND VILLAGE
3RD VILLAGE
3RD WINTER CAMP
1ST VILLAGE
BIGHORN RIVER
TONGUE RIVER
N
TOQULIXLA'S ROUTE
RIVERS

CHAPTER 20

Strife

A lone, hairy man, wet from the waist down and carrying bags and spears, strode to the edge of the encampment, where children played under the watchful eyes of three women. The children did not know him and ran to the women, who picked up their own spears and eyed the man warily. One of them called something over her shoulder, and a man emerged from a nearby hut. Upon seeing Toq, he called something of his own and in an instant was joined by five others.

Toq, the stranger, signed as a friend and stepped forward. Grinning, he called out the names of the first man and all of the women.

He then said, "I'm Toquuxla!"

Their expressions morphed from concern to joy. They ran to him, greeting him warmly, touching his hands, hair, and skin. A few of the men held back, not smiling or welcoming, although they knew who Toq was. The friendly group led Toq to the center of the village, where the chief talked with people outside his lodge.

The chief looked at the procession coming towards him. He stood and quickly recognized the newcomer. The villagers had not seen anyone from the outside in well over a year, and they were happy to see a new face. The chief appeared older and more somber, and he did not smile, but he greeted Toq graciously, more so than when Toq had left their former settlement more than a year ago. Soon, the entire village surrounded Toq, some smiling, some looking grim. One of the Asshole's stooges pushed through, causing several people to back up, their smiles vanishing.

The stooge interrupted Toq's discussion with the chief, demanding, "What are you doing here? You were told to never come back."

Toq was about to give him a smart answer—that of course he hadn't come back to the same place—but the chief scowled at the stooge and said, "He is our guest now. I welcome him in."

Some of the chief's relatives stepped in front of the stooge, who flushed with anger. The chief motioned for Toq to join him inside his hut, and another man and woman—the chief's cousins—also came in. It was dark and too warm inside, but Toq's eyes adjusted, and when the door flap closed, he knew the chief wanted their conversation to be private. Toq waited for the chief to speak.

"Toq, I am sorry I was not better to you and the Traveler. I have not been a good leader. I would not normally say these things to an outsider, but you once were with us, and I know you had troubles with some here in our tribe. And my wife liked you. We have big problems here. Most of the tribe is still with me and my wife, but the Asshole and his people are stirring up trouble, turning one family against another. He says he is a chief and that my time is up. I would like to stop being chief, but nobody will challenge him. They fear him. I don't want him to lead our people."

Toq found it funny that the chief now referred to his own enemy as the Asshole, too.

"Where is your wife?" Toq asked, thinking she ought to be a part of this discussion.

The chief's voice cracked. "Gone." After a long pause, he added, "Nobody knows where."

Toq's stomach twisted. *He* knew.

"She rarely went anywhere by herself, but she was strong, and yesterday she went south along the river and never came back."

He waved at his cousin, who said, "We looked for her first on this side of the river, but no sign. Some people saw a pride of lions across the river this morning, and they were afraid the lions would find and kill her, so a large party of men crossed the river. At first, the lions didn't know what we were, but we made them nervous because they had cubs. Each of us had four spears. The lionesses saw us coming first, and they stood and stared. Then, the two males stood and roared, but only one came toward us. When he charged, people scattered, and when he was near enough, everyone threw their spears. Four spears stuck in him on the first throw. He tried to turn around and run, but we threw another batch of spears—so many spears. That lion was done. He died quick. Half of our group charged the pride, and the lions turned and ran off up the hills to the east. They were gone."

"So that's why they ran from me . . ." Toq said. "I saw them up on top, and they ran from me. Unbelievable."

The cousin said, "We brought the beast back here, so we will have his power and strength. Then, more people went out searching on the other side of the river. You didn't see them?"

"Oh, yes, I saw them but far away." This was not exactly true.

The chief said, "I think the lions got her."

The woman cousin whispered, "The Asshole and his men got her. She hated them, and she never missed an opportunity to knock them down. They wanted power, and she stood in their way. They wanted her gone. I hate them, but everyone is afraid of them. Now, they are out pretending to look for her."

The old chief could barely hear her, but he knew what she said and simply looked at her in silence.

The cousin said, "The Asshole was good with his spear, and it was one of his that stuck the lion. He was the first to run up to the dead beast. He pulled out his spear and plunged it into the heart of the animal with a holler. He was a maniac. Everyone was happy, but he was crazy, and his men became crazy with him, yelling, screaming, stabbing the dead lion. They ruined the skin and much of the meat. The Asshole is one bloodthirsty bastard. He loves to kill things, and he loves having control over people, having people fear him."

Toq listened quietly. Clearly the Asshole had enemies here as well as followers, and it seemed like the village was about to tear itself apart because of him.

"Why don't you go your own way?" Toq asked. "This village has always been too big anyway. There must have been over a hundred people when I left."

The chief said, "A group did leave last year—about twenty-five people."

The cousin said, "Another larger group wanted to leave this spring, but the Asshole said, 'No more splitting of the village, and if anybody tries to leave, they will be considered enemies.' He said he would hunt them down. He says we need a large village to fight other tribes and to hunt mammoth."

Toq thought to himself, *What a mess. Life was so simple and easy off by myself.* He considered telling the chief good luck and goodbye. He didn't want to be involved, but he did feel compassion for the chief and his people, as well as anger at the assholes. He weighed his next words carefully, knowing he would likely be accused of murdering the chief's wife.

Toq reached over and grabbed the chief's right hand, saying, "Listen carefully. I do not lie. Your wife was good to me. The Asshole threatened me. It would be easier for me to leave the village, but you must know this." He nodded toward the woman and said, "I think she is right. When I came down to the valley, I found a poorly made grave. A woman's body was there. There were no clothes. I did not know it was her. She was clearly beaten and stabbed through the chest. She was not dead long. I am sorry, but it must be your wife."

The chief said nothing. He bowed his head, brought his hands to his face, and sobbed deeply. Toq looked at the cousins, and even in the darkness, he could see their tears and grief.

After a few moments, the chief lifted his head and said, "We have to go get her. We can't leave her there." He looked at the three people in front of him. "You are my friends. Don't tell anyone else about this; let me. We will go in the morning."

They exited the lodge to breathe cool, fresh air. The sun had set, and dusk enveloped the outer world. The chief told his cousins that when his sons returned, he wished to speak to them. Toq presumed the chief's sons led one search party while the Asshole led the other. A few people had gone to bed, but most of the village waited for the searchers to come back.

The chief said, "Toq, I want you to sit and wait with me. Tonight, you will be my guest in my lodge. They will not attack you here with me." Toq nodded, accepting the offer.

A few people came to sit with the chief and build up the fire. The stooge passed by a couple times, glaring at Toq, wanting to make sure Toq knew he was being watched. Toq missed the company of the wolf and the mammoth.

Darkness surrounded the camp by the time the Asshole's group showed up. People met them and then quietly dispersed to their lodges. The stooge spoke to the Asshole at the edge of the village to tell him about Toq, and the Asshole, followed by a small group of his men, walked straight to the chief's lodge. Some of the people around the fire stood up at their approach, but the chief and Toq remained seated.

The Asshole pointed his spear angrily at Toq and said to the chief, "I told him I'd kill him if he came back to us."

The chief calmly said, "I told him you would not. Did you find my wife?"

"She is gone. We will never find her. The lions got her. You have to accept reality," the Asshole responded. He looked at Toq and said, "You're leaving tomorrow or you're dead." He started to leave but then turned and added, "We found the little shrine you set up for your stupid, dead partner. I didn't kill him, but I would have. So, you've been wandering alone out here all by yourself. A pathetic, stinking idiot of a human being."

He walked back to Toq and spat on him. Nobody said a word. Nobody moved a muscle. Not even Toq, who simply looked at the Asshole with disdain.

Sauntering away, the Asshole said to two of his men, "Watch him."

When the other search party returned, the chief told his three sons what Toq had found and what he planned to do. Nobody argued. They all quietly retired to their lodges for the night.

••••

Only the children slept well that night. Everyone else felt the tension and feared the coming day. Before daybreak, while the chief lay snoring softly, one of the chief's sons entered the lodge and whispered, "Toquuxla, here is another spear. I was told you only carried one big one. You may need this. You are with us, yes?"

Toq replied, "Yes, I am with you."

The son said, "I hope there will not be a fight, but I fear there will be."

The sun came up, quickly heating the fresh, cool morning air.

The chief warned Toq, "Don't go anywhere by yourself—not even to take a piss."

Toq learned that the young man who'd lodged with him and the Traveler had moved on during the split, as had one of the Traveler's lovers. The other woman who slept with the Traveler was now with the Asshole, who had two women.

The chief said, "One is a quiet, nice girl. But stay away from the other one. She is mean. She'll cut your throat. She is just like her husband."

The chief's close family members—men and women—gathered in front of his lodge to eat. He spoke briefly to them, in a hushed tone, before anyone else came near.

"My dear family, you all know what sad news Toq has brought to us. After we eat, we will go find my poor wife, and we will take care of her so she can live at peace in the next life."

Toq dreaded this, but he knew it had to be done.

He quietly told the chief, "I am sorry to tell you this, but the birds had gotten to part of her body before I got there, and the flies were everywhere. The smell will be bad. This will be terrible for you and your family."

The chief looked down and nodded, saying, "I know. I know," as tears fell from his eyes. Then, he grabbed Toq's arm and said, "Come with me."

He waved for several men to come along, and they walked to the Asshole's hut. The Asshole sat outside eating with his women, two young children, and a baby in the quiet woman's arms. He watched them coming and stood to meet, or confront, them. The mean woman stood as well, and she picked up a fist-sized rock. A few men came over to stand with the Asshole.

The Asshole spoke first, asking Toq, "Why are you still here? Are you on your way out?"

"No, he isn't," the chief replied. "He is going to show us where my wife is."

The chief studied the Asshole's face, but the man did not grimace, wince, or twitch. Everyone on the Asshole's side stared stone-faced at the chief and Toq.

The Asshole said, "How is he going to find your wife? Is he a shaman now? *Our* shaman couldn't find her."

The chief said, "Not 'find.' *Show.* He already knows where she is."

Toq thought the Asshole's face turned a bit pale.

The Asshole said, "Alive?"

"Alive?" the chief said. "You think she's alive? You said the lions got her."

"Probably. Maybe."

"You're coming with us," the chief said.

"Why? No, I'm not. It's a waste of time. I've searched enough. She's gone, and I have other things to do. This jerk isn't going to find anything. You're wasting your energy with this idiot."

Toq looked beyond the Asshole to several furs hanging from poles on his lodge. One was a fresh skin from the top of a lion's head to the mane across its shoulders, and one was a wolf with a familiar-looking pattern of fur. But then he thought, *A lot of wolves look like my wolf.*

The chief finished the conversation abruptly by saying, "Come if you want. I don't give a shit," and he turned around and walked away.

On the way back, Toq asked one of the chief's sons, "How did the Asshole get that wolf fur? Trap it? Surprise it?"

The son replied, "Naw. It was weird, according to him. He was out with one of his guys, scouting for large game, when this wolf came trotting right up to him. He thought it was going to attack, but instead, it acted friendly and even seemed to want to play. But you know that asshole. He said he didn't want to compete for game with wolves, and he wanted its fur, so, he said, 'I stuck my spear in that stupid wolf.' He's such an asshole. He didn't have to kill that wolf."

Toq clenched his fist and gritted his teeth, and he turned to glare at the Asshole and his lodge.

The son stopped and looked at Toq, asking, "What's wrong?"

Toq snarled, "That was my wolf."

• • • •

Toq led a large procession of about thirty people—nearly half the village—out to the river. They waded across a wide, shallow section; a couple of people helped the chief across. They walked along the river until they came to the first spot by the stand of spruce.

Toq pointed to the bloody ground and told the chief, "I think she died here." Then, he pointed up the draw going east, and said, "They dragged her up there."

A woman came up to the chief, pointed behind them, and said, "The Asshole is coming."

Everyone looked to see the Asshole leading a group of seven men toward them.

The chief asked him, "Changed your mind?"

"I want to see what the hero has to show you," the Asshole sneered.

The chief pointed his spear at the ground. "Blood!"

"So what? It's animal blood!"

"We'll see." The chief pursed his lips and motioned with his head for Toq to lead the way.

Toq started, but the chief suddenly said, "Wait." He stopped and removed a large, brown and gold eagle feather from around his neck and tied it just below the stone point of his spear so it hung loose and waved in the breeze.

"Let's go," he said.

They went up the depression, into the coulee, and up onto the knoll above the grave. No animals had disturbed the site. Toq motioned for people to spread out on the hill above it while he and the chief's sons uncovered the body. The smell was worse than the day before, and Toq made the sons back away while he uncovered her head and upper torso, intentionally keeping the rest of her covered.

Many people gasped, then looked away, and the smell made a couple people feel sick. Many tears fell, and some family members began to cry out loud. The chief took a bladder of water from his cousin, and he went down to wash the blood and dirt from his wife's face and body.

"It does not look like her," he muttered, but when he took her hands, he saw the old scars that he knew belonged only to her. He closed his eyes, held her cold hands, and with tears running down his cheeks, quietly uttered a prayer. Everyone looked on.

The chief opened his eyes and said, "Oh, my dear woman, now you are free."

He touched the wound on her chest. Then he stood and looked at Toq and his sons. He leaned on his spear as he turned to look directly at the Asshole.

He pointed and said, "You did—"

But the Asshole blurted, "How did Toq know she was here? He was the only one who knew. He killed her and buried her! Now, he thinks he can get away with it by blaming someone else. She disappears, he shows up, and now he finds her dead? Come on! He did it! He killed her!"

The chief answered, "Why would Toq kill her? She liked him, but she hated you."

A few women retreated down the coulee, where they stopped to watch.

The Asshole tossed his head and scoffed. "*Shiiit.* That doesn't mean I would kill her. But him! He and his old dead buddy would happily rape women. That's why he would kill her. Lots of people here know he is a rapist. He pretends to be a nice guy, but he is only out for himself."

The Asshole repeatedly pointed his spear at Toq. His voice grew louder, his face reddened with anger, and veins popped out on his head and neck.

"He has you all—"

"*Oh, shut up, you fool!*" shouted the chief. "We've all heard enough from you! We're—"

"*You're* the fool, you stupid old man!" the Asshole screamed. "What are you going to do, old man?"

The chief said, much more calmly, "We're going to go back, after properly burying my wife, and we will decide if you are to be banished from our village or killed."

The Asshole said, "Horseshit! This is *my* village!"

He feared no one, especially with his men backing him, and now his temper overwhelmed any prudent thought in his brain. His head tilted back, he looked to the sky, and with his mouth opening wide, baring his teeth, he let out a rising roar like a lion. Then, he snapped his head down, his eyes focused on the chief, and with the speed of a flapping wing, he yanked his spear back and let it fly with such force that it became a blur.

Toq and one of the chief's sons tried to knock the spear off course, but neither was quick enough. The chief tried to turn away, but the Asshole's aim was true and the chief's reflexes were slow. The stone spearpoint entered his left side below his arm, breaking through two ribs, just missing his heart, but piercing his lungs, slicing arteries and his diaphragm, and sticking out of his front right side. The force knocked the chief to the ground, but he caught himself, and he held himself up on all fours. He looked down between his arms to see the bloody spear sticking out from his body. Blood poured down the point onto the ground. The chief tried to take a breath, but blood filled his lungs, and his damaged diaphragm could barely pull in any air. He vaguely heard a commotion and felt somebody's hand on his back, but he was desperate to get a breath. He inhaled but only heard gurgling sounds, and he immediately coughed a large spray of blood onto the ground, accompanied by terrible pain. Panic made him pull at the spear, but soon, everything turned fuzzy, then dark, and he collapsed, his body depleted of oxygen and blood. In a few moments, the chief's heart stopped beating, and he died with the Asshole's spear stuck through him. His own spear lay by his side, the eagle feather flecked with beads of his own blood.

Three women ran to him, two women ran away, and the others joined the fray. Loud human voices—yelling, screaming, and cursing—desecrated the peace of the valley. The land, which had never seen people before now, witnessed the violent side of human nature for the first time—not in the killing of an animal, but in the killing of one of their own. People brought their murdering, destructive ways to the new land. Dust rose into the air above the scuffle. Spears and rocks were thrown. The Asshole and his seven men fought against twenty-five of the chief's people, and while they started well, it was a suicidal battle. Toq and one of the chief's sons threw spears at the Asshole, but he dodged them, just getting nicked by one.

The Asshole quickly grabbed both spears and threw one at Toq, who ducked. Toq picked it up, but the point was broken, so he grabbed the chief's spear from the ground. The chief's son charged the Asshole. A spear flew in from the son's blind side, striking him in the hip, dropping him to his knee. The Asshole lunged, swatted the son's spear away, and drove his spear into his chest. Spears and stones rained down on the Asshole's men, three of whom lay dead or dying on the ground. As the larger mob descended, courage fled from the hearts of the remaining five men, and they ran. Toquuxla and the mob gave chase. They downed the first man and then the second, but Toq did not stop. Some men reached the third man, and Toq passed them by. Toq caught up to the fourth man and pushed him hard to the ground, but he didn't stop. A couple of men behind him speared the fallen man and rejoined the chase.

The Asshole was strong and fast, as well as good with a spear, but Toq was faster. The Asshole raced toward the big river, running over flats, hills, and gullies. Toq knew he would be pinched between the river and the high, steep walls of the breaks. Adrenaline coursed through the bodies of all the men, propelling them beyond what was normal. Toq spotted movement up a sidehill as a small herd of bighorns ran away from the activity. He was catching up to the Asshole, and he wondered what he would do once he caught him. As he considered all the trouble and death the Asshole had brought, he gave in to his fury and knew the murderer deserved to die.

One of the chief's sons was behind Toq, and he wanted revenge before all others. But Toq had nursed his own grudges against this man for so long—his hatred and threats against the Traveler and Toq, the murder of the chief and his wife and now of the chief's eldest son, how he'd divided the village against itself, and how he'd killed Toq's wolf.

The Asshole kept looking behind him, which slowed him down. He saw Toq with the chief's spear and several more men behind him. To his right, he could go up the hills, but he feared Toq would catch him. He angled toward the big river, instinctively thinking it was his best option for getting out of this alive—if the river didn't kill him. Throughout the chase, he never had a single regret about what he had done.

Toq was within throwing distance of the Asshole when he saw him turn toward the river—likely thinking they wouldn't follow him into the water. Toq thought the river would most certainly kill him. He considered throwing the spear to hit him before he reached the water. Then, from a treeless, domed hill, a flash of blond fur—powered by long legs and with a long tail flying in the air—bolted straight for the Asshole. Toq stopped running, breathing heavily. The Asshole didn't see the cat coming, and with stunning speed and power, it slammed into the running man, knocking him to the ground, his spear jolted from his grip.

The cheetah-cat wrestled with the man, who screamed, "Help me! *Aaagh*!" until the animal got a grip on his throat and clamped down.

The Asshole kicked and tried to roll away. He swung his fists at the cat's head and tried to gouge its eyes, until the cat pinned his arms with its front legs. Toq held his spear ready and approached the man and cat with a cold, pitiless heart.

Several men came running up, including the chief's son, and Toq heard one of them say, "Kill him! Kill both of them!"

But Toq held out his hand and his spear and said, "No! Leave it be. Let the cat take him. It is better this way."

The Asshole couldn't speak. The cat spun around to face the men, never letting go of its prey. Although the men made it nervous, it had no intention of giving up its meal.

The chief's son walked closer and spat upon the man on the ground. "This death is too easy for you, you pile of shit!"

The cat growled, and the son backed up. The Asshole's body went limp, as blood and oxygen were cut off from his brain. As much as Toq hated him, in that moment, he finally felt sorry for him and everything that had happened. Toq turned around and began walking away.

But one of the men cried, "Shit, Toq! We can't just let this beast eat him! We have to kill it and bury the Asshole or he'll haunt us forever. And now the cat has a taste for human blood."

Toq stopped and looked back.

The son said, "We're not killing the cat. It's on our side. Surely, the spirits sent it. We will come back later, find his bones, and bury them. That's good enough for him."

Toq nodded. So, one by one, they all left the cat with its kill, and they walked in silence back to the rest of the group.

Toq was deep in thought. How ironic it was that one of the wolf's enemies had taken out his wolf's killer. *The Asshole claimed lions got the chief's wife, and then a cat got him.* Toq did not feel victorious; all he felt was loss and a sense of emptiness for the people who'd died.

As they approached the site of the fight, he asked the son, "Now what will you do?"

The son said, "I don't know. I can't think right now. There will be no more killing, no vengeance. But our village cannot stay together. The Asshole's people and family will have to go their own way. Do you think that is right?"

"Yes, I do. You are wise for seeing that. I hope your people go along with you."

In his heart, Toq burned with anger at the people who'd backed the Asshole. The man would have been just like any other rotten person, ignored or rejected, except that his people had given him strength and power, and now they had nothing left but death and heartache. Ignorance and idiocy and arrogance—three qualities that tend to go hand in hand—brought suffering to innocents who did not pursue power, fame, or glory, who only wished to live simple, happy lives of peace in a land that seemed eager to give it, if only they could find contentment without wanting more and more.

CHAPTER 21

Contemplation

Toquuxla helped the people clean and prepare the dead for burial. They put spears, stone tools, stone knives, clothing, and furs in the graves, along with any pendants or necklaces of bone, tooth, claw, or ivory that the person had owned. The shaman carried only a little ocher, and they used it all, decorating the faces of their loved ones. The dead were buried where they were found, except for the chief, his wife, and his eldest son, who were laid next to each other in graves on the hill above where they had died. More care and preparation were given to their burials; stones and ashes were placed beneath their bodies as well as on top. They received spears, clothing, spearpoints, ivory figures, ceremonial items, bear claws, feathers, and furs. Toq did not believe the dead needed all these things, but it was customary. After the singing, praying, chanting, and tears, the villagers walked away from the graves, but Toq stopped and looked back. He wondered how long it would take for the earth to cover and hide them. He wondered if anybody in the future would ever know what had happened here, or if all knowledge and memory of it would eventually be lost. Would someone, someday, find the graves, and if so, what would they think of the items found? Would the items remain, or would the earth absorb them? Would the bones turn to stone?

He followed the group, knowing he would never know. *At least, I don't think I'll ever know.* The villagers looked for the bones of the Asshole but did not find them. A piece of broken rib was found, and somebody said it was his, but no one could know for sure. The shaman said it was the Asshole's, and he gave it to the man's mean wife. No one knew what she did with it. Toq pondered the fact that this man was gone, and nothing remained of his body. Except for his personal items and the memories of him, it was as though he'd never existed.

The village split into two groups without further violence. The Asshole's group went back west. Toq stayed with the chief's family group through winter. Following Toq's advice, they moved south along the smaller river (Judith River) because it had better water and more timber. The group thrived. Although most people had left the horror and sorrow of last summer's violence behind, many still struggled with the loss, the viciousness, and the fear of another confrontation from within or from without. Toq had his own bad dreams and images of that awful day, but with each passing month, the vividness began to fade.

The men of the group talked of hunting mammoths, but Toq convinced them it was too dangerous for a group of their size. "Besides we can find all the meat we need hunting easier animals."

This new clan had nearly forty people, with more women than men, some elders, and a good number of children. Toq noticed that, even with a group this size, wildlife gradually moved farther and farther away. The winter he'd spent alone did not have so dramatic an effect on game animals.

He told people, "There are too many of us in our clan. The animals are leaving."

But whereas they normally listened to him, on this subject they simply said, "We're not going to split up again. These animals have always been here. There are countless numbers of them. They'll always be here to feed the people."

Toq had heard these arguments before, but he did not believe animals existed to "feed the people." He knew that not everyone could live as he had, having little to no effect upon the land, so he didn't really know what he wanted from them. One thing he was certain of was that if people kept coming, they would completely change the lands they were moving into. While it was hard to imagine, he believed it *was* possible to wipe out all the animals.

During the winter, Toq brought a woman—a little younger than himself—into the lodge he shared with an older man and his wife. While he appreciated having human company, conversation, and companionship, he missed the solitude, living with the wild lands and wild animals. He and the rest of the tribe had plenty of time to tell stories of what they had seen and done and the close calls they'd had. His stories of the massive prairie glaciers to the north intrigued people the most, while those of the tribes to the south created the most trepidation.

In contrast to his time alone, Toq felt safe within this little village. Certainly, a bear, lions, or something, could attack, but these human hunters asserted their dominance over other predators quickly. They went after the big carnivores to send them the message "We are not prey," and as long as they went out in numbers, the bears and lions kept away. Toq wondered about that as well, realizing, "We are even affecting the mighty bear, lion, and wolf."

When setting up their winter camp, the humans successfully drove a lion pride from its territory and into a less favorable area. Here, they battled another pride, leaving both weakened, and a deadly winter with little shelter diminished both prides. The only thing that saved them was the large number of vulnerable, dead, or dying prey animals.

Hard as the winter was, it did not kill any of the villagers. By the time spring came, the people were ready to move on to a new place, having worn out the spot they'd settled in.

"Let the lions come back. It was theirs before us," they said.

Toq especially felt the urge to go, to travel, to explore new lands, or to go back to places special to him. No one place was his favorite—he considered all of it magnificent. He longed to see his own people, too, far to the west, but he did not see himself returning anytime soon. More and more, he felt a part of this clan, and now that he was with a woman, he felt the added pull to stay. He'd lost the freedom of being alone, and he pined for that time when it was just him and the land, the sky, the stars, the great and small beasts, the birds, the wind, and the glaciers. He loved the woman he was with, but in his heart, his greatest love was for wandering, and wondering, about the lands that had no people.

••••

Toquuxla stood on top of a hill with a light breeze blowing his long, straight, black hair. His woman had shaved and plucked his whiskers, giving him a smooth, clean face. Wearing only pants and moccasins on this glorious morning, the sun felt good on his bare brown skin. He held a spear, and no bugs pestered him. He closed his eyes and breathed deeply the fresh, early summer air, rich with new grasses and wild prairie flowers. He opened his eyes and beheld the vast prairies stretching off to the west, north, and east. The little mountain range on the western horizon (Sweet Grass Hills) and the mountains to the south (Bears Paw Mountains) were all familiar sights to him. Below, straight north, lay the valley holding the river (Milk River) that flowed from the great prairie ice sheets. Lightning had killed the bison on the ridge to the southeast. Nearly two years had passed since he had come this way. The prominent, long, rocky butte with the gouge in it lay below to the northeast (Saddle Butte). The wide valley below—lush, green, treeless, where mammoths grazed and wolves and bears and lions fought—lay partially flooded by glacial meltwater.

Way north, just out of sight, Toquuxla knew the glaciers beamed in the summer sun. On the green hills and prairies and wetlands, mammoths, bison, caribou, musk oxen, pronghorns, horses, deer, camels, wolves, bears, lions, cheetahs, bighorns, wolverines, rabbits, marmots, ground squirrels, lemmings, weasels, foxes, coyotes, llamas, and countless smaller creatures, strove to survive, to breed, and to raise young. In the air and on the water and land, more birds of different sizes and colors and kinds than he could ever count filled the empty spaces.

"The land lives!" said the man. "No people anywhere to claim this land as theirs. I am free to go wherever I want." He waved his open hand, palm to the gigantic sky, in an arc toward the horizon, and said, "I do not worship a god or gods, or spirits or demons, the unseen, imaginary things dreamed up by humans. I revere the beautiful world that lies before me and that my eyes can see. This world gives life. It feeds my belly and my soul. This is not fantasy. This is what's true, what's real. *This . . .* is the truth!"

But, "One day," he feared, "people will be here, and it will all change."

A massive bull mammoth with two giant, curving tusks sauntered up the hill nearby.

"I love this, all of this," he said, and then he looked at the mammoth and said, "I love *you*," and he grinned at his daft statement, but he felt it in his heart.

Content and happy, he looked down the hill to where five other people were just getting out of bed. One of them was his woman, his partner. They'd camped on a ridge above a pond, well below the hill Toquuxla stood upon. She looked up and waved to him, and he smiled and waved his hand in a high arc over his head. The small group was traveling to the ice sheets before returning to the larger village far to the south and across the big river. To Toquuxla, the humans looked strange and inharmonious in this land. They were invading the land of no people, though he knew that he too was an invader.

He gave a good, long look around and contemplated the past.

"Was it always like this? Were there ever people here? Did they come and go?"

The answer was no. He'd been the first and, for a while, the only. Time before him went on for hundreds, thousands, and millions of years. Life and landscapes changed without the hand of humanity and without any concern for humanity. He contemplated the future—his own, the immediate, and the far-off. Human numbers were growing and expanding. People were coming.

"What will it be like in a hundred, a thousand, or ten thousand years? How many people will be here? A hundred? A thousand? What can stop them?"

He looked at his feet, "I won't be here. But I still care."

Among all the stones the glaciers had left behind, an unusual marble rock of orange and pink, and speckled throughout with crystals, lay nestled in the grass. Toquuxla bent down and picked it up; it fit neatly in the palm of his hand.

"I remember you. I picked you up two years ago."

He turned it over and over, examining every small detail.

"So, what made you? And how did you get here?" he asked the rock. "You're beautiful. I love you, too," he said somberly.

Then, he laughed at himself, in his euphoria, saying, "It's okay. I love it all, corny or not," and he put the rock right back where he'd found it. His thoughts drifted to his two friends, the Traveler and the wolf, and he said, "I wish you both were here."

Finally, Toquuxla takes a deep breath and looks at you and says, "You can stop watching now."

CHAPTER 22
After Toquuxla

Toquuxla experienced many more adventures and visited new lands and people, but for the rest of his life, his greatest fondness was for the first lands he'd seen on his solitary journey. People said that during his last few years, he would often be found off by himself, wistfully staring toward horizons he had explored, thankful for the life he had lived, and despite his troubles, he was unable to imagine how it could have been any better.

Time passed, and so did Toquuxla and all the people he'd known. People kept on coming and growing in population, and they flourished in the lands rich with wildlife. A hundred years went by, and generations were born, lived their lives, and died. Another hundred years went by, and all the rivers and mountains and lands that Toquuxla did not name were named. Clans and tribes and villages laid claim to certain territories, dividing the lands.

For a while, tribes told stories of Toquuxla and his people, but after a thousand years, any memory or thought of him had vanished, replaced by new stories of more recent heroes. With nobody watching, and with time, nothing is remembered: not personal experiences, not names, not people, not wars, and not Toquuxla. A remnant of their customs and traditions carried on in some form, morphed by time, but Toq's language changed into something vastly different from his native tongue. And after another thousand or two thousand years—it's hard to say precisely how long it took—Toquuxla's fears about the future were realized: The mammoths were gone, as were the mastodons. The giant ground sloths, the huge, short-faced bears, the peccaries, camels, llamas, horses, dire wolves, and cheetahs were all gone. Periods of cold came and went, but over time, the glaciers melted away. Birch and spruce forests moved north while prairies expanded. The long-legged bighorn sheep and musk oxen and caribou left the land, either going extinct or migrating north. The great lions, bigger than the African lions, were eventually gone, and even the vast numbers of bison that Toquuxla's people had hunted were replaced by their cousins, the smaller, modern American buffalo. The teratorns and storks were gone, and numerous other eagle, hawk, and bird species moved, changed, or died out. Plants and fish changed. Certainly, Toquuxla would recognize much of "his" land and many of the remaining animals, but taken as a whole, it was an entirely different world. Time and people reduced the mighty bones and tusks of the mammoths to the point where not a trace of them remained unless they were fortunate enough to be buried and preserved in the earth.

Toquuxla would have said, "Humans did it. Everything was fine with the world until we showed up. There are too many of us, and we're too greedy."

Time moved forward without Toquuxla. More than ten thousand years passed. Five hundred generations of people came and went—living, surviving, fighting. Populations went up, then down, then up again, multiple times. People left, new migrants moved in, and sometimes new people pushed out those who'd been there before. Technology changed. The land and wildlife changed. Trails turned into roads. Permanent towns and cities formed. Power lines crossed the landscape, dams created lakes, and communication towers topped hills. The land filled with railroads, fences, telephone poles, industrial and commercial buildings, farms and ranches, feedlots, mines, power plants, giant wind turbines, solar farms, golf courses, stadiums, highways, bridges, landfills, clearcut forests, water and sewage treatment plants, ski hills, parking lots, campgrounds, airports, and countless homes—spreading from the cities into the forests and onto hillsides. Apparently, there is no end to the expansion of humanity.

••••

Today, perhaps fifteen thousand years after Toquuxla—nobody knows for sure—a man climbs a hill to have a look around. He is not free to go wherever he wishes, because someone else "owns" the land; permission must be acquired. He is a little older than Toquuxla was when he climbed this same hill. It's late spring, and the early morning sun feels warm on his face as he looks around. The horizon off to the east, north, and west is the same horizon Toq gazed upon, as are the Sweet Grass Hills to the west and the Bears Paw Mountains to the south. The long butte with the gouge, Saddle Butte, is still there, and although time and erosion have changed it a little, Toq would still recognize it.

Upon hearing a jet high above, he looks up. Several white contrails cross the blue sky, and the distant drone of a small plane carries for miles. A loud pickup truck driving up the highway and the distant sound of train engines express the tone of this world, dominated by man, not by nature. There are birds, even some species that Toq knew, but not as many. Still, the man enjoys the singing of the meadowlark and the soft, sweet chirps of horned larks along with the honking geese and cawing crows.

Down below, to the north, in the valley formed from the meeting of Bullhook Creek and the Milk River, lies the city of Havre. It completely fills the valley bottom and spreads out onto the surrounding hills and plains, its tentacles reaching farther and farther into what was once countryside. When Toquuxla passed through, the valley was a rich wetland flooded by gray, silty, glacial meltwater. Mammoths grazed, and giant bears, wolves, and lions fought for food and territory.

Vast chunks of prairie are now farmland, and in the shining spring sun, it is a beautiful, lush green, but compared to what it used to be and the wildlife that thrived here, it is dead. The wheat fields are especially bleak in winter, and while a few pronghorns and deer manage to eke out a living here, the land does not support the great beasts that the natural, native prairies used to.

The man on the hill looks down to the hillsides and coulees untouched by plows. Isolated patches of dark-green brush dot the light-green hills. Wildflowers grow, scattered thinly about, white, yellow, and purple, but invading plants from other continents have taken root and are taking over. Humans wage war on these plants in an effort to control the damage they themselves have brought upon the land. The man on the hill hopes that one day people will find solutions to nature's problems without destroying it.

The man tries to imagine what this world must have looked like fifteen thousand years ago. What a sight it must have been to see a huge Columbian bull mammoth, with gigantic, curved tusks, sauntering up this hill, or the massive herds of buffalo spread across the plains. He looks down at some deer in the coulee below and sees some cattle on a ridge.

"All the big, wild animals are gone from here. This is what's left," he says to himself. "We have always worked to manipulate and control nature. We still do it, more than ever, and we will probably do it even more in the future. Will all that make life better for us? Material wealth demands that we grow, grow, grow. Where is this leading us and the world? I don't know. I have no answers. Maybe the man living fifteen thousand years ago had a better, more interesting, more exciting, more dangerous, and shorter life than we do, but maybe he also felt more peace and contentment. How rich he was compared to us. Now, we go to the park, or we fish or hunt or hike or birdwatch or recreate in 'the great outdoors' just to get a taste of what it used to be like to live outside with nature. We even use nature to 'test ourselves'—our knowledge, our skills, our endurance, and we obsessively take photos and videos of ourselves out in nature to show the world what we have done. Some use nature to get their adrenaline fix. We write blogs and books and magazine articles to supposedly get more people out there, to get them in shape, to enrich their otherwise dull lives, to get them to love, and then to protect nature. And then they go and trample the hell out of it.

"So, here we are. Can't go back in time. Have to learn to 'live in the present.' Can't spend our lives mourning what is lost and long gone. Can't worry too much about the future. Restoration? Maybe. It's possible but difficult. There are just too many people. I don't know. Is it simple sentimentality to care about the natural world, or is it imperative to conserve and preserve what is left? Does the future of humanity depend on what we do to the natural world? Are we better off if we 'conquer' nature? I doubt it. Maybe it doesn't matter. While there have been some small victories for nature and some species, the overriding trend continues to be slow—though sometimes fast—chipping away at the natural world. Humans want too much, and centuries of preaching, educating, writing, filming, and reporting on how nature and its wildlife are threatened has not stopped man's progress, mankind's eating away at the planet. Where does it end?

"And it's not just the miner or oilman, the developer, the farmer or rancher, the hunter or fisherman. It's *all* of us, rich and poor—including the masses of recreationists and tourists and the least intrusive, the hiker, who supposedly only leaves footprints and takes pictures. It's pretty bleak, pessimistic, but is destruction of the natural world our inevitable reality? Maybe, maybe not. Humans have the capacity to completely alter life on the planet. Yes, other living organisms have radically changed the world, but not like us, not this fast. Possibly, the natural world is doomed. The land has been radically changed, yet those who radically change it call environmentalists 'radical.' And why do all these people have to move to the country, to build their homes and cabins in the pretty spots? They *wreck* the pretty spots.

"Humans are a force of nature, a product of natural selection, an offspring of life on this planet, a force much like the movement of tectonic plates, earthquakes, volcanoes, erosion, ocean currents, storms, and asteroid strikes. All these things happen to the planet. They shape and change the planet, and now we humans are happening to the planet.

"Microorganisms happened to the planet billions of years ago, and they changed the atmosphere, over time, pumping up the oxygen levels so life of other kinds could take hold. They, one would argue, were a force for good—for life—on this planet. We shall see if humans are a force for good. So far, we do not appear to be. Those microorganisms changed the world unconsciously. Humans—though conscious individually—are collectively, unconsciously changing the world, while also being aware that we are doing it (is that a contradiction?), oftentimes denying that we *are* doing it, often claiming we change the world for the better, and perhaps most importantly, seem to be powerless to stop ourselves.

"I'd like to come back in a hundred years. No, a thousand years! It's impossible to predict the future, and what this planet will look like in a thousand years. How about fifteen thousand years in the future? That's a long time—at least for us and our short lives. Just as the first man to come here would not know this place, so I am certain that I would not know this place one thousand years from now. Someday, people will ponder and study what it must have been like to live now in my time.

"Oh well. It's all idle daydreams. You will never know the future."

He sits on the ground and picks up a rock. It is an unusual marble rock of orange and pink and speckled throughout with crystals. It fits neatly in the palm of his hand.

"You're beautiful," he says to the rock, as he turns it over and around. "I know where you came from. You're not native. The glaciers brought you here from Canada. You're a remnant. You're proof of the ice ages. You give me the chance to touch the past."

He ponders the ice ages, imagining what the land below looked like covered by the ice sheets. Then, he thinks about the glacial floods in eastern Washington state and wonders if evidence that humans were there to witness the floods will ever be found or if it has already been found.

He puts the rock back down in its place without realizing the first human to come here examined this same rock and that the rock enabled him to touch not only the past, but also the future. He is tied to all time—and everyone and everything *is* the connection to the past and the future.

CHAPTER 23

Fifteen Thousand Years in the Future

THREE WORLDS

WORLD NUMBER ONE

A young woman climbs to the top of a hill to get some exercise and a good view of the surrounding country. The woman picks up the unusual marble rock that Toquuxla picked up thirty thousand years ago and that another man picked up fifteen thousand years later. The woman immediately recognizes it as one left behind by the last ice age a long, long time ago. The woman is tempted to take the rock but decides to leave it for someone else to admire.

She speaks an entirely different language than the man of fifteen thousand years ago, and neither one of them would know the words spoken by Toquuxla. She is fit, healthy, and happy. Everyone is healthy and happy. It has taken thousands of years, but mankind, with the promise of science, technology, and wisdom, has solved most of the world's problems.

She looks out at a horizon unobscured by pollution. The air above and water below are pure and clean. The Sweet Grass Hills, the Bears Paw Mountains, and Saddle Butte are all still there, although a bit more worn down. The human population of the world is less than a tenth of what it was fifteen thousand years ago. Humanity has found balance, living at peace and in harmony with nature and with themselves.

The late spring sun warms her face and bare arms. One lone aircraft streaks silently across the blue sky. Lower-flying planes infrequently zip above and down into the Milk River valley, while the only sound coming from the highway is the faint hum of wheels on the road. Loud combustion engines have not existed for thousands of years. Birds thrive and there are more than in the past.

In the valley bottom, the town that was once called Havre has moved. It has spread out onto the hills and plains around the old site, and except for a few buildings that were allowed to stay, the bottom land has been given back to nature. With fewer people, the land used for agriculture has been remarkably reduced. Wildlife numbers have grown and humans tolerate and love them. Wild plant ecosystems thrive without too much help, interference, or manipulation from people.

From her hilltop, she looks down upon some deer. Farther down on the flat, there are pronghorns and a few bison, while to the north, a small group of wild horses graze in a steep ravine. A coyote watches the horses.

She says, "What a perfect day. Well, about as good as it can get, anyway."

She wonders what it must have been like to see a big bull mammoth wandering up the hill, and she wonders about life here before humans. She shakes her head while recalling history lessons that spoke of the masses of humanity over the last fifteen thousand years and the destruction they wrought. But history will not have a lot to say about her time, because it has no wars or conflicts. It is calm and peaceful—at least for now.

"Things are better now," she says to herself. "Things will get better yet. I wonder what the future will be like."

She bends down and again picks up the orange-pink marbled rock.

The heart of Toquuxla lives in her, and she says, "You're so beautiful."

WORLD NUMBER TWO

A man and a woman climb to the top of one of the few remaining protected hills around. Set aside a long time ago as a monument to the past, the hill also serves as a place where people can get some "natural" exercise. You can hike the trail from the huge parking lot, or you can take the boardwalk with stairs, or you can ride the chairlift. It is illegal to fly your personal aircraft to the hilltop. Lines of people move up and down the trail and boardwalk, while another line waits for the chairlift. The distance from the parking lot to the top of the hill is less than a mile.

The man grumbles about "all the people on the trail," while the woman cheerfully smiles and greets those she passes. Upon reaching the sprawling summit, packed with humans, they see a long line waiting to get food and drink and seating at one of the three indoor/outdoor restaurants.

"Gawd," the woman says. "Forget that."

They instead wait in a line to get a view to the north. Artificial stones completely pave over the hilltop, and a railing encircles the summit, keeping people corralled and "safe." After almost an hour, the couple finally obtains an unobstructed view at the railing, where they look out upon the land. The late-spring sun, high in the sky, warms their skin. Fresh green leaves fill out the trees below. Though the sky is cloudless and sunny, smoke, haze, and humidity ruin what used to be a common sight—the far horizon, rendered invisible. And even if the air were clear, they would not be able to see the Sweet Grass Hills because those mountains are gone, taken down and used up. To the northeast, what remains of Saddle Butte, only a bump on the flatlands, has been completely built over with homes.

The Bears Paw "Mountains," now flattened and rounded off, are higher than the surrounding flatlands, but they are no longer mountains, and buildings and roads cover them. Humanity has smoothed everything out, so mountains are merely highlands and valleys only a dip or slight depression. Barely visible through the haze is Baldy—the only mountain in the entire range saved from the miners and developers. It stands tall and alone, and the man and woman know people crawl all over it like ants on an anthill. People seeking peace, solitude, nature, or something spiritual will never find it on Baldy.

The sun dims slightly then brightens again as massive structures in orbit pass overhead. Every level of the sky is busy, from super-fast planes booming through the upper atmosphere, to low-elevation personal aircraft zipping around to more local destinations. No birds or bugs fly through the air. A couple of species of small but colorful birds, genetically modified, survive down below in the residential neighborhoods. People love them, and if people do not feed them, they will die, because there is nothing natural for them to eat.

Down in what used to be called the Milk River valley lies the city (Havre) with a hard-to-pronounce modern name, one of a long succession of different names periodically handed out by new generations who want a change. Its massive, shining skyscrapers rise higher than the hilltop the people stand upon, and airports, bridges, and aboveground rail systems make it a sight to behold. The city spreads across the landscape, the residential zones reaching to the bottom of this hill. It has gobbled up the surrounding lands and towns and stretches as far as the couple can see. Every visible piece of land holds a house, a street, a business. The people of the city planted all the leafed-out trees below; nothing grows naturally. And where the city ends, the next city begins. No open country remains—hence the crowds on this hill and on Baldy.

The woman says, "Oh, isn't the city beautiful?"

The man responds, "I guess."

She glances at him with irritation. He is thinking about what it might look like without the city.

It has been many thousands of years since nature could supply all the food that humanity requires. Farms and ranches went extinct along with all of the natural world, and now food is not grown outside. It is manufactured, and there is plenty of it. Apparently, science made it healthy, because—along with other advances in medicine and genetics—people rarely die. Disease and aging have become things of the past. Even mental health problems are fixable—meaning violence, criminal behavior, depression, you name it, have a cure. If someone feels like they have lived long enough, there is a way out and society will accept their decision, but only after much counseling and chemical treatment to try to resolve their irrational desire to die. Severe trauma, like in an aircraft crash, will end your life, but in this superbly safe world, it is extraordinarily rare. The man and woman both know healthy one-thousand-year-old people. People don't have many babies, but according to the man, "Nobody dies! So, we've run out of room!" Death, if people think about it at all, is so unusual that it terrifies people more than ever in human history and is no longer accepted as "part of life." Of course, anyone gripped with debilitating fear or anxiety regarding death can see their doctor and get that fixed. Everyone is happy.

Except this man. He does not like this crowded world.

He says, "It isn't natural, the way we live."

His girlfriend tells him, "If you're not happy, why don't you go see your doctor? They can help you. I don't understand why you fantasize about the past. It's gone, done, history. Life is better now. You think it was fun to be chased and killed by wolves or bears or to get sick and die? You're delusional."

It is hard for him to argue with her, or anyone else, about the wonders and achievements of humanity, but he often feels that people are now simply happy imbeciles.

Humanity controls the natural world completely. Wildlife is gone—except in zoos and national parks. Glacier and Yellowstone National Parks are half their original size. People pressured the government to develop more of those lands, claiming they were just going to waste. The small fragments of wildlife left there are little more than caged animals trapped in an open-air zoo, put on display for tourists.

People have animals for pets, but the few small birds flying around the city are the closest most will ever come to seeing wildlife. Mankind has become so adept at manipulating the genetic code that natural selection and evolution are considered quaint, imperfect processes of a long-dead world. People have wiped out most all wild animals, large and small; they have wiped out most wild insects and fish, most of the native plants and trees, and they've even changed the microbial universe to better suit humanity.

Even *people* are no longer naturally selected, instead their own DNA has been artificially changed, and so people do not look the same as they did fifteen thousand years ago.

Cities cover the terrestrial globe and extend out even into parts of the oceans. Thousands live in orbit around Earth. A million live on the moon. Many millions live on Mars, and for some time now, huge ships have been leaving the solar system, scattering humanity across the galaxy like seeds in the wind, to find new worlds on which to live. All those living in space have had their DNA changed so they can better survive off of their home planet.

But humans do not just control life on the planet—they control the planet itself. Humans have learned how to manipulate the geological forces of Earth so that earthquakes and explosive volcanic eruptions are a thing of the past. Humans determine the weather; they adjust the temperatures, gasses, and humidity in the atmosphere. Hurricanes, tornadoes, floods, fires, and blizzards never happen anymore. Snow falls only on occasion at the north and south poles. All the planet's glaciers and frozen oceans are long gone. Violent storms have been replaced by periodic gentle rains. Thunder and lightning are rare. The man complains about the weather but not in the same way people have throughout history.

He says, "Yeah, it's another beautiful, boring day. Nothing exciting will happen."

While the day's length still changes with the seasons, the temperatures outside are only slightly colder in winter than summer. Everyone knows what the historians and Earth scientists taught about the past, and the man and woman try to imagine what it must have been like to see snow covering the land—or continental glaciers.

The woman says, "I don't know how they did it. How they survived in that cold with the primitive technologies and clothes they had. I think I would die."

The man only says, "No, you wouldn't. You'd find a way to survive."

The man thinks often about trying to get on one of those ships to another solar system just to see a new world, but he doesn't know if he wants to be stuck on a ship for so long, in suspended animation or not. He vacationed on Mars, but it bothered him to see how humans were changing the little red planet. In some people's minds, humans going to new worlds would be bad for those worlds, just as we'd been bad for this world.

In an out-of-the-way spot, a ranger gives a presentation to a small group. He points out different landmarks and speaks on the history of the area. To the man and woman's surprise, a few people are incredulous about what the ranger says, and they argue with him, claiming their religion told them what's true and what's false.

The woman rolls her eyes and whispers, "Shit! Will we ever be free of these stupid religious fantasies?"

"I doubt it," the man says.

Science and society have found a way to alter people's tendencies to believe in the unbelievable, but it is not forced upon anyone, and many relish the opportunity to be counted as a member of the faithful, superior to unbelievers.

The religious ones leave, and the ranger brings out a couple of objects of interest—historical things collected over the past fifteen thousand years. He passes some of them around for people to touch. One is a beautiful, unusual, orange-pink, speckled, marble rock.

The ranger tells them it's one of the oldest objects in his collection and that it was found, long ago, "Right here on this hilltop. Geologists tell us it was brought here from the far north, riding in the glaciers from one of the past ice ages. You are holding something that gives us proof of a continental ice sheet."

The man and woman take turns examining the rock, and their minds each try to reach back into a world more than thirty thousand years ago. The man wonders what it must have looked like when the first people came here. But humanity no longer has any relationship with the natural world and so is unable to imagine it. It took thousands of years of steady erosion, but now there is no natural world on the surface of the planet. Were it not for medicine, humans would be very dissatisfied with their lives without any connection to nature. They would not feel alive.

And what, he wonders, *will the future look like?* He rolls the rock over in his hands, and he says to the rock, Toquuxla's rock, "You're beautiful."

The woman looks at him and asks, "You okay? You're talking to a rock. You think too much."

WORLD NUMBER THREE

On a sunny, early summer day, a light breeze blows against the short green grasses and wildflowers struggling to grow in the chill air. A lone man in furs, carrying a long, metal-tipped spear and a bow, climbs up a prominent hill. He wears a backpack made of tough, woven hair, bark, sinew, and leather. Upon reaching the summit, he looks down into the valley at a massive expanse of ice stretching to the northern horizon where it meets a clear blue sky.

The great continental glaciers are pushing south, advancing into the old Milk River valley. They lie upon the land like a blanket a thousand feet thick, extending to the northwest and east as far as the eye could see. A lake has formed to the northwest, nestled against the ice sheet, still mostly frozen with only a sliver of open blue water around the edges. The ice sheet has pushed across the river valley and now sends arms up into the coulees, filling them until its gargantuan bulk will eventually overwhelm the hills.

The man is spellbound and nearly blinded by the reflection of the sun on the brilliant ice. He was told of the glaciers and wished to see them, but nobody has been here in a long time, and so no one knew the ice had advanced this far. The high points of Saddle Butte are slowly being engulfed, and they poke above the ice like little islands in a sea of white. The Sweet Grass Hills sit on the western horizon, and the Bears Paw Mountains rise in the south, where white patches of snowdrifts dot the greening mountains. The old town site of Havre lies buried under ice growing thicker by the year.

No planes fly through the sky, and all the nation's satellites crashed to earth long ago. The air possesses only birds and bugs. The man hears a couple of geese and numerous prairie songbirds. A hawk circles above, and he watches an eagle and two ravens fly by. On the ground, squirrels and badgers dig holes, deer, pronghorns, and elk graze, and buffalo once again dominate. Some say that caribou and musk oxen have even come down with the glaciers, but the man has yet to see any.

Wild horses roam the land, the descendants of the old, domesticated horse. The man began his journey on a horse, but wolves spooked it, and it ran off. A toughened, wild version of domestic cattle has also survived, evolving to live in small herds here and there.

Coyotes, foxes, bobcats, wolverines, and cougars have all done well, but wolves and grizzlies have assumed the role of top predators. The man wants to see one beast more than any other: the mammoth. And one wanders up a hill below him. A large bull with long, sweeping, curved tusks and thick reddish-blond hair swings its trunk into the air and down to the ground.

"Magnificent," says the man, watching the giant. "That's one thing we did right."

He recalls the stories of how a thousand, or maybe five thousand, years ago, scientists cloned and manipulated genes to bring back this extinct animal, placing them in zoos and wildlife parks and eventually releasing them or allowing them to escape. Perhaps activists set them free. No one really knows, but now here they are. The land has not yet fully recovered from mankind's onslaught, but it is well on its way.

As for people, there is nobody here. Only him. Humans left this area long ago, and there is little to be seen of their past existence unless one digs or knows what they are looking at. Nature has eroded or grown over or buried most of the scars and structures humans created. Stories and legends abound regarding what happened to humanity and civilization: wars, starvation, disease, overpopulation, social problems, environmental destruction, asteroids, supervolcanoes, the start of the new ice age, aliens, and, of course, God's judgment and wrath. The man tries not to think too much about the hows and whys regarding the near complete annihilation of humanity and civilization. He doesn't know and he doesn't believe that he, or anyone, will ever truly know what happened, but he rejects the ideas of aliens and God's wrath.

He told his friends, "It would be nice to know. That way, if humans ever do come back, maybe they can keep from repeating the stupid things they did the first time." Then, he cynically added, "Nah, if humans come back, I'm sure they'll do the exact same things and ruin their world again."

"No people," he says, looking about the huge landscape. "Completely extirpated. I am it, the last one, and I'm not staying here long. From the time of the first human to set foot here, we have been exterminating thousands of nature's creatures, leading them to extinction. And now where are we,

Almighty Humanity? Nearly extinct ourselves. We probably deserve it. We shed few tears for the species we destroyed, and the planet will shed few tears when we are gone. We dominated for so long, but geologically, not long at all. I shed no tears for us, either."

It's odd, he knows, for a man to not really care for his own species. Perhaps that's one reason humans are nearly all gone.

At this moment in time, only one man remains in what was once called Montana. The names and governments and people and cultures changed several times, over thousands of years, and now, only a handful of people are left living far to the south and on the coasts, having returned to simpler lives of hunting, gathering, and growing a few of their own foods. Most of humanity's accumulated knowledge has been lost.

The man sits in the grass, and a hard rock interrupts his soft seat. He reaches underneath him and picks up a beautiful, orange-pink, marble rock with crystals. His fingers wrap a bit past halfway around it where it sits in his hand. He looks it over, wondering how it was made and how it came to be on the hilltop. He has no knowledge of the previous ice ages. Fifteen thousand years ago, a "present day" man picked up this same rock. Thirty thousand years ago, Toquuxla, the first human to come to this land, picked up the same rock. They all said, "You're beautiful," and put it back down.

This man stands, contemplating the past and the future, asking himself if any human will ever see that rock again. He leaves the hilltop, walking north to the ice sheet. Hardy and fit, he covers a lot of ground. He approaches the big mammoth, but when it becomes obvious the bull is irritated, he circles around the beast. He walks down a ridge and across a coulee where erosion has exposed some old concrete and steel that once formed a small bridge. A few large animals are scattered in the distance, but it's nothing like in Toquuxla's time.

He reaches a place where the ice has pushed up onto a hill, and a large mound of dirt and rock sits bulldozed up at its front. He climbs up the moraine and presses his hand to the ice. It's too steep and slippery to climb, so he contents himself with just touching it. He climbs back down and walks west along the glacial front, going around low spots holding marshes and ponds, some frozen, some not. From a distance, he sees a section of ice with large, dark, protruding objects. When he gets there, he is astounded to see a huge area littered with the rubble of a city—a city far to the north, in old Canada, pushed and carried to the south. The ice crushed and ground up buildings constructed of material resistant to decay, but some large blocks remain intact in the glacier and on the moraine. Some type of composite beams, twisted and bent, poke into the sky. The glacier carried the surviving detritus of civilization, including a few headstones, and slowly wiped from the land most, but not all, of what people left behind.

"Incredible," he says, his gaze sweeping across the site. "They had so much." But he only sees a vestige of what they really had. "I wonder what it was like to live back then with all that stuff."

The man spends a good portion of the day digging interesting old objects out of the moraine. Most items have been severely damaged or are too heavy to carry around, but he finds a small cache of children's toys, and among them are a little toy man and a toy mammoth, made from some unknown, unbreakable material.

"Ah, that's perfect. Splendid tokens from the past. I shall take you with me."

To him, they will come to symbolize both humankind and nature, and perhaps, one day, what they might become together.

"Tens of thousands of years people have been in this land. A lot has happened over that time," he muses. "Impossible to ponder each individual life."

The man starts walking away from the glaciers, believing it is time to get back to his people. He relishes the isolation in this beautiful land, but the short, cool summer and coming relentless winter forces him to get moving. For him, like Toquuxla, his first love is nature, people are secondary, and he has no relationship with any god, because he does not believe there is a god or spirits or anything else like them, and no one watches him from afar.

He wonders about the next thirty thousand years. Will humans come back?

He says, "I'm not too sure where I'm headed, and we, the human animal, are not too sure where we're headed. Nobody's steering the ship."

The sun drops toward the horizon. He turns to see a single, young wolf following him. The animal doesn't appear to be a menace, but nonetheless, he'll keep an eye on it. He remembers a dog he had as a child and thinks perhaps this wolf will be "his" wolf.

He smiles at the wolf and says, "Come along, then. Let's get out of here," and the last man leaves the land.